Part Two
Blood Sanctuary
Blood Grace Book IV

VELA ROTH

FIVE THORNS PRESS

ISBN 978-1-957040-05-9 (Ebook)
ISBN 978-1-957040-10-3 (Paperback)
ISBN 978-1-957040-11-0 (Hardcover)

Edited by Brittany Cicirello, Suncroft Editing

Cover art by Patcas Illustration
www.instagram.com/patcas_illustration

Book design by Vela Roth

Map by Vela Roth using Inkarnate
inkarnate.com

Published by Five Thorns Press
www.fivethorns.com

Visit www.velaroth.com

CONTENTS

Momcat, this book is still for you.

CONTENT NOTE

BLOOD SANCTUARY Part Two includes some fantasy violence, but also themes that are tragically real for many people, including suicidal thoughts and peer abuse.

In particular, "Hypnos's Brink" and "Crossing the Veil" (12 Nights Until Winter Solstice) are an emotional, but not graphic portrayal of characters intervening to prevent a loved one's death by suicide. "The Greatest Mage" (Festival of Sanctuary) includes graphic bullying and shows one character supporting another who is experiencing suicidal thoughts.

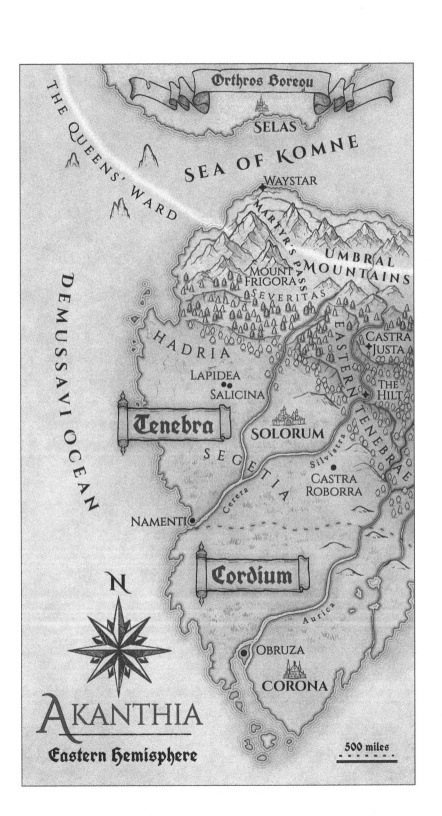

13

nights until

WINTER SOLSTICE

MORTAL NEEDS

THE SUMMIT GAMES WERE at an end, Lio had done much better in the races than the battles, and his Grace had celebrated his performance in both with equal enthusiasm. Alas, they must now get out of bed.

He tried to convince himself. It was almost moon hours. They were expected to be at the embassy's tour of the Healing Sanctuary. Chrysanthos was a disgusting excuse for a person who had to be stopped. Lio had already had his breakfast.

Cassia needed her breakfast now. That got him moving.

Her skin caressed his as she slid off of him. She pillowed her head on her arms and watched him go, her eyes sleepy and warm with enjoyment. Cup and thorns, it felt good to have nothing but her gaze on him. His breakfast might be over, but his dessert was the sight of her lying there on her belly in a pile of silk cushions and rumpled sheets, dawdling her dainty, freckled feet in the air.

He decided not to put on his robe just yet. He turned around and sauntered away from her, all but levitating across the marble floor. He floated over the step down to the lower center of the room.

Cassia fell back asleep watching him spoon fresh-ground coffee into the pot. Lio listened to her heartbeat echo softly through his tower.

Knight woke her with dog kisses. She accepted his greeting with her usual affection, but whispered to Lio over the dog's head, "Don't tell Knight, but I would like a cleaning spell from you."

"We'll keep it our secret that you prefer my kisses." Lio obliged her with a touch of his magic.

"Thank you." She joined him in the sitting area.

He swept his gaze over her. "You look lovely this moon."

She paused to kiss him before she sat her bare bottom down on a silk-padded chair. Lio handed her a large glass tankard of coffee.

"Is that cassia sprinkled on top of Deukalion's Blend?" she asked.

"Yes. I've put your spice on my coffee."

She wiggled her eyebrows at him and put the coffee to her lips, mouthing the mug's rim as she took a languid swallow. She let out a little moan. "I don't know how I used to wake up without your coffee. As strong as Polar Night Roast, but without any bitterness. Pure, rich darkness through and through."

"I think cassia's bite compliments the flavor perfectly." He watched her throat work. If this was how she enjoyed a cup of coffee named after him, what would it be like when she enjoyed a drink of his blood?

Her stomach growled loudly.

He grinned. "My plan is a success. I have helped you work up a healthy appetite."

"Prepare yourself. I shall drain your coffee pot and lay waste to your cupboard."

"It's only fair, after I've just done the same to yours. I'll go get your breakfast out of the cold vault."

Lio threw on his veil hours robe and went out the side door. He opened the hatch in the snow and wondered how much of its overflowing contents he could poke into Cassia's mouth in the next hour. The pile of food in the cold vault soothed an unbearable urge inside him. She might insist she was fine, but he doubted she was fully recovered from her frequent fasts in the king's household and living in fear of being poisoned.

It would take longer than a few weeks in Orthros to make up for her lifetime of hardship in Tenebra. It would take more than food to ensure she had what she needed. What she deserved.

Until he could provide for her from his own vein, he could at least continue to supply her with healthy mortal fare. He chose some of Orthros's thick, strained yogurt and four large cassia pastries made with almond flour and honey. When he went back inside to put the rolls on the warmer, Cassia was no longer in the sitting area, and her coffee sat unfinished on the table. Lio set it on the warmer as well to keep it hot. She must be in the privy.

Knight had stolen her spot in the bed. With his head on his paws, he gazed at Lio innocently from amid the silk sheets, while the wool blanket and chew toy lay abandoned on the floor. It was a good thing Hesperine cleaning spells worked on liegehound messes, even when Hesperine magic didn't work on liegehounds.

Lio reached into a storage basket under the table for a dog treat. The dry, solid bar didn't look very appetizing to him, but the animal healers swore it was not only a healthy supplement to the canine diet, but irresistible to doggy cravings. Lio dropped it on the carpet at his feet and devoted his attention to the coffee.

The next thing he knew, Knight was sitting beside him and devouring the treat. While the dog was busy, Lio quickly worked another cleaning spell on the bed. The treat was gone before he finished. Knight's eyes filled with pleading more pathetic than anything Lio's diplomatic career had prepared him for. He gave the dog another bar to tide him over until Cassia was ready for Lio to retrieve some meat out of the vault for her hound.

While they waited for Cassia to return, Lio heard a courier enter and leave the front hall. He went into the entryway to see what had been delivered and found a few scrolls on the table under his Ritual tapestry. Glancing through them, he returned to the library. He dropped a couple of the messages on the coffee table on the way to the discreet door behind the dressing screen. He trotted down the stairwell that led to the bath and halted on the landing halfway down.

Through the privy door, he said, "The information you wanted about Hesperine transplanting methods just arrived. The initiate agriculturalists we met on the greenhouse tour have sent you copies in Vulgus and Divine, with the original diagrams. Would you like me to hand this in?"

The spell over the privy might ensure privacy, but no veil could ever interrupt his Union with Cassia. Her aura turned eight shades of embarrassment. "No. I'll be right out."

"Do you need anything?"

"Certainly not. Thank you."

Lio hesitated a moment longer. "All right. Take your time."

They slept skin-to-skin every night, and yet she was self-conscious about her mortal needs. It would also be more than a few weeks in Orthros, it seemed, until she felt entirely comfortable with some aspects of sharing a home with him.

Returning to the library, Lio counted how many nights she had been here and arrived at the same concerning result as each time he had counted before.

When she rejoined him at the coffee table, she had put on her beloved, comfortable gardening dress. She sat back down on her chair and hid behind her mug of coffee. He slid the papers about transplanting across the table to her, along with a plate of pastries. A blush still flamed in her aura and on her cheeks. There were times when he was reminded just how nonsensical Tenebran standards of modesty were.

But that nonsense could be dangerous. There was something she might need to talk about, and he was certain she would not feel at ease broaching the subject. If, Goddess forbid, she needed a healer, she might not acknowledge it to herself, much less confide in him about it.

Should he encourage her to talk about it? Would he cross the veil if he asked her about that particular aspect of her body?

How had his education in Tenebran ways and his conversations with his parents about mortal women not prepared him for this?

Well, trying to put Cassia at ease was never the wrong decision, and reminding her she could speak openly with him was always all right. He must try.

HEAD TO TOE

"I S THERE ENOUGH PAPER in the privy?" Lio asked.

Cassia choked a little on her swallow of coffee. "Ah. Yes. Thank you."

Lio opened another scroll, as if they were talking about the night's diplomatic correspondence. "Is there anything else you need in there that I forgot? As a Hesperine, I am imperfect at anticipating mortal requirements."

"I still wonder why you even have a privy," she blurted. When he had shown her where it was on her first night in his residence, she had felt too awkward to comment on it at all.

He set the letters aside. "Of course I have one for the helpless humans I seduce into spending the night with me. If I don't keep a woman comfortable, she might try to escape from my lair."

"Of course."

"There's no need to blush, my rose. I hope times like last night show you how much I appreciate every inch of you."

"Privy needs aren't the same."

"Just because I don't have them doesn't mean you should feel embarrassed that you do. My fangs and peculiar diet don't disturb you."

"That's different too. Only mortals must worry about unpleasant breath in the mornings."

Lio breathed into his hand and sniffed. "I'm sure I have blood breath sometimes."

"Never."

"Well, our bodies absorptive properties are quite different from human digestion. I suppose we can't properly appreciate how humans feel about such matters. That's why the privy has its own veil over it to ensure absolute privacy. I suspect sleep isn't the only basic need you had no time for in Tenebra. You know I want you to be able to relax here."

She must rid herself of this ridiculous awkwardness. She would do what always worked with Lio. Talk about it anyway. "I can't believe you provide your human guests with paper for their privy needs. Wouldn't you rather spare such a luxury for your scrolls?"

He chuckled. "It's a different kind of paper more suited to the purpose, compliments of the Empire. But I would gladly sacrifice my scrolls, if I didn't think you'd find them scratchy."

"That's sacrilege."

He gave her a broad grin. "Nothing is too fine for your sweet ass."

Lio hadn't used such words with her before. They meant something entirely different coming from him than from the men who said crude things about women's' bodies. She put her hands to her flaming cheeks, but she smiled.

The teasing light in his eyes gave way to gentleness. "You know you can talk with me about anything. Nothing you choose to say is outside the scope of our Oath of honesty. Our promise takes precedence over all Tenebran strictures, as we've often agreed."

"Yes."

He grew more serious. "If you needed a healer, I hope you would mention it. You could see a proper physician in the Healing Sanctuary. You don't have to make do with mortal medicine."

"What are you worried about, my champion? No enemy mages have tried to poison me this week."

"Thank the Goddess," he said gravely. "But I wasn't referring to that. There are more usual reasons to need a healer, and if you did, it would be nothing to be embarrassed about."

"So far, frosty Orthros agrees with me exceedingly. I'm not going to catch cold." She pulled her feet up onto her chair, sipping her coffee again.

He was quiet a moment, but the furrow in his brow told her he was not satisfied. He took a swallow of coffee before speaking again. "You've been here longer than twenty-eight days."

"That's right, the month of Daedala is about to end, isn't it?" she was able to say without looking at the Hesperine calendar in the back of her dictionary. "We're almost to the month of Anastasios, so important to your bloodline."

"There's something that hasn't happened since you arrived. My understanding is that it's usually every twenty-eight days, but I know it can sometimes vary. Is that usual for you? Is there any reason to be concerned?"

Oh. *Oh.* He was not referring to colds or the Orthros calendar. He was, in his well-reasoned and meticulously respectful way, referring to *that.*

She shouldn't be surprised. This was Lio. Concerned, protective, and utterly free from shame. He would think of it, even before she did. Even though, as a Hesperine, he couldn't sire children and needn't pay attention to whether her courses came.

She had no words for this occasion. She seldom spoke of the matter with other women. She had no idea how to broach the subject with a man.

Not a man—a Hesperine. Lio. But for once, his Hesperine nature made it more difficult to talk with him. Or did it?

Although her embarrassment was spiraling downward into the deepest mortification, she made a jest. "No, don't worry. I'm not with child."

Lio laughed, a surprised, affectionate sound. "Thank you so much for setting my mind at ease. I was beside myself. I'm not usually so irresponsible, you know."

"We really must stop forgetting to hang the barrenness charm over the bed."

Their laughter began to unravel the mess of humiliation within her and to banish the voices of generations of Tenebran mothers reciting superstitions in her head. Her time with Lio had long since drowned out the contemptuous words of men.

She shook her head in wonderment. "You, a Hesperine, are more aware about mortal females than most mortal men."

"It would ill behoove us to be insensitive to the needs of humans. Especially those upon whom we depend. Also, we're not squeamish about blood."

This time she choked on a laugh. "The mere mention of this subject is enough to send most hardened Tenebran warriors running in terror."

"I did notice Tenebrans seem to have an irrational fear of females in general."

"I'm glad you're not frightened of me, dangerous as I am."

"How could I be uncomfortable with anything about you, from your head to your toes? Need I say this is also something you needn't feel any embarrassment about?"

With all her might, Cassia pushed away her memories of apologizing on her knees before her father that her monthly courses had arrived at the wrong time. Of carefully counting how many days it had been since she had last used feminine weakness as an excuse.

She looked into Lio's tender, dark blue eyes. "I'm not—that is, I don't…" She took a deep breath, then sighed, then got stuck on the knot in her throat.

Lio wouldn't care.

The beginning and end of his interest in the matter was to make sure she was in good health. Beyond that…no judgment. No pity. No consequences.

"I'm barren," she said. "I don't have monthly courses."

And she found herself able to shrug about the lack of that bane, which was in itself a bane of her existence.

"Are you well?" was Lio's first response. He leaned forward, his expression full of concern. "If it's because of a women's illness, you could confide in one of our female healers."

Cassia shook her head. "That illness I had when I was fourteen made me barren. My courses had only come a couple of times, and after I was sick, they stopped. Good riddance."

He pulled his chair closer to her and took her hand. "It wouldn't hurt to talk with one of Orthros's healers, in any case. It might be reassuring for them to verify what the Tenebran healers told you at the time."

"Oh, I made *very* sure the Tenebran healers never knew a thing about it."

"You weren't even given proper attention from female Tenebran healers? After you nearly died?"

"Can you imagine how hard it would have been to bribe them from then on, to make sure they never told anyone? It was trouble enough to make believably stained rags every month so my handmaidens never caught on. I'm so glad Perita and I trust each other now, and I don't have to go through that nonsense with her anymore."

He held her hand tighter, brushing his thumb ever so gently over her knuckles. "I'm aware that barrenness carries a terrible stigma in Tenebra, but I confess, I never imagined you would have to go through so much to hide it."

"If anyone ever found out, they would hold the secret over my head to get what they wanted from me—or go straight to the king with the information. Then he would know I'm no use for childbearing. It might have been to my favor, since I couldn't bear sons with claims to his throne, which would make me less of a threat to him. He might have gone on bartering me to suitors, never letting on they wouldn't get heirs from me. But there was always the risk it would decrease my usefulness to the point that he didn't consider me worth the bother anymore. I decided it was better for him not to know. It's always better for the king not to know."

Lio pulled her close, his embrace sure and tender, but when he spoke, she was shocked at how much anger she heard in his voice. "First, they tell you to be ashamed of something healthy that your body does. Then they tell you to be ashamed if it doesn't do it. Then you have to live in fear because a lot of men want to know, for their own ends, what your body is doing. Shame upon *them*. That is repulsive, even for Tenebra."

She had never thought of it that way. She had never meant to tell Lio all these details about bloody rags that weren't hers and the king's obsession with the vessel labeled Cassia, in which bastard claimants to the throne might grow. She had never realized how sick and angry it had always made her, until now.

"They have no notion of sanctity." He cupped her face in one hand, his expression stricken. "I hope it's all right with you that I asked."

"Thank you. For asking. For being concerned about *me*." The emphasis landed on the last word without her intending it.

He paused again, clearly considering his words. Careful Lio. Gentle Lio. "I'm so sorry if it causes you personal disappointment. Apart from everything you've endured because of how others would react, I'm sorry if you're unhappy with what your illness took from you."

She shook her head. "For my part, I never minded. It's a relief that I don't have to go through that every month or fear the dangers of childbirth." She pushed aside the other specters. Refused to think any more of the king ending her life because of the life that could not be gotten out of her. They were talking about her, not others. They were in Orthros, where the only misfortune that could come of this was disappointment, which she had never felt.

"So," Lio said slowly, "bearing children of your own isn't...something you would look forward to?"

She tilted her head, looking at him. "Does it bother you that you can't?"

"Actually, I never gave it a thought."

"Even though you're bloodborn?"

Now it was Lio who shrugged. "Father enjoyed doting on my mother while she was pregnant with me. I suppose that would be a wonderful experience. It's not something Hesperines expect or imagine for ourselves, though. We look forward to Solacing children like Zoe."

"That's worth looking forward to."

She liked the new light in his eyes. The significance in his gaze. They way he took a breath, as if to ask something else.

"Speaking of Zoe," he said, "she'll be here for breakfast any minute, I suspect."

Cassia smiled. "Time to lift the veil."

She was looking forward to that something else, whenever he decided it was time to ask it.

THE GRAVEST DANGER IN ORTHROS

LIO PAUSED AT THE foot of one empty sickbed. Its sturdy iron frame and cotton bedclothes made it identical to every other that lined this wing of the Healing Sanctuary. The tall, narrow windows on either side of this bed were the same, and the moons touched it with the same light. But Lio would never forget awakening here when Queen Soteira had pulled him back from the brink of fatal Craving, after he had collapsed in front of the Firstblood Circle during his proposal of the Solstice Summit.

Now he and his Grace were accompanying the Tenebran embassy on Queen Soteira's tour of her Healing Sanctuary.

Cassia slowed and drew nearer. "This bed has some particular significance, Ambassador?"

"It is empty. A powerful testament to victory." Lio smiled and moved onward, a step behind Queen Soteira. "Thank you, Annassa, for personally welcoming us to your Healing Sanctuary tonight."

"I have looked forward to showing our neighbors what we do here." She beckoned to the mortals behind her.

Javed walked in attendance on her other side. "Your great works on behalf of humankind should have taken precedence on the itinerary, Annassa. The Week of Service should rightfully have begun here."

"Your protests on my behalf are noted and appreciated. However, my correspondence with the Empress obliged us to delay. We shall make this tour the finale instead."

The negotiations would begin tomorrow night. At last. Every time Lio thought about it, it felt like a kick in the gut.

They had done everything they could. Tomorrow night, they would know if these weeks of effort by all of Orthros had been enough to sway the mortals. And change history.

This was their last night to change hearts and minds. It was only right that Annassa Soteira make her people's closing argument.

She paused at a pair of side doors and turned to the embassy. "This is the entrance to the wings where our Imperial patients stay when they need to accompany us north to complete their convalescence. When the time comes, they go south with us once more and return to their homes."

"I can scarcely believe how many wings they have here," Ariadne murmured to Pakhne.

"Would that we had one such wing in our temple," Pakhne whispered in reply.

"How well I understand you." Queen Soteira spoke directly to the deferent attendants. "If I were to give you an account of my mortal years, it would be a chronicle of those I could not save."

Pakhne hesitated, but then looked to the Queen. "The weight of so many lives is heavy to carry, Annassa."

Queen Soteira nodded gravely. "My life was a constant journey to those who needed me. There were always villages where I arrived too late, people I did not reach in time, or catastrophes on opposite ends of the land that forced the most painful of decisions upon me. However, becoming a Hesperine has ensured I have all the time necessary to use my magic for the benefit of others. My people have made it possible for me to establish my Healing Sanctuary here in Orthros and bring those in need to me. Best of all, I am no longer one pair of eyes and one pair of hands. Our healers who have completed their education here constantly scour the Empire for the sick and wounded, treating them where they are if possible and ensuring the most difficult cases reach me in time."

Master Gorgos gesticulated around him. "I hear bold claims of great works, but I see no evidence."

"Alas," the Queen replied, "I cannot show you through the occupied wings. I have debated the matter at length with Her Imperial Majesty, our sister monarch, but she wishes for her people who are patients here to remain undisturbed. I delayed your visit for as long as I could in the hopes that she would soften her stance, but she is adamant."

"How convenient," said Chrysanthos.

Lio ignored the Dexion's acrid comment and admired the lingering bruises on the mage's face.

"Aye." Lord Gaius looked askance at Chrysanthos. "We wouldn't want the tour to go on too long, for the sake of the injured."

"You know, Honored Master," Lord Adrogan drawled, "why don't you ask the Hesperine healers for some help while we're here?"

There was a rare glint of sarcasm in Lord Severin's eyes. "He's too manly to accept healing, even from the Semna."

Lio congratulated himself that Chrysanthos was unable to sneer at the men's mockery. If the Dexion allowed any hint of expression on his face, it was certain to hurt. His pride must be even more damaged, if it would not allow him to submit to the Semna's spells.

Tychon looked offended on his master's behalf, but he had no other allies here tonight. The guest house fire had provided justification for excluding Skleros from this tour to keep him away from the alchemical supplies. Lio rather regretted Eudias's absence, though. The apprentice's informed, sensible comments were always an asset. Lio suspected the young mage had pleaded he was unwell just to avoid another long night of listening to his masters' tirades.

Master Gorgos was peering at the closed doors to the next wing. "Sight unseen, one must wonder what goes on beyond this hall."

"I share in your disappointment," said Queen Soteira. "It was my hope that you would have the opportunity to meet our Imperial patients personally, so that they might share their experiences with you firsthand."

"It's your Healing Sanctuary," Lord Adrogan said. "Surely you can show us anywhere you like."

"They are the Empress's people," Queen Soteira replied. "We would never disregard her decrees regarding the safety of the guests she has entrusted to us."

"Is their condition so fragile?" the Semna inquired.

"Some are in critical condition," Queen Soteira answered, "but many are well enough for a visit. Alas, it is not to be. Come, you are welcome to join me in the wings where our Hesperine healers work. I will introduce you to a number of my initiates who are studying here and the masters who assist me in training them."

Javed bowed. "It will be my pleasure to accompany the Annassa as we show you through the apothecary, where we prepare medicines."

Queen Soteira turned to lead everyone onward, but Cassia hung back, one hand on Knight.

"Annassa," she said innocently, "I am certain we would be willing to prepare ourselves in any way necessary for the honor of meeting your Imperial guests. Would it be possible for us to see them if we donned Sanctuary robes, or if I left my hound here?"

The Queen paused, a knowing light in her aura. "That won't be necessary, Lady Cassia. I'm afraid this is a matter of diplomacy, not health."

"What a shame. May I ask what danger there could be in visiting the patients, if they are well enough for our company?"

"I am loath to discuss the unfortunate matter further." Queen Soteira shook her head. "Ambassador, you may shed some light on the delicate position in which Orthros finds herself between her Imperial and Tenebran guests, but take care to show both the honor we owe them."

Lio bowed. "I will do my best, Annassa. Honored guests from Tenebra, the Empress's foremothers issued very particular decrees regarding contact between their people and your own, and Her Imperial Majesty sees fit to maintain that policy. I am sure you respect her determination to ensure her people's safety at any cost, and you understand the matter is out of our hands."

"Oh, I see." Cassia gave a curtsy. "We regret the situation deeply."

The lords and knights looked at her, their expressions ranging from concerned to confused to clueless.

Benedict cleared his throat. "I am sure we do, Your Ladyship, but perhaps you could shed some more light on it."

She glanced among the lords. "Did no one discuss the matter with Princess Alexandra's distinguished guest, Harkhuf Khemkare? No? Ah." She gave them all a rueful look, folding her hands with poise. "You see, the Empress regards *us* as the gravest danger her people may face in Orthros."

Lio watched the realization dawn on the Tenebrans. Their gazes went to Chrysanthos.

"Honored Master," said Cassia, "I am sure you could tell us more about the disastrous voyage by the Order of Anthros that made it necessary for the Empress to turn away all visitors from our part of the world."

Chrysanthos straightened his mastery mantle. "Whatever misunderstanding led to her unjust policy of isolationism, a Tenebran master from Solorum such as myself is as ignorant as you are. Those are the sorts of secrets the Akron keeps locked up tight in Corona, I'm sure."

"Ah, of course," Cassia said. "At least the Hesperine account is educational."

Lio wanted to laugh, but he knew he must brace himself. Chrysanthos would find a way to retaliate for that, he was certain.

"Indeed, this tour is quite revealing." The Dexion's gaze roamed the hall, then landed somewhere near Queen Soteira's forehead. "Wing after wing full of mortals, out of sight and out of reach. How many of them are destined for eternal darkness?"

"Only as many as choose the Hesperine path," Queen Soteira answered calmly. "We do not hand out the Gift as a cure-all. It is true that, in extraordinary cases, the Gift is the only power great enough to restore a person's body, but we reserve that offer for our very last resort. Long before that point, we apply every healing art within our power for the preservation of mortal life. The overwhelming majority of our patients return to their families and lives in the Empire. We bring mortals here to serve them, not ourselves."

"How magnanimous of you," the Dexion replied.

How forbearing of you, Dalos had once said in the very same tone, when Lio had tried to impress upon him Hesperines' reverence for life. Never before had Chrysanthos sounded so much like his late rival, whom he so vocally derided.

Among the rest of the embassy, stifled murmurs and doubting auras echoed the war mage. Lio strove to emulate Queen Soteira's patience. He had known that when she handed out moonstones, the men would bite them like false coins.

"You deny this Healing Sanctuary is a prime source of new Hesperines?" the Dexion challenged.

Lio cleared his throat. "Annassa, if I may?"

The Queen gestured for him to continue.

"Honored guests," Lio went on, "kindly recall the facts my mother related last night, when she walked the embassy through the typical adjustment process each newcomer to Orthros experiences."

"Ah yes," Cassia spoke up. "Those population reports the Chamberlain discussed with us. The sources of Orthros's population growth, from *least* to greatest, are: Imperial patients who can only be healed by the Gift; adult Tenebrans seeking Sanctuary; abandoned children Solaced from Tenebra; and adult guests from the Empire who choose to stay, either to avow Hesperines or pursue professions here."

"Why, Basilis." The Dexion gave her a deep nod. "You missed your calling as a temple schoolgirl."

"If basic census data baffles you, Honored Master, I wonder what useful knowledge is taught in temple school."

"A true scholar learns to question not merely a source's assertions, but the validity of the source itself."

Queen Soteira looked at Chrysanthos. "Do you trust the validity of your own magical senses?"

"Of course," he retorted, but he did not meet her gaze.

"Question my aura," she said. "I do not need the Gift to save mortal lives, only my affinity for healing."

Lio bit back his protests. That his Queen should condescend to suffer the mage's doubts! But it was not for him to question her.

The tide of her power whispered through the hall. Then her magic, the rhythm in her people's veins, rushed and flowed around them, yet never crashed upon them. Beautiful and deep, massive and gentle, her power inundated them. Lio felt as if he had swallowed a whole ocean of moonlight. He heard Cassia gasp.

Queen Soteira looked from one human to another, taking in each and every man and woman. A quiver went through their auras and reverberated in the Union, and Lio shivered.

Lord Adrogan met the Queen's eyes for but an instant before his own widened, and he turned his face away. Lord Gaius dared her gaze with chin high and feet braced while sweat broke out upon his brow. But Lio saw Cassia look into Annassa Soteira's eyes the way he so often did, as if searching for something she could almost grasp. She was not the only one. The Semna neither flinched nor looked away.

"The beds in this empty wing are for you," Queen Soteira told them. "Know they will always be here for you, should you ever have need."

Chrysanthos's eyes flashed with the same fury Lio had sensed in the mage after his first conversation with Queen Alea. "Rest assured, we are not so desperate for aid as Imperials. Our Orders of Kyria and Akesios will continue to see to our needs."

Queen Soteira gave him no reprieve from her full attention. "I marvel that there is such a surplus of healers in your lands. Do you mean to say that not a single mother forfeits her life to bring a child into the world? That not a single child dies in infancy? That not a single man survives battle, only to perish from his wounds while a healer works on him? That no warrior struggles on with a missing eye or finger or leg?"

Lio flinched with Callen. Perita tucked her arm tighter in her husband's.

"I seem to recall," said Queen Soteira, "there was recently great fear over an outbreak of Frost Fever in Tenebra. What wonderful tidings, that the Kyrians and Akesians were so completely prepared for this disaster that all people could rest assured their needs would be met."

The Semna let out a *hmph* in the Dexion's direction.

Chrysanthos's aura was hot with the anger he so carefully controlled in his voice and on his bruise-mottled face. "Hesperines are not the only ones keeping tally of how many mortal lives you add to your numbers. Do you keep records on the mages whose lives are forfeit when they try to prevent you from bringing so-called Sanctuary seekers over the border? Do you take a census of the mortal casualties of the so-called rescue efforts by your Hesperines errant?"

The words were hardly out of his mouth when a wail split the air. The Blood Union screamed with a fellow Hesperine's suffering. Queen Soteira shut her eyes and grimaced. Lio shuddered with her.

Panic consumed him. He searched the suffering aura for the presence of someone he knew. But he had never met this Hesperine. Not until this moment, when he would do anything in his power to help his brother in the blood.

Javed sounded out of breath. "They have brought him to the West Oktagonon. Shall I go on your behalf, Annassa?"

Lio unclenched his teeth. "We will leave you to your work. I will escort the embassy out."

Queen Soteira shook her head, already striding to the end of the wing. The double doors there flew open before her. "Come. They may observe."

As they followed, Javed explained, "The West Oktagonon is the receiving chamber for those whose lives are in immediate danger."

"We must remain quiet and orderly," Lio urged the mortals, "and do nothing to impede the healers."

Cassia answered for the embassy. "You have our word."

If the Dexion was angry at her for so binding him, he said nothing. Lio would have locked Cordium's filthy spy here in the empty wing, but Annassa Soteira had summoned them all. Lio and Javed guided the embassy after her, through the double doors and into the spacious, eight-sided chamber where the western wings converged.

The air smelled of seared flesh. The afterburn of war magic made Lio's stomach turn. Another cry echoed up to the high ceiling and through the Union, the howl of a fully grown male enduring unimaginable agony. It took Lio a moment to surface from the Union and remember Hypnos's fingers were not clawing through his own veins.

Lio ushered the embassy to stand along the perimeter of the chamber, while Queen Soteira and Javed joined the Sanctuary initiates and Chargers who hovered in the center of the room, whence the currents of suffering emanated. The group parted for Annassa Soteira.

The wounded Hesperine lay atop Rudhira's gray wool cloak on one of the Sanctuary's levitating litters. Annassa Soteira leaned near over him. His cries quieted.

What Lio was seeing sank in. The charred figure was a Hesperine, a person.

A patch of his hair had survived. The soot-stained lock was tangled with a Grace braid. Only that and his canines were still recognizable.

He bared his fangs, and his silent plea keened through the Union. As if to caress him, Annassa Soteira ran her hand over the air a hair's breadth from the blistered, oozing visage that had been his face. The vast depths of her magic enfolded the one person before her. He reached a blackened hand up toward her. His finger brushed her cheek, then fell away into ashes.

A tear slid down Annassa Soteira's face. "And I am so happy to meet you, dear one. Welcome home."

Grief welled out of Cassia and filled Lio. Her sympathy shone through the Union, focused and deliberate, a silent act of support for all the Hesperines there. Lio touched her mind, taking solace in her.

Emotion rippled through the Tenebrans around her. So they were not unmoved. Whatever they assumed, whatever they believed, they did feel what they saw before them.

"Who is he?" Cassia's voice quavered.

The Queen gazed into his eyes. "He says his name is Alkaios."

Lio watched Cassia turn to stone beside him and could not reach for her. He felt all the turmoil inside her that she hid with an iron will.

They were looking at one of the Hesperines who had saved her and given her sister the Mercy.

Lio could do nothing to give his Grace the support she needed. He could scarcely do anything for Alkaios, either.

A Charge healer calmly, efficiently explained, "Annassa, some burns are several nights old, others fresh, all of magical origin. We had no chance to do more than stabilize him in the field. We brought him straight to you."

"You did the right thing," the Queen said. "He is too fragile to move any further until I have a moment with him. Tell me what happened."

"He was trying to make it home. Two war mages were on his trail." The Charge healer glanced at the embassy. "We brought Alkaios through the ward while one of our comrades headed off the mages who were pursuing him."

Queen Soteira was quiet for a moment. "One of your fellow Hesperines errant stayed behind alone to hold off two war mages?"

The Charge healer cleared her throat. "He's our best, Annassa."

So it had come to this. Rudhira and war mages in open conflict. Lio could not find the words for a prayer. He sent up a silent plea to the Goddess.

Anger thrummed in Cassia's aura like a spell ready to unleash. "We need to know where this skirmish took place."

"The northern forests of Severitas," the Charge healer answered.

"Not the northeastern wilds?" Lord Gaius murmured. "Not even the frontier."

"Right in Tenebra proper," whispered Benedict.

Cassia exchanged a look with Lord Severin.

"I do not know," Lord Severin said. "I cannot say whether my father or the king authorized it, or if it was merely a circumstance of our domain being on the border."

"What was Alkaios's business there?" Lord Gaius asked the Charge healer.

"He was trying to get home," she answered. "He was *leaving* Tenebra. They could have just let him leave."

"Perhaps the mages were rogue apostates," Benedict suggested without conviction.

The Charge healer did not look at the Dexion. "They were Aithourians. Even if I hadn't seen their robes myself, what renegade has the training to do this to a Hesperine?"

"We've seen enough," Chrysanthos announced.

Queen Soteira shook her head. "You asked to meet our patients. We shall take this unexpected opportunity to oblige you."

"That won't be necessary." The Dexion turned to go.

Lio stood in his way. "The Annassa has issued you an invitation."

"We should not forgo this opportunity to learn about each other's techniques," said Queen Soteira. "Surely many of you here have had occasion to treat burns in the field."

Lord Severin took a step toward Queen Soteira, holding out a hand. "If I am always to be picking up the pieces my father leaves in his wake, I shall pick up every last one. I have indeed cared for my men's war burns. Can I be of assistance to you, Annassa?"

Queen Soteira met his gaze. He did not look away.

Master Gorgos, his face flushed, opened his mouth to bluster about something. The Semna silenced him with a pat on the arm and shuffled forward.

"Allow me to do the honors on your behalf," she said to Lord Severin. "Let it be known that Kyria has seen your compassion. Watch with a clear conscience."

He bowed his head. "Thank you, Semna." He hesitated, then nodded to Queen Soteira, almost bowing to her as well. "Annassa. My father will hear about this, I assure you."

"I say before your gods and mine," the Queen replied, "you are a good man who has already saved many lives with that outstretched hand. Semna, we are honored for you to work your magic in our Sanctuary."

"Two pairs of old hands will set this child to rights, eh?" said the Semna. "My fingers are not so steady these days, but my spells are my goddess's hands and shall not fail."

Queen Soteira smiled at the Semna over Alkaios. "With two goddesses giving him back his life, he is blessed indeed."

CAPABLE OF ANYTHING

NO ONE IN THE main hall of Rose House felt talkative except Master Gorgos. Cassia sat on her side of the table they had arranged out of the sideboards and wondered if any of the silent lords would speak up and tell the mage no one had the heart for his exhortations.

The mage stood at his place, farthest from Lio's window, and hadn't sat down since they had gathered. "Let us not forget the divine bliss with which Anthros rewards those who please him. A long life of suffering is the mere blink of an eye compared to an eternity in his Hall. No momentary relief in this worldly life is worth being forsaken by him and forfeiting the glorious future he has in store."

Lord Severin threw down his spoon beside his untouched porridge. "Tell that to the Imperials who bring their dying wives or malformed children to Orthros."

"All they care about is sparing those they love the unbearable," Cassia agreed.

"We know so little about the ways of these Imperials." Master Gorgos waved a hand. "No telling what heretical entities they worship."

"According to all the tales," said Benedict, "their lands are blessed by the sun."

"If that is the case," Master Gorgos replied, "then it grieves me for their once-noble spirits to be tainted by the blood goddess. Like Queen Soteira herself, they turn their backs on the sun and follow Hespera into darkness. The heretics seek always to rob the godly of their divine rewards."

Lord Gaius looked up from his mead. "Do you have a wife?"

Master Gorgos gave an uncertain laugh. "No mage may have a wife. We proudly take vows of celibacy to dedicate ourselves wholly to the gods."

"Do you have any children?"

"Certainly not!" the mage sputtered.

"Then you don't know whereof you speak, and I'll thank you to say no more." Lord Gaius shook his head. "I keep thinking about how many more children and grandchildren I'd have if we hadn't lost so many of them as babes."

"There isn't a man here who hasn't watched someone he loves die," Lord Severin said. "Someone he was supposed to protect."

The mage leaned forward. "Then it must certainly trouble you deeply to imagine if your own were subjected to perverse Hesperine magic. Would you forfeit the chance to meet them again in Anthros's Hall? Would you surrender their minds to the domination of the Queen of Darkness? Would you let her drag them into her world, never to return?"

Cassia heard Callen mutter, "It would be a wonder if they wanted to return, if this is the welcome the mage and his ilk have in mind for them."

Cassia glanced at him in time to see him rub his thigh under the table in a rare demonstration of discomfort. Perita clutched his free hand in hers, murmuring something in his ear.

The mage paid no mind to anyone except those of rank around the table. "Think of how many Imperial patients have been taken prisoner to swell the heretics' numbers! Impressed into Hespera's army of darkness! It does not bear imagining that Tenebrans would submit to the same!"

Lord Adrogan snorted. "I'm sure it will take a mind mage to convince them a life of luxury in Orthros is preferable to living in fear of starvation and brigands in Tenebra."

The mage tucked his hands into his sleeves which, no one could fail to notice, rested on his rotund belly. "Had they a choice, I am certain such godly folk would prefer a humble and virtuous life to wealth and wickedness."

"Oh, aye," Lord Adrogan replied. "No one in their right mind wants unholy fine food and corruption by silk sheets."

"Do not be deceived," the mage repeated. "All of this is a show to make us believe the Hesperines are compassionate and worthy of our friendship. Once they win our trust, the conniving Queens will betray us."

It grew harder each night for Cassia to swallow her outrage and keep a civil tongue. She must not allow the Solorum mage to hinder her progress with the lords and knights, although she considered it a victory that Master Gorgos held court with her and her supporters at Rose House, rather than joining the Cordian mages at the New Guest House.

Even poor Eudias came here to eat his meals in peace, but she must let him retreat to his post in the gallery afterward. None of them could be sure how much he might repeat to his master under duress.

Cassia managed to assume an earnest, innocent tone. "Master Gorgos, if the Hesperines' power is so great and fearsome, could they not have done whatever they wish to us already? Why go to such trouble to create a ruse when they could merely flick their fingers and tear us away from Anthros, condemning us all to an eternity of darkness?"

"You are wise to fear for your spirit every moment we are here. Only Anthros's protection has preserved us this long."

"I said," Lord Gaius warned, "that's enough, mage. We know our own minds. Take care you do not make your own attempt to twist our thoughts."

"We all know what we saw tonight," Lord Severin said. "The Queen restored that Hesperine's flesh and bones before our very eyes. She was *regrowing his skin* when we left. If she can do that, is there anything she cannot heal?"

Cassia sat back in her chair and listened to her supporters testify.

"Of course she can work such magic on her own minions," said Master Gorgos.

"One of her own kind destroyed by their greatest weakness," Lord Severin returned. "Magefire. If she can save a Hesperine from Anthrian magic, healing a mortal must be a trivial task for her."

Master Gorgos scowled. "She snatched the blood goddess's spawn from the reach of Anthros's justice. The god of war is angry."

"Master Gorgos," said Pakhne, "have you forgotten Kyria's own power helped save Alkaios? I shall not listen to any healing of the Semna's be called displeasing to Anthros."

Ariadne wrapped a warm woolen mantle closer around their mentor, who sat dozing off the great magic she had worked.

Master Gorgos looked on sadly. "How well I know my sister mages' tender hearts, which urge them to bestow Mother Kyria's mercy on the undeserving."

"You can't teach anything to a dead Hesperine," Ariadne said. "If you want him to hear of the goddess's forgiveness, you have to save his life first."

"I believe Kyria sent us this opportunity," said Pakhne. "When have we ever had such a chance to demonstrate our goddess's power to Hesperines? We have planted a seed that will grow into great good."

Master Gorgos sighed. "The Semna exhausted herself for a lost cause. That Hesperine was already doomed to the pyre the moment he sprouted fangs."

Cassia rose to her feet. "Who could look upon Alkaios tonight without feeling compassion for his suffering? Who could see a fellow creature in that much pain and dare suggest he deserves it?"

"You are a true daughter of Kyria, moved to pity by the goddess," Master Gorgos replied. "I am a mage of Anthros, charged with dispensing godly justice."

Cassia stood as still as she could, so he would not see her shaking with anger. "What justice could there be in such torture?"

"A Hesperine's punishment at the hands of war mages is not a fit sight for females. Do sit down, Basilis, and rest yourself. This is why Anthros entrusts such difficult tasks to the strong wills of men."

Cassia did not sit down. "You forget how many burn victims the healers of Kyria treat in the temple."

"Lady Cassia has worked in our infirmary," Ariadne said. "She is the last woman you should accuse of having a weak stomach."

"We have faced death together, haven't we?" Cassia replied. "All of us here have faced death."

Lord Severin sighed. "I once lost a dozen guards in a few moments to heart hunters' fire arrows. A rival warband's feud with my father's hunters brought them too close to the keep. Men and Hesperines burn just the same."

Lord Gaius took another swallow of his mead. "We lost the Siege of Tenth Coin to fire arrows and boiling oil."

Master Gorgos delivered his tidy answer without batting an eye. "There is no comparison between men who fall honorably in battle in Anthros's name and the wicked who meet with divine judgment."

Benedict's leather journal snapped shut upon his notes. Cassia glanced at him. He had not looked so forlorn since the Autumn Greeting.

One of the lords spoke up, a young, brazen, and scheming rival of Lord Adrogan's who was also out for whatever he could gain from this venture. "Hear the Master out. Everything that happened tonight was too convenient. What are the odds an innocent Hesperine was harmed by war mages and brought to safety here at the precise moment when the Almighty Healer Queen was trying to win our trust?"

Of course a man like him would suspect that. A chorus of ayes arose from both the unscrupulous and the devout.

Lord Adrogan's rival raised his voice over the troubled murmurs. "It was all conniving, not coincidence, if you ask me."

"Never forget they are Hesperines," came Chrysanthos's voice from the doorway. "They are capable of anything."

Cassia turned to see the Dexion and his apprentice enter the hall under the rose window. They had collected Eudias on their way through the gallery, it seemed, for he now lurked in the doorway.

"Honored Master," she said, "what a surprise. How unusual for you to join us."

"I could not shirk my duties as the embassy's spiritual guide." He circled the table and stood opposite Cassia. "Tonight's events might cause confusion. Even lead men astray."

Tychon imposed himself next to the Dexion, and Master Gorgos gave them room.

"Master," Tychon asked Chrysanthos, "what insight can you give us?"

Cassia readied herself to undo whatever damage the mage was about to deal. With the official negotiations commencing tomorrow, she was not about to let Chrysanthos have the last word tonight. She could not allow him to knock the Summit off course at this critical moment.

The Dexion took a seat and poured himself a glass of Hesperine wine. He lifted the goblet to his nose and breathed. Then he set it away from him.

Corks popped all around them, and every flask of wine in the entire hall began to spill its contents. Cassia was the only person who did not jump.

Chrysanthos watched the massacre of dark red wine stain the white silk tablecloth and pour over the tile. "My nephew is three years old. Too young to have any memories of his father—my brother." He gave them a cold smile. His injuries made the expression macabre. "My brother has been in his grave less than a year, and the boy's mother struggles to raise him alone. I do what I can for my nephew, but within the walls of a temple, I am frequently out of reach."

"I am sorry for your loss," Cassia said in the silence.

"It is the Hesperines who should be sorry," said Chrysanthos. "By the time they were done with my brother, there was little more left of him than of the Hesperine errant you saw tonight. I would ask Queen Soteira where her people's compassion for mortals was when Hesperines deprived a mother and child of my brother. I would ask any man here if the Hesperines who murdered him do not deserve to burn on Anthros's pyre."

Cassia had no reply to that. To such grief, such blind hate, she could make no argument.

She'd had no idea. This was the enemy she and Lio faced. Not just an Aithourian. One with a deep, personal grudge against Hesperines, wrought by loss.

She had no doubt Chrysanthos was somehow mistaken. But that didn't matter. He blamed the Hesperines for his brother's death.

The Dexion didn't seem to notice the wine that had splashed onto his robes. "That is why I am here. For my brother. You would all do well to remember why you came, as well."

With that, he stood and quit the hall.

BLESSED TRAITORS

WHEN CASSIA SLIPPED OUT to the courtyard, she told herself she was not surrendering. She had done all she could to strengthen the embassy's faith in the Hesperines despite Chrysanthos's condemnation. If she said anything more, it would be too obvious whose side she was on.

There wasn't any more she could do. The damage was done.

Chrysanthos hadn't even explained the circumstances of his brother's death. It didn't seem to matter. His emotional speech had taken root in the men's minds and given fruition to all sorts of doubts, speculation, and second thoughts.

Cassia took refuge among the Sanctuary roses, only to discover she was not alone. So this was where Benedict had disappeared to. He sat on a bench by the fountain with his elbows propped on his knees, contemplating the amulet of Andragathos in his hands.

"Forgive me for interrupting your solitude," said Cassia. "I shall bid you good night and proceed to my rooms."

He looked up. "Not at all, Your Ladyship. No need to go inside on my behalf."

She had yet to ascertain how he had taken Chrysanthos's declaration. Was there still hope of keeping Benedict on her side? Against all odds, it might yet be possible to sway him by appealing to his conscience. There had to be a chance. She could not afford to lose Benedict.

In fact, it would hurt to lose him. It would hurt not just her plans, but also…her.

"May I join you, then?" she asked.

"Of course, Your Ladyship." He looked in the direction of her rooms.

Through the glass, Perita and Callen were visible inside. Apparently satisfied as to propriety, Benedict moved over to make room for Cassia on the bench.

She sat down next to him. "Does Andragathos offer you any clarity of mind regarding tonight's events?"

He shook his head. "I am no more certain of the Hesperines' motivations than any other man here. Or woman."

She waited to see if he would say more. But he sat in silence with her, worrying his amulet between his fingers.

"When Master Gorgos tries to teach us a lesson on guilt, he exhorts the Scions, doesn't he?"

"Indeed," Benedict said without expression. "I know all about how much better it is to die than to live in shame."

"You and I do know. Yet neither of us has lain down and died yet, have we?"

"That would be a poor way to repay those who let us live."

"'Let us live,' you say, as if we did not already have a right to. Do you really believe that? Will you really sit here and think any human would be better off dead than restored to life by Hesperines? That you and I would be better off dead, because my mother was a concubine and your father a traitor?"

"I have always been grateful for your forgiveness. But I fear neither you nor I have the power to absolve each other. Only the gods can do that."

"Is that why you pledged yourself to Andragathos? Because you were trying to atone? I think not, Benedict. I think the real reason you made a vow to your god is because you aren't like your father. You want to protect others. To be needed by someone."

"I deem this quest to Orthros a worthy fulfillment of my promises. I am not afraid to lay down my life for the gods. I may yet be called upon to do so, if the mages of Anthros are right about the Hesperines' intentions."

She was losing him to his own conscience. Time to win him back. Nothing short of the truth would be enough. It was time to counteract Chrysanthos's revelations with her own. For Benedict, hers would be far more powerful.

"Are you all right?" she asked.

"Why shouldn't I be?"

"When we saw Alkaios," she said, "I know what you were remembering."

"Fearful memories often come to mind in spite of us, whether or not what we see before us should remind us of our own experiences."

"You are too hard on yourself, Ben."

At her use of Genie's affectionate name for him, his hands stilled. "It is wiser not to think of that night, much less speak of it."

"Why? We are no longer children. We need not be silent. In fact, I think we need to stop being silent."

He turned the amulet again in his hands, and again. "The catapults."

"Yes."

"Gods." He closed his fist over the amulet. "The thought of catapults must mean something entirely different to you."

"Yes. When I think of catapults, I think of the ones that fired my sister's body over the walls. I know you think of the king's catapults, which hurled fire upon the ramparts where your father stood."

"We truly should not speak of this."

"I never saw my sister's body," she went on. "Did you see your father's?"

Benedict looked away. "No. The king does not allow traitors a blessed burial."

"Sometimes what we imagine is worse than what really happened."

"Nothing could be worse than the truth we must live with. I am so sorry."

"You have no reason to be sorry. You were only eight when you watched your father dance the Autumn Greeting with my sister. In Bellator and Solia's betrothal promise, you saw nothing but your own bright future. You would not merely be the next Free Lord of Roborra, but a prince. Best of all, you would have a mother again, and what a kind and loving one."

"You needn't remind me."

"No, I think I must. Tonight is one of those nights when we must remember."

"There's nothing more to be said about it."

"But there is, Ben. You don't know everything."

His gaze snapped up, and he looked at her with furrowed brows. "What can you mean?"

"You weren't at the Siege of Sovereigns. As we all know, you were safe in the care of Lord Titus's family, which saved your life. Whatever else can be said of your father, he loved you and wanted to keep you safe, to give you a good future. He succeeded in that."

Benedict let out a bitter sigh. "How can you say one good thing about him?"

"Because you're sitting here next to me."

He would not meet her gaze.

"Lord Titus paid dearly that night," she said. "By refraining from intervening, by abandoning the rebel free lords to the king's justice, he let members of his own faction die to prove his loyalty to the king once and for all. But Lord Titus won, too. He won you, when he convinced the king an eight-year-old boy should not be punished for his father's crimes. He promised he would raise you to be loyal, so you would not grow up to cause problems later. But I think you are often the one who teaches Lord Titus's family about loyalty. You have repaid your life debt to them over and over. Flavian and Genie's love for you is proof of that."

"They are generous to me, as you are."

"It's not just generosity, Ben."

"Why?" he demanded.

"No one is ashamed of you but you. Stop prostrating yourself before the gods. Get on your feet and strap on your sword, Knight of Andragathos. You will need all your courage to confront the difficult truth I am about to tell you."

He looked startled, and he straightened beside her. Good. She had his attention.

"I was at the siege," she reminded him. "I witnessed what happened."

"A grievous experience for a girl. I regret my father subjected you to that."

"*My* father subjected me to it."

At the mention of the king, Benedict tensed.

"He can't hear us," Cassia said. "And even in Tenebra, whenever you think it, he cannot hear your thoughts."

Benedict recoiled. "I would never entertain thoughts against the king. I know better."

"So do I. How well both of us have been taught to know better, even as we quietly bear the truth. There are too few truth bearers, Ben. We cannot afford to let the torch we carry in silence snuff out."

"I don't understand what you mean."

"My father is a tyrant who has made all of us suffer. He is no better than your father."

Benedict did not appear shocked. He did not glance nervously around to see who was in earshot or jump to his feet and refuse to listen to her treason. He solemnly put his hand over hers with his amulet hanging between them. "Let us speak of it no more, Your Ladyship. For your sake."

"I appreciate your concern. But I do not need you to protect me. I need you to defend the truth."

"I'll lay down my life, but not yours."

"My life is of no use to anyone laid down, nor is yours. We have to keep ourselves and the truth alive. Will you hear me out?"

He looked stricken now. "Such matters are better left in the grave. But I already carry it with you. It would be cowardly of me to shy from it now."

"Thank you. I knew I could rely on your courage. I am going to tell you something only I know—I and Lord Hadrian."

Benedict sat up straighter. "We cannot leave truth at the mercy of Lord Hadrian. One of Segetia's own ought to champion her. Tell me what's weighing on your heart, Your Ladyship."

"I have uttered these secrets to no other man but you in all these years." Only to a Hesperine. "The king's cruelty on that night rivaled the free lords'."

"He had to make an example out of Castra Roborra." Benedict recited the teachings that had been graven into them their whole lives. "The lords who set themselves up as sovereigns—my father included—behaved without a shred of honor. Even after he met their ransom demands, they still struck down the princess."

"He didn't meet the ransom demands, Ben. He lied. The king refused all their terms and let them carry out their threats upon Solia without lifting a finger to stop them."

He went silent. His face went blank. She understood. It took time for truth to shift beneath one's feet.

She pressed on, "When the rebel lords sent the hostages over the walls, my father didn't collect the bodies. He left them on the field. He abandoned my sister."

"But—" He shook his head. "The funerary rites at Solorum. I was there for those. The crypt in the temple—I visit it myself every year, you know I do."

"They didn't carry her in a covered bier because her body was damaged. There was no body to carry. Her tomb has been empty all along."

"By all Fourteen Scions." He went a shade paler than the moonlight, his face twisting into a sickened expression. "That was her true fate? Our future queen never even received a blessed burial?"

"I could not bear the thought, so that night, after the catapults fell silent, I went to find her."

"You? On your own? A seven-year-old maid? It's a miracle you survived."

"I almost didn't. Someone fired at me from the walls. There I was, a child alone, with no one to save me from that oncoming arrow."

He listened in silence now. She watched the first hint of realization dawn in his eyes.

"Do you know who saved me from that arrow?" she asked.

"I can think of few who would be on an abandoned battlefield in the depths of night, except..."

"A Hesperine. She snatched me out of the way before the arrow touched me. And when I told her my father was near, do you know what she did? She and her two fellow Hesperines errant took me back to him and laid me in my own bedroll to sleep."

Benedict shook his head, opened his mouth to speak. But he said nothing.

"You may wonder," Cassia said, "if they returned me for political ends, because there would have been consequences for their people if they took the king's daughter. But they didn't know that's who I was. They didn't know if the castle or the camp was in the right. They didn't know your father was a lord and mine a king, or that they were both monsters. All they knew was that I was a lost child with a parent nearby, and that my sister lay dead on the field."

"They took her body," he breathed.

"No. They commended her remains to the gods with rites they hold sacred. How can I condemn their practices, when the Champion of Anthros was so cruel to my sister, she who was worthiest among us all?"

"I can scarcely believe it."

"If nothing else, believe what you beheld in the Healing Sanctuary tonight—a brave and honorable person who does not deserve to suffer. Alkaios was one of the three Hesperines I met that night. The one who recovered Solia's belongings from her body for me."

Cassia sat with Benedict, waiting with him while what she had said sank in. It seemed he did not know what to say. It might take him a long time to find the words to speak of that horrific night, if he ever did. It had taken her a long time, and she had needed Lio to help her.

Even as she held Lio in her thoughts, she felt the touch of his familiar hand on her shoulder. How long had he been here in the courtyard, keeping watch over her? She relaxed under his touch, willing him to feel how grateful she was for his presence.

"Ben, if you're thinking you must now question everything you have ever been taught, you are right. If you are thinking it is our deeds, not our origins that mark us as godly or not, I believe you are also right." She closed her hands over his pendant. "Wear this with honor. You are worthier than the king."

He had no reply, but when she eased the pendant out of his hands, he did not stop her. He let her put it over his head once more.

THE FATE OF GRACES

THE MOMENT BENEDICT LEFT the courtyard, Lio took his place on the bench and pulled Cassia into his arms. "Are you all right?"

"Is Alkaios doing any better?"

"Annassa Soteira continues to treat him."

"Tell me what Rudhira will do to the mages."

"I doubt they were still breathing by the time Alkaios arrived."

"I hope there's nothing left of them for Chrysanthos to put on a funerary pyre. I must go to Alkaios, as soon as we may see him."

"Annassa Soteira has already asked us to come to his room after the half hour. We don't have long to wait."

"Veil hours already. I missed bedtime stories." Disappointment crushed Cassia's aura. "I must apologize to Zoe tomorrow."

Lio silently cursed politics for denying her the comfort of seeing his sister. "What you spoke of with Benedict was especially difficult for you tonight."

"I'm glad you were here."

He ran his hand down her stiff, straight spine. "You have given me as much of an education as you gave Benedict. I had no idea he was Lord Bellator's son. Now I understand your regard for him."

She frowned. "Were you troubled by my 'regard' for him?"

"It was difficult for me to understand your friendship with him, for in my eyes he represents Flavian. But it is clear to me now why you care about Benedict."

"We are bound by that night. It was not his fault, any more than it was mine."

"I should have known that anyone fortunate enough to earn your trust is worthy of it."

"He is an honorable man. Tenebra needs every one of those it can get. *We* need him, if we are not to lose the embassy's hearts and minds to the Dexion." She pulled back. "Lio, did you hear what Chrysanthos said about his brother?"

"Mak, Lyros, and I were listening. We felt his aura while he said it. I couldn't help but hear what he was thinking, although I didn't invade his mind with my magic. He was all but shouting his thoughts. He wasn't lying. Or at least, he certainly believed his own words."

Cassia nodded. "That was not some tale to produce a desired effect. He blames Hesperines for his brother's death. Of course mortals, in their infinite perception, don't realize how preposterous that is."

Lio shook his head. "Hesperines wouldn't risk entering Cordium, much less assassinate a son of a princely dynasty, leaving his widow and small child to grieve. Since Prometheus's death, no Hesperines errant dare venture into the Magelands, except for the most careful and clandestine forays, which must be personally sanctioned by Rudhira."

"Of course you would never incite conflict. I wish I could make the rest of the embassy understand you have nothing to gain by striking against the Cordian aristocracy. We need to find out the truth."

"We've already informed Aunt Lyta. She will consult with the envoys and try to learn more about what really happened."

"Whatever befell his brother, Chrysanthos's grief explains why he has been emotional and uncontrolled. There's no telling what he'll do. He isn't here for his circle's politics. This is personal. His chance to avenge his brother."

"Revealing his personal grudge was a mistake. He has handed us an accurate assessment of how dangerous he is and a better understanding of what motivates him."

"Thank you for reminding me. I fear my first thought was not how to use his personal feelings against him, but how difficult it will be to combat them."

"We will keep the Tenebrans from falling once more under his sway. You have worked tirelessly at it tonight."

"I am uncertain how much I accomplished." She shook her head. "We were so close!"

"We *are* so close."

"I can't believe Chrysanthos has struck this blow the very night before the first official proposal of treaty terms. Tomorrow seemed like such a good time to finally begin negotiations. But now I am uncertain."

"Our plan is still sound." If Lio managed to convince Cassia of that, perhaps he would feel more sure of it himself. "When the Winter Solstice festivities start next week, we'll have another chance to win their favor and demonstrate the benefits of a new Oath."

"We have no time to judge how much of our good work Chrysanthos has undone in one move."

The bells tolled the half hour. No more time.

Lio rose to his feet and helped Cassia up. "This will not be easy, but we will do it together. Are you ready?"

Cassia took a deep breath. "I don't know if I will ever feel ready. To meet one of my rescuers at last... It is hard to know how to honor him. What thanks could be enough?"

"What greater deed could you do for him than to be at his side now, when he is suffering?"

She nodded, then held up a hand. "Wait, there is one thing..."

She darted back into her rooms, then returned a moment later carrying Solia's pendant. How well Lio recognized the wooden triquetra of ivy from the night Cassia had first confided in him about her sister.

He could feel the dread, hope, and sorrow knotted inside her as he stepped them to the Healing Sanctuary. The hall outside Alkaios's room was deserted and lit by gentle spell light. No sound emerged from behind the veil of fabric and magic that hung over the doorway.

The curtain did not stir as Queen Soteira stepped out of the room and joined them in the corridor. "It is good that you are here."

Cassia's lip trembled. "He is Alkaios."

"I know." The Queen pulled Cassia into her arms.

Cassia gasped, then held on to Annassa Soteira for a long moment. Lio put a hand on his Grace's back.

"How is he?" Cassia asked at last.

"Go in and see. I would warn you this is not an encounter for the faint of heart, but your hearts are right where they need to be."

"Thank you, Annassa." Lio gave her the heart bow.

She blessed him with a kiss on the forehead before she disappeared.

Lio pulled back the curtain for Cassia to go first. As soon as they set foot inside Alkaios's room, moans of agony and the smell of blood washed over them. Cassia froze in her tracks, and Lio pulled her close, ready to take her right back out the way they had come if she needed him to.

Despite the wonders Annassa Soteira had worked upon Alkaios, a long, guttural cry of pain worked its way out of him, as if he did battle with every breath. But he did not suffer alone. Rudhira sat on the bed with both arms around him.

Alkaios had skin again. The stub of a finger was regrowing on his hand. Someone had cleaned his Grace's long, blond braid and the remaining lock of his own shoulder-length, light brown hair, and he wore a fresh Sanctuary robe. Even so, he shivered hard amid the twisted bedclothes. As each shudder came over Alkaios, Rudhira braced him. The Hesperine errant clung to his prince, his face turned against Rudhira's shoulder.

Cassia seemed unable to look away. "Why does he still suffer so? Annassa Soteira healed his burns. Did the mages leave some malign spell on him?"

"We should let Rudhira continue tending to him," Lio cut in.

He knew the answer to Cassia's question. He should have realized it the moment he had first felt Alkaios's pain through the Union earlier that night. Alkaios suffered no curse but the one Lio himself had felt as ice and fire in his own blood, a force rending him from inside out.

"We have done all we can." Grief edged the prince's voice. "His malady is simple. He has been starving for months."

"What?" Cassia asked. "How could he be so deprived? There were many ways for him to procure the Drink in Tenebra, surely."

Rudhira glanced at Lio. "Based on my experience as a healer, I would say he has been without his Grace since sometime this spring."

Lio tightened his arm around Cassia. Spring, when he had parted from her. So he saw before him what his own fate might have been, if she were not in Orthros now.

BOND OF GRATITUDE

CASSIA TRIED TO SEE her childhood rescuer in the Hesperine before her. Alkaios's body was emaciated and contorted with anguish, his newly grown skin still glossy and ruddy. He bore no resemblance to the strong, gentle protector who had braved the field below the ramparts of Castra Roborra so Cassia did not have to.

"Is it all right for us to be here?" Cassia asked.

"You are welcome to remain," Rudhira answered, "although you need not."

"I will stay." She would not abandon Alkaios to his pain. She would not flee this room. He was the one who had rescued the ivy pendant from Solia's remains and put her sister's last gift to her in her hands.

Cassia stepped forward. A shiver moved through her, as through the Hesperine on the bed, as through a cold and frightened child in the woods in the Tenebran winter. Tonight she had not her father's camp behind her, but Lio's warmth. Not an enemy fortress ahead of her, but the prince and his promise of support. Tonight it was Alkaios who needed her.

"Will it hurt him if I touch him?" she asked Rudhira.

"Just be gentle," the prince advised.

Cassia reached out a hand and caressed Alkaios's forehead. Hollows under his eyes. Gaunt cheeks. Furrows of strain on his brow made him look like a careworn man, not a Hesperine who should be eternally in his prime. As she turned his head gently toward her, he uttered a low moan.

Shadows cast by moonlight and spell light. Furrows of regret on his brow. A confident, kind voice, promising her Solia was in a better place.

"Alkaios?" she queried softly.

His eyelids, no longer melted shut, flew open. His gaze darted about. Then his brown eyes focused on her. When she touched his wounded hand, he slowly released his iron grip on the blankets. She turned his hand over and placed the ivy pendant on his palm, then held his hand in both of hers.

"Do you know me?" she asked.

His gaze fixed on the pendant. His jaw moved. At last his voice emerged in a hoarse murmur. "Solia."

She heard Lio and the prince let out a breath.

Cassia nodded. She would not cry. "My sister."

Alkaios's eyes lifted to meet hers again. *"Cassia?"*

"Yes! I am Cassia." She smiled at him. He needed her smile right now. "I'm here to thank you for everything you did for me. You have my gratitude."

Alkaios's expression eased, and his body relaxed. He had understood her. Her words had mattered.

Her smile widened in spite of the ache in her throat. "See what you have done for me? I survived, and I grew up strong, and I came home to Orthros. I am so glad you have come home to us now."

Alkaios's fingers closed around the pendant, and his eyes slid shut. A sigh rushed out of him, and then he seemed to stop making the effort of breathing. But in the quiet room, she could hear his heart laboring on.

Lio put his arm around her again, and she leaned against him.

"He remembers. That is the only good sign we have had tonight." The prince shook his head. "My mother Soteira tells me this is the first time Alkaios has been to Orthros. A Hesperine errant must have Gifted him in the field. What a homecoming."

Cassia didn't let go of Alkaios's hands. She knew the answer to her question before she spoke it. But she refused to accept the answer. "How can he be starving? Now that he is home, can you not give him as much to drink as he needs?"

"He will want for nothing," said Lio. "The Imperial guests who come to the Healing Sanctuary for training also give their blood to Hesperine patients."

"I have given him the Ritual Drink myself." There was no reassurance in the prince's voice, only regret.

Lio's face mirrored the same. "I'm not surprised, Rudhira. I know you would shed your blood for any Hesperine errant. You have done a great thing for Alkaios tonight."

Rudhira gave one shake of his head.

The blood of the Queens, delivered by their firstgift, must hold astonishing power. If that was not enough to bring a Hesperine back from the brink of starvation, what was?

Cassia was angry at her own tears for encroaching, furious that all she could do was stand here and hold Alkaios's hands. "How many of your kind follow Hylonome's path?"

"Who told you that story?" Lio demanded.

"Your Trial sisters." The tears spilled over. "How can he fight so hard for others, but not for himself?"

"We still fight for him," said the prince. "I will not stop fighting, whether with blood or healing magic or my sword."

"Did you deliver justice upon the war mages?" Cassia asked.

Rudhira was silent for a long moment. "What I did to them tonight was one of the hardest things I have ever done." He sighed and looked at Lio. "I was mindful of dealing a blow to the Summit, if I executed Chrysanthos's brethren while their Dexion is here in Orthros. So I chased them back to Solorum and left them unharmed."

"Rudhira, I…" Lio shook his head. "I am as grateful to you as I am disappointed."

"A wise decision, First Prince," said Cassia. "Thank you. I only wish I felt wiser tonight."

"Do not give up on your Summit," Rudhira replied. "You two are fighting for Alkaios as well. Whatever you do, do not surrender."

Just then, a Hesperine appeared on the opposite side of Alkaios's bed. He looked about Javed and Kadi's age, but he wore Tenebran attire in the browns and greens of the woods. "You called me out of the field, My Prince?"

"Not without reason," Rudhira replied. "Cassia, Lio, I would like you to meet Kalos, the best scout in my Charge."

Kalos didn't meet their eyes, just angled a slight bow in their direction.

"Well met, Kalos." Lio bowed. "It is an honor. I have heard much of your deeds."

Before Kalos could reply, Knight broke away from Cassia and went to greet the Hesperine errant. Kalos took a step back, his expression astonished. She opened her mouth to command Knight to heel.

But Kalos held up his hand. "No, don't call him off. Please."

Knight was all over him, sniffing and slobbering and wagging his tail, although it was clear Kalos was not of the Queens' blood. Cassia watched, a command on the tip of her tongue in case Knight overstepped.

Kalos crouched down in front of the liegehound and eased his hands out. Tentatively, he slid his fingers into Knight's ruff. The Hesperine's sober face softened. "It's been an awfully long time since a fine dog like you wanted anywhere near me."

"You are clearly a dog person," Cassia said. "That must be why Knight likes you."

Kalos ran his hands along Knight's shoulders, back, and rump. "Well, look at your conformation, Sir. You are Solorum Royal through and through, except…" Kalos took one of Knight's paws in his hand. "That's quite a footprint for a palace hound. I think a randy Severitan had a roll in the kennels with one of your fine lady ancestors."

"You're exactly right." She relaxed and smiled at Kalos. "A few generations ago, a Lord of Severitas gifted a stud to the then-king to add hardiness to the royal pedigree. The crown waged a lot of mountain campaigns in those days. You do know your dogs. You must have spent time with liegehounds before you came to Orthros."

The pleasure in his eyes faded. "I had a hound of my own."

She gentled her tone. "Losing them is as hard for us as losing us is for them."

He shrugged. "I imagine it was easier on him this way. Always thought he'd rather go down fighting than live on in a world where his master is a Hesperine."

"I don't believe that."

Kalos scratched Knight's chin. "You think his liege bond might have survived my Gifting?"

"Master Arkadia partnered with Knight for a round of training exercises in Hippolyta's Gymnasium."

Kalos's eyes widened, and he shook his head.

"What pedigree was your hound from?" Cassia asked.

Now Kalos scratched the base of Knight's tail and watched the hound wag it. She wasn't sure the Hesperine errant would reply.

"Same pedigree as mine," Kalos said at last. "But now I'm a Ritual tributary of the Charge, and that's my bloodline. Fine thing about the past—it stays behind you."

"I apologize. I did not intend to cross the veil."

"Look at liegehounds laying down beside Hesperines," Rudhira said. "There are no prejudices in this room, Kalos."

"You're a wonder," Kalos told Knight.

"Cassia is going to tell you a great deal about her past," Rudhira added. "She knows Hespera's verdict upon you. You survived your Gifting."

Kalos kept looking at her hound. "I was a heart hunter."

She hoped Kalos did not misinterpret the surprise he must sense in her aura. She wanted to tell him he had just restored a great deal of her faith in humankind. If a heart hunter could become a Charge scout, there must be no lost causes after all.

If a heart hunter could survive the Gifting, then surely a hardened survivor of the king's court could, too.

She knelt down and stroked Knight, her hand just inches from Kalos's. "I was a palace bastard who might have sold out anyone to save my own skin had Hesperines not shown me kindness. Instead, I am a traitor to the King of Tenebra and an advocate for Orthros."

Kalos met her gaze for the first time. He had kind green eyes.

"Kalos disobeyed his hornbearer's orders to raze a village," Rudhira said. "His warband turned on him. His hound fought to the last, defending him against his former comrades, and fell at his feet. I am sorry we were too late to save such a faithful companion."

"The band left me in the remains of the village," said Kalos. "Staked me out for the Hesperines. See how they answered."

A smile ghosted across Rudhira's face. "Now Kalos devotes his skill for tracking Hesperines to finding those of us who go missing Abroad."

"I'm sorry it was so hard for you to get here," Cassia said, "but I'm glad you made it."

"Allow me to thank you," Lio said. "On behalf of my family, you have our gratitude for your dedication in searching for Nike."

Kalos got to his feet and looked to the prince. "The trail will go cold yet again if I let it out of my sight for long."

Rudhira gazed at Alkaios. "We must trust Nike to protect herself awhile longer. I must retask you to find Nephalea."

"My Prince, it's my duty to advise you what your orders will cost. You've other scouts tracking Nephalea, and their skill is equal to the task. I'll be of greater use to you if I continue to search for your Trial sister."

"I know, Kalos. You are the only person who has even the slightest chance of finding Nike." Rudhira let out a hopeless, affectionate laugh. "She is expert at using our own strategies against us. The first Master Steward of the Stand, with her mother's warding and her father's thelemancy, with nearly sixteen hundred years of life experience and eight hundred as a Hesperine errant, does not wish to be found."

"I'm afraid so, My Prince. My latest efforts suggest she's using the same methods to evade us as the Blood Errant used to avoid the attention of hostile mages."

The prince rubbed a hand over his face. "Meanwhile Nephalea's trail has disappeared as if it never was, despite her Grace stumbling all the way home to Orthros. Do you know why he didn't simply step home? Why he took the journey in stages, making himself vulnerable to repeated attacks by war mages?"

"His injuries," Lio guessed. "I assumed he was in such dire condition, he could not manage the Will to step all the way to the border in one act."

Rudhira shook his head. "It appears he was deliberately leaving a trail—for Nephalea to follow him home or for us to follow back to her, we are not certain. Our other scouts traced his difficult passage back to the point where he and Nephalea were last together—and found nothing. You see before you what our failure is costing him."

Kalos studied the prince's patient. "I fear I must be the one to speak words no one wishes to hear. Are you certain Nephalea—"

"She lives," Alkaios ground out. "Our Grace Union…"

"There is our answer," Rudhira said. "If all were lost, Alkaios would know."

Alkaios heaved a breath. "I must not die."

"You will live," the prince promised.

Kalos took a step nearer the bed. "Alkaios, can you ask her through your Union where she is? Can you sense anything about her location?"

"She is weaker than I."

"Where was Nephalea when you last saw her?" Kalos's voice was quiet and even.

"With Iskhyra."

"Can you tell me where Nephalea and Iskhyra were?"

"I live for Nephalea. Please. Keep me alive. For her."

Kalos touched a respectful hand to Alkaios's Grace braid.

"How did Nephalea's braid survive the war mages' spells?" Cassia asked.

"Nephalea probably warded it herself," Lio answered. "It's a ritual when you go errant. You or someone you trust wards your Grace braids."

"That is usually all we bring back to the families," Rudhira said.

Kalos withdrew his hand. "I've got an impression of Nephalea's aura."

"Rest now." The prince lowered Alkaios's head to his shoulder once more. "While we discuss our course of action, I will put Alkaios into a slumber, so he can have some relief. Is there anything else you wish to say first, Cassia?"

Cassia bent close to speak in Alkaios's ear. She reached within her for all the kindness she had ever known herself to possess. She tried to put into her voice all the strength Alkaios, Nephalea, and Iskhyra had given her that night, which could make it seem like there was hope in the face of utter despair. "Don't give up, Alkaios. Nephalea loves you, and she needs you to be here waiting for her when the Charge brings her home. Please, don't give up. We will help you stay strong. You don't have to do any of this alone."

He clenched his hand around Solia's pendant as another shudder wracked him.

The prince made no move, but he must have worked his spell. Alkaios relaxed, and his tortured expression faded into one of serene rest.

"I wish he could tell you more, Kalos," said the prince, "but what you have heard is all we have managed to get out of him since we found him."

Kalos shook his head. "I don't mean to tax him with my questions. It's testament to his strength that he's still capable of speech."

"I know, my friend. Too many of our comrades did not last this long in his situation." Rudhira eased off the bed, settling Alkaios there. The First Prince of Orthros straightened the bedclothes around his patient with the efficiency of a commander and the tenderness of a father. "We cannot know what danger our other missing Hesperines may be in, but we must have faith in their capabilities and respond to the immediate threat to Alkaios."

Kalos was quiet for a minute. "I understand, My Prince."

Was that a moment of silence for his months of progress on the search for Nike, which were now for nothing? This must be an excruciating decision for the prince. No doubt one of many he must make to protect his Hesperines errant from the dangers of Tenebra. From the king, who sought to barter their lives to the mages and bolster his throne with the pyres of their executions.

"We won't surrender," Cassia promised.

"I'm sure this is what Nike would want," Lio said. "She wouldn't want you to spend time looking for her when Alkaios is in danger."

The prince nodded. "Cassia, I must ask you to tell Kalos everything you can about when you met Alkaios, Nephalea, and Iskhyra at Castra Roborra. I know how demanding it is for you to speak about that night, however—"

"Their lives may depend on it." Cassia turned to Kalos. "I will spare no detail, if it will help you find them. But that was over fourteen years ago."

"So recently?" Kalos asked. "That's good news. Did they use much magic?"

Lio gave Cassia another reassuring touch on her back. "Iskhyra performed the Mercy for Cassia's sister."

"I'm sorry, I didn't know. I carry your grief in my veins." He shifted on his feet, an unusually awkward gesture for a Hesperine. "The Mercy is a dramatic act of blood magic. I could ask for no stronger evidence of their passage."

"Solia's memory lives on," said Lio, "and can now help guide us to those who carry it."

Cassia tucked Alkaios's hand and the pendant he held under the bedclothes. "I hope the way they rescued me will now help us rescue them."

12

nights until

WINTER SOLSTICE

OPENING THE CIRCLE

UPON ESCORTING THE TENEBRAN embassy into the amphitheater, Lio discovered it was possible to feel more trepidation than he had when proposing the Summit to the Firstblood Circle. The last time he had spoken before the firstbloods of every family in Orthros, he had experienced a brush with mortality. This time, the lives of countless mortals and Hesperines could depend on the Circle's negotiations with the Tenebran embassy.

But tonight he was free of the Craving. There was no vertigo to trip him. No pain to halt his thoughts and rob him of his words. No danger of collapsing at the podium from life-threatening withdrawal from Cassia's blood. Sustaining power coursed through him, feeding his determination to bring all his best abilities to bear, to bring his best efforts to fruition tonight. Thank the Goddess he did not strive alone.

His greatest ally was in his very veins and at his side. Cassia stood and stared at the amphitheater spread out before them and the crowd of ancient power personified. A thrill rose in her aura, stronger than her anxiety. She would soon experience for herself how differently Orthros was governed than Tenebra. She would not kneel, voiceless, before a king. Here, she would stand before the Queens and be heard.

Whatever happened, neither he nor Cassia would end this night on their knees.

Lio felt as if the entire Blood Union swelled within his chest. Whenever he was in the Firstblood Circle, his own people always inspired awe in him, but it meant more when his Grace beheld it for the first time. And when Orthros's enemies must behold as well.

The Dexion was actually silent for several moments before he found his voice. "I see Hespera's temples loom large in Orthros's memory. But then, memories are all that's left of them."

"Her Great Temples are alive and well." Lio spoke the undeniable truth the mage must see.

He followed the Dexion's gaze down to the Firstblood Rose emblazoned on the floor of the amphitheater. The vast marble rendition of Hespera's Rose pointed its thorns, the arrows of his people's compass, toward the statues that bordered it.

"The first Hesperines keep vigil yet," Lio said. "My father's memorial sculpture of Ritual Firstblood Anastasios, his Gifter, stands before the seats of our bloodline and our Ritual tributaries, so we may always honor our origins at Hagia Boreia, the Great Temple of Hespera in the North, where Anastasios was Prismos. You see the statues of Ritual Firstbloods Daedala and Thelxinos before the seats of Blood Timarete and Blood Kitharos, heirs of Hagia Zephyra, Great Temple of the West. And there are the memorials to Ritual Firstbloods Eidon and Ourania in front of Blood Argyros and Blood Hypatia, who hail from Hagia Anatela, the Great Temple of the East."

Tychon looked greener than usual, and Lio knew it was not only the toll of being his master's channel. Eudias's teeth were actually chattering from the force of the Firstblood Circle's magic. The apprentice could not blame his distress on the cold. Geomagical warmth drifted up from the stones beneath their feet. Tonight a ward shielded the entire amphitheater from the elements for the mortals' sakes—and closed them in with the most powerful blood mages in the world.

Lio looked at the Dexion. "There are more Hesperines than statues."

Chrysanthos would not look at him, only at the two southerly memorials. "The Prismos and Prisma of Hagia Notia in Corona have naught but a wall behind them."

"A wall inscribed with Ereba's name. She did not survive to become an elder firstblood of Orthros and carry on Ritual Firstblood Eukairia's Gift. The only living mage of that temple failed to honor Ritual Firstblood Khariton's legacy and is unworthy to have his name spoken within the Circle."

"No wonder you have shoved the statues of Khariton and Eukairia aside."

"The better to devote the southern section entirely to Elder Firstblood Kassandra and her many Ritual tributaries."

"A prescient reminder of your Imperial allies to the south," Chrysanthos commented, as if upon a move at the game board.

Indeed, the time for subtle moves was past, and they both knew it. Tonight, they would see each other closing in for the win.

The Dexion had best remember the Queens were the most powerful movers on the board.

"Prisma Alea is not a statue," Lio said.

The top thorn of the Firstblood Rose pointed straight to the Queens. To the rows upon rows behind them filled with the royal bloodlines. To all the power Annassa Soteira had built beyond the temple where her Grace's Gift had begun.

Lio informed the embassy of the arrangements Cassia already knew. "Your seats await you on the Circle floor. Each of you will have a place before one of our bloodlines befitting the part of Tenebra you call home. Solorum's royal representative shall sit before our royal family."

She gave him a deep curtsy. "I hardly know what to say, Ambassador. I am highly unaccustomed to such honors. You recall my seat at last year's Summit."

"This is not the Equinox Summit, Lady Cassia, and we are not in Tenebra. This is the Solstice Summit in Orthros. Allow me to escort you to your place of honor before our Queens."

Cassia's shoulders were tense as they prepared to descend from the gallery, and she held her skirts tightly in her fists. He could sense her bracing herself against the anxiety that beset all of them who were young and trying to add their voices to this ancient chorus. He had counseled her thoroughly in preparation for this night, but this was not the circle on the Queens' Terrace, and there was no preparation that could make one immune to the splendor of all the firstbloods.

Xandra and Nodora smiled encouragement from below, and Kia waited with stacks of notes in front of her, ready to subtly cue Cassia and Lio about any historical facts they forgot. Mak and Lyros stood guard behind the embassy. Lio hoped Cassia would draw as much confidence as he did from their friends.

The Queens nodded to Konstantina. Lio could only imagine the Second Princess's reluctance as she acquiesced to her mothers and signaled Lio.

"The Circle is ready for us," he announced.

Mak led the eastern Tenebrans away, and Lyros commandeered those from the west, while the northern Tenebrans had the honor of being escorted by Lio's mother. A small army of Kassandra's Ritual tributaries approached the southern Tenebrans—and surrounded the mages.

Lio met the Dexion's gaze. "In honor of Cordium, where we were once neighbors and all our cults began, our colleagues from Tenebra's temples of Kyria, Chera, Anthros, and Hypnos shall sit before the southern section."

The smoke in Tychon's aura suggested he was about to erupt in defense of his master's authority over the Summit, or perhaps to reiterate their ruse that they had nothing to do with Cordium. What worried Lio more was that Chrysanthos calmly put a staying hand on his apprentice's shoulder. The Dexion acquiesced to his and Cassia's seating arrangements without protest. He had sacrificed the throne to the hounds like a strategist who intended to bring the sun into play.

When one group of mortals was in position at the top of each of the five aisles, Lio led Cassia, Knight, Perita, and Callen downward. In five processions, the embassy descended into the amphitheater between the ranks of firstbloods and their bloodlines. All along the way, the Hesperines who had welcomed, celebrated, and challenged the mortals since their arrival in Orthros turned in their seats or stood to greet them, as they would Hesperines arriving to join the Circle.

At each friendly word, Lio felt Cassia's tension easing. She must see this tapestry of power was made up of familiar faces. She must feel, as he did each time he spoke here, that she had a right to be here. That she was among *her* people, unlike when she had braved a hostile crowd of Tenebran warriors to win a few moments of their time at the men's council table at Solorum. By the time they reached the chairs between the podium and the royal seats, where Cassia gave the Queens a deep curtsy, Lio could tell her knees were no longer shaking.

Konstantina spoke Vulgus in the Firstblood Circle for the first time in

Orthros's history. "Lady Cassia, on behalf of our beloved Queens, as their eldest daughter and the voice of their Will, I bid you and each of our guests from Tenebra welcome to the Firstblood Circle of Orthros."

"For inviting us to attend the highest governing body of your land, you have our gratitude."

"No mortals from your part of the world have ever set foot in the Firstblood Circle, save those who await their Gifting. Tonight, just as we have often welcomed mortal dignitaries from the Empire to treat with the firstbloods, so too do we now welcome you, Tenebra's embassy. May these nights of negotiation bring about a successful conclusion of the Solstice Summit and the promising beginning of a new era."

"We hope to set a precedent tonight that will benefit us all."

Konstantina nodded to Lio. "Ambassador Deukalion, Firstgift Komnenos. The Annassa empower you to act as master of ceremonies and call forth each speaker."

He bowed to her. "Thank you, Royal Firstblood Konstantina, Second Princess."

Although Lio could not touch Cassia, he filled her mind with encouragement as he seated her. Her response was a flare of determination that warmed him as surely as her blood. She reached into her worn oilcloth satchel, which she wore, garden stains and all, with her formal gown in Tenebra's royal colors of blue and gold. She pulled out the notes she had painstakingly penned for this occasion over many weeks.

As Lio ascended the podium, he withdrew his own notes from his scroll case. He unrolled the program for the evening before him, with his proposal and his list of Cassia's deeds tucked behind it, just on principle. How far they had come.

My Goddess, it still amazes me how, through these events, you have brought the two of us to such prominent seats before this exalted circle. I am glad you are with me in my blood at the final step on the path, as at the first.

"Princess Konstantina," he said, "I am ready."

She addressed the crowd. "The Goddess hears all of us, from the mightiest firstblood to the smallest child, Hesperine and human, her own and those who worship other gods. Let all Hesperines remember, and let it be known among our guests, that this is the law of Orthros: in this circle, everyone may speak, and everyone must be heard. Any may take the stand, and their words shall be considered and voted upon by each bloodline. While the final vote rests with the firstbloods, the young are not voiceless, but may make their wishes known through demonstrations of partisanship. While the final determination of Orthros's path rests with the Hesperines, Tenebra is not voiceless here and shall join with us in deciding our joined futures." She took her seat and nodded for Lio to continue.

He looked all around him, this time at careworn, sun-blemished mortal foreheads as well as familiar Hesperine ones. Quick human hearts fluttered among the slow, powerful pulse of Hesperine blood.

Lio began, "Annassa, Firstbloods, and heirs of the blood, and guests from Tenebra, thank you for hearing me under the Goddess's Eyes. By Alatheia's light, I shall strive to speak only truth, according to my conscience, and I ask that our Tenebran guests do the same, speaking their truth according to their consciences with their gods as their witnesses. Make the circle petition at any time to indicate you wish to participate in negotiations." Lio extended his hand on the podium before him, palm up in offering. "If we run out of time for everyone's contributions tonight, rest assured the discussion will continue for many nights to come. With orderly and respectful proceedings, all shall have the opportunity to speak for their lands or temples. It shall be considered how relations between Orthros and Tenebra affect each and every one of those under your care—your lieges and vassals, families and comrades, mages and worshipers."

Although the mortals had been in Orthros these many weeks, they had not run out of surprise. Murmurs went up, heads bent together, and Lio's ears brought him hints of many spontaneous speeches being prepared in light of this revelation that all would have a say. The mages of Kyria and Chera spoke amongst themselves most busily of all. This would be quite a different Summit than last year's, indeed.

Lio went on, "Allow me to first submit my own people's terms for you to consider and debate as the negotiations progress. Orthros's hopes for this Summit are simple. As you have witnessed in our homes and libraries, our music and arts, our warriors and healers, we have in common with you the deepest regard for tradition. We desire only to keep Orthros and Tenebra's traditions strong.

"In this spirit, we ask that Tenebra join us in renewing the age-old Oath that has always benefitted both our peoples. Let the Solstice Oath echo the words of the Equinox Oath. Let this resurrection of our treaty stand witness to my people's reverence for human life, to which we remain committed in the field in Tenebra as surely as in our own Healing Sanctuary. Let us give you our solemn vow to never lift a finger against your ways, just as we have rejoiced to see your ways brought to life here within our own borders. In return, we beseech you to promise us the safety of our Hesperines errant, who strive only to protect both our peoples from the dangers of this world.

"Let the negotiations begin."

Cassia was the first to signal she wished to speak. Her other hand shook a little as she smoothed her notes before her.

"Lady Cassia," Lio responded, "the Circle hears you."

"Thank you, Ambassador. I have taken the liberty of drawing up a list of terms gleaned from careful consultation with each member of our embassy. It is my hope that these recommendations address the needs and concerns of all Tenebrans regarding the Hesperine presence in our lands. I would like to present what I judge to be an accurate representation of my people's wishes for relations with yours, then invite my fellow Tenebran ambassadors to add to or revise what I have said on their behalf."

The nods and "ayes" among the Tenebrans gave the Circle a rough head count of who was still on Cassia's side. Wary or indignant auras warned of the hard cases who would need to hear compelling arguments if they were to rally to her banner rather than the mage's torch. The embassy was deeply divided. But not lost.

"We thank you for your devoted efforts," said Lio, "and we look forward to hearing your terms. You have the floor, Lady Cassia."

Lio listened to her draw breath to speak and awaited her voice, which would announce their final charge. The voice that cried out when he loved her and whispered words that brought down fortresses. In that little breath, he could hear their promise to win her fight.

Behind Lio, metal clanged on metal. Had he been mortal, he would have jumped. But he turned smoothly with Hesperine composure to look at Chrysanthos, who sat with his hand out, having announced his intention to speak with a blow of his rings against the table before him.

The mage did not wait for Lio to acknowledge him. "Allow me to present my temple's terms."

Lio bowed. "We are glad such an esteemed colleague from the Sun Temple at Solorum will do us the honor of participating, and we look forward to a mage of Anthros lending his voice to the cause of peace. Would you be so kind as the take the floor once the king's representative has made her presentation?"

Chrysanthos laughed. He reached into an inner pocket of his robes, and Lio tensed. The Dexion withdrew a scroll whose worn appearance bore witness that it had spent the entirety of the Summit on Chrysanthos's person.

"Ambassador, let us not waste the Firstblood Circle's time. The hour has come when Orthros must hear Lucis Basileus's real terms, which he has empowered me to state, and I assure you, you want to hear them right away. It is an irony of immortal existence, is it not? Mortals can still wield time against you. There is very little time left for the Hesperine prisoners whose fate I have come here to negotiate."

The shock that went through the Blood Union rocked Lio's power to his foundations. So this was what Chrysanthos had been plotting all along. How long? If his words were true, how many weeks had these Hesperines languished while the Solstice Summit sailed slowly onward, as if time were a luxury?

It didn't matter. Lio did not have a moment to waste reassessing his decisions or entertaining what-ifs. All that mattered was that he was on the stand, which made him the Hesperine hostages' first line of defense.

Lio demanded of the mage, "Explain yourself. Who are these prisoners you claim to know of and what proof can you offer us that you speak the truth?"

Chrysanthos eased his chair back, then got leisurely to his feet. "First, know that if I do not return from Orthros safely, it will be a death sentence for the seven Hesperines errant who are in custody. Second, know that my colleagues are holding the prisoners in a location unknown to me, so any attempt to extract that information from me will be fruitless. These points are what should inform every step you take from this moment forward. I urge you not to do anything reckless."

"Say what you will about the threat of time," Lio warned, "but we are eternal. No one considers their responses more carefully than Hesperines, but once we do respond, beware the decision behind which the full power of Orthros is brought to bear."

Four figures neared the mages' seats. The entire Stand mustered around Chrysanthos, their silent approach a louder warning than any stunts of magic. Aunt Lyta, Kadi, Mak, and Lyros stood in formation, clearly ready for anything. From the direction of his own bloodline's seats, Lio sensed his father ready his power.

Chrysanthos did not glance at them. "For an ambassador who was so recently a mere initiate, you do not disappoint. The elder firstbloods' power and teachings run strong in you. I cannot tell you how I have looked forward to this debate. Count yourself fortunate to be Hespera's instrument in this, Orthros's first and only negotiation with Cordium."

Hot, acrid power burned into Lio's senses, and the floor of the amphitheater shook beneath his feet. Through the ward the Stand had already raised around Chrysanthos, Lio saw the mage's face contort in either agony or ecstasy.

But no wall of fire rolled out to consume them. The tremors of power rocked only through the mage, one blow after another to Hesperine senses, each one breaking open the man's aura until the full power of an Aithourian war mage blazed before everyone.

Chrysanthos was more adroit than Dalos. Neither his face nor his voice had given any forewarning. But Lio had no doubt he had just witnessed the same perverse magical process that Dalos had enacted at the Equinox Summit. Chrysanthos had just reclaimed his full power, rendering Tychon unconscious in his seat and, no doubt, leaving the helpless vessel back in Tenebra dead.

Lio showed his fangs. "We wondered if you would find the courage to identify yourself to us. This debate will be more fruitful now that we do not have to pretend we did not know you are Chrysanthos, Dexion of the Aithourian Circle."

Chrysanthos panted, his eyes glazed and dilated, his hair plastered to his brow with sweat. "My clever enemy. Too devious to let me catch you unawares."

"What now, Dexion?" Lio asked. "Will a mage of your circle once more sabotage the Tenebrans' negotiations of their own affairs? Not with an assassination, this time, but with hostages?"

"We cannot stand for this!" Cassia cried at Lio's back. "My fellow Tenebrans, will you let a foreigner decide our fates? Will we let another mage like Dalos make us kindling for the pyre to which Cordium wishes to consign the Hesperines?"

The entire Tenebran embassy was in a tumult, but Chrysanthos raised his voice above theirs. "If you care at all about your own fates, you will be silent. I doubt our hosts will take kindly to you if we cannot reach a resolution about the Hesperine prisoners. I am certain my Order will not take kindly to you if you interfere. I am not only your king's ambassador, but also the appointed agent of the Akron himself."

Lio held out a hand to indicate the lords. "We hold no Tenebrans accountable for Cordium's crimes. The Tenebrans we invited here are perfectly safe. I cannot say the same for the Cordians who usurped Tenebran mages' rightful places among the embassy."

"If you care at all about the prisoners' fates," Chrysanthos reminded him, "you will be silent and hear me."

"You have yet to offer evidence this is more than a mere bluff. Never in the history of conflict between Anthros and Hespera has the god of war found the patience to keep prisoners. We must have proof if you expect us to believe your circle has managed to resist their insatiable thirst for offering sacrifices on the Akron's Altar."

"One of our hostages gave us a message for you. She assures us you will not doubt its veracity. I hope she has not misled us, otherwise she will find herself in even worse condition when I return than she was in when I left."

"Deliver her words," Lio ordered.

"A touching message, to be sure. She says, 'I am Nephalea, Hesperine errant, and I will remain steadfast for as long as I can. My love for Alkaios is proof that I yet live, and that I yet live is proof of my love for him. All seven of us will gladly lay down our lives for Orthros, but for the sake of those who depend upon us, we pray for Hespera's deliverance.'"

With all the subtlety it had taken him to hide the Craving from his family, with all the determination that had kept him on his feet when he had been starving, Lio let none of his reaction show on his face.

No mortals from Tenebra or Cordium knew the secret of Grace, least of all the Aithourian Circle. This was one aspect of Hesperine nature they had always succeeded in keeping from the enemy. No Hesperines would reveal it under any torture, lest they sentence their own Graces to death. Nephalea knew Alkaios's best hope was for her captors never to learn that killing her would end his life as well.

Nephalea's message alluded to the secret of Grace without giving it away. There was no way the Aithourians could have contrived such words.

"Do you accept this proof?" Chrysanthos prompted.

Lio turned to Konstantina, although he knew what she would say. "Second Princess, as our legal authority, do you deem the evidence presented to us sufficient?"

"With a heavy heart, I do."

Lio could not keep himself from looking at Cassia. For the barest instant, their gazes met, their pain joined, and he saw in her eyes a plea for Alkaios and Nephalea, even as he felt her heart swearing retribution upon Chrysanthos.

Lio's prayers to Hespera for the prisoners' deliverance were not words. His grief and anger were his prayers. That he turned toward Chrysanthos once more was his promise.

He would not give up. Not until every Hesperine errant was safe behind the ward.

Lio faced the mage. "For what purpose have you imprisoned our people and taken them from their loved ones here in Orthros?"

"For their crimes against mankind. Nephalea alone sent two of my brothers to Anthros's Hall the last time she tried to lead the hostages in an escape."

"Do not your own laws deem violence justified when someone fights in self-defense?"

"What justification brought these intruders into Tenebra in violation of that kingdom's wishes? The Oath lapsed four hundred years ago. None of these Hesperines had the Tenebrans' permission to enter their lands."

"Nor has Tenebra refused us permission by revoking the last Oath we swore with their king four centuries ago. The aggressors our Hesperines errant most often combat are bandits, apostates, wild animals, and the elements, all of which bring the honest and hard-working people of Tenebra to great harm. Do you have Tenebra's permission to hunt Hesperines in their lands?"

"Time, Ambassador. Time. Do not waste yours wondering how and why she came into our hands. Think instead of the fate that awaits her. Her fight for your goddess's perverse cause will soon be at an end."

Lio made his final petition to the Tenebrans. "Hesperines do not give up. When cornered, we rally. When desperate, we stand. For we would rather meet a noble end fulfilling the divine tenets we hold dear. It is something I believe we have in common with our courageous neighbors from Tenebra, the land where our own people began. What neither Hesperines nor Tenebrans do is capitulate, least of all before the Orders."

Would the embassy unite with Hesperines against their common enemy? Or would the Tenebrans unite in prejudice with their fellow mortals?

"As determined as you are to fight for the prisoners' lives," said the Dexion, "you are certain to accept the Order of Anthros's terms for their release."

"State your terms. Present them before the firstbloods and our Queens. The vote of the bloodlines and the Will of the Annassa shall decide whether we accept."

"You had the audacity to quote Order law to me. Let me educate you on it. Our law mandates a life for a life. The sentence for murder is that the murderer's life be forfeit to the victim's family." The mage's breathing was even now, his face less flushed, but the vehemence in his aura struck Lio with all the force of another spell.

"Take note we have admitted no fault. Of what crime do you accuse us?"

"The murder of Dalos, Honored Master of the Aithourian Circle. If you submit to justice, our Order is prepared to spare Nephalea and the other prisoners the sentence all Hesperines deserve. We will return the seven prisoners to you—in return for Dalos's seven murderers."

Aunt Lyta and Kadi's ward swelled with power. Lio felt Uncle Argyros's aura rumble like a storm. Lio was certain that Javed, at House Argyros with the sucklings, must have halted in his tracks. Perhaps even Basir and Kumeta, wherever they were in Tenebra, felt the ripples of the mage's demand.

But it was the waves of Cassia's outrage that engulfed Lio. In her, he felt an echo of the promise she had made to him when Dalos had threatened his life. *I will not let him touch you.*

"How fitting," Lio said calmly. "It is for my own life that I am to negotiate tonight. I do not fear your demand, Dexion. But you should. For you have also asked for the lives of my family and their Ritual tributaries. For my part, I shall defend them with all I have to give."

"What will you defend, Ambassador? Peace or their lives? You cannot choose both."

Chrysanthos unrolled his scroll and held it up. The document bore not only the blue wax seal of the King of Tenebra. Burned upon the vellum with magic were the flame-red emblem of the Aithourian Circle and the Akron's golden glyph of Anthros.

"I speak for the Akron of the Order of Anthros, for the Synthikos of the Aithourian Circle, and for Lucis Basileus, King of Tenebra. If you fail to meet our reasonable demands for hostage exchange, both Cordium and Tenebra will regard your refusal as a willful rejection of our attempts to reach a truce with you. Should you commit this act of war upon mankind, the king will have no choice but to bring the Cordian Order of Anthros into Tenebra to ensure his people's safety from you. This is the only way Orthros's ambassadors can secure peace—by sacrificing their own lives on the Akron's Altar."

Before Lio could reply, Konstantina's voice filled the amphitheater, beautiful as a spell, forceful as a gavel. "Allow me to educate the Dexion on Hesperine law."

Lio kept his eye on Chrysanthos as the mage raised his brows at the princess.

"Our law," she declared, "also mandates a life for a life. The price for murder is rescue. The only atonement for destroying a life is to restore one. How many Hesperine lives will you give back to us as justice for those you have taken? How many human lives will you make better in order to atone for your abusive reign over the mortal world?"

"Heretics have no life price."

"The decision lies with the Circle and my mothers. But I, Royal Firstblood Konstantina, hereby vote for my bloodline. I shall not hear of paying in the blood of our ambassadors, who labor for peace. Your destruction of Hesperine and human lives has sunk you deep in debt, and I will accept no payment from you but the compassion you owe to this world. I will accept no terms from you but repentance."

The whole amphitheater hushed, silenced by the rustle of the Queens' robes. The Annassa stood, their hands on their daughter's shoulder more emphatic than a Tenebran monarch laying a sword upon a noble warrior to knight him for his bravery.

The Queens descended from their bench. Annassa Soteira paused to wipe a tear from Xandra's eye. Annassa Alea's bare feet were the only sound as the Queens reached the floor of the amphitheater.

They walked among the Tenebrans as they did among their own people each time they attended Circle. The lords came once more to their feet, while the Anthrian mages' gazes followed the Queens. Cassia watched them approach Lio. He bowed with his hand on his heart.

Annassa Alea put a hand upon his head in benediction. "Well done, Ambassador Deukalion. Take your place with Anastasios."

"I would remain at your sides."

"Your life is in the bargain and has long been ours to protect," said Annassa Soteira. "Recuse yourself and let Prisma Alea negotiate for her temple, this time with her Grace at her side."

"Of course, Annassa."

No sooner had he stepped to his seat than his mother took his hand, and his father reached back to grasp his shoulder. Lio squeezed their hands in reassurance and, like Anastasios's statue, pinned his gaze on the Queens.

Annassa Alea stood at the podium with Annassa Soteira, looking down at the young mage who dared challenge them.

"Do you know who I am?" Annassa Alea asked.

"Indeed. I stand in awe." The mage's elaborate bow was a mockery. "You are the Sanctuary mage who thieved the greater part of your cult from Aithouros's grasp. Your temple was the last bastion where Hespera's worshipers fled with our fire at their heels. Those who managed to survive us found their last hope of safety behind the Sanctuary ward of Hagia Boreia, the temple farthest from Cordium." Chrysanthos flung a hand at Anastasios's monument. "He is the healer who spent every last drop of his power until he died, keeping you alive while you fortified the wards against the siege of our most powerful fire mages. But you could not run far enough from us. Orthros is not far enough, Prisma Alea."

"Do you understand what you are truly doing here, trying to wound with your words?"

"I understand you all too well. Dalos made the critical mistake of thinking he could stir the mother beasts of the Hesperines to vengeance. I know your nature much better. You will never lift a finger for revenge, but you will stop at nothing to rescue your own when they are helpless and facing destruction. For it is you who bargained yourself, the last Ritual firstblood, to Aithouros as a prisoner so your spawn could escape and go into hiding. Hesperines are devious, but you most of all. You even managed to escape custody in Corona and flee all the way to the Empire, out of our reach. But the witch you brought back with you can no more save you than Anastasios. Your Imperial allies do not frighten Anthros."

"I have been called many things," Annassa Soteira replied, "many worse than 'witch' by men more powerful than you. With those words, they only betrayed their own weakness. All I see before us is a man trying to prove he is strong. If you must prove it, you are not. All I hear in your voice is fear of our power."

"Do not think you can bring me to my knees with a gaze!" Chrysanthos cried. "I am not afraid to look into my own soul. If I answer to Anthros today, I will bare my soul to my god proudly."

Chrysanthos boasted of this? This was what the mage believed made his god proud? Lio could not fathom the Will of Anthros, and he did not wish to. But he had to wonder which of the war god's faithful had misheard him. Aithouros, who had rejoiced in destruction, or Laurentius and his king, who had made war to end suffering? Chrysanthos, who held Nephalea's plight over the Hesperines now, or the Tenebran men who had felt moved by Alkaios's suffering?

"Are you satisfied?" Annassa Alea asked. "Have you troubled our ears enough to feel like a master of your Order?"

"You would do well to heed me, Prisma. Go ahead. Deliberate and wring your hands and cast your votes. But do not take too long. If I depart Orthros without the Hesperine embassy in custody, I will return to mortal lands to give an order of execution. What is it to be? Shall my sacrifice to Anthros be seven diplomats or seven Hesperines errant?"

"There will be no vote." Queen Alea held out her hand to her Grace.

Queen Soteira rested her hand in Queen Alea's. "We invoke our power of veto."

Annassa Alea stood in her temple vestments on the podium of the Firstblood Circle, as she had once stood on the walls of Hagia Boreia. "I will give you the same reply I gave to Aithouros himself: Hespera does not give up on a single life. In her name, we will sacrifice no one. We will surrender none of our own to you, and we shall not rest until all our people are safe behind the ward. Do not think we will let this ward come down, as we lowered the defenses of Hagia Boreia to break your Order's siege upon us and make our escape. We have created our refuge on these shores, and this is where we shall remain. Orthros is Hespera's Sanctuary that will never fall, and you stand within it on her benevolence. You have chased us as far as you can, and you shall go home empty handed."

"You sentence your prisoners to death!" Chrysanthos warned.

"You cannot give an execution order from here, and your Order does not expect your return until the mountain passes thaw. You will remain here under house arrest until spring. Let us see if our prisoners are still in your custody by then."

"Send a rescue party, if you will. They will only swell the ranks of our prisoners."

"You have truly done your master proud today. Aithouros once promised me I would swell the ranks of his sacrifices to Anthros upon the Akron's Altar."

Chrysanthos launched no defiant retort this time. But of course the bloodless war mage had to have the last word. He raised his hands, even as the Stand reinforced their ward. Inside their umbrous shield, golden light flashed, harsh and blinding. The smell of smoke roused a primal fear in Lio. When he could see again, he beheld Chrysanthos's closing remarks.

On the stone at the mage's feet, vandalizing a petal of the Firstblood Rose, a glyph of Anthros burned.

"How dare you!" Xandra cried.

She appeared before Chrysanthos, right inside the ward, standing at the edge of his glyph. With the rest of the crowd, Lio came to his feet, not daring to make any further move.

Chrysanthos gave her a sardonic smile. "Have you come to challenge me to a mage duel, Princess? Shall we really test how well your education holds up against mine?"

"I have come to cleanse my temple of you. How dare you defile the Circle in the presence of our Queens?"

The floor beneath her sizzled, and crimson light traced the lines of the war god's glyph. Her fire ate Chrysanthos's and burned away his spell, leaving a gleaming red glyph of Hespera in its place. The mage's mocking smile twisted with rage.

Konstantina looked at her youngest sister with admiration in her aura. "Chrysanthos, Dexion of the Aithourian Circle, our Queens have rejected your terms. May the Goddess's Eyes watch the gates of your prison."

HYPNOS'S BRINK

THE COURTYARD OF THE New Guest House was deserted like a battlefield in a stalemate. Lio's ears brought him many sounds from within the mortal's lodgings, where they hid in the wake of the mage's successful takeover of their embassy. Heated arguments, fearful murmurs, and the silence of despair echoed through the halls. Lio's nose brought him the various stenches of apathy, desperation, and grief—all smelled like the alcohol in which the men now drowned their consciences or their sorrows.

Chrysanthos's quarters smelled like undisguised war magic. The Dexion's new rooms were now lurid with Aithourian battle wards. Was he daring the Hesperines to retaliate against his ultimatum?

"Challenge accepted," Lio murmured.

Lio sensed Mak and Lyros approaching via the gallery from Rose House. Their patrol was bringing them his way. He was curious to know if his veil could get him past them. How would a concealment he had learned from Uncle Argyros measure against Aunt Lyta's training? How would a ruse of Lio's measure against the insight of his Trial brothers? He could not afford to take chances. This was one of those occasions when it was better to carry his secrets in plain sight.

He dropped his veil and approached his Trial brothers as they paused at the gallery's exit. Instead of standing at attention on either side of the archway, they kept watch with an arm around each other.

"Lio," Lyros said. "Are you all right?"

"No. Are any of us?"

Mak shook his head. "He didn't tell us the names of the other prisoners."

"Nike can't be one of them." Lyros sounded like he was repeating a line of reasoning he and his Grace had already worn out. "Chrysanthos would have bragged about having one of the Blood Errant in custody."

"Unless she's kept her identity a secret for that very reason." Mak lifted his gaze to the heavens.

Lio tried to shift the weight of his guilt into a better position, so he could find the strength to keep carrying it. "Mak…"

"Don't apologize," Mak threatened. "You may have proposed the Summit, but that does not make the hostages' plight your fault."

"You're right. Wringing my hands, as Chrysanthos instructed, would be a waste of time. I was only going to say this isn't over yet. The Queens are convening a circle tonight to determine our course of action. I'm on my way there now."

None of Mak's emotion abated. "We got word. The envoys, the Charge, and the diplomatic service are all to mobilize. The Stand is to stand here."

Lyros rubbed Mak's back. "That is our purview. We protect our home. The hostages are in the capable hands of those who operate Abroad."

"Our family is always the Stand's purview," Mak returned.

"The life of every Hesperine is the Queens' purview," Lio said. "The hostages are in their hands."

At last a bit of reassurance appeared in Mak's aura, turbulent though it remained, and he said no more.

"Isn't Cassia going to the circle with you?" Lyros asked.

"The circle is starting before she can get away from the Tenebrans," Lio lied. "I'll go on ahead for now, so at least one of us isn't absent, then come back later to pick her up. Could you keep an eye out for her? If she comes out before I've returned, tell her I'm on my way."

"Of course," said Mak. "We'll patrol back to Rose House in a moment."

Lyros glanced around the courtyard. "While Grace-Mother is inside the New Guest House breathing down Chrysanthos's wards, Mak and I are to keep the rest of the guests in line. I doubt we'll hear a peep out of them, though. The Dexion has broken them."

So the Guardian of Orthros was also between Lio and his target. This would be a challenge indeed. "Thank you both. Reassure Cassia I won't be long."

Lio stepped away, yanking a heavy veil about himself as he went so they would lose track of his aura between where he departed and where he arrived. They would never guess he had gone not to the Queens' Terrace, but to the common room right across the courtyard from them.

Now to put his power to the true test. Uncle Argyros's teachings against Aunt Lyta. But Lio had something more. Queen Alea's teachings.

A fitting night for him to put her lessons into practice. It had taken him years to master the illusions that had once formed part of her fortifications of Hagia Boreia, methods that lived on in the ward over Orthros even now. He could not craft the warding component of her spells, of course, but with his light magic, he could make veils the way the last surviving Sanctuary mage had taught him. Lio reached for his power and meditated upon her words.

They call us shadow mages because they fear the night. We call ourselves light mages because we do not.

He breathed in, and the shadows around him stirred. A shiver went over his skin. This was magic you could stake lives on. Lio must do that now.

Hespera is the goddess of darkness and light. Rejoice in both.

Lio exhaled, releasing the light in his veins. The moonlight in the room gleamed brighter, as if the sky had cleared of clouds. Lio watched his own body disappear into shadow before his eyes.

He passed through the room as a fleeting length of darkness that touched Cassia's chair, then blended into the gloom that clung to one wall. He slipped around the perimeter of the room and into the dim hallways beyond. He crept nearer Chrysanthos's sun-bright wards.

But as he neared, he sensed no trace of Aunt Lyta. A different aura, just as familiar, loomed outside the Dexion's door.

It seemed Rudhira had relieved the Guardian of Orthros and taken up watch himself.

Why would he do that, when he was due to arrive at the Queens' circle right now?

Lio fed his sense of warning to his spell, dissolving himself into finer shadows. He would have to put a Queen's magic to the test against the First Prince.

Rudhira stood in a shaft of blood-red light that came down through one high stained glass window. Lio crept up behind his Ritual father, occupying the deep shadow just outside the light's reach. Rudhira hadn't even changed clothes. He stood before the Dexion's door in chain main and Tenebran riding boots.

As Lio watched, his Ritual father reached out a hand as if to open the door.

"Rudhira," Lio said.

He froze. He cocked his head, then turned slowly around, scanning the shadows. "It was bad enough that my little sister Konstantina always used this spell to win hide and seek when we were children. Imagine how I feel about my Ritual son casting it to sneak up on me. Care to stop lurking, Lio?"

Lio adjusted the shadows to make himself visible only to a Hesperine's sight. "Rudhira, what are you doing here?"

"It is unlike you to ask me to explain myself."

"It is unlike you to miss a circle with the Queens that concerns the fate of your Hesperines errant."

"On the contrary. I am a very lax prince. I do nothing but miss crucial events in Orthros."

His Ritual father's words were edged in bitterness Lio had seldom heard, but often suspected was there.

"Rudhira, I'm not here to admonish you, so you certainly needn't admonish yourself. Don't mistake me for your sister or your conscience haunting you in the shadows."

"Why are you here, Lio?"

They gazed at each other in silence for a moment.

"I am a very lax diplomat," Lio said at last. "I am here to take an Apollonian course of action. I'm sure my uncle will grieve that I'm using the magic he taught me to do so. But you will appreciate this."

"What are you talking about?"

"Chrysanthos may not know exactly where his order is keeping the prisoners, but he's the sunbound Dexion of the Aithourian Circle. His mind is the foremost library of all their secrets, after the Synthikos's own. Chrysanthos probably knows more about how the Order works than the Akron does. The captives' precise location is not in his mind, but the information I need to figure out where they are is certainly somewhere in his thoughts."

"Lio, go home."

"The Dexion may have surrounded himself with a fortress of Anthros's own fire, but I have no doubt I can retrieve what I seek. It's not that I underestimate the challenge of breaking through Aithourian battle wards. I simply don't care what it costs me. I can do this. I will do this. Whether there will be anything left of Chrysanthos's mind by the time I am done, I cannot say. I hope there isn't."

"It isn't necessary," Rudhira said.

"You have a better plan?"

"The matter is taken care of. Please go tell the circle I will be late. Reassure the Queens I won't be long."

Dread closed around Lio and disturbed the tendrils of darkness he held near. "Rudhira...what are you going to do?"

"My mothers called me home to help resolve the stalemate regarding the captive Hesperines errant, and that is what I intend to do. When Orthros calls upon me, they must be prepared for how I will answer."

"I see." Lio waited to see if his conscience would intervene. He found his Will only pushed him onward. "If that is your intention, then our success is assured. The Dexion's Will is no match for your means of persuasion combined with mine."

"Lio! I am not here to interrogate the mage." Rudhira rubbed a hand over his face. "Please. Will you give my regrets to the Queens?"

"If that is not what you intend, then what?" Lio took a step closer. "What regrets?"

"As your prince, I ask that you do as I have bade you."

The conviction came over Lio that the worst was not yet to come—it was upon them. He stood where he was.

"Ambassador Deukalion, Firstgift Komnenos, I have given you a royal command to depart my presence at once."

"The royal family of Orthros doesn't give commands. You ask, and we obey, because we love you. This time I am going to disobey for that very reason. Father told me of the one and only time he ever heard you issue a royal command. That was when you ordered him and Nike to go on with the inquisitors' prisoners so you could go back and die with Methu. They had to drag you out of there by might and magic. What in Hespera's name are you here to do tonight?"

"Nothing you are responsible for. Know that. In those moments we've spoken of, when we Hesperines relive each turning point in our long years and wonder what we could have done differently...never wonder if you could have changed this."

"Rudhira, whatever it is you are here to do, I will go with you. We will do it together."

"Where I dare to tread tonight, you cannot follow."

"I will not leave your side, My Prince."

Rudhira took a step away from the mage's door. "Lio. You have too much to stay for."

A crack in Rudhira's voice, in the Union, in his armor, revealed a flash of love and despair that knocked the breath from Lio's lungs.

He was speechless. It was unthinkable.

But if he was going to stop it, he must find his voice. Now.

"Rudhira, please tell me what's wrong. We need your help, but you don't have to solve this alone. We can plan and help one another find the best solution."

Rudhira's next step brought him out of the light and into Lio's cloak of shadow. "There is only one solution. The Order's most-wanted Hesperines are not the embassy. The criminals the Aithourians would do anything to capture are the surviving Blood Errant. How much more valuable a hostage if one of them is a royal. I drive an even harder bargain than Chrysanthos. He is certain to take one Hesperine for seven, if that Hesperine is me."

"No." It was the only word Lio could find at first. "Rudhira, *no*."

"Think like a diplomat, Lio, not like my Ritual son. This is an effective resolution to the problem."

"As a diplomat, I know this won't solve anything. The Aithourian Circle doesn't want a hostage exchange. They want war. They'll contrive any excuse to put more of us to the pyre. We cannot trust the Order of Anthros to relinquish the hostages, no matter what demands we meet. Turning yourself in will gain us nothing—and cost us *you*."

"May I remind you this is how my mother Alea saved all of Hagia Boreia?"

"Annassa Alea would never sanction one of her children going willingly into the Order's custody. This is not some plan of yours with the Queens. Rudhira." Lio's voice broke. "You are right about one thing. You are notorious. There will be no escape to the Empire for you. You know what they will do to you."

Rudhira put a hand on Lio's head and pulled him close. "I am sorry to cause you this pain."

"I can't let you go in the embassy's place. In my place." Lio held fast to his Ritual father.

Rudhira embraced him for a long moment, then set him away from him. "This is my choice."

Think like a diplomat, Lio, not like my Ritual son.

No, Lio had to stop thinking like a diplomat. Rudhira didn't need a diplomat to explain this to him. He knew the Aithourian Circle. He should know that if he offered himself to the war mages, neither he nor the hostages would ever see Orthros again. He should know not to come here looking for a way to end the hostage crisis.

He had come here looking for a way to end his life.

He will wither in the soil of Tenebra, she says. She must rescue him before he becomes a martyr.

Konstantina had been right. Of course. She was a theramancer of Annassa Soteira's blood. She was Rudhira's sister. She had seen the signs.

She wasn't worried Tenebra would martyr him. She knew he would one night martyr himself.

How had Lio not noticed? He had gone to his Ritual father for support countless times without ever realizing Rudhira was desperately in need of rescue himself. He had known Rudhira still mourned, not knowing how close they were to mourning him.

Rudhira served and served and served until there was nothing left inside him. Until the suffering he beheld night after night and the Hesperines he lost year after year and the mortals he could never save grieved him so much that he couldn't bear the pain anymore.

Even as he sought escape in death, he would not permit himself Sanctuary unless he gave his life for others.

Konstantina was trying to save him from himself. She knew he would never lay down his sword, so she was trying to wrest it from his hands before he threw himself on his own blade. She had masterfully wrought Orthros's politics in an attempt to do what was best for everyone while saving the life of one person she loved. Just as Lio, still a student of her craft, had tried to save Cassia without starting a war.

"Remember what I told you when you proposed the Summit," Rudhira said. "Our bond of gratitude cannot be broken. My work with the Hesperites is done, thanks to the time you and Cassia have bought us. I have made the Charge into all I have ever wished for it to be. My Fortress Masters are fit to continue what I have started."

"No one can fill your boots."

"Konstantina has Orthros well in hand. She is our mothers' true heir."

"Never doubt you are necessary to us in every way."

He thought his sister was ashamed of him, when she was his greatest protector. Lio did not know where to begin to approach that rift. He might cross the veil, and he feared if he prodded at the wound of the royal siblings' differences, it might cause Rudhira more pain than comfort.

One word out of place, and Lio might drive his Ritual father closer to the edge.

Lio might be a mind mage, but he was no mind healer. He was in no way qualified to coax a hurting soul back from Hypnos's brink. Least of all Rudhira, whose heart bore nearly sixteen centuries of war wounds.

But Lio was on the stand. The Goddess only knew why, but it was Lio who was alone in the dark with her First Prince, standing between him and certain death.

What had he learned from his mother about what to do in this situation?

He started asking questions. "Why is your heart so heavy tonight, Rudhira?"

"I'm tired, Lio. With Orthros, I will soon turn sixteen hundred. You cannot fathom how heavy the years are. They will never be this difficult for you because you will face them all with your Grace."

"Is that what weighs on you? That you have not found your Grace yet?"

Rudhira leaned back against the wall opposite the mage's room, gazing at the door through which he intended to go. "My Grace is dead."

Horror robbed Lio of his words once more. Into the silence, he uttered a prayer. "Hespera. This cannot be."

"Tonight, I asked Kassandra if she could divine where the Aithourians are holding the hostages. She answered me with an entirely different prophecy. You know the difference between her predictions of amorphous futures and those rare moments when she speaks with absolute confidence about what is not subject to change. She has explained to me, as if it is divine law, that my Grace is a Sanctuary mage. We will be true heirs of the Queens, she congratulated me—I with Annassa Soteira's dual affinity, my Grace with Annassa Alea's. We would have been. I envy Kassandra that vision of the life that is out of my reach."

"Why would it be out of your reach? Are these not wondrous tidings for you and our people? A Sanctuary mage!"

Rudhira shook his head. "The truth is clear. All the Sanctuary mages died in the Last War. My Grace can only have been one of the mages of Hespera who never made it to Orthros."

"Is that what Kassandra said?"

"No, but history speaks for itself. My Grace died before we met. Yet somehow, I survived over a year of perilous mortal existence for the Queens to pull me, a helpless, dying child, from the ruins of a Hesperite village. Somehow they brought me to safety here and made me the most powerful and fortunate of their people. I have been so blessed. But I think sixteen hundred years is long enough."

"The prophecy doesn't have to refer to the past. A Sanctuary mage must be in your future."

"It would be a delusion to believe there will ever be another one among us after all this time."

"I can well understand why you're struggling with what Kassandra has revealed to you. We've all been troubled by her prophecies at times. But she loves you. She knows you. She would never tell you this to cause you despair. There must be a reason she prophesied about your Grace tonight. She must have known you needed cause for hope."

"I cannot find it in myself to take heart in her words."

"Then take heart in my father's experience. I believe with all my heart you will have happiness as he has found. What if he had given up even one hundred years ago? What would have become of my mother and me? Your Grace awaits you, and she will need you as much as you need her."

"Your father's hope has been well rewarded with the finest son he could ask for. Have I told you I too am proud of you? Not often enough, I think. I'm sorry we never got to ride together in the Charge. But I think you will not wish to go back to Tenebra for a long time to come. Ask Konstantina and Adwene to be Cassia's Ritual parents. It will mean a great deal to my sister."

Lio was losing him.

"Your Queens have already invoked their veto," Lio said. "Their Will is that not a single Hesperine be sacrificed in exchange for the hostages. As their only spokesperson here at this moment, I will not stand aside. I will spend all the words I have reminding you what your life means to us. Your *life* Rudhira, not your death. Do you know how much it matters that one of our heroes is not a constellation or a statue? That we can reach for his flesh-and-blood hand when we need his help?"

Rudhira's brow furrowed, and he looked down at his hands.

"How many lives have those hands snatched from death?" Lio asked.

"Enough. I am satisfied with my life's work."

If that was the case, then what could Lio offer to hold Rudhira to this life?

What could he learn from Konstantina's example?

"Then come home," Lio said.

Rudhira raised his head.

"Come home and celebrate with us," Lio pleaded. "Have coffee around the Ritual circle at House Komnena and watch Zoe grow. Warm yourself by the fire Xandra keeps burning in the hearth in your residence. Vote in the Firstblood Circle and ruffle everyone's feathers. Play with Konstantina's descendants, so they can love you as she does. Let us stop missing you."

Rudhira swallowed. "I can't stay here."

"An abundant life awaits you here, with or without your Grace. We will help you. Your years can be full of purpose and happiness. You have so much to look forward to."

Again, Rudhira shook his head. "I had all of that."

"You haven't lost it," Lio said as gently as he could, "even though you lost your Trial brother."

"When I am in Orthros, Methu's memory is all I see. There is no comfort in the familiar for me anymore."

"Far be it from a mind mage to make prescriptions to a mind healer, but I can pass on some advice from one of the greatest theramancers in Orthros. Talk to a mind healer if you need to. My mother can refer you to one of her colleagues, if you need to speak with someone who has some distance from the event."

Upon hearing his own words quoted to him, Rudhira did not answer, and Lio did not know if his plea had fallen on deaf ears.

Lio tried again. "Know this. In those moments we've spoken of, when we Hesperines relive each turning point in our long years and wonder what we could have done differently...never wonder if you could have changed what Methu did that night."

Rudhira flinched.

"Where he dared to tread," Lio said, "you could not follow."

"He had just as much to stay for as I did."

"Ioustin," Lio said for the first time, "this is not that night. These hostages are not those prisoners. Trying to imitate Methu's sacrifice in this situation will not save any lives. What happened to him was not your fault, and throwing away your life now will not make anything right."

Ioustin stared at the mage's door as if it were the portal to Anthros's own Hall, and he might charge through it to throw all of his power against the god of war himself. "Now my Trial sister might be one of their prisoners. I will not let this happen again."

"Then don't let it happen. Don't surrender. Come to the circle, where we will make a plan to save her."

Now Ioustin looked at Lio, and his gaze cleared. His hand came to rest on Lio's shoulder.

He was shaking. "Thank you, Lio. Let us...let us go to the circle. As soon as Lyta returns."

Lio put his hand over Ioustin's. "We'll go together."

The grip of Ioustin's gauntlet was heavy as he leaned on Lio for support.

The shadows in the corridor shook with Aunt Lyta's arrival. "Thank you again for keeping watch while I broke my fast, Ioustin. I prefer to be at my full power at all times when dealing with the Dexion."

"A teaspoon of your power would be enough, but I was happy to assist."

As she glanced from him to Lio, her gaze softened. "I see I am not the only one fortunate in your support tonight."

Lio did not correct her assumption that he was here to seek his Ritual father's counsel. Ioustin said nothing as he released Lio and straightened.

"Are you all right, Lio?" Aunt Lyta asked.

Ioustin answered for him. "He should not have had to bear tonight's events, but the way he has done so is a credit to Orthros and our Goddess."

Aunt Lyta put a hand on each of their shoulders. "May her Eyes light a path to safety for the hostages. I will not keep you two from the circle any longer." If she was thinking of Nike, there was no waver in her grip or voice to give it away. She took up her watch at the Dexion's door in the ready stance of her statue in the harbor, her Will unwavering as stone.

Lio prayed for strength like hers and wished he were as confident in his role in tonight's events.

When Ioustin stepped away, Lio hurried to follow. He would keep his promise not to leave Ioustin's side until he was sure his Ritual father was truly going to the circle and not seeking another route to endanger himself.

Ioustin did not veil himself on the way. They arrived side by side at the foot of the stairs leading up to the Queens' Terrace.

"You'd best go get Cassia," Ioustin said. "I'll see you both in a moment."

Lio waited until his Ritual father made it to the top of the steps. He listened to the Queens greet their son.

Relief made Lio's knees feel weak. His Ritual father was safe. For the moment.

Lio must now save the hostages.

How much could Aithourian wards hurt, really? They weren't true wards, he knew, not like the protective magical barriers cast by mages of Anthros who had the affinity for warding magic. No, Aithourians were war mages, and they had devised very effective, very painful ways of using their fire spells as armed defenses. If true wards were the walls of a fortress, battle wards were the rows of stakes all over the field leading up to it. And the fire arrows raining from the ramparts. And the boiling oil coming down through the murder holes.

Lio had felt the pain of Dalos's fire magic. He had even survived the Craving for half a year. He could surely withstand interrogating the Dexion.

But if he didn't?

He was the sole bearer of the knowledge that Hypnos was tempting Ioustin.

Lio must warn someone now.

CROSSING THE VEIL

LIO VEILED HIMSELF AGAIN, retreating from the terrace to the shadows under the royal evergreens. He must hurry, but he must not sacrifice discretion.

He knew to whom he could and should entrust Ioustin's private battle. Konstantina had the knowledge and power to save her brother. But how to approach her? She would already be on the terrace, advising the circle on legal precedents relevant to the unprecedented hostage situation.

As the city bells rang, an idea occurred to him. He counted the chimes. There was just enough time before the last couriers went home to their youthful Slumber.

Lio cast a red-and-white spell light that would not be visible from the terrace. He had barely pulled his writing supplies out of his scroll case when a courier appeared. He remembered her from a few weeks ago, when she had delivered notes to his Trial circle. She covered a jaw-cracking yawn with one hand, her eyelids drooping.

When she saw where the summons had brought her, she grew more alert and beamed at Lio. "A summons to House Annassa? What a way to finish the night! How can I help you, Firstgift?"

Lio levitated a slip of paper in front of him, wondering what in the world would convince the Second Princess to leave a critical circle with the Queens to hear out the young ambassador who opposed her vision for Orthros's future.

He addressed her as he had all his life until the Summit, hoping to invoke that time not so long ago when no politics had stood between them.

Aunt Kona,

There is something I must confide in you right away. This is a family matter too private to discuss at the circle, too important to commit to paper, and too urgent to delay. Please. You can find me just beyond the terrace.

- Lio

Lio sealed the note with his blood, veiled it, and held it out to the courier. "Have you delivered a veiled blood seal before?"

"Yes, Firstgift!" The courier took the note with great reverence. "I know to deliver it without delay, only into the recipient's hands, and never, ever reveal to others who the sender is. You can rely on me. Who is it for?"

"The Second Princess. She is up there on the Queens' Terrace."

The courier's whole aura lit up. "For the Second Princess! She tips in *storybooks.* They say this week she's giving out *The Adventures of Laiya and her Fanged Familiar.*" She was gone in a blink.

Zoe had been over the moons when Lio had presented her with his entire collection of all the storybooks he had received from Aunt Kona as a boy.

The bells had not chimed another quarter of an hour before Konstantina appeared before him. She had come, and what she allowed him to sense through the veil over her aura was her concern.

"Thank you," he said at once.

"Come to my garden."

He stepped, following her powerful presence to her neighboring grounds. She halted in her greenhouse, where the ancient glass walls were foggy with veil spells and moisture. The spell lights reflected a thousand tiny sparkles in the damp panes.

"What could you need to confide in me?" she asked. "It must be dire, for you to call me out of this circle."

"Ioustin needs help. He won't ask for it, and I doubt he'll welcome my effort to do so on his behalf. But if he continues to fight this battle alone, he'll—he won't win."

"Which of my brother's many battles has caused you to fear for him so?"

Lio took a deep breath. "Aunt Kona, he tried to end his own life tonight. I was there."

She touched his shoulder and sat him down on a bench under the Sanctuary Rose. It wasn't until then that he realized how his blood was pounding and his heart was aching. He had come here to offer help, not ask for it. It had not occurred to him that he, too, had been through something tonight.

"Who else was there?" Aunt Kona asked.

"Just him and me."

"You say he tried. But he did not succeed, for he stands safely in the company of our mothers as we speak. Did you have something to do with that?"

"I...I believe so. I did everything I could think of to talk him out of it. I made sure he got to the circle. But the moment he sets foot off the terrace, he will be in danger again. There is no telling how short-lived his reprieve from despair might be. I know death could beckon to him again at any time, if he doesn't get the healing he needs. He will try to keep it from everyone that he is in so much danger, but the veil be sunbound. I will cross it to protect him."

"Would you show me what happened?"

"Yes. You should know exactly what he said and did so you can assess his mental state. If I only tell you, I might leave out details I don't realize are significant."

Her magic unfolded and filled the Union with deep, fragrant light. He sealed his plans for the Dexion behind his mental defenses, then offered up his memories of the night, showing her in stark thelemancy what had passed between him and Ioustin.

When his mind returned to the greenhouse, he tried to think of sufficient words to offer comfort and support to her. She had almost lost her brother tonight.

She spoke first. "That was a terrible situation to find yourself in. You did well, and you did the right thing to ask for help."

Her hand on his shoulder was not seeking, but giving. In her eyes, he realized, he was a Ritual son in need of wisdom, a patient in need of theramancy, a Hesperine in need of leadership. The power of her sorrow was a mystery to him behind her royal veil, and when she confided her private pain to someone tonight, it would certainly not be one of the youngbloods.

"The only help I can give him isn't enough," Lio confessed, "but how I wish I had given it to him before. There's no telling how long he's been like this—whether we've come close to losing him before tonight—"

She held up a hand. "When someone you love is in this situation, it is very easy to feel you are to blame. You must be kinder than that to yourself."

"You knew. You've been trying to bring him home all along, because you could see what was happening to him."

"I knew what would eventually happen to him. Even I did not realize he is already at this point. If I had, he would already be home."

"I'm sorry he has kept this from you, when you are the first person he could have trusted with it."

Konstantina sighed. "I am the last person he would trust with it, because he knows I have the power to keep him out of the field. Clearly he has gone to great lengths to hide this from our mothers and me. As you know, every Hesperine who serves in the Charge is required to visit a mind healer on a regular basis to ensure their service has not wounded them too deeply. Ioustin is not exempt. The Queens receive regular reports on his mental health from Fortress Master Baruti."

"Firstblood Baruti is one of the most qualified theramancers in history. How could he have missed the signs?"

"He wouldn't. Unless Ioustin deliberately deceived him. Few theramancers are more powerful than Baru, but…"

"None are more powerful than Annassa Soteira and those of you who have inherited her power."

Konstantina nodded. "Ioustin used his power to make Baru believe he is well. You see why you should not blame yourself for not realizing your Ritual father needs a mind healer?"

Lio looked down at his hands. "Thank you, Aunt Kona."

She gave his shoulder a squeeze.

He looked up. "Only the hope of saving Nike was enough to convince him to step away from the mage's door. The next thing he will want to do is ride out and not return until he has rescued the hostages himself."

"As we speak, he is making his case to the circle for that very course of action."

"The mages are not the gravest danger to him. We cannot let him ride into his worst memories. He might not come back. He might make sure he doesn't."

"He will not set foot outside the ward until our mother Soteira pronounces him in a fit state to do so. Do not fear. I will make sure we do not lose him. Go get Cassia and join us at the circle. You will see."

Lio's duty was done. That meant the Dexion awaited.

He was just about to rise from the bench when she stayed him with a hand on his. "Lio. You have my gratitude."

"That is a gift beyond price, My Princess."

She would not release his hand to let him make the heart bow. "Also, you should know I have always taken it as a compliment that you and Kia chose one of my scrolls as the object of your magical experiment. You were trying to devise a way to use magic to transcribe text more quickly than scribes can, to foster the spread of knowledge. Imagine what it means to me that my legal writings were your first choice."

Her gaze twinkled with amusement. Surprised silenced Lio for a moment, then he laughed.

"Of course it was one of your writings. The law of our land. All we hold dear."

With a smile, she released him.

He stood, unable to quell the urge to give her the heart bow. "I'm still sorry we ruined your scroll."

"I'm sorry we still don't have a way of magically transcribing text. Bold experiments frequently result in destruction, but your heart has always been in the right place."

"I was not planning to raise the subject of the Summit with you tonight, Aunt Kona."

"You did well," she said again. "Ioustin's plight will only strengthen my resolve to invoke the Departure, but you put the well being of others ahead of your political ends tonight, which is precisely why I am glad you are in politics."

"I was under the impression my foray into politics did not meet with your approval."

"If you think I love you any less from the opposite side of a political debate, you need to live through a few more upheavals in Orthros's history. I codified the laws that uphold Hesperines' freedom to disagree. Do you think my Ritual mother and I love each other any less because she cast the deciding vote that turned your Summit idea into a reality?"

"Of course not, Aunt Kona. You and Kassandra both have my gratitude, many times over."

"Now we have work to do. I will see you at the circle."

Lio hesitated a moment longer. "Aunt Kona, if I may ask, why do you disagree with Kassandra about the Summit?"

"She knows what she is doing. So do I. Orthros needs both of us, whatever shape our people's future may take. Keep doing your part."

With that dismissal, that blessing, Lio stepped out of her greenhouse.

He returned to the New Guest House, raising his concealment yet again. Mak and Lyros were not in the courtyard at the moment, but he would have to get past Aunt Lyta after all in order to interrogate the mage.

Out of the shadows Lio had conjured around him, his Trial brothers materialized, girded in the Hesperine warding magic they held ready. They blocked his way into the guest house.

"We're not diplomats," said Lyros. "We won't try to talk you out of your plan."

"We'll just stop you in your tracks," Mak promised. "Be glad we're going to use wards and not a Grace Dance. You deserve to have your nose broken again. Rudhira's in need of a mind healer, but you're just being an idiot."

"He sent you."

"Actually," Lyros corrected, "we followed you after you tried to make us believe that nonsense about going to the circle ahead of Cassia. I never thought we would need our training in stealth attacks to spy on our Trial brother and our prince."

"You talked the Blood-Red Prince out of something!" Mak crowed. "A feat of the ages. Too bad you're not smart enough to take your own advice."

"All right," Lio said. "I'll make you the same offer I made him. Would you like to help me break Chrysanthos? I won't deny I could use your help. This won't be easy. But you can't tell me we have another option."

"We aren't going to tell you that," Lyros said. "Mak and I don't have another option for you."

"Lio."

At the sound of Cassia's voice, he spun away from his Trial brothers. She stood behind him, looking for all the world like a goddess who had manifested out of the moonlight and foliage.

"Cassia is going to tell you," Mak clarified. "While you were escorting Rudhira to the circle, we called in reinforcements."

She held out her hands to Lio. "We can do better than this."

"Do you really think we can?" Lio asked.

"I'm out of ideas," she said. "But if you come away from here and we try together, perhaps we will find a better one than you throwing away everything you've worked for."

He took her hands and pulled her to him. "I'm so sorry about Alkaios and Nephalea."

"So am I."

"This is how I repay them for keeping you safe. By playing ambassador with Nephalea's captors while she and Alkaios waste away."

"Destroying one of the Aithourian Circle's key mages while he's on a diplomatic mission to Orthros will only bring more retaliation upon all our Hesperines errant. Don't give up on your path of peace, Sir Diplomat."

"It has accomplished nothing."

"You saved your Ritual father's life tonight. Is that nothing?"

"Listen to your Cassia," Lyros said. "And hold fast to her."

"She'll set you to rights," Mak agreed.

With that, his Trial brothers left him and Cassia alone, wrapped in his shadows and the garden.

"Come to the circle," Cassia said. "Then come home and tell Zoe a story. Then come to bed with me. Because Lio, I need you to hold me tonight."

With Cassia close against his side, Lio turned away from the door that led to the mage and didn't look back.

PRISONERS OF WAR

AT LAST LIO JOINED the circle on the Queens' Terrace, hand in hand with his Grace.

"Ah, here they are." Annassa Alea sat alone on the Queens' bench.

Annassa Soteira and Konstantina were absent. Even now, Konstantina must be privately informing Annassa Soteira of Ioustin's plight.

Kassandra occupied the chair beside the Queens' bench. To her right stood Ioustin, the embodiment of the Charge. Basir and Kumeta were at his side, representing the envoy service. On the Annassa's left waited four Hesperines Lio did not know personally, all heads of bloodlines whom he had spotted at the Firstblood Circle before. With them stood Uncle Argyros and Lio's father.

Of course they would call upon Uncle Argyros at a time like this. He was much more qualified to address the hostage situation than Lio.

Cassia gave the heart bow. "I beg everyone's pardon for our late arrival. I had difficulty escaping the embassy tonight and kept Lio waiting outside the guest house."

Lio held his veil steady and hoped everyone there assembled would accept Cassia's excuse without too much thought.

Annassa Alea nodded to Lio and Cassia. "You had important work to do there, as well."

Queen Alea never accepted anything except with a great deal of thought. Lio, too, gave her the heart bow. "Thank you, Annassa."

"Thank you for your deeds on behalf of our children tonight."

The others listening would assume she was referring to what he had done for their people when he had confronted the Dexion at the Firstblood Circle. Lio knew she meant what he had done for Ioustin, for even now, thanks to Grace Union, she was privy to Annassa Soteira's conference with Konstantina.

He gathered Annassa Alea's gratitude to him like a light, a shield. A Sanctuary ward.

"Cassia," Queen Alea asked, "in the aftermath of the interrupted negotiations, how have our guests reacted to the Dexion's plot?"

"They are afraid," Cassia answered, "too afraid to resist Cordium's might, even when it only amounts to one man, and the only magefire he waves at them is a scroll from the Akron."

Annassa Alea's age-old sadness sighed through the Union. "How much has changed in sixteen centuries, and yet how little. One of the truths that remains is this: Hespera has always rescued the children of Kyria from Anthros's wrath. May we yet rescue the Tenebran embassy from the Dexion."

"Yes, Annassa," Lio and Cassia agreed.

Lio's father drew near and clasped his arm. "You had to leave the Firstblood Circle so quickly earlier tonight, we scarcely had a chance to tell you how proud we are of how you handled the situation."

Lio gripped his father's arm in return.

"How are you, Cassia?" Father asked her.

Cassia had yet to become at ease in his father's presence, but she managed a smile. "Angry. Therefore I will be of great use to the hostages, for anger is productive."

"A woman after my own heart," his father replied.

The glass doors behind the Queens' bench opened, and Queen Soteira and Konstantina emerged from House Annassa. Queen Soteira rejoined Queen Alea, while Konstantina went to stand next to Ioustin. She put a hand on her brother's arm. He turned to her.

Annassa Soteira addressed the circle. "Much is at stake tonight. War or peace. Victory or surrender. The very balance of power between Orthros and Cordium. But none of those are *why* we are gathered here tonight. We are here for our people."

Annassa Alea slid her hand into Annassa Soteira's. "Son, tell us of the

Hesperines errant we are here for. Let us hold their names, their faces, and their loved ones in our hearts with every step we take from this moment forward."

Ioustin bowed his head and recited four names Lio didn't recognize. "These Hesperines errant have all gone missing Abroad in recent months and are presumed to be in the Order's custody. I have informed their bloodlines accordingly."

Annassa Alea turned to the Hesperines on the left. "Thank you all for being here tonight. It is only right that the firstblood of each family affected by this crisis be party to our decisions."

One of the four unfamiliar Hesperines bowed, her hand on her heart. "Ever since the First Prince informed me my great-granddaughter had gone missing Abroad, all our family could do was hope and pray—and offer all possible support to the Charge from home. I will not say it is better to know nothing than to know she is in the Order's custody. At least now we can act."

"Who are the other three hostages?" asked the bearded firstblood next to her. "What other bloodlines share our sorrow?"

"As the Dexion has confirmed," Ioustin answered, "Nephalea, Alkaios's Grace, is in custody. That leads us to believe the sixth hostage is their comrade Iskhyra."

"They have no family in Orthros," Cassia spoke up, "except me."

The other hostages' families surrounded Cassia in Union. Although she might not be able to feel their sympathy and support, she could certainly see it in their expressions, for her aura strengthened.

Lio's father looked at Ioustin. "There is indeed no comfort in unanswered questions. Tell us, what are the chances the seventh hostage is Nike?"

Ioustin rubbed a hand over his face. "For a time, Kalos assured me her trail indicated she had gone into hiding, not disappeared. But he was running out of signs to follow even before I asked him to look for Nephalea instead. I cannot say with any certainty whether Nike is at liberty or in the Orders' custody. I can say that if Kalos finds Nephalea, he will find all the hostages."

Uncle Argyros remained silent. He didn't meet Ioustin's gaze.

He wasn't here as a diplomat, after all. He was here because he was the firstblood of a family affected by the crisis. One of his daughters was almost certainly a hostage. The Orders had demanded his other daughter, his Grace-son, his own Grace, and him as payment.

Lio's father was here because the Order had demanded Lio as payment.

Here tonight, representing the entire diplomatic service of Orthros, was Lio. But not alone. As if she sensed what was going through his mind, Cassia squeezed his hand, and the thought that she felt their Grace Union even as a mortal almost brought a smile to his face there on the terrace in the midst of their despair.

Annassa Soteira spoke. "Firstbloods, do not fear for your missing family. Ambassadors, do not fear for yourselves. Hespera has made our people rich in power, and we have only begun to tap it. Here is what we will do." She turned to Lio and Cassia. "We do not seek a diplomatic solution to the hostage crisis. Negotiating the hostages' release would be ideal, but that opportunity is not available to us. The Dexion has made it clear he will twist any of our attempts at diplomacy into a trap to cause greater harm."

"Cordium does not negotiate," said Queen Alea. "I know this firsthand."

"Annassa," Konstantina said, "if I may?"

"By all means, Daughter," Queen Soteira answered, as Queen Alea nodded.

The Second Princess opened her hands, casting a glance around the terrace to include everyone. "At this heartbreaking time, with the Dexion of the Aithourian Circle in our midst, I invite everyone to draw from the wisdom of our laws, especially regarding the treatment of prisoners."

Her gaze rested an instant longer on Ioustin. Then on Lio.

Cup and thorns. He had veiled his thoughts so closely. Could she know what he had intended to do to the Dexion?

"No matter how foul a person's deeds," Konstantina counseled them, "whether he is a fallen elder firstblood or an impudent war mage, he must be treated in accordance with Hespera's tenets, with the compassion and dignity all creatures deserve. So long as he is under our power, his basic needs will be provided for; he will not be made to endure any harm or suffering of the body or mind; and his imprisonment is the greatest extent to which his Will may be impeded, unless further action is necessary to prevent immediate harm to himself or others."

Apollon sighed. "Some of us may need to be reminded."

"Hespera gave us fierce hearts," Konstantina replied, "as surely as she gave us tenets to guide them."

"For the sake of those tenets," said Annassa Alea, "Soteira and I wish for our diplomats to stay the course of the Solstice Summit."

"Certainly, Annassa," Lio and Cassia answered.

"You must concentrate your efforts on the original purpose of the negotiations: peace between Orthros and Tenebra. This is not a Summit between Orthros and Cordium. We will not allow the Dexion to make it so. Continue to work toward the renewal of our people's truce with Tenebra."

Lio made a heart bow. "Yes, Annassa."

He voiced none of his disappointment, but Queen Soteira addressed it. "Never doubt you are helping the hostages by seeking to revive the Oath. Our diplomats are the open hand stalling Cordium's advance and giving us the time we need to bring our people home."

Lio knew this, but when one of his Queens reminded him, he felt the truth of it. "We will redouble our efforts."

"Formal negotiations are now suspended. Take this as an opportunity to do the work that cannot be accomplished on a grand stage. Then, when Winter Solstice begins, use the events to your advantage, as you have done with the fair, the games, and our other demonstrations for our guests."

"We will not give up," Cassia promised.

"Very good," Queen Alea said. "After careful consideration, Soteira and I have deemed it best to hold the Winter Solstice observances as planned, even at this time of crisis. The Vigil of Thorns is appropriate, given the situation, and we should take those five nights as an opportunity to pray for the hostages and offer our support to their loved ones. As for the Festival of the Rose to follow, it is true this is not a time for celebration. However, those five nights are key diplomatic events as well, and we cannot risk any more damage to our relations with the Tenebrans. Let it be known that these revelries are dedicated to our hostages as surely as the Vigils, for we must use these events to advance the cause of peace, for the sake of our Hesperines errant."

Queen Soteira looked to Ioustin. "We do not seek the Charge's solution to the hostage crisis, either."

His expression betrayed his astonishment. "Annassa?"

"Until we know where the mages are holding the hostages, it is unwise for the Charge to mobilize."

There was a furor in Ioustin's eyes. "There is only one place mages take Hesperine prisoners. As we speak, the hostages are surely in the inquisitors' prison, one step from the Akron's Altar."

"You have made your case for an expedition to Cordium, but we cannot take that course of action except as a last resort."

"*Bamaayo,*" he began.

She shook her head.

"I have taken into consideration it could be a trap," he said, "but even if my riding into Cordium is precisely what the Aithourian Circle intends, I must do it nonetheless. I must go, now, and I must not return until I have found them and liberated them."

Kassandra smiled. "The Blood Errant are the only ones who have ever successfully rescued heretics slated for execution in Corona. You may yet repeat your greatest deed."

Ioustin looked into the eyes of their Ritual mother, their oracle. Lio wondered if she had just now voiced her opinion—or given Ioustin the second prophecy of the night.

"But not tonight," said Annassa Alea. "Envoys, we will rely on you."

Basir and Kumeta gave the heart bow.

"Find out where the hostages are," Queen Soteira bade them. "Then we will know where to send their rescuers."

"Yes, Annassa," Kumeta replied. "Our envoys will act with the greatest speed and discretion—and the least danger."

Ioustin took a step nearer his mothers. "If the envoys *and* the Charge are searching, we could find the hostages in half the time. Kalos is already making progress searching for Nephalea."

"Leave Kalos on her trail," Annassa Soteira agreed, "but the rest of your people must continue their current endeavors."

Annassa Alea's tone was urgent. "There are still Hesperines errant besides the hostages who did not heed our Last Call. The Charge must reach them and convince them to return before it is too late."

That imperative, spoken by a Queen, struck Lio with dread. He looked from Konstantina to their mothers. Were they nearer the Departure than ever before?

Annassa Soteira continued, "Once the envoys have located the hostages, then the Charge can liberate them from the mages' custody. That undertaking must be flawlessly planned to the last detail. That is why we need you to remain in Orthros, Son, to discuss the rescue effort with your mother and me."

Some tension left Ioustin's posture. "Of course, *Bamaayo*. As soon as this circle concludes, if you wish, I will lay out each point for your approval, before I return to the field to lead the Charge's search."

Queen Alea leaned forward. "Are not your Field Masters the most experienced, powerful, and trustworthy of our Hesperines errant?"

"Of course, Mother." An unspoken protest hung at the end of his words.

"They may lead the search."

"You need to be here," said Annassa Soteira.

Annassa Alea nodded. "Until the envoys return with answers. It will take at least that long to plan for anything you might encounter when you go to rescue the hostages."

With those few reasonable words, the Queens ensured the protection of Ioustin's life and his privacy. No one would question why they wanted him at their sides at a time like this. No one need know he had come so close to death tonight. While Orthros thought he and the Queens coordinated a rescue effort, he would, Lio had no doubt, find Annassa Soteira and Konstantina coordinating his time with the mind healers.

The Queens had spoken, and no matter his anguish at being bound behind the ward, Ioustin could say no more. Silence reigned on the terrace.

Lio could imagine how his Ritual father felt, after having spent half a year trapped in Orthros while Cassia was on the other side of the border.

When every path had closed before Lio, he had tried to make a new way. He had tried the Summit.

Now that path was crumbling beneath them all.

THE THORNS OF HESPERA'S ROSE

Show Mercy to those who suffer,
give Solace to the lost,
guard the sanctity of each person's Will,
strive to live in Union with all,
offer the Gift to any.

VIGIL OF
MERCY

5 Nights Until Winter Solstice

ALKAIOS'S FAST

THERE WERE NO BLOODSTAINS on Alkaios's Sanctuary robe, but the smell of potent cleaning spells told Cassia the starving Hesperine had not been able to keep anything down tonight.

"I'm so glad I'm here now," she said to Lio. "All these events transpired to bring Alkaios and me together on this night so I can keep the Vigil of Mercy at his side."

With his chair pulled up against hers, Lio held her as he had during their vigil in the ruined palace garden on the anniversary of Solia's death. "You are doing Alkaios a great honor. No Hesperine errant could ask for more than to have someone he saved bear witness to his deeds."

"I wish my gratitude could feed him." Cassia stroked the back of Alkaios's hand. All she could see of Solia's pendant was the tattered ribbon trailing out of his fist.

"My best intentions won't feed him, either."

Cassia turned to Lio. "This is not your fault. The Solstice Summit was our best hope."

"Yes. It *was*."

"We've done everything we can this week to keep our promise to the Queens to rescue the Summit. We'll keep trying."

"*You've* done everything you can. You've spent every moon hour at the guest houses trying to change minds, while I've been making arrangements for Winter Solstice events." Lio rubbed his face. "So much time wasted with the culinary crafters for a guest banquet the embassy is unlikely even to attend, all while Alkaios lies here."

"It was a good plan, to let me work alone among the embassy for now.

The persuasions I've employed would have had them begging for scraps from your table, if they weren't such cowards. Instead they brood in their cups and pray for their escape from Orthros."

She felt she was back at the Equinox Summit, sitting helpless in a chair at Callen's bedside while the threat of a war mage hung over everyone's heads. Except this time, she had no more secrets to wield against the enemy. His secrets and theirs were all on the table. There was no trap to spring—they were in it.

Lio shook his head. "How neatly I cleared the way for Chrysanthos to corner us."

"Forgive me. I should not lament our situation. It only rubs salt in your wounds."

"And yours. Do you think it helps anyone for you to blame yourself?"

"No," she realized. "No, it does not. It only makes you blame yourself more as well."

He was silent for a moment. "Guilt won't feed him either, will it?"

"You are right." She released Alkaios and took Lio's hands. "You and I are doing our best with the Summit. We must trust the envoys to find Nephalea and the others."

Lio rested his head on Cassia's shoulder, turning his face against her neck. "What a time for the one night of the year when Hesperines indulge a rare ascetic urge. It would feel wrong to feast during the Vigil of Mercy. But I wish I could drown my sorrows in you tonight."

She caressed his head. "Let my gratitude to you sustain you through your fast."

"Gratitude does feed something inside all of us."

"No matter what happens, I will never regret the Solstice Summit. I will never believe for a moment you made the wrong decision. Because if you had done anything differently, I would not be here in Orthros now."

Lio cast a glance at Alkaios. "I would be lost, if you had not come."

She saw all her own despair in Lio's eyes. They were drowning in it together. She repeated their creed, which had pulled him away from Chrysanthos's door. "Together, we can fight better. Everything would have been much worse if we had not come together and tried."

He bowed his head to kiss her palms. "You are right. I cannot regret what we have done together. The Goddess knows I cannot regret having you with me."

Suddenly Cassia became aware they were not alone. She looked up, and Lio raised his head. On silent feet, his Trial brothers and sisters had slipped into the room to surround the bed.

"On this Vigil of Mercy," said Mak, "we have come to honor Alkaios and your sister."

Cassia looked from him to Lyros, from Xandra to Kia to Nodora. "Thank you all. I'm so glad you're here. But...you are still planning to go to Nike's monument, I hope?"

"In a little while." Mak put a hand on Cassia's shoulder. "It's all right if you don't want to leave Alkaios's side."

"It's so important to me to honor your sister as well, but..."

"Plenty of us will pay tribute at Nike's monument," Mak reassured her. "Alkaios doesn't have any family here to keep Vigil with him, though."

"Yes he does," came Komnena's voice from the doorway.

Cassia looked to see Lio's father and mother just inside the entrance to Alkaios's room.

Komnena came to the bedside and put a hand to Alkaios's clammy forehead. "Since he has no relations in Orthros, we shall gladly fill those shoes."

Apollon nodded. "When he is strong enough to consider such matters, we will offer ourselves as his Ritual parents."

"I can think of nothing more fitting," Lio said. "I look forward to welcoming Alkaios into our Ritual family."

"For rescuing Cassia," said Komnena, "Alkaios will always have our unconditional support."

Cassia took Alkaios's hand again. "I...find myself at a loss for words. Alkaios deserves no less. But for you to do so much on my behalf..."

Komnena took a seat on the other side of the bed. "Your bond of gratitude is ours, Cassia. I will share in your Vigil over him. Zoe is staying at House Argyros with Bosko and Thenie. Lyta and Argyros feel the need to dote on the sucklings tonight."

"Blood Argyros needs some time together at home." Apollon's smile was not one of tender affection. "I shall take a turn guarding the mages so no members of the Stand need be at the guest houses. My presence should also be sufficient to relieve the Charge from their watch there so they can patrol the border instead."

Mak's face brightened. "Thank you, Uncle. We were struggling to arrange our shifts so that everyone would have time for Vigil."

"Should you wish to join Mak and the others at Nike's statue," Komnena reassured Cassia, "know that Alkaios will not be alone for a moment."

Just as Lio said, gratitude was a kind of nourishment. Cassia found her cup running over with it.

She stood and turned to Mak. "Whenever you are ready, I would be honored if you would introduce me to your sister."

VICTORY POINT

THE SKY ABOVE THE cliffs was so clear it hurt Cassia to look above her. The aurorae blazed vivid under the full Light Moon, and the fallen Hesperines' namesake stars shone stark and bright around the waxing crescent of the Blood Moon. A blizzard had left the sea restless and thrashing below and flooded the grounds of House Komnena under a second sea of white.

The snow banks would have swallowed her if Lio had not levitated her at his side. The young Hesperines walked lightly upon the surface of the snow, their feet barely disturbing the glittering white path along the cliffs, and Cassia felt nothing more beneath her silk slippers than the soft crush of rime.

A shadow appeared ahead of them, deep and translucent. It looked as if a shield wrought of night had alighted upon the cliff before the dark statue that stood there. Stone and magic rested weightlessly on the very tip of a rocky outcropping that jutted over the sea.

Mak gestured ahead of them. "Here it is. Victory Point."

Hand-in-hand with Lyros, he led the way out onto the spear of rock. They came to a halt behind the statue.

A tall, broad-shouldered lady of black granite guarded the cliff in Stand regalia, her feet planted as surely as her mother's in the harbor. She stretched one hand out before her, her palm toward the sea, as if conjuring that shield of shadow, as if declaring to the world she would halt them all at Orthros's gates.

Cassia said nothing to disrupt the reverent hush, which was punctuated only by the crash of the waves far below. As if in silent agreement, they all let Mak decide whether to speak and what to say.

"Kadi says Uncle Apollon made a perfect likeness. I'm glad to know what Nike looks like, to have a true image of her in my mind when the family tells me the stories about her." He sighed. "Mother and father have never set foot here, as far as I know, and Kadi never came back after the night Uncle Apollon dedicated the statue. So when Uncle said he didn't feel the portrait was finished, I offered to help. I cast this ward to last."

"It is beautiful," Cassia said. "A true tribute to your sister."

She wanted to say she was sure Nike would soon come home to see what her brother had done for her. But she couldn't find the confidence to say the words, and she would not shower Mak with platitudes she didn't believe.

Lyros tugged Mak's hand. "Let's sit with her awhile, shall we?"

Mak nodded, and everyone followed him into the shelter of his spell. His ward felt as reassuring as the magic that had shielded Cassia the night of the Siege of Sovereigns, as inviting as the power that had guarded the Hesperine embassy in Solorum Fortress during the Equinox Summit. She paused with his magic at her back and faced Nike for the first time.

Cassia stood transfixed and stared at the unchanging, unforgettable Hesperine.

Although sculpted in black granite, instead of revealed in living color by spell light, there was no mistaking her beautiful oval face, her proud brow and full lips. She had worn a hood and robe then. But here she was fully revealed, her long, ancient hair flowing behind her, her Stand regalia whipping around her powerful body as in a wind. No tears on her face now, only an expression of bold and joyous defiance.

"Cassia, what is it?" Lio asked.

"I know her."

Their gasps and murmurs of surprise broke the still night.

Cassia turned to Mak. As she had to Nike that night, she reached out a hand to him and touched the tears trailing down his cheek. "I have met Nike, and I can tell you she is all her legend holds her to be. Your sister gave mine the Mercy. Nike is the Hesperine errant who rescued me from that arrow."

Mak shook his head, then laughed aloud. "She knew what she was doing all this time, staying in the field. It was all worth it. For if she had come home, she couldn't have saved you."

Cassia suddenly found herself enveloped in a bear hug. Mak smelled like cloves and made her feel as safe as his magic, as safe as his sister had that night.

"The brother she spoke of was Methu," Cassia said. "Now I understand her pain."

"To think, my sister has been traveling with Alkaios and Nephalea."

"Nike *is* Iskhyra," Cassia realized, "she must be, for I met the three of them together that night."

"Nike must have taken a different name so Rudhira wouldn't hear of her whereabouts." Mak's momentary joy left his voice.

Cassia held Mak. She didn't want to say the rest aloud, although they must all be thinking it.

Mak pulled back, rubbed a hand once over his eyes, and then his tears were gone. "Lyros and I will notify the Charge and the envoy service of this new information right away, so they can get word to Kalos, Basir, and Kumeta. Now we know for certain that Nike is in the Aithourian Circle's custody with Nephalea and the other hostages, using the name Iskhyra so the war mages don't realize they have one of the Blood Errant, the heir of two elder firstbloods."

Lyros took his Grace's hand once more. Their Trial sisters stood in silence, while Lio put an arm around Cassia's shoulders and pulled her close.

Cassia took it upon herself to be the first one to say it. "Mak, I'm so sorry."

"Don't be. You've given us the most valuable lead we've had in decades. We can't lose sight of the hope you've given us. Kalos and the envoys can now put together everything they've learned about Iskhyra and Nike. That's twice as much information as they had before. It may lead them to her and the other hostages."

"I wish there was more I could do," Cassia said.

"There is," Mak replied. "Will you go tell Kadi and our parents? I know it won't be easy, but it is an honor that should be yours."

"Of course I will. In the name of my bond of gratitude with Nike, I will tell your family she saved my life."

"Thank you. Lyros and I must not waste a moment getting word to the Charge and the envoys."

"Let's go." Lyros squeezed Mak's hand. Together, they stepped out of sight.

Lio wrapped Cassia in his arms. "It was all worth it. For if you hadn't come home, you couldn't have saved them."

But Nike, Nephalea, and five other Hesperines with grieving families were not safe, not yet. Not until the envoys found out where they were, and the Charge brought them over the border, alive and well.

The truth was staring Cassia in the face, set in stone. If Nike had stayed in Orthros, many lives would have been forfeit.

If Cassia stayed in Orthros, how many would she fail to save?

SOLSTICE GIFT

LARGE, SOFT FLAKES OF snow swirled around the terrace at House Argyros, alighting on the abandoned coffee service. Beyond the railing, the orchard was still and quiet.

A giggle startled Cassia. She glanced down. From under the pristine white tablecloth, Zoe, Aurora, and Moonbeam peeked out, smudges of dirt on their faces. Zoe looked up at Lio and wiggled her fingers, motioning at herself.

Lio smiled at his little sister. Cassia sensed his magic at work, and then Zoe disappeared.

"They're playing veil and step," Lio murmured. "Aunt Lyta is it. No one stands a chance."

"Is it cheating for your big brother to use his magic to help you?" Cassia asked.

"Oh, no. Unlike in the gymnasium, any and all magic is allowed in children's games. Funny thing is, they only get more fun as you grow up and get more powerful."

"If your uncle is playing, too, then I doubt we'll find him before my gift to him needs transplanting again."

"Uncle is on the tree bench with Thenie," came Zoe's whisper from under the table. "Are you giving him his Solstice Gift right now?"

"Yes," Lio answered. "Why don't you bring the rest of the family to the tree bench when your game is over?"

"All right."

Cassia kept a hand on the veiled gift to guide it along while Lio levitated it before them. It would have been too heavy for her to carry, even with all the strength she had built up gardening. Hand-in-hand, they descended from the terrace and went into the orchard.

They hadn't gone far when she spotted Lyta leaning against a pomegranate tree. The Guardian of Orthros grinned and put a finger to her lips, pointing above her. Cassia could make out a curly head hidden among the pomegranates. Suddenly Lyta levitated and grabbed Bosko's shoulders. He let out a startled yell, then a laugh, and tumbled out of the tree.

A cocoon of shadow broke his fall, and he hit the ground running. He made it about three paces before Lyta caught up to him and snatched him up in her arms. To Cassia's surprise, he didn't struggle to get away. He just kept laughing and kept letting her hold him longer than necessary.

"One down!" Lyta crowed. "One to go."

"Three, if you count the goats." Bosko dusted off his hands. "I'll help you find them!"

"We may be outnumbered, but we shall triumph. Let us interrogate these innocent bystanders. Perhaps they saw something." Lyta crossed her arms and strolled toward Cassia and Lio.

"If we did," Lio replied, "we are honor bound not to reveal what we know."

"We are but pilgrims on our way to the tree bench," Cassia said, "bearing a Solstice Gift."

Aunt Lyta's smile wavered. "A kind thought for tonight. Argyros will appreciate it."

"I have a gift for both of you."

"Doubly kind. I'll be along in just a moment."

Bosko tugged his grandmother's sleeve. "This way. I'll show you one of Zoe's favorite hiding places."

He turned and loped toward the terrace. Lyta winked at Lio and Cassia, then followed her grandson.

Lio and Cassia went onward to the center of the orchard, where a stone bench ringed the starflake tree Argyros had said was the first and oldest on his grounds. The founding tree's modest size belied its age. Its smooth trunk and pristine fruits appeared fresh as new snow. In the shelter of its branches, Argyros sat with Thenie on his lap.

Thenie never met anyone's gaze, but here she was, looking right into her grandfather's eyes while she made sounds. He listened to her with rapt attention and a delighted smile, nodding occasionally. It occurred to Cassia that someone who loved the child without reserve, who was also an ancient thelemancer, could probably understand what went on in Thenie's mind as no one else could.

"Cassia, Lio." Argyros looked up, resettling Thenie on his lap. "To what to do I owe this unexpected pleasure?"

Lio gave Cassia an encouraging touch on the shoulder.

She cleared her throat. "I thought this would be a good time to give you my Solstice Gift."

Argyros's expression, so often unreadable, softened into surprise. "How kind of you, Cassia."

It wasn't long before Lyta and Bosko joined them under the old star-flake tree. Bosko's attention went to Thenie. Argyros handed her to her brother, and Bosko, without any sullen looks, gave a nod that look suspiciously like a gesture of thanks. Thenie was clearly the Equinox Oath in Bosko's relationship with their grandfather. A moment later, Zoe came along the path with Kadi and Javed in tow, and they too gathered around the tree bench.

Cassia looked at Lio. He nodded, and the gift became visible.

Argyros actually gasped. He got to his feet and came near to peer at the sapling.

"Oh, well done, Cassia," Javed said.

Thenie cooed and reached out, and Bosko held her where she could touch the leaves with her clumsy baby hands.

Zoe scooped up Moonbeam and Aurora an instant before they hopped onto the bench. "No eating Uncle's plants."

Lyta drew near to admire the young tree. "What manner of plant is this?"

"You mean you don't recognize it?" Cassia asked.

Argyros spread his hands. "In all our years together, she has never seen a live one."

A look of consternation crossed Lyta's face. "You don't mean to say this is a coffee tree."

Argyros couldn't seem to take his eyes off the sapling. "I cannot fathom how, in the middle of Orthros Boreou when all our trade with the Empire is at its seasonal standstill, you not only managed to procure a coffee tree, but also kept this prime specimen alive between your door and mine."

"It's your coffee tree," Cassia said. "The pot is different because it needed transplanting into a larger one, twice."

His eyes widened. "*My* coffee plant? This thriving masterpiece cannot possibly be the pathetic creature I entrusted to you for study."

"You asked me to fix it. I couldn't leave it like that."

"I thought you might discover something from it that would inform future attempts." Argyros let out a laugh. "I never imagined you would bring it back to life."

Cassia couldn't hide her smile. "Surprise."

"That's the coffee tree from your desk?" Kadi asked.

"The very one whose unsightly presence your mother has been generous enough to tolerate in our home."

Lyta grinned. "What did I tell you about every experiment of yours?"

"And how many of my successes have been possible only thanks to your support, my love? But in this case, the credit for such a triumph goes entirely to Cassia."

Argyros turned to her again. "However did you manage it? You must tell me everything. No, wait—I will retrieve writing supplies from the library. I would like to take notes."

"You don't have to do that," said Cassia. "It was really quite simple. I couldn't have done it without Lio, though."

"It was Cassia's idea," Lio was quick to say. "I was happy to assist."

"I suggested we do for your coffee tree what revived the lost roses we discovered in Tenebra."

Argyros frowned. "The biology and care requirements of roses and coffee are entirely different. How could the same techniques work?"

"This method always works." Lio smiled.

"We gave it our blood," Cassia explained.

Argyros's brow furrowed. "I don't understand. That shouldn't have affected the plant at all."

"It was my idea," Cassia answered, "but I think it was mostly Lio's power. Hesperine blood can revive anything, can't it?"

Javed shook his head. "Blood magic only works on creatures with blood. That is why we feel no Blood Union with, for example, jellyfish or flatworms. It's also why Hesperine blood does not heal plants."

Lio was looking at her, a slight smile on his face, his brows raised expectantly. "Your green thumb."

"Thank you," Lyta told her.

"It's the least I can do," Cassia began, "for you and your family. There is something I came here to tell you tonight. I know how it feels to face painful memories. I do not wish to disrupt your peace and call to mind what you would rather not remember on this night…but it is only right that I tell you this upon the Vigil of Mercy."

"They won't want you to wait," Lio said gently. "We have all waited far too long for this already."

Lyta did not hesitate. "What is it you need to tell us, Cassia?"

Cassia took a deep breath. "We all went with Mak to the beautiful statue Lio's father made of Nike."

Argyros's face became still and obscure once again. Lyta just nodded.

"I'm glad," Kadi said, her voice thick.

Cassia knotted her hands. But Hesperines had taught her much better work for her hands than that.

Cassia reached out. She took one of Aunt Lyta's hands in her own, and one of Uncle Argyros's in her other.

"I recognized her," Cassia said.

Uncle Argyros's hand tightened on hers.

Aunt Lyta's breath caught. "You've seen our daughter?"

"She is the Hesperine errant who saved me fourteen and a half years ago. She's the reason I'm standing here right now. Everything I have done in my life, she made possible. I am so sorry you've had to do without her all these years, but I hope I can be of some comfort to you."

The air around Cassia swelled with power. The deep, safe darkness of warding magic she had first felt in Nike's arms. The brilliant tide of mind magery Lio had taught her to trust. She found herself enfolded in an embrace between Aunt Lyta and Uncle Argyros, and she realized where

Mak had learned to embrace others. She heard someone crying; Kadi was too strong to hide her tears.

Orthros was full of people who would feel Cassia's absence. It was full of love she must give up.

She would give Nike's family as much comfort as one small person could, before she must cause them the same pain Nike had and leave the Sanctuary.

VIGIL OF
SOLACE

4 Nights Until Winter Solstice

DECLARATION

UNCLE ARGYROS SAT IN silence by Alkaios's bedside, and Lio wished he could find the right words to say to his uncle. When Cassia had broken the news about Nike, none of what Lio had added to the conversation had felt sufficient. At the moment, his uncle seemed to find the greatest comfort in devoting himself to Nike's ailing comrade.

Alkaios's room was full of family. Lio had managed to squeeze himself into a corner to sit cross-legged on the floor with Zoe on his lap. She and Thenie were engrossed in a make-believe with the animal figurines Father had carved for them from colorful stone. Bosko was feeling very impressive wearing his new speires and holding up the back wall with Mak and Lyros.

Lio was glad the children's Vigil of Solace gifts kept them distracted from their troubled elders. The visit to the Healing Sanctuary was not dampening the sucklings' spirits, not after all of tonight's gifts and games dedicated to celebrating Orthros's children. Lio wasn't sure how the rest of them would have gotten through the night, if they hadn't had the sucklings to focus on.

Cassia felt too far away. It had been so hard to return her to Rose House without breaking his Vigil of Mercy fast. But now that veil hours had once more released her from the embassy, he could not begrudge his relatives a chance to spend real time with her, despite the raw edge of his hunger.

He just hoped she did not feel too overwhelmed by demonstrative family members. Aunt Lyta did not look likely to let Cassia out of her arms any time soon.

"Thank you for indulging me," Aunt Lyta said to her. "I have not felt this close to my daughter in ninety years."

Cassia made no move to escape the embrace. "It's the least I can do."

Lio sensed she was holding up, despite confronting the night of her sister's death yet again. In fact, not all the fraught emotions in her aura were difficult ones. She was not without solace in this, either. Given time, she would take comfort in the family, as they did in her, he was certain. The love everyone felt for her would smooth the painful edges Tenebra had sharpened inside her.

"Alkaios definitely understands what we're saying to him," Javed was telling Uncle Argyros. "Make no mistake, he will have memories of this time, despite his condition."

"Good. I want him to remember he was not alone." Uncle Argyros slid a hand under the nape of Alkaios's neck, and Lio could feel his uncle's thelemancy at work, easing the starving Hesperine's pain.

"I think it only right that he be our Ritual son," Aunt Lyta said again. "He was Nike's comrade in the field. She may well be his Gifter. He is one of Blood Argyros's own, just as Cassia is through her bond of gratitude with our daughter."

"But through Cassia, our bond of gratitude with him is deepest," Lio's father insisted. "A place is waiting for him in Blood Komnena's section of the Firstblood Circle."

"Can he not have four Ritual parents?" Mother looked to Uncle Argyros for confirmation. "Is there anything in the law which limits him to two?"

Uncle Argyros raised his eyebrows. "It would be best to consult Konstantina on this matter, but I believe tradition, not law, is the basis for each Hesperine having two Ritual parents."

"Well," she replied, "Blood Komnena excels at bending tradition."

"With a claim on both our bloodlines, he has a truly bright future awaiting him." Lio cast a glance at Alkaios, trying not to see himself. That was in his past. He could only pray it would soon be in Alkaios's past as well.

"We shall see he gets to enjoy that future," Aunt Lyta said. "Receiving the Ritual Drink from four elder firstbloods, he will be able to endure until Nephalea returns."

Just then, Kadi and a wisp of snowflakes appeared in their midst. They all shifted to let Javed squeeze over to his Grace's side. Thenie did not have to squeeze anywhere, for she was delivered to her mother from one pair of hands to the next.

Cradling Thenie in one arm, Kadi tugged Bosko's speires, which won a smile from him.

"How are things at the ward?" he asked her importantly.

"The envoys made contact to bring us word of their progress."

"What news of the search?" Aunt Lyta's voice was tense.

Kadi delivered a solemn report while Thenie played with her mother's Grace braid. "The envoy service is searching all over Tenebra. Basir and Kumeta themselves have established a forward outpost just inside the border of the Magelands at one of our few remaining Sanctuaries there. They hope to find evidence of whether or not the Aithourians took the hostages into Cordium."

Bosko scowled, muttering, "Why do we have to wait here for them to find Aunt Nike? The healing Sanctuary is boring."

"Just you wait," his mother told him. "As soon as you're old enough, I'll take you on ward patrol myself."

"As soon as you're of age," Javed said firmly.

Kadi and Bosko shared a conspiratorial glance. Mak grinned at Lio, shaking his head behind his sister's back. *Just like his uncle Mak*, Lio mouthed, to which Lyros nodded emphatically.

Veil hours waned and eventually brought Cassia close to Lio again. Zoe smiled and turned over the flower globe he and Cassia had made for her. Together they watched the betony petals flutter inside the enchanted glass. Lio decided to do himself a kindness, just this once. He left politics outside the door and focused on the moment.

It was not until Queen Soteira came to check on Alkaios that they all headed for home upon *the* healer's orders. Kadi and Javed picked up their Slumbering sucklings to step back home with Aunt Lyta and Uncle Argyros. Zoe had fallen asleep in Cassia's lap, and she let Lio pick up his sister and hand her to their father.

When Lio and Cassia were finally alone in his residence again, they found a delivery in the entry hall. She frowned at the warded canvas bag on the table under his Ritual tapestry.

He opened the scroll that accompanied it and read it aloud to her.

Dear Lio and Cassia,

The Charge does not admit defeat. We shall call this instead a temporary pause to regroup. My Fortress Masters inform me that all the talents under my command have been unable to open the enchanted box you recovered from the Dexion's chambers, so they have returned the artifact to me here in Orthros.

While I was still at Castra Justa to oversee the Charge's experiments, we even tried crushing the thing with Apollon's hammer. Admittedly, the Hammer of the Sun is less effective in any hands other than Apollon's, but I am still astonished it did not leave a scratch on the box. Should we tell him? I will leave it to your judgment whether he can sustain this blow to his pride.

Since I now find myself occupied at House Annassa, I am returning the artifact to you. I leave it to you to seek the aid of Selas's experts. Perhaps some of them will have more success.

I am satisfied the box is not an immediate danger to you in its present state. No one in the Charge suffered from our attempts to open it. However, it remains to be seen how it might respond to further experiments.

Since you two are as reckless as I am lately, warnings are in order. Keep the box in the warded bag when you are not working on it. Do not under any circumstances make an attempt upon the artifact without Mak and Lyros present to ward you. And do keep the sunbound thing out of the reach of the goats.

Cheers,

Rudhira

Cassia raised her brows. "He sounds as if he's in remarkably good spirits."

Lio shook his head. "Gallows humor. He's never flippant, except when he's in pain. The mind healers must be keeping a very close eye on him, if he wasn't even able to deliver this in person." Lio hesitated. "Unless he chose not to come because he's avoiding me."

Cassia touched a hand to his. "You think he knows what you told Konstantina?"

"If so, he knows I am, in part, to blame for keeping him here, when he wants only to be in the field, looking for the hostages."

"However he feels about it, you did what is right. He is safe."

"I should talk to him."

Cassia eased the scroll from Lio's grip and put it away beside the warded bag. "That can wait until tomorrow. You're starving."

Lio couldn't resist her invitation to enjoy this night just a little longer. He drew her into the library. "Do you want something to eat or something hot to drink before we go to bed?"

"Oh, no. I don't think I could eat anything. You must be looking forward to ending your fast, though."

"It's been a long night." He rubbed her tense shoulders. "My family can be rather overwhelming at times."

"No, they are wonderful in every way. Your people are very…physical. They embrace. They show what they feel. When the children are loud, no one scolds them or commands them to be silent. Your dignified elders just smile and laugh and play with them. These are things I had no way to learn until now. I want to know how to show you the kind of affection you were raised to want from others."

"Your affection, however you feel comfortable showing it, is what I want. You don't have to work at it."

"But this Hesperine way is wonderful to me. I want it to become my way."

"Then I will shower you with it."

"I will treasure this time, despite what hangs over us."

He put his thumb to the furrow between her brows. "I am so sorry anything taints your time with us."

"No, I won't let it. I shall not allow anything to ruin this." She reached up and touched his braid. "There is something I need to tell you. I have needed to say it since I came, but…I think now is finally the right time. I can't wait any longer, Lio."

He caught his breath, scenting her sweet distress and heated resolve. How he had waited for this! Yes, surely this would be the moment when she told him one part of the negotiations had been a success—his effort to persuade her to stay.

The most important part of the negotiations. They could weather whatever came. They could bear their fears and grief together. They could find a way through to joy.

He said their private invocation. "By our Oath, I am listening."

"But it isn't enough to say it." She tangled her hands together, then unwound her fingers deliberately, hesitated, then reached out and rested her palms on his chest. "I have said things in the past that would give you cause to doubt my words. I must show you, so you know I mean what I say."

He rested his hands on hers. "I never doubt your words."

"This is different. This is so important. I've never said anything like this to anyone."

Goddess bless. He could taste her words on his tongue, feel them in her aura already. Rich and powerful as her blood. How could she think he would doubt her, when she finally spoke aloud of what had been blossoming between them since the nights they had spent together in Tenebra?

"However you wish to show it or speak it, Cassia, I treasure all that you say to me."

She took both his hands and pulled him further into the room. She led him to his desk. Bemused, he let her sit him down in his chair.

Still holding his hands, she slid to her knees before him, gazing up into his eyes. Cup and thorns, she didn't have to say anything. Just that look she was giving him, that was a feast in itself.

Goddess, he was so fortunate. The way Cassia buried her hands in his hair promised he would count himself even more fortunate by the time she was done with him. She trailed her fingers over his scalp, and he shut his eyes to enjoy the sensation.

"Lio. Your mind is the most brilliant I have ever encountered. But its power has never frightened me. Only amazed me." She slid her hands out of his hair to caress his brow. "I have always admired your wisdom and knowledge, which guide all your decisions." She kissed both his eyes. "You have helped me see so many things clearly. Including…me." Her fingers came to rest on his mouth, then her lips feathered kisses over his. "You were the first ever to speak your mind with me and make me feel safe speaking mine in return."

He opened his mouth to speak, but she kissed him more deeply. With an effort, he kept his hands on the arms of his chair. It was so important to her to demonstrate what was in her heart tonight. He did not wish to disrupt this gift she was giving him.

She unfastened his collar slowly. "Your voice is magic to me. Bewitching, reassuring. Every time you speak, you seduce me, as surely as you make me feel that all is well."

He held his breath as she kissed his throat. Slow and luxurious, she tongued his vein, sucking gently. Desire gripped him, and joy shivered across his skin. He knew what she was trying to say. He knew it.

She kissed her way down his chest. Over his heart, she halted. She rested her cheek against him there. He gazed down at her, feeling his heart beat against her skin.

"But it is your heart, Lio, where your greatest power lies. Your greatest strengths are your love for what is right, your courage in the face of wrong, your devotion to all you hold dear, and your ferocity in protecting it. I did not know someone so good-hearted existed in the world, until you proved all my bitter certainties wrong. You have confronted all that is ugly and cruel in our world, and you have proved those things have no power in the end, by the very fact that you continue to be kind."

He could not refrain from lifting a hand to her head to hold her against him. "Thank you, Cassia."

She looked up at him again, opening his robe further so she could slide her hand down his belly. "But there is another way you showed me how much real beauty there is in the world. Another way you gave back to me what ugliness seeks to ruin."

She laid his robe open, baring him to her from head to toe. She wrapped her fingers gently around his rhabdos and slid her hand up and down his shaft. He gripped the arms of the chair once more, clenching his fingers upon the iron.

She ran her thumb along the length of his rhabdos, tracing his vein. "You showed me that desire is not a weapon. With you, I learned how divine passion can be. Every inch of your body is Sanctuary to me."

He gasped, smiling around his fangs as they shot out of his gums. She kissed the head of his rhabdos, then drove her point home by taking into her mouth as much of him as she could hold. Pleasure tightened his skin and gripped his muscles, then flooded through his blood in a heated wave as she sucked him and pulled her head back. He braced his feet against the floor, and she supported him with her hands as he arched up out of the chair.

She loved him with her mouth in one long, deep adoration after another. She lulled his self-discipline into Slumber and brought his hunger wide awake. But he held on to his control. Just a little longer. This moment, this blessed instant in his eternity. He did not want it to end too quickly.

When his fangs unsheathed to their fullest and every hot, wet stroke of her tongue on his rhabdos was an agony, she withdrew her mouth and got to her feet before him. He bit back a groan, staring up at her with his rhabdos jutting between them.

The windows behind her were a vivid blur of light and color to his dilated eyes. Shards of light played about her as she disrobed before him. His senses raw with hunger, he gazed upon her bare body and braced himself to keep from climaxing at the sight of her.

She slid onto his lap and straddled him, holding her krana just out of reach. She caressed his face, tilting his head back, and teased his lips open with her fingers. She lifted her hand to his mouth and drew her palm across one of his fangs. She traced the tip of his tooth over the same place she had cut herself the first time he had smelled her blood. The very place she had opened her own flesh to feed the Hesperine magic that had saved them from Dalos.

He felt his fang open her skin. She flexed her hand, and warm, rich droplets of her blood slid into his mouth. He swallowed and parted his mouth for the next sip.

Cup and thorns, yes, at last, she eased her krana down upon his straining rhabdos. She began to ride him as slowly and thoroughly as she had pleasured him with her mouth. Swallow by swallow, she hand-fed him her blood while she worked the muscles inside her krana to massage his rhabdos within her.

"Open your mind to me," she invited. "Feel what I am saying to you."

He felt it. He knew it. He reached for it, surrendering to her irresistible profession.

When his mind touched hers, it was as if he tapped another vein. All that was inside her flooded out and into him. He felt her speaking to him in their Union, as surely as she spoke to him with her hands and her krana. In his mind, she whispered it. To his body, she showed him how it felt. In her heart, she declared it. And although he had believed he knew it well, she taught him anew what it meant, and he drank it down.

"I love you," she said.

With that, she arched her back, stretching up toward him, and brought his face to rest upon her neck. With a cry, he gripped her to him and sank his fangs into her.

He had known pleasure, but this was ecstasy. It consumed every inch of his body and roused every ounce of his power and flooded every corner of their minds. They rocked together in the chair with the force of his climax, and he bit down with all the power inside him. He heard her cry out, and suddenly she was undulating in his arms.

Her love flooded his veins and became a part of him. Their natural union flared and pulsed within that vaster, deeper Union.

"I love you," she said again. Nestled on his lap, damp and panting, she kept feeding him those words. "I love you so much I cannot contain it all. I fell in love with you before I even understood what was happening to me, and when I realized what it was, I felt as if all I'd thought impossible was suddenly true. As if all that was wrong could be righted."

He framed her face with his shaking hands. "Thank you for describing it so perfectly. I have been struggling to put it into words myself."

A stunning smile spread across her face, and she let out a beautiful laugh he would never forget.

"I love you," he told her.

"I know. All this time, you have been loving me better than anyone ever has."

Cassia, who believed in nothing, had faith in his love.

"I want to love you like that in return," she said.

"Goddess, after tonight, I think *I* must catch up with *you*."

The last remnants of her fears faded from her aura. "In the past I said so many heartless things about how romance was nonsense. I feared I had cast doubt on any confession I might make in that regard."

He shook his head. "You have shown me over and over again. You have risked your life for acts of love on my behalf. No one has ever loved me the way you do."

She let out a sigh, and relief and wonder breathed through her aura.

"Will you come to bed?" he whispered. "It is my turn to say it to you, and it will take me the rest of the night."

VIGIL OF
WILL

3 Nights Until Winter Solstice

OUT OF SCHEMES

Cassia was accustomed to dreading dawn. But when she awoke to the bells of moon hours, the realization that she dreaded them made her feel she had lost a piece of Orthros already.

"I know." Lio kissed her neck. "I don't want you to go back to Rose House either." He mouthed his way across her shoulder. "But it's only for a little while." His hand drifted down her belly as if he had ambitions of venturing further.

As she had hoped, he was still caught up in the afterglow of last night. Like a more powerful spell covering a more subtle one, her declaration of love had blinded Lio's senses to her pain. At least for now.

"I love you," she whispered, weaving the spell tighter. Reveling in the words. Just a little while longer.

He lifted his head, meeting her gaze. "I love you, my rose."

She looked into his eyes, memorizing the expression there. This was how Lio looked at the one he loved. This was boundless affection. Friendship unconditional. Passion without inhibition. Devotion for the ages. "The minstrels didn't invent love, as I once scoffed. But it deserves much more heroic songs than the foolish ballads they sing."

He smiled slowly, and his voice wrapped around her, deep and low, weaving his own spell. "You've never heard a Hesperine love ballad."

"Alas, we have only ever danced to Tenebran songs."

"It is high time we remedied that." He sat up beside her and nudged Knight with his foot. "Do make room for me, if you will, Sir Knight. I have something very important to ask your lady."

With his head on his paws, Knight looked up at them, unmoving.

Cassia swung her legs over the side of the window seat and sat up next to Lio, patting the bed on her other side. Her hound wallowed into a sitting position and rested his head beside her. Lio only chuckled.

Then he slid out of bed and went down on one knee in front of Cassia. His humor faded, and on his face she saw the earnestness she so loved in him. Was she about to witness another important Hesperine tradition? Did one's lover always perform it wearing not a stitch, or was that just a happy circumstance in their case?

Lio took her hand. "A week from tonight, Orthros will hold the Festival of Grace, a whole long night of music and dancing. It is a celebration of all lovers. A time for making promises…and keeping them. Will you do me the honor of attending Grace Dance with me?"

Yes, oh yes. It was selfish of her to accept his invitation, when she knew how much pain she would soon cause him. But she wanted to undo the Autumn Greeting she had danced with Flavian, one step with Lio at a time, to remind herself she was his. To show him that she left her heart here with him.

She gave Lio the true smile she saved for him alone. "It is my joy to accept."

He smiled back, the smile of someone who has won the prize at life's carnival, and his kiss was so full of promise she could scarcely bear it. "Cassia. I love you."

"I love you so much," she answered.

Now that the words were out, they came so easily between them. They kept saying them, just because they could. She kept saying them over and over, as if that could make up for all the years in which she could not say them.

Lio stood, pulling Cassia to her feet with a touch of levitation. "I might be able to bring myself to take you back to Perita, knowing I shall have your hand in mine all night at the festival."

She kept up the spell of their love as they dressed each other, as they stepped back to the guest house, right until the moment he left her at the door of her room and disappeared amid the roses.

Then it came over her. She went inside and sank down onto the edge of the bed. She had no idea how she would ever get to her feet again.

The pain was too great for tears. She sat and stared out at the courtyard until she could not bear to see the roses anymore, and she had to go and close the curtains. The paralysis came over her again there. Knight whined, twining around her skirts. Her hand slid to rest on his ruff, but she found no words of reassurance for him. She stood at the covered door, leaning her forehead against the drape.

"Oh, my lady, you're still in your clothes?"

At the sound of Perita's voice, Cassia jumped. She must rally her frozen mind to her defense, and quickly. But the apathy had set in as she had never felt it before, and she found she did not care what Perita thought.

Cassia had to find a way to care. She would have many cares in the years to come, and they would demand all her capabilities.

Perita clicked her tongue and came to Cassia, taking both her hands and sitting her down at the dressing table. "Didn't I tell Callen you wouldn't get a wink of sleep last night? You've been pacing all night, haven't you, trying to think of a way out of it before today dawns."

"What's today?" Cassia asked blankly.

"You know you don't have to put on an act for me, my lady. This is the thirty-first of Kyria's Loom, and I know how you must have been dreading it."

"Of course. Weaving Day. When the women of Tenebra finish the new blankets for the cold weather, and men tie up their debts and agreements in case Hypnos takes them before winter ends. The day the king and Lord Titus will finalize my betrothal to Flavian."

"I know all you can think about is Lord Pretty Breeches the Elder and His Majesty sitting down over a pint and dooming your future with Lord Fancy Soap. Here, stand up for me, my lady. I have to get you dressed."

"But there are no Summit events tonight."

Perita sighed. "I have done everything I can to talk them out of it, but they are determined. Your well-wishers are just down the hall, waiting to come in with food and drink to celebrate your betrothal."

"Benedict," Cassia accused.

"I'm afraid so. He's had a gift hidden for you in his packs all this time." Perita patted Cassia's shoulder. "Shall I tell them you're ill?"

Cassia swallowed. "They're trying to be kind. Help me get ready."

Within half an hour, Benedict descended upon Cassia's sitting room leading a party of merry Kyrian mages and a solemn Callen.

With an uncharacteristic flourish, Benedict presented Cassia with a parcel wrapped in velvet and ribbons. "Congratulations, Your Ladyship. It is my honor to be the first to officially welcome you into Segetia's most noble family."

Cassia must put it on. The Smile. Her court mask, horribly believable and appealingly false. She had thought it had been difficult to put on the Smile at Solorum during the Greeting. But no, it was so much more arduous to wear it now, here, in Orthros. She felt she betrayed Lio a little more every second she wore the Smile, and she felt she dishonored Benedict's kindness a little worse the harder it became to keep the expression on her face.

She glanced around her to see if it was even working. The young Kyrians' eyes gleamed with delight over their veils, the Semna chuckled, and Benedict watched Cassia with anticipation on his face. The Smile might be costly, but Cassia was still good at it.

She accepted his gift, discovering it was quite heavy. She felt the shape inside the velvet. "Has our sober Knight of Andragathos brought me a jug of wine?"

He blushed, smiling. "From His Lordship's own cellars. My lord Flavian couldn't be here to toast you, so we shall do it in his stead. I've brought a deck of his cards, as well, although we needn't gamble."

The Semna patted the basket on Ariadne's arm. "These resourceful young mages were kind enough to bring some provisions for my health from Kyria's own larders."

"Our little secret," said Pakhne.

Benedict's customary glower showed itself again. "Eudias shall not be joining us, I might add. He has been persuaded to spend the day among those with whom he came."

"And that's all that shall be said of *them* for the rest of our celebration," the Semna declared. "We shall not allow all that has happened to disrupt this occasion."

"Her ladyship may relax among her own," Benedict assured her.

Cassia told herself this was good practice. If she could get through this day, she could get through another. And another. And another after that.

But what a long day it was. As long as the Autumn Greeting and just as lavish in its own way. Even Lord Gaius stopped by with a bottle of Hadrian spiced wine to congratulate her on her upcoming marriage, although he offered no customary compliments to the groom-to-be.

As moon hours wore on, Callen's frown deepened, and Perita fussed over Cassia all the more. Knight did not move out of her reach for even a moment. She redoubled her efforts to seem delighted over the Kyrians' singing and Benedict's card games. Her fear mounted. What would she do if she lost control and wept in front of everyone?

It was almost veil hours when Benedict rose at last, swaying a little on his feet, and gathered their empty wine cups with deliberate care. "This whole journey has been exceedingly tiring for you, Your Ladyship. We shall depart and leave you to your rest."

If they hadn't all been tipsy, they would surely have seen through the good-nights Cassia barely managed to utter. She hid behind Callen's insistence and Perita's shooing. As soon as the invaders were gone, she fled into the bedroom and took refuge at the dressing table again.

Perita put her hands on Cassia's shoulders. "There now. It's over."

"For now."

"Don't tell me you haven't got any ideas for un-Ladyshipping yourself. You were probably scheming all last night trying to decide how you and your owl will escape the hawk."

"Scheming?" Cassia asked. "Is that really what I am? A schemer?"

"Aye, the finest schemer in Tenebra. I know what's going on behind that blank expression of yours when you're wearing a hole in the floor. I often think to myself, 'Every step of her slippers gives the lords of Tenebra more reason to shake in their boots.'"

Cassia reached over her shoulder and clutched Perita's hand. "Thank you."

Perita faced Cassia and leaned against the dressing table, her expression clouded with worry. "Is it so hard this time?"

"It's impossible. I've thought of everything—*tried* everything. I cannot see a way for me to be with him."

Anger crossed Perita's face. "Where is he to help you when you need him? If he loves you so much, he shouldn't leave it all on your shoulders."

"He hasn't. He has done so much for me."

"I had hoped he was working on something for you back in Tenebra, while you've been here."

"During the entire Summit, he has worked tirelessly for our cause. But some forces are too great to overcome. Even for him."

"This isn't right! A lady ought to be happy on a day like this."

"There are many of us who have not rejoiced upon our betrothals."

"My lady ought not to be among them."

"Do not feel sad for me, Perita. I am fortunate, if not in my betrothal, then the reason for my unhappiness."

Perita stowed a brooch in the dressing table with a vengeance and slammed the drawer shut. "If he can't fix this, then he isn't good enough for my lady."

"Don't be angry, Perita. He is…the best."

"I am angry. I'm angry at the bird in the bush for spoiling your chance for happiness with the bird in the hand. Flavian may be Segetian, but I think he has it in him to rise to the occasion, once he realizes how fortunate he is in you. Benedict is a good sort. He'll knock sense into his lord and see you're treated right. And I can't really say anything bad about the family, even if I can about the title. Lord Titus is a generous man, and Lady Eugenia will be a good friend to you."

"Risara and I understand one another well," Cassia said.

She recalled what Titus's concubine had told her the day of the Autumn Greeting. *Don't ever forget what you deserve.*

"See there," said Perita. "I think you might have been happy today, if not for Lord Fancy Soap beguiling you with illusions that aren't real."

"If not for him, I would have regarded myself as fortunate and never known I was unhappy. I would have deemed Flavian an advantageous choice and dismissed love as of no use. I would have resigned myself to my duties to Flavian and never had a taste of real passion."

If she had never known Lio? She could not bear imagining such a life. She must give up their future. But no one could rob her of their past.

Nor the last, precious remnants of their present, before the Summit must come to an end.

Again. She was going to lose him again.

Perita's indignation did not abate. "Will happiness and love and passion take you out of your father's household and see to it you've one of your own? And enough to eat? And family to fill the house and the years, to care for you as you grow old?"

"He would give me everything."

All she had to do was ask. Speak her desires. Tell him how much she wanted.

"Woulds and might haves aren't enough," Perita concluded. "Not for my lady."

NIGHT TO LAST FOREVER

T HE BIRD IN THE bush stood just outside Cassia's door. Rose foliage and a curtain were not enough to keep Lio from hearing the end of Cassia and Perita's conversation. Was it wrong of him to eavesdrop? He thought not, for Cassia had been glad of his nearness during her heart-to-heart with Benedict the other night. Even now, she must know Lio was nearby.

So this betrothal nonsense was what had upset her, while she pretended everything was fine, as if he couldn't tell. Didn't she realize that meaningless agreement was no threat to her now? Perita need only depart, and he would deliver the cure for Cassia's fears.

But when Perita left, Cassia did not come out. Her aura lingered in her shadowed room, as if she were hiding from all that lay without.

Never mind tradition and asking her at Grace Dance. She needed assurances now. Had he really failed to make his intentions clear? If his actions had not convinced her, it was high time he spoke. It would not take long to banish her tears.

From the other side of the glass, he Willed her curtain to open slowly, letting her see he waited for her. He held up the perfect white rosebud he had selected from the bushes in the courtyard. She met his gaze. Tears streaked her face.

He didn't bother opening the door, only stepped to her side and knelt before her. He took her stricken face in his hand. "Cassia. Do not cry, my rose. All is well."

"My betrothal to Flavian is final as of today."

"His father's bargain with the king is a puff of air. Flavian's pretensions toward you have no validity here. Tenebran marriage vows, much less betrothal promises, don't even carry legal weight in Orthros."

"I hoped it would not matter."

His Grace thought a handshake in Tenebra mattered between them! "Of course it doesn't. Our Oath came first, and it shall outlast everything."

"I—I can't bear for this to change everything."

"This night is no cause for weeping." Lio pulled her to her feet. Kissing her tears, he summoned her cloak from nearby and bundled her up. "Come with me. Just the two of us. There's something I've been waiting to show you."

"*Baat*, Knight." Bidding her hound to stay, she wrapped her arms around Lio.

He held her close, letting their feet leave the floor. With a thought, he opened the glass door ahead of them and levitated them out into the courtyard. He spun her around. They need not wait until the festival to dance. He swept them up toward the glass, where the sky seemed to surround them, and the ground was far below.

"Hold on tight," he said.

He stepped them to their destination, setting them gently down on the observation deck. Cassia clung to him as if to steady herself, or perhaps only because of the cold.

She looked all around them at the expanse of white stone and the vast, dark reaches of the sky. "Where are we?"

"The top of Hypatia's Observatory, the tallest structure in all of Orthros Boreou. You can see everything clearly from here." He turned her toward the south. The city's glow slept, and stars no one could see during moon hours gleamed at them, rising over the Umbral Mountains and a veil of aurorae. "On the eve of the Autumn Equinox, I stood here alone for hours, watching for the Summit Beacon. I feared I would never see you again. Now here you are in my arms, safe with me in Orthros. Look how far we've come."

She was silent a moment, as if staring the mountains down.

"Now look at all that lies ahead." He kept his arm around her and led her to the edge.

He heard her suck in a breath. Then she looked down.

She let out a soft exclamation, almost like when he loved her. He stood behind her and wrapped both his arms around her, holding the white rosebud close against them. Together they gazed down upon Selas and into the deep darkness of veil hours. Scattered secret lights shone at them like jewels from windows here and there. Snowy roofs and marble works of art gleamed white and red and black, reflecting or drinking the moons' light.

Lio spoke to Cassia the way it pleased her in their private hours, touching her mind and deepening his words with magic. "Behold Orthros, my love. It is yours, and it always has been, and it always will be."

The wind swept over them, and her scent, salty with tears, sweet with wonder, wrapped around him. She tightened her arms over his.

"No one can take Orthros from you, Cassia. Nothing in Tenebra has power over you anymore. Leave all of it on the other side of those mountains."

She took a breath that was almost a sob. "I wish veil hours would never end."

He kissed her neck. "Tell me you want the night to last forever, and I will make it so. I have that power."

"I want you so much."

"I will take you from your father's house and give you House Komnena," he promised. "I will not merely see to it you have enough to eat. I will give you a feast, night after night. Our happiness and love and passion will be so great that mere years will not be enough to hold it all. We will fill eternity with it…and with our family. We can have happy, safe, beloved children of your blood and mine. You will never grow old. Only more powerful, happier, and more loved."

"I don't want to go back," she cried. "I want to stay in Orthros."

He rested his cheek against hers. "Stay with me. Stay *for* me. Stay for *you.*"

Her chest shook. "I can't. No matter how much I want to. I cannot."

"You can. You need no longer hold yourself to your promise to fight. That time is past. We fight together now."

"We lost."

Lio held her more tightly. "We have lost nothing."

"I can't sacrifice lives for our happiness."

Her pain tore through the Union. Lio took a step back.

She pulled out of his arms as if it burned her to touch him. "If Nike had stayed in Orthros, I would be dead. How can I justify staying here, when I could save so many lives?"

Lio stood where he was as the wind buffeted him. "What lives, Cassia? The envoys are looking for Nike, Nephalea, and the other hostages. When the Order's wrath descends, we shall all be here together, safe behind the ward."

Cassia wrapped her arms around herself. "Even if the envoys succeed, who will the Aithourian Circle endanger next to rile Orthros? The war mages are nothing without war. They will never give up trying to draw Hesperines out to battle, and the king will serve his people up to the Orders."

"What-ifs," Lio countered. "Nothing more. But all the more reason why you should be here with us. The 'Hesperite sorceress' of Solorum will be the first target of persecution."

"What did we expect to happen, even if the lords and knights agree to an Oath with us? The nobility is not strong enough to stand against the king and the Orders, not without leadership to keep the free lords united. The Oath will die the moment they return home. The king will not suffer any hope of peace to live."

"Cassia, don't lose faith in our Summit. Not now."

"We've been dreaming, Lio! The Dexion's takeover of the embassy has shaken us awake. As long as Lucis is on the throne, there is no hope."

The wind tore at her now-tousled hair, which she had worn in the same braid since the night of the fair. Lio reached out to her, but it was too late. The wind unraveled the promise she'd had him weave into her hair.

"You cannot be considering going back."

"You must be wondering what could be gained, if I go return to the way things were, hiding in the shadows and waiting to strike at the king's plan where I can. What more could I do, when the effect of my best efforts was already waning when you intervened with the Summit? You are right. I have no intention of continuing as I was. It is time for me to change everything."

"I don't understand."

"I know," she said, so gently it hurt. "Even you, my mind mage, have yet to see. No one has ever thought it possible. But I can do it, Lio."

"What is this plan of yours I have not seen?" he asked helplessly.

"I am going to make myself Queen of Tenebra."

NO OTHER WAY

THEY LANDED BACK IN the courtyard with a stagger. Cassia watched Lio sink down onto a bench by the fountain. He put his head in his hands.

He said nothing. The silence between them stretched on, terrible in its certainty.

"Can you do it?" he asked at last.

"Yes."

"Can you do it without Flavian?"

"No."

His head snapped up, and he looked at her, his hands out in a gesture of protest, of plea. "You cannot really be thinking of—not that. Not Flavian."

"The free lords will never accept a bastard daughter on her own. But she can provide the path to the throne, and a popular lord at her side can win her the nobility's approval."

Lio's face flushed. "This is the future you envision for yourself? A life as Flavian's shadow queen? As his *wife?*"

"It will be a political union only! I have already made it clear what he shall not expect of me. He and Sabina know they have my blessing. Heirs can be adopted. Or produced by his sister, if I can persuade Titus and Risara to acknowledge that Eugenia is their daughter."

Lio shook his head as if someone had struck him. "You have it all planned. You've had this in mind all along. The whole time you've been here."

"No. Yes. It was always my last resort. I thought I would have to go through with it when the Dexion arrived at Solorum. I believed it was the only way to prevent war, until you convened the Solstice Summit. As soon as we were together again, I hoped I wouldn't have to do it. That we could find another way. But you must see, Lio. There is no other way. This is what I must do."

"No, I don't see." He surged to his feet. "This cannot be. Orthros needs you. You belong here, with us."

"Yes. I do." She could scarcely bear to look upon the shock and pain on his face. She had known she would hurt him. But now that she had dealt the blow, it was so much worse than she had dreaded.

"You cannot do this to yourself—to me—to all of us!" he cried.

"I don't know how I will do it. I don't know how I'll bear to give you up a second time. But I must find a way. I wish it were not so, I wish there were anyone else to take up this burden, but there is not. I am all we have. I am the only one who can save us from the king."

"Is that what this is about? The king? Of course. It is too much to ask of you, that you leave him in power, after all he has done."

"No. He has no place between us," she told Lio, as she had one night in Tenebra. That time he had refused her blood, she had felt so angry and humiliated.

This was infinitely worse. She was the one making him angry.

But she was also right, as she had not been then. She must hold fast to her conviction, to her conscience.

"Perhaps you think I want revenge," she said. "If that were the case, I would not go back. You know there was a time when all I cared about was surviving the king. What better way to have the last laugh than to survive him forever?"

"There was a time when you wanted revenge."

"And I banished that specter. You know I did, for if I had not, you would never have taken your first drink from me. As I asked you that night, I shall ask you now. Is revenge what you hear crying out in my thoughts?"

His mind descended over hers, a beautiful darkness. Her resolve trembled. She could lie beneath that darkness forever. He had promised her she could.

"No, there is no revenge in you." His voice brought his mind deeper into hers. "Only want. You are so full of want. What I once told you was true. Tenebra will never be enough for you."

She could feast on his words, his voice, his presence in her mind and never run short. Everything she wanted was right here, standing across from her in the courtyard, within arm's reach, within her mind.

If she let herself want him, if she let herself drink him down another moment, it would be too late.

"I cannot have what I want!" she shouted.

He withdrew as if the sun had risen and banished the night. She stood burning a few paces away from him.

He looked away, his breathing too quick for a Hesperine. "Going back to Tenebra will give you one thing you want. Justice for Solia."

"I would rather show my gratitude to the Hesperines who honored her than punish the king. I would rather keep my sister alive by"—Cassia's voice wavered—"by being a sister to Zoe the way Solia taught me. That's enough for me. I'm not such a brave and selfless avenger after all. No victory could be sweeter than seizing for myself all the king has sought to deny me—freedom, safety. Love. My anger is not strong enough to withstand happiness."

"All I have sought to do since you came to me is make you happy."

"You have. You have given me everything, and it breaks my heart to repay you so. But I cannot in good conscience remain, knowing I have the power to stop what is to come. This conscience of mine is still a young creature, but she is strong. I find her as pragmatic as the lack of conscience that once ruled me. I know bringing down the king will not bring Solia back. But it will save many others from him—Hesperines and Tenebrans."

"How, Cassia? Lucis is the most formidable king Tenebra has seen in generations! How can you dethrone him?"

She did not blame Lio for wondering. He did not doubt her, not really. He never had. He simply wanted to believe it could not happen. He wanted impossible odds to mean this was not their future.

"Poison," she said. "A little of the right plant in his fire. Smothersweet smells just like maple. He will breathe it. He will be found dead at his desk. And it will all be over."

"You will be standing in that fire."

"Not for long. I don't mind that I must depart quickly. I actually don't want to see it happen." She swallowed. "But I'm not sorry. Not even about the guards who will be there. I know their abuses too well."

"You're going to assassinate him. By your own hand."

"I am not Skleros! I take no pleasure in it! But even a Hesperine errant must sometimes resort to ending a life to protect the innocent."

"What about Caelum? He is the king's heir."

"When I give the word, Lord Deverran will come forward and reveal that Caelum is his son with the late queen, who was his betrothed before the king stole her from him."

"Caelum isn't Lucis's son?"

"I have no idea, but it does not matter. My brother will be better off as Lord Deverran's son. I have no qualms about taking the throne from him to give him a better life. I will *not* make him the Solia at my Siege of Sovereigns."

"Then you have already cleared your way."

"All the preparations are in place. I can put them into motion as soon as I return."

"I have been so blind," Lio said. "I, the expert on your deeds. All this was right there all along, and I did not see."

"Neither of us wanted it to be true."

"It can't be true."

"I am so sorry. I hope you will be able to forgive me one day. Because I am going to need you."

"Are you really going to ask me to come back to Tenebra next spring for an Equinox Summit? You want me to swear the Equinox Oath with Queen Cassia and King Flavian?"

"Before the Solstice Summit, I thought that might be the only way I would ever see you again. I would have taken the throne just for that, Lio."

"For one more spring? You think it would be worth it, to give up your life for one more tryst? You think it would be enough?"

"Nothing short of forever is enough. But I can promise you one more spring. At least we will have that."

"I can't do this."

"Please, Lio. I can't do this, either, if you do not help me. I cannot go back to Tenebra unless I know I won't die there. When my work is done, when peace is secure, please. I need you to come back for me. I just need to know there is still a place waiting for me here. I need Orthros ahead of me, or I cannot take one more step forward."

"And how long will that be, before your work is done?"

"I don't know," she confessed. "Only ten years, if I am effective. Fifteen, perhaps, if unforeseen obstacles arise. I will have to finish by fifteen. I would not want to try to last for twenty, even with a liegehound and a Sanctuary ward to protect me. There will be no threat of childbirth, thankfully, but there are still diseases, age, and assassinations."

"Goddess," he ground out. "How could you expect me to live like that? With you in constant danger, and me never knowing if Hypnos would snatch you from me before I had a chance to bring you home?"

"I don't know. I am still trying to find how I will live with it."

"I don't need you in ten or fifteen or twenty years, Cassia! I need you *now*."

"After we restore the Oath, it won't be so dangerous for you in Tenebra. You've sneaked into the palace to see me before."

He gave his head a shake. "I didn't want to tell you until after I'd dried your tears. I thought the news would be easier to bear after we'd talked about our future here together."

Her mouth had gone dry. "What news?"

"Konstantina is proposing the Departure." Lio still held the white rosebud in his hand. "After the Dexion delivered his ultimatum about the hostages, she quietly set the formalities in motion. She moved so fast that many within the royal family didn't even know until tonight, when Xandra warned me. Konstantina is only waiting for Solstice to be over to convene the Firstblood Circle for a vote on her proposal. She will cite the capture of our Hesperines errant as proof of why it is too dangerous to remain involved in Tenebran affairs."

"She might lose the vote."

"She has spent the entire Summit securing votes. Every time she and her Trial circle were absent from an event, they were behind closed doors with other firstbloods, negotiating pledges of partisanship. Konstantina has already secured a majority. Xandra is trying to change minds now at the last moment, but her influence can't overcome her eldest sister's. Ioustin is with the mind healers, in no position to try to sway the outcome. It's too late. The vote is a foregone conclusion. As soon as the hostages are rescued, Konstantina will close the borders. There will be no embassy from Orthros in the reign of Queen Cassia. There will be no more Hesperines in Tenebra."

There would be no Hesperines to come back for her when her work was done. Lio would live on. Without her.

Cassia let go of the last shred of the spell that had sustained them all these nights. All it left behind was a sick feeling deep within her. "Then I must save the mortals on my own."

"Not again," Lio warned. "Don't tell me to be safe and happy in Orthros."

"I wanted so much to make you happy. I wanted to be the one." There it was, her anger, coming back to her now that happiness had quit the field. This time, she must not let the anger win. "But I know you are the one who will understand, when no one else will. You know politics, and you know heroism."

"No, Cassia. I cannot understand how this could be our future. I cannot last a year without you, must less ten. I. Cannot. Do this."

"This is the only way. We must give up what is good for us to do what is good for everyone."

"You told me you love me!"

"I will always love you."

He pressed the rose into her hands. "How can you give this up? After the way you showed me how you feel last night, after the way I—"

"Please." She pushed his hands away. "Don't. This is hard enough. My resolve is almost gone. Do me the kindness of not trying to persuade me to stay."

He dropped the rose at her feet. "If all I have done since you came has not been enough to persuade you, I have nothing more to say."

"I am so sorry."

"If this is the right thing to do—if this is what the Goddess requires of us—then I am no hero and no devout."

He turned on his heel and quit the courtyard with a crack of power that made Cassia shiver and the glass quake.

VIGIL OF
UNION

2 Nights Until Winter Solstice

EYE TO EYE

L IO HALTED IN HIS tracks in front of Prometheus and braced his hands
on his knees.

As soon as he was still, his thoughts got the better of him again.
For the first time, he noticed the trail his bare feet had left in the pristine
white around the monument. His passage across the grounds at a break-
neck run had gouged the snow.

Lio remembered when he had grown as tall as Prometheus. As he had
often done since, he now cut in front of his childhood portrait and faced
the first bloodborn. The view was very different when they stood eye to
eye. It was a view no other Hesperine but Lio was tall enough to see.

Queen Alea's words upon the night of his Summit proposal now came
back to him. *Why look into stone eyes for wisdom?*

Prometheus's eyes had shut on this world for the greater good. Could
that decision be understood? Had he understood it, when he had made
it? Or had he simply done it, because he must?

You need only seek it in your veins.

"I am angry," Lio told Prometheus.

The last drops of insight his own veins had to offer.

"Why did we have to lose you?" he demanded. "If you had made it
home, your monument would not be all I have of you. Goddess, why must
this be all that's left of us?"

Despair rose within Lio, as crippling as a Craving chill. He braced his
hand on Prometheus's shoulder for support.

"I don't want this to be my future."

Would Zoe one night stand before a statue of her brother, grieving for him as Nike had for Methu? How many years would it take Zoe to become tall enough to reach Lio's stone shoulder? Years he would miss.

Would Mother ever recover from the loss of her son, whose survival she thought she had secured? What shape would her pain take, as Kassandra's had taken on life as a hopeless prophecy?

Could Father bear one more loss without his rage consuming him? When the family that had healed him was broken, what would his grief break?

And for what?

To save lives. One more time, from one more strike by the Orders. Cassia's palace would be the inquisitors' prison of Lio's legend. All the Tenebrans she saved from tyranny would be the prisoners whose freedom his sacrifice made possible.

"I cannot stomach the medicine I gave your Trial brother," Lio said. "All the arguments I made to Ioustin sound different when it is my life at stake. When I know my sacrifice would not be a waste. I could change everything."

Lio could secure the peace he had worked for his whole career, which his people had tried to build for their entire history. There would be a good monarch on the throne of Tenebra who would usher in a golden age as there had never been since the Mage King and the Changing Queen. No orphans would need the Solace when a kind queen provided for them. No soldiers would wait for the Mercy on battlefields when a strong queen stopped the wars. No mages would persecute heretics when a woman who had loved a Hesperine wore the crown.

Lio's role in this golden age was easy. All he had to do was give up his Grace. All he had to do was lay down and die.

"This can't be right," he railed. "What of your Grace? What if she is alive now, doing without you? What of all those you might have saved, had you lived?"

Lio pushed away from the stone hero, only to stumble over the children that surrounded him.

"Why couldn't you have lived to rescue us with Nike, Rudhira, and Father? What if a different quest had brought you all to us, a happier one than avenging you? Why must this be truth? Why couldn't there have been a different truth for you?" Lio backed away. "I cannot live with this one."

The question was, was Lio prepared to die for it?

"You shouldn't have died. You deserved better."

Lio looked at the smiling legend who was glorious in death.

"What did you want for yourself?" Lio asked Methu for the first time. "I have never heard your truth from your own lips. All I know is the truth Orthros has made of your memory."

Only the wind answered.

"What have we done to you? How have we reduced you to this? Are you and I not worth more than memorials? Do we not deserve more than stone?"

The sound of footsteps told Lio he was no longer alone. Large, graceful feet barely brushed the snow as they approached. Mak. Lio tossed aside the veil that had kept his rant from echoing along the cliffs, while he fortified the spells that hid his anger from the Union.

Mak came out of the trees and joined Lio before the statue, but it was Lio whom Mak studied. "Ouch. Is this your first quarrel with Cassia?"

"Well." Lio flushed. "So much for my powers of concealment."

"Claiming Cassia can't get away from the embassy may work on Zoe, but not the rest of us."

Lio shoved his hair out of his face. "This isn't just a quarrel. This isn't like the other times she was angry with me."

"Heh. You always did have a taste for hot tempers."

"She's not angry with me. I—"

Mak whistled. "You're angry with her! Now there's a first. That's all right. It's good for you to get angry now and then. You don't do it often enough."

Lio could hear the conversation in his head now. *She's going back to Tenebra, Mak. She's going to make herself the queen.*

She can't do that!

Oh, but she can. Her expertise knows no limits. There is only one thing she cannot do. Stay in Orthros.

But he would not tell Mak. He would not ask his cousin to become Ioustin and leave Methu to die for the sake of the prisoners. That was too much to ask of any of his friends and family. How well he knew, after Ioustin had asked such a thing of him.

Lio was right back where he had begun at the Autumn Equinox. He could tell no one of Cassia's plans. The moment he did, they would intervene to save his life.

If he was going to make this sacrifice, it must be his decision, and his alone.

"Do you want to tell me what's wrong?" Mak asked.

"I cannot."

"I won't cross the veil. Just let me ask you this. Have you told her yet?"

Lio let out a humorless laugh. "I had romantic notions of waiting until Grace Dance."

"Tradition be sunbound. Tell her already! Whatever has come between you is sure to be irrelevant as soon as she knows."

Irrelevant, that she would choose a throne over Lio? That she would doom herself to Tenebra when she could have happiness? "Forgive me if I would like her to feel moved by something other than my certain death."

"You know what moves her. She loves you."

"Yes. Yes, she does."

Lio knew that. But even though she loved him like this, she could still find it in herself to give him up for the sake of others.

How could he do any less?

"I have never needed your father's advice more than I do tonight," Lio told Mak. "The very time when he and I are barely speaking with one another."

Mak stood in silence for a moment. "Well?"

"Well what?"

"Are you going to ask me why he's been acting like this?"

Lio gave his cousin a long look. "You've known all along."

Mak nodded, his expression rueful. "I was wondering when you would stop wallowing and ask me for advice."

Lio let his regret speak for itself through the Blood Union.

Mak snorted. "It never even occurred to you, did it?"

"This Vigil of Union, I think I should begin by apologizing to you. I'm so used to mediating between you and your father, I have given you too little credit in this situation and dishonored your bond with him."

Mak waved a hand. "Apology accepted, if it makes you feel better. I'm glad for your patience with both of us over the years. I'm really glad to be able to return the favor for a change. You know, just because he and I don't always get along doesn't mean I don't understand him."

"Of course. Besides, the two of you seem to see eye to eye more than ever of late."

"Being Graced changes a person's perspective on things. So do children."

"Everyone is grateful for your influence on Bosko."

"He's the best fun." Mak grinned. "He and Thenie have given Lyros and me a lot to discuss about our own future."

Lio would *not* let his troubles rob his cousin of that grin. He managed a smile of his own. "Two questions. Am I still under consideration as a Ritual father? And when do I start?"

"There was never any consideration. Of course you'll be our children's Ritual father, although it will be awhile yet."

Lio wanted to be here for that, too. He didn't just want to spare his family pain. He wanted all the things he had looked forward to.

"The position of Ritual mother is still vacant," Mak added. "You'd better get busy recruiting Cassia for us."

Lio had expected life to be so sweet. He had thought it would never end.

Mak cocked his head at their childhood portraits. "It occurred to me that parents need their children just as much as children need their parents. So I made some effort at being what my father needed. And I'm glad."

"I can imagine how much that means to him. You know, your directness holds a kind of wisdom neither he nor I possess. I would be grateful for as much of it as you can give me now."

"I'm going to surprise you and take a leaf out of Father's book by asking you a question instead of giving you an answer. What was my first reaction when you told me about Cassia?"

Lio lifted his eyebrows. "You were worried for me."

"Terrified," Mak corrected, but he nodded. "And my second?"

Lio thought back over the muddle of that night, when he had been nearly too ill to think. His heart sank. "You were hurt that I didn't tell you."

"You always were a quick study. Well done."

"By the Blood Union. I hurt Uncle's feelings."

"He does have them, you know."

"Well, of course he does. But most of the time he is..."

"Impervious? He seems so, yes. That's why this sort of thing is so hard for him. Mother and Kadi and I wear our wards for all to see. But he wears a veil."

"I'm beginning to think he and I have done nothing but wear veils with each other this year."

"He took it hard that you told everyone but him about Cassia. In fact, you went out of your way to keep her a secret from him until—"

"The Firstblood Circle." Lio rubbed his face. "Thorns. What possessed me to let him find out with the rest of Orthros? Him, my mentor?"

"You weren't thinking clearly because of the Craving," Mak reminded him. "That isn't an excuse, it's a real obstacle."

"Yet somehow I managed to present a plan for changing the history of Orthros without stumbling over my words, while I couldn't even see the nose in front of my face and realize I did wrong by my own uncle."

"You did collapse after presenting said plan. Imagine what might have happened if you'd tried to make amends with Father then. It would have been even worse than vomiting on his fruit trees, and that was *bad*."

"Well, I did have reasons for not telling him."

Mak counted them off on his fingers. "Keeping our elders from kidnapping Cassia. Keeping the Queens' Master Ambassador from kicking you out of the diplomatic service for getting your fangs polished by the king's daughter..."

"I was afraid he would talk me out of my plan for the Solstice Summit. He is the soul of caution."

"Maybe. But contrary to popular belief, he is not reason incarnate. He's just as volatile as the rest of our family."

"Well, I wouldn't exactly call your father 'volatile,' but..."

Mak shook his head. "Why do you think all his children turned out like we did? Why do you think he's a match for Mother? How do you think he managed to hold off an army bent on razing his temple with only his mind? Not by being reasonable."

"I never thought of it that way."

"You should know this. You're the one who's so much like him. What makes you a match for Cassia? How did you get the idea for the Solstice Summit?"

"Sheer benevolence on the Goddess's part and sheer impertinence on mine."

Mak chuckled. "A very Argyran answer. But the real answer is you're so passionate about everything you don't know what to do with yourself half the time. You care so much. There. I have educated you, without even needing to raise a fist to prove my point, I might add." He patted himself on the back.

"I think you have taught me as much as about myself as your father."

"Now go use what you've learned and apologize to him. The Vigil of Union is supposed to be a time of reconciliation. Veil hours are waning, and I want the two of you to end this night on good terms."

"Is he in his library?" Lio asked.

"No, he's in yours, waiting to apologize to you."

Lio gave Mak the victor's salute. "Are you sure you aren't a mind mage?"

Mak shuddered. "Definitely not, thank the Goddess."

"For your help tonight, you have my gratitude."

"Good luck." Mak gripped Lio's shoulder, then turned him around and gave him a gentle push toward House Komnena.

MORE THAN STONE

LIO STEPPED TO HIS tower, then climbed the front steps to his door on foot. His uncle's aura within was evident in the way of a mind mage politely disclosing his presence.

As never before, Lio contemplated how much his uncle kept hidden beneath the surface.

As soon as Lio set foot in the entry hall, he found himself drawn in by a coffee aroma unlike any he had ever smelled. It must be a new creation of his uncle's. If it was a peace offering, it was a spectacular one. If it tasted like it smelled, Lio might never drink another kind of coffee again.

Uncle Argyros waited at Lio's coffee table with the glass service laid out for them. Two empty tankards sat between them in invitation.

"I'm so glad you've come," Lio said.

"The element of surprise is not on my side, I see."

"A remarkable night, when a warrior brings two diplomats to the negotiation table, isn't it?"

"I am fortunate in my son."

"And I in my cousin and Trial brother." Lio took a seat across from his uncle.

"I would value your opinion on this new attempt of mine." Uncle Argyros reached for the coffeepot.

Before he could pour, Lio held up a hand. "I have something to contribute to the occasion. I...didn't have time to wrap them, but..."

He stowed the empty tankards under the coffee table and took out the pair of new glass coffee cups he had made. He set his uncle's Winter Solstice gift on the table between them.

Emotion stirred in Uncle Argyros's aura. "You have continued our tradition, just like every year."

"Of course."

The emblematic cups sat between them. Every Solstice, Lio designed a new piece for his uncle's collection of fine coffeeware. Each time, Lio crafted two so they could celebrate together. This year, it had taken hours of painstaking glassblowing to cajole the multicolored glass into an intricate pattern that resembled thorns. Lio watched the colors change as dark coffee filled the vessels, then as pale cream swirled within the glasses.

"This new drink is a gift for a young person," Uncle Argyros said, "the next one I intend to invite into diplomatic service to Orthros."

"A generous gift for a new student, to be sure." Lio's hopes faltered. His uncle had been scouting for...his replacement?

He tried not to appear reluctant as he lifted his cup. The coffee was a thick, auburn brew, heavy with cream and frothy on top, an uncharacteristic way for Uncle Argyros to craft his drinks. Lio could not deny the aroma enticed him, so familiar, yet new and strange at the same time. Not for the first time, he wondered how much magic Uncle Argyros put into his craft.

Lio obliged his uncle and took a taste. His mouth filled with an echo of a flavor he knew better than any other, and in the steam curling around his face, he recognized a tribute to the fragrance that had changed his life. "Cassia."

"It would not do to merely dust her namesake across the top. It was necessary to roast and blend beans that would suit her, brew them extraordinarily strong, and make cassia, sugar, and cream an integral part of the final beverage."

"You envision a future for Cassia in diplomatic service."

"I will count myself fortunate if I snatch her talent before she commits herself elsewhere. You two must have the opportunity to continue such a stellar partnership. Do you think she will accept my offer?"

Lio set down his cup. "She has other plans."

"Then I am too late."

Grief settled over the Union, heavy as Orthros itself.

"No," Lio said. "I cannot bear this any longer. I love you, Uncle. Regardless of all that I have done, I want you to know that. I know it seems I haven't shown it. But it has never changed."

"Lio!" Uncle Argyros sounded surprised.

Lio made himself look at him.

There were tears in his eyes. "I am so proud of you."

Lio let out a breath of exclamation. The next thing he knew, his uncle closed the distance between them, pulled him to his feet and hugged him close.

Lio held on to his mentor. "I was so afraid I had lost you."

At length, Uncle Argyros released him. "It takes more than a scandalous speech to deal me damage, Nephew. You might have told me the young lady was so important to you. I would have borne the shock. I can understand why you would confide in your friends and your parents first, of course. But I assure you, I too have the fortitude for the announcement."

"I'm so sorry I didn't tell you. My address before the Firstblood Circle was not how I wanted you to find out."

Uncle Argyros sank back down onto his chair. "I wish I could have helped you prepare your proposal."

Lio took his seat again, leaning forward over their coffee. "I should have trusted you. Please accept my apology for keeping the truth from you for so long."

"No, do not apologize. Not for anything. This is not about my wishes. You have done the right thing, from start to finish. I wish I could have helped you, but I could not. *You* had to do this. Your way. Not ours. Not mine."

Lio could feel that his uncle's hurt remained. That open wound in the Union had not yet sealed. "Forgive me. I thought you wouldn't consider such a dangerous scheme."

"I wouldn't. I would never have imagined it in my wildest dreams."

His uncle's stone expression was gone, and so was his veil. Lio beheld his uncle's anger, anguish, and love.

"I have never been so disappointed in myself," Uncle Argyros said. "I have robbed myself of taking part in what you have done this winter. I have let myself grow old."

"That couldn't be more untrue," Lio protested. "You taught me everything I know."

"On the contrary, your greatest triumph has come from doing the exact opposite of everything I taught you. No sooner had you made your address than I realized I must take my hands off your entire plan. As difficult as that has been."

"I would have valued your involvement. I can't count how many times I wished for it."

"I would have run the risk of steering you in the wrong direction."

Was this what Uncle Argyros had been thinking all this time? That he had…lost his touch? That his rudder was somehow not fit for this voyage?

Argyros doubted himself?

"You can't mean that, Uncle."

"Clearly, I have already misguided you somewhere along the way, at the very least about myself. I gave you the impression that I am so prone to disapproval, I would reprimand you for your genuine love for a worthy partner simply because it was against the rules. I come across as so heavy-handed that you believed I would interfere with her plans instead of appreciating them. I led you to believe I am reactionary enough to talk you out of what is clearly one of the most brilliant innovations in the history of Hesperine diplomacy. If this is how I seem to you, I have done something wrong. What is worse, I am not sure any of it is untrue."

Lio had never known his uncle to have such a crisis as this. But then, until their journey to Tenebra, he had never heard his uncle express uncertainty about anything. "My intention in all of this was never to cast doubt on how I value your teachings, your opinion—your support. I meant what I said the night we all decided to stay and battle Dalos at the Summit. Do not imagine for a moment I love your teachings any less than I ever have…but think what else I have learned as your initiate. To that I must add, think what I have yet to learn."

"The last time I attempted to share a life lesson with you, it was a complete disaster."

Oh. One of the wounds that remained in the Blood Union was Lio's own. "You are alluding to what you told me after Martyr's Pass."

"I thought it was time for you to learn the truth of what happened after my thelemancy saved my temple during the Last War. You outgrew the enthusiastic chronicles of my heroism very quickly that night and needed to understand the consequent tragedy. It seems, however, it was not what you needed to hear after all."

"Uncle, you *are* a hero for taking control of the army's minds and repelling them from your temple. It was not your fault they broke free afterward. You must never blame yourself for what they did to Aunt Lyta's village. I'm glad she helped you see that, for I know no one else could convince you not to torture yourself these many years."

"You defend your mentor to the last. Even though I hurt you when I revealed the truth."

"I admit, that conversation still pains me. That does not change the fact that I am honored you confided in me."

"I think I need to explain that I did not recount my most spectacular failure to you because I believed you had failed."

"Why, then?" Lio shook his head. "At the gymnasium, what did the thorns on that rose mean?"

"That I was proud of you!"

"I took it to mean you approved of my self-control against Chrysanthos, because I had surpassed my previous lack of discipline at Martyr's Pass."

"Hespera's Mercy. Dialogue has completely broken down between Orthros's two foremost diplomats. Why would I bestow the thorns upon you, unless I regarded your previous achievements as worthy of the white rose?"

"I thought you believed I lost control of my power in Martyr's Pass and killed hundreds of mortals on accident."

"It did not matter to me whether you had or hadn't. But it mattered so much to you. Losing control of your magic is your worst fear. Your heart was breaking at the thought that you might have done such a thing."

Lio swallowed. "You did understand."

"I was trying to tell you what I learned from my own failure during the War, what Lyta teaches me again and again with her forgiveness and love. Even if you make the gravest mistake you can imagine, it will be all right."

Lio put his head in his hands. "Uncle, I am failing tonight."

"It *will* be all right, just as it was in the pass."

"I am at a loss. Please, if it is not too much to ask, you would have my gratitude if you would be generous with your advice once again."

"This time, let there be no doubt I have every confidence in you. You will find your way through. You have done so in the face of every obstacle so far."

Lio released his grasp on the veil that held his despair in check. "I need your help."

The throbbing injury in their Union began to ease at last.

Mak had said parents needed their children. This must be part of what he meant. Elders needed to feel needed.

"There is no one else I can turn to," Lio said in all honesty. "I can trust no one but you with the truth. Only you will understand this burden and the demands of our era that have placed it upon me."

"Is it the Departure that weighs on you so?"

"Even more than that. Can I tell you this in the strictest confidence?"

There, at last, Lio sensed it. The bond of blood and wisdom between them, a current of heart and mind in the Union. It opened, strong as ever.

"Of course you can," Uncle Argyros said.

Lio lifted his head and looked at his uncle. "Cassia intends to make herself Queen of Tenebra."

What he hadn't predicted about this admission was how much it would humiliate him. He was losing his Grace. No failure had ever been so painful. No confession to his mentor had ever been so excruciating.

There came neither shock nor censure. The warmth of his uncle's love and concern enveloped him. How could Lio have forgotten this was what Uncle Argyros was really made of?

"How can I help?" Uncle Argyros asked.

"Having observed Tenebra's politics and history, do you think she will succeed?"

"Success is not guaranteed in such a dangerous endeavor, but her plan is certainly possible, even probable, and undoubtedly brilliant. In the current situation, I would predict her as the victor."

"This is the same conclusion I have reached. No insurmountable obstacles offer a basis for argument against her plan. As for the long-term impact of her reign, we would be heartless to deny her people such a just and skilled queen, and we would be fools to prevent a Hesperine sympathizer from taking the throne of Tenebra."

"She would be their finest monarch since the Mage King and the Changing Queen and an even greater champion of the Oath. She would work tirelessly to heal Tenebra and their relations with us in the face of Cordian aggression. In spite of the obstacles before her, I have no doubt she would succeed in enacting her policies by influencing the Council… and the king she selects as her figurehead."

Lio couldn't bring himself to say it.

Uncle Argyros said it for him. "She has positioned Flavian expertly."

"How am I to bear this?"

"Are you to bear it?"

"My fears for her safety and happiness have fallen on deaf ears."

"What about your pleas for yours?"

"She does not know what it will cost me. I had not told her yet, before she broke this news to me. Can you blame me for hesitating to reveal a truth so precious in the midst of our strife? Is it not understandable that I wish for her to choose me?"

"You now know I kept secrets from Lyta that were far less sweet than the truth you withhold from Cassia. It was wrong of me. It was not my failure, but my dishonesty that almost cost me her love."

"But your love triumphed. Please, Uncle, tell me I may find hope in your history. You are two Hesperines who survived to be happy."

"You need only look all around you for plenty of examples of that."

"All I see is Bloodborn's Path."

"No." The finality of Uncle Argyros's word echoed in the Union. "That is not your path. Not you."

"I'm losing her. You have confirmed all my thoughts about her plan. You see."

"What I confirmed was the political situation. All I see is that Tenebra will have to do without her, because Orthros has a prior claim on her."

"I cannot wrestle politics out of our way this time. What more can I do?"

"Stop wrestling politics."

"What?"

"Forget politics," said the greatest diplomat in the history of their people. "Devote all your powers to what you and Cassia need."

"But can we, in good conscience, put our needs ahead of politics?"

"Try as we might, there are some things we cannot change."

"But if we *can* change things, is it not selfish to do otherwise? Cassia could change so much, if I…"

Uncle Argyros shook his head. "Out of the question."

"Are you saying this as my uncle or as an ambassador?"

"Both. Would you sacrifice Nike for the safety of the rest of Orthros? Would you sacrifice Nephalea—and thus Alkaios? Would you sacrifice any of the hostages?"

"Of course not!"

"May I also remind you that you are the one who talked our esteemed, reckless prince out of making just such a sacrifice?"

"Mak told you about that, too."

Uncle Argyros sighed. "No. Ioustin told me about it."

Lio straightened. "You spoke with him."

"When I think of what might have happened, had you not stopped him that night… We have already lost one of Nike's Trial brothers. I could not bear to forfeit another."

"Uncle, I am glad to hear you say this."

"Cassia is…a most beloved proof that I should not question my daughter's decision to remain Abroad. I miss Nike so much that I have been unjust to her, and to her Trial brother. This Vigil of Union, I made things right between Ioustin and me."

"That is an answer to many prayers."

"Ioustin and Nike, just like you, have done right in disregarding my wishes. If any of you had acted differently, Cassia would not be with us now. Do not think I intend to let her out of my sight, not when she is so precious to us all."

"I am not certain we have a choice."

"What is the purpose of diplomacy?" his uncle asked.

"To ensure the safety of all our people and peace with all others," Lio answered without thought.

"*All* our people. You and Cassia among them. The time comes when we exhaust ourselves asking what we can do about the political situation. We must begin to ask what we can do in spite of it. What good can we create in the midst of so much wrong? The answer is always the same, although it takes on many forms: love."

"You certainly never included a lesson like this in our discourses on balance of power or the influence of economics upon human suffering. But now that I hear you put it into words, I must say you have been teaching it to me by example for many years."

"Then I hope you have learned it in an easier way than I did. During the Last War, a little love pushing back against immense suffering was all that kept us sane. Love was our only hope of survival."

"But so many chose to lay down their lives for others then."

"Many of us managed to survive instead," his uncle said dryly. "I did not found Orthros for my nephew, my student, my friend to be the one who sacrifices himself. And I do not believe you established the Solstice Summit to let Cassia pay the ultimate price to Tenebra."

"No. I did not. How can she do this to herself? Am I, who should be the first to strive to make her safe and happy, to sit by and watch her destroy her heart?"

"Are you?"

"She is worth more to our people *here*. I…I am worth more to our people alive than as a memory. I have devoted my life to Orthros—how will it help for me to die for them instead?"

"How will it?"

"This isn't what I want for any of us—and not for myself." Lio faltered. "I can recite countless justifications to soothe my conscience, but in truth, they are all excuses. I am not the altruistic idealist I thought myself to be. I just want to be happy. Is that wrong?"

"Is it?"

"I don't know."

"Cassia struggles to reconcile her conscience to her happiness. You cannot do that for her. Nor can I do that for you. But I can remind you of what I have taught you. Why did we found Orthros?"

"To give our people Sanctuary."

"What is Sanctuary?"

Lio had dwelt on the words night after night as he had crafted them in glass for the window at Rose House, and again when he had emblazoned their adaptation upon a window in this very room. They had taken on new meaning when he had translated them for Cassia. "'Come unto me, to my certain embrace, under my wing of darkness, where you shall find shelter, against my heart, where you shall find strength, in the light of my eyes, which shine with joy, in my endless sky, where you shall be free.'"

Uncle Argyros stood before him and touched his head, lifting his face. The light from Lio's own window shone in his eyes.

"Forgive us," his uncle said, "for walling you in with memorial statues. Forgive us for tempering the beauty of the sky by naming the stars after our fallen."

Lio got to his feet. "I have always been grateful for your legacy."

"We have tried to teach our children gratitude, compassion, and responsibility. But in so doing, it was never our intention to teach you guilt. We never wished for you to deprive yourself of what you must show to others. Be Merciful to yourself. Give yourself some Solace. Respect your own Will. Revel in your Gift and rejoice in your Union."

"It is so hard to shake the fear that I will hurt others in doing so. So much is at stake. If I make one mistake, so much will be lost."

"Whatever I have failed to properly explain, I can say with absolute certainty there is one thing I never taught you. Fear. I did not teach you to fear your mistakes. I did not teach you to fear your power. I impressed upon you that you must use it wisely, yes, but…"

"You taught me to *use* it."

"You have done so since you stood before the Firstblood Circle and proposed the Summit. What did you do then, when caught between two unbearable alternatives?"

"I rejected them both and created my own."

"Do not falter on this path now. I will not say I have faith in you, although I do. I will say, have faith in yourself." Lio's uncle gripped his shoulder, which he had always taken as a sign of approval. Had it also been his uncle reaching for support? "If you need one more reason, I cannot bear to lose you."

"You will not," Lio promised. "No one is going to lose me or Cassia. I will not lay down and give up, nor will I let her."

RECONCILIATION

"I OWE YOU AN apology."

Lio looked up at Prometheus. The crimson veins in the black stone pulsed. As Father had crafted the statue, how much of his own blood had he shed to pour life and magic into this portrait of his friend and Ritual son? Father swore this work was no memorial to Methu's death, but a tribute to his life. Father had not relegated Prometheus to Bloodborn's Path.

Lio had.

"I was so preoccupied with how you died," Lio confessed, "I failed to heed how you lived."

He pulled out a votive beeswax candle. He had commissioned a small fortune in them for the Tenebrans' comfort during their stay. It was so much like the one Cassia had lit for her sister during their vigil in the princess's garden.

He pulled back his arm and hurled the candle over the cliff into the sea.

"You lived with all your spirit. You loved with all your heart. You *never* laid down and surrendered. You went down fighting."

Lio reached into his pocket again and pulled out Skleros's tinderbox.

"There should never have been an inquisitors' prison. The people there should never have been doomed to die for their beliefs. Your life should never have been the price of their freedom. But it was. You chose to pay it. You are the best of us."

Lio struck flint against steel. Over and over again. Anthros's element resisted him. But he shielded his tinder from the wind with his hand, and at last, a spark caught.

"Because of you, Methu, we are here. We are here to tear down the walls of the prison. We are here to make it safe for everyone to worship as they choose. We are here, living in freedom."

From his scroll case, Lio took the document the Dexion had presented to the Firstblood Circle.

Lio set fire to the scroll and watched the war mage's terms go up in flames.

The King of Tenebra's blue wax seal dripped onto the snow. The emblems of the Synthikos and the Akron burned away in their own fire.

"Because of you, I am here to change the price." Lio dropped the flaming offering at Methu's feet. "We will live."

VIGIL OF THE
GIFT

1 Night Until Winter Solstice

A SAFE PLACE

Lio knelt on the silk cushion across from Kassandra and placed his present before her. "Good Vigil of the Gift, Ritual Mother. I hope you like what I came up with this year."

With a smile, she crossed her legs on her cushion and pulled the gift box of opaque glass to her. The box was nothing more than a basic piece to draw out what little surprise remained regarding what lay inside, but he knew she would store yarn in it. Lio and his Ritual mother had their private traditions, as he and his uncle did.

"You always know what I'm going to give you," he said.

"But it's the design that's new each time."

"I think you know that, too."

"I make a point never to foresee gifts. It ruins the fun." She opened the lid of the gift box, and her face lit up. "Ah, Lio, you have outdone yourself this time."

"Thank you, Ritual Mother. I'm glad it pleases you."

She lifted out this year's stained glass lantern and turned it each way, studying the designs he had crafted on its four sides. "The finest ships in my fleet, sailing in miniature. Such perfect detail. I shall treasure it."

"Shall we light it?"

She placed the new lantern on the coffee table beside his previous gift. Last year's round globe painted with silk moths gleamed with a golden spark of her spell light. She opened the tiny door in the sides of both lanterns and moved her hand, coaxing.

The light inside the moth globe flared, and a new bauble rose from it and floated over into the ship lantern. Light shifted across Kassandra's weaving room and shone across her loom in ocean blues and the scarlet of her fleet's sails.

Kassandra fastened the door on both lanterns and gave Lio a knowing smile. "The Vigil of the Gift is not only a time for giving your Ritual parents presents. This night is also dedicated to seeking their advice."

"I have a matter of great import to discuss with you. Perhaps the most important question I have ever asked you."

She waited and listened, as always. If she already knew what he was about to say, she gave no indication. Lio had learned long ago she would let him tell her. She often said speaking with one another was more important than anything they had to say.

Lio rested his hands on his knees. "I cannot sit idle while the envoys search for the hostages. I will do everything in my power to help them from here. I know the Queens have bade me pursue the Summit's original purpose, but bringing our people home may prove the key to rescuing the Summit as well. If I can secure the hostages' release through negotiation, it will not only save them, but might also restore Orthros and Tenebra's faith in the Summit."

"You intend to bargain with the Dexion for the release of our Hesperines errant."

"Yes. If I can diffuse the situation he is using to ruin the Summit, there will still be a chance for peace with the Tenebrans—and a hope of halting the Departure. To accomplish that, however, I need bargaining power." Lio gentled his tone, wary of causing her pain. "The one thing the Order might be willing to trade for is the Akron's Torch."

Kassandra smiled. "Now that is a bold idea."

"One worthy of a bloodborn, I hope."

"Tell me more."

"The mages are only using the hostage crisis to incite conflict. They will construe any response as hostile. They do not care whether we meet their demands or not. But if we meet their demands with the Akron's Torch, we will make them care. The Torch not only holds great power, but it is a *symbol* of the Order's power."

"And their humiliation."

"To be sure. To gain such a real advantage over us, but especially to restore face, they might be willing to sacrifice the opportunity to justify war that the hostage crisis presents. Of course, they will try to start the war some other way, and they will have the Torch to wield against us."

"But our hostages will be home."

Lio nodded and pushed away all the doubts it was too late to consider. "I have often asked Rudhira and Father what became of the Torch, but Methu only told them he put it somewhere safe. So I wanted to ask you, although I know it is difficult to think back on that time, if Methu mentioned anything to you that might give us a clue as to the Torch's whereabouts."

"I would do much more for the hostages' sake than face a few painful memories. I'm glad you've asked."

"Thank you, Ritual Mother. If Methu said anything, or if your sight has revealed a hint about the Torch, it is our best hope. I realize the odds are slim that we will be able to discover an artifact that's been missing for over a hundred years. Even if we can, who knows how difficult it may be to retrieve it from its hiding place, or if it's even possible to reach it in time. But we must try."

Kassandra tapped her chin. "Let me think. Hmm."

"Any detail, however insignificant, might prove relevant."

She poured herself another cup of coffee, then reached for the silk storage box she always kept under her loom. She flipped back the lid and pulled out a skein of yarn. She always said she could see more clearly with silk in her hands. She took hold of the loose end that had escaped the skein and began to wind it round and round.

Then she tucked the end in, set the skein aside, and began to methodically remove each skein of yarn and spool of thread from the silk box.

When light began to shine out from between the skeins and spools, a chill went down Lio's spine. He watched his Ritual mother lift away the silk that was so potent with her magic to reveal what she had hidden underneath.

She grinned. "I am a very safe place."

Lio let out a breath of wonder and bent over the box with her.

The Akron's Torch was a pillar of solid gold inlaid with precious gems and engraved with tiny, detailed scenes from Anthrian myth. Inside a filigreed cage at the top, a mass of spell light flared and ebbed. Lio looked into it, but it did not make his skin crawl or fill his mouth with the taste of destruction. How strange. It reminded him of how sun had felt on Cassia's back in her memory of gardening.

"It looks the part of a fabled treasure, doesn't it?" she asked.

"The Order of Anthros would come up with such an opulent symbol of their might. You've had it right here all this time?"

"If you want to keep up with something, entrust it to your mother."

"Isn't it dangerous?"

"Only if you fear it." A tiny bauble of light floated out of the cage and into her hand.

Lio looked from that bauble to the dozens of stained glass lanterns gleaming around her weaving room, on the coffee table, from the rafters, atop her scroll racks and over her loom. "It's been right here in front of me all these years."

"I have been acclimating you to it gradually, in case you ever needed to wield it."

Lio kissed his Ritual mother's hand. "I promise to use it well."

"Take it now. There is a negotiation that requires your attention before you begin your dealings with the Dexion."

"What could be more urgent?"

"Konstantina will not wait until Solstice is over to propose the Departure. She will convene a special circle. The announcement will be in every firstblood's hands half an hour from now."

"She's holding the vote *tonight?*"

"My vote will not save you this time. Adwene and Khaldaios have great influence among the Imperial bloodlines. My tributaries are as divided as the rest of Orthros. You must win our people's hearts with your words alone."

"I haven't secured the hostages' release yet. I have no argument. I don't know what I'll say."

"Just keep speaking truth. That is all any of us can do."

Lio looked into the strange and powerful light coming from the artifact. With a deep breath, he took up the Torch.

FIRE IN THE CIRCLE

THE INSTANT LIO STEPPED into the amphitheater, a startle and a shudder went through the Blood Union. Every Hesperine there turned in their seats, looked up to the highest gallery, and stared at him.

Among the auras of the firstbloods, the Akron's Torch felt like a bell booming the wrong hour. The Torch's magic emanated down Lio's arm and heated his chest, bizarre and invigorating. He lifted Prometheus's legacy for them all to see. Its light blazed brighter.

Many Hesperines threw up their hands to shield their eyes. Gasps and murmurs rippled through the crowd, while some of the firstbloods rose to their feet.

Lio's father gave a triumphant laugh and began to applaud.

Lio's mother was the first to join in, then Uncle Argyros and Aunt Lyta. Mak and Lyros let out a cheer. The applause spread in a wave among the Ritual tributaries, relatives, and allies of Lio's family. At the podium, Hypatia turned to the Anatelan section to see Kia leading a rebellious round of applause there. Among the Zephyrans, Kitharos blinked at Nodora, as if dismayed to discover his daughter could make so much noise. A few seats away from the Second Princess, Xandra gave a solitary but symbolic round of royal applause.

"Firstgift Komnenos!" Konstantina's voice carried over the clapping. "How dare you bring the Akron's Torch into the Firstblood Circle!"

"You recognize it, Second Princess."

"I have lived long enough to have seen it in Prometheus's hand. I am shocked to discover it ever crossed the border into Orthros."

"Thank the Goddess it did. Prometheus has provided us with ample ransom for seven Hesperine hostages."

The applause and cheers resounded once more.

"Recover your dignity!" Konstantina demanded. "This is the Firstblood Circle, not a fighting match at the gymnasium."

Queen Soteira lifted a hand. The amphitheater hushed.

Queen Alea beckoned to Lio. "You may bring the Akron's trinket into the Circle."

Lio gave them a deep heart bow. "Thank you for your forbearance, Annassa."

"Take your seat," Konstantina bade him.

"Second Princess," Lio addressed her, "I request a place on the speaking schedule."

"You must wait until all those ahead of you conclude their remarks. You know no time limit is imposed on speakers, and until the current one acknowledges he or she is finished, the next may not take the podium."

"The matter of our hostages is of the utmost importance. With respect, I would like to discuss their plight with the firstbloods without further delay."

"Our Queens have already entrusted the hostages to the envoys. Tonight's vote strictly regards the Departure."

"We cannot address one unless we address the other."

"Elder Firstblood Hypatia has the podium at present. You must wait."

Uncle Argyros made the circle petition. "Hypatia has already acknowledged her cession of the podium to me and was about to return to her seat. I hereby give my place on the schedule to my nephew."

Konstantina rounded on him. "Argyros, it was purely out of respect for you that I agreed to allow you some brief remarks before I take the podium to present my proposal, despite the fact that you oppose the measure. This is how you reciprocate?"

"Of course you would invite a dependable and cautious ancient such as myself to be the obligatory voice of dissent. I must tender my excuses."

Hypatia subjected him to a glare of betrayal.

He looked back with a mild countenance and piercing eyes. "By my right as an elder firstblood, I appoint my nephew to speak on my behalf at the podium."

"My gratitude, Uncle. Second Princess, is that in accordance with the rules of the Circle?"

A moment of silence stretched across the Firstblood Rose between Konstantina and Lio.

"For in accordance with the spirit of the Circle," he said, "I have come to do my part."

Her sigh was barely audible. "So you must."

He gave her the heart bow. Then, bearing the Torch high, he circled the gallery and descended the aisle next to the Imperial section. As he passed the front row, he would have saluted Kassandra with the Torch, but she was not there.

Hypatia made him wait beside the podium while she gathered her scrolls with affronted precision. "I will not insult the memory of one of our greatest heroes by pointing out the dreadful consequences of that Torch coming into our possession. However, I have no qualms voicing a forthright analysis of Firstgift Komnenos's recent actions. Remember, my fellow firstbloods, it is youthful recklessness that drove us to this point of crisis in the first place. I pray you will not allow blind idealism to lead Orthros to further destruction."

With that charming introduction, she left the podium to Lio and returned to her seat.

Lio set the Torch on its end upon the podium before him, then released it. It hovered upright of its own power. *Thank you for your partisanship, Methu.*

"Annassa, Firstbloods, and heirs of the blood, thank you for hearing me under the Goddess's Eyes. By the light of Prometheus's greatest victory, I shall strive to speak only truth, according to my conscience. I will not dissemble. I am here tonight to convince you that we must never invoke the Departure. For the sake of our elders who have dreamed and bled these long years to craft us a better world. For the sake of every reckless young Hesperine in Orthros who dares imagine that what is set in stone can change."

Lio had stolen a place on the schedule ahead of Konstantina. Until he was finished, she couldn't take the podium. She couldn't propose the Departure. The Circle couldn't vote in favor of it.

All Lio had to do was keep talking.

THE ORACLE SPEAKS

THE CITY BELLS TAUNTED Cassia. Orthros was slipping through her fingers. She was certain Lio would not come to get her, just like last night. The truth had spoiled all that was left of their time. Would they while away the rest of this stalemate, unable to bear being together because they knew they must part? When she departed Orthros, must she leave without the solace of these final nights of their life together? It would have made her sacrifice so much harder, but so much easier, if she could only have enjoyed Lio to the last.

The emptiness of the guest room dragged at Cassia. The bed called. If she but lay down upon it, the paralysis would overcome her, and she would find no reason to rise again.

No. No, there might be one more reason to stay on her feet.

I so enjoyed our evening together during the Vigil of the Gift, Kassandra had said, the first time Cassia had met her. According to Kassandra, their encounter on this night had already come to pass. Cassia had never put any faith in diviners, whether the Oracle of Chera or the Tenebran fortune tellers who claimed they could read the future in a bird's entrails. But she had also put no faith in kindness or love, until she had met Hesperines.

Cassia made herself put on her cloak. She hesitated, casting a long look at the empty bed. No illusion of her would sleep there tonight to deceive eyes and minds.

Cassia went to the couch in the sitting room and put a hand on her friend's shoulder. Perita didn't startle. She must not have been asleep.

"Do you need something, my lady?"

"I need to scheme. I'm going to shut my bedchamber door and not come out till I think of something."

Perita sat up. "That's my lady. Callen and I will make sure nobody crosses that threshold until you call for me."

"Thank you, my friend. You know I would be lost without you."

Cassia caught a glimpse of her friend's smile in the gloom as she retreated to her bedchamber. She closed the door firmly. "*Dockk,* Knight. We will find our way to House Kassandra."

He perked up and followed her out into the courtyard, and she drew the curtains behind them before securing the glass door as well. She paused by the fountain and assessed the archways. With Hesperines always stepping her to and fro, she had lost track of which led where. On her walk with Kia and Nodora, however, that arch there had led them on foot out of the guest house. Cassia took a chance on it.

A gallery led her to a gate, the gate led her to another courtyard, and a nest of gargoyles watched her make her way out onto a lane that ran behind the guest houses. She thought about all the maps of Selas that had passed before her eyes during many circles with the Stand, and she got her bearings.

Cassia found her way out of the Docks District and onto the broad thoroughfares and snow-covered agoras of Selas. The first few streets she crossed were deserted. Everyone was at home, she thought, spending time with their Ritual parents. She had learned that the Vigil of the Gift was for meditating on the lessons of your Gifting and honoring those who guided you on the immortal path.

She might have had a Gifting. Friends and family might have showered her with welcome all through moon hours. Then, when veil hours descended, she might have made her journey into eternal night. In Lio's arms.

Anger filled Cassia until she didn't know what to do with it all, and her body shook. She halted, reaching out for the nearest support. Her hand closed over a lamppost that lit the corner of two lanes. Above her head, a stained glass lantern shone, bright and beautiful.

Cassia wanted to hurt someone. The person who had made it so she could not stay in Orthros.

But that person was her.

If she stood here a moment longer, the paralysis would catch her right here in the middle of Selas. She had to make it to Kassandra's.

Kassandra might be the only person who could tell Cassia if she would ever make it back to Orthros.

By the time Cassia neared House Kassandra, she was running. Her lungs burned for air and her face with cold. The map in her head brought her to a short stone wall and a broad iron gate, which stood open.

She took that as an invitation and entered. Before her lay a path lined with knotty, twisted evergreens. She had never seen the hardy little trees before, but they looked like they had endured sixteen centuries of blizzards and lived to tell the tale. She drifted between them, catching her breath.

The gate behind her slipped out of sight sooner than she expected. She looked back, but all she saw was the ordered chaos of a garden.

Snow and shadow cloaked Kassandra's grounds, but scents dry and sharp, spicy and green hinted to Cassia of the wonders she could not see. She followed one smell after another, wondering which would lead her to tonight's fated encounter. A hint of roses made her detour along a side path.

Warm spell lights emerged from the night ahead and revealed a pavilion of red and purple silk. Cassia came to a halt under a tasseled awning. Fabric walls fluttered in the polar wind, but beneath the pavilion's shelter, she felt only warmth. The fragrance of roses settled over her, heavy and sweet.

"Cassia! Come in," came Kassandra's voice.

Stained glass lanterns hung everywhere and sat on every surface, each one different from the last, filling the room with countless unique shades of light. Cassia trod across thick carpets and crept behind a silk curtain.

The oracle knelt at her magnificent loom. There was a silk box at her knees and a pile of yarns and threads scattered about it. Silk cushions surrounded a low table beside her, where a copper coffee service emanated warmth and rich aromas.

In a glass dish on the coffee warmer, rose oil quivered, golden in the spell-light, releasing curls of fragrance. Cassia stared at the oil, wanting to look away, unwilling to stop breathing its beautiful smell.

"In Orthros, even oil is made of roses."

Cassia tore her gaze from the oil dish. Where was her courtesy? "Thank you for inviting me here tonight."

"I'm so glad you've come. Make yourself comfortable."

Cassia arranged herself on a cushion, which puffed more coffee and rose fragrance around her as she sank onto it. Knight went into a down-stay beside her before she asked.

Kassandra gave Cassia a little smile of anticipation and reached behind her. She pulled forward a large pack constructed of thick, sturdy tapestry woven in a botanical pattern. She set the bag before Cassia.

"For me?" Cassia asked.

"Go ahead. Open it."

"You already gave me a welcome gift," Cassia protested, although she would prefer to forget the historical Tenebran banner.

"As an oracle, I reserve the right to give gifts out of order. These are some presents for many occasions that have not yet come to pass."

Cassia hesitated over the tapestry bag. Would something so beautiful hurt her if she opened it?

She had come here to face the truth. She unfastened the straps and opened the bag.

Within was a bundle of red-brown silk with a pattern of brilliant yellow flowers. Cassia laid the garment upon her lap with great care, only to discover there were more in the bag. She felt the urge to wash her hands before touching them. "These can't all be for me."

"I think it's enough to get you started. I'm quite relieved I finished them in time. I started selecting the fibers as soon as Apollon and Komnena asked me to be the Ritual mother for the son she was carrying, but I didn't finish the sewing until Lio's entry into diplomatic service. I was starting to think you would arrive earlier than I expected, but it turns out tonight's schedule prevailed."

Cassia caressed the flawless fabric with reverent fingers. "Elder Firstblood Kassandra, that means you started these…ninety years ago?"

"You must call me Kassandra. Silk holds up well in Orthros."

Cassia could not fathom this bag full of luxuries had been nearly a century in the making—for her. "I am humbled that you would make something like this with me in mind."

"Well, go ahead. Shake them out and tell me if you like them."

Cassia stood and carefully unfolded Kassandra's first gift. It was a robe in the Imperial style, with a high collar and a front that unfastened all the way to the hem.

"It's the perfect size and length for me." Cassia held the robe up to herself.

Kassandra grinned. "I always did have an eye for a person's measurements."

"It's a masterpiece."

"It owes its beauty to the nature that inspired it. Do you know what kind of flowers those are?"

Cassia nodded. "They are the blossoms that appear on cassia trees. I don't know what to say. I have never had anything like this."

"You need something more Hesperine to wear on special occasions."

Cassia should fold it up and hand it back to her right now. But she stood there with the robe laid over Solia's Tenebran dress, looking down at herself.

Kassandra examined the hem of Solia's dress, testing the fabric between her thumb and forefinger. "Our eagerness to trade in Tenebran textiles is no flattery, you know. There is a substantial beauty in craftsmanship that is achieved despite adversity." She flipped the hem up an inch to study its stitches. "Tenebran velvet. A luxurious nap. For a part of the world lacking the sea snails that produce Imperial purple, this violet dye is quite exceptional. Strong seams, too. This has lasted through some travails."

"It was part of a gown that once belonged to my sister," Cassia explained, "although it was since reworked for a queen, then for me."

"This is a fine piece, but heavy to wear. Once you've worn silk and felt its weightlessness for yourself, you never want to wear anything else." Kassandra smoothed Cassia's hem into place once more and sat back. "I used to enjoy long walks in the Imperial cassia groves with my sister."

"You had a sister in your mortal life? Before you were the Queens' sister?"

"Yes. My sister and I loved one another as you and Solia will."

Cassia began to understand the longing and even jealousy she heard in others' voices when they spoke of Kassandra's prophecies. Cassia, too, would like to live in a state of mind in which Solia was a part of her future, not her past. "If I may ask, your sister did not come to Orthros with you?"

"She exiled me here to secure her claim to the throne over mine. Such was her love for me, that she bargained with the Queens for my eternal future, and kept for herself forty years as the Empress."

"You are a member of the Empire's royal family? I…forgive me, I did not know."

"I am Kassandra, the Imperial elder firstblood of Orthros, and you need not apologize for anything, my dear. Sit down and let me pour you a cup of coffee."

Cassia sank down onto the cushions, still holding the robe to her.

Kassandra set a steaming cup of coffee before Cassia. "Have a look at the rest."

Cassia returned to the bag and discovered yellow silk dancing shoes and a pair of those comfortable-looking trousers in red-brown silk. Beneath them waited a set of practical cotton work robes. Then a green veil hours robe the exact shade of her gardening dress. Cassia sat back. She could not bear to look any further.

Kassandra had made her an entire wardrobe fit for a new Hesperine. After she had given her a banner fit for an upstart queen. What was Cassia supposed to make of all this?

"My gifts and my prophecies are two different things."

Cassia blinked and shook her head. "I was given to understand your power is foresight, not mind magery."

"There was a possibility of this conversation in which you said more of your thoughts aloud. It was a shape your present might have taken that would have made you more forthright with me tonight. But I think your thoughts are the same, although you are more hesitant to speak them than you would have been."

Was there a more forthright version of herself Cassia had failed to become? A less honest Cassia she had avoided? Or were the past, present, and future all somehow true, as Kassandra seemed to perceive them? Would that mean Cassia was both honest and dishonest, and always had been, and always would be?

"You must know," Cassia said, "why I am not certain it is right for me to accept these robes. I fear they would be wasted on me."

"That is not how gifts work."

"I do not wish to dishonor your gift."

"You want them. That is enough reason for you to keep them."

Cassia did want them. She wanted so much. Was it all irrevocably out of her reach? "I am not sure of my right to petition Orthros's oracle and Lio's Ritual mother. But if you could see fit to also give me the gift of your advice, you would have my gratitude."

"Whomever's oracle or Ritual mother I may be, I invited you here, and that gives you every right."

"Then, may I ask you to tell me my future?"

"You may certainly ask. But you don't need to."

"Oh, but I do. I have never needed insight into my future more than I do now."

Kassandra folded her hands in her lap. "My foresight is for navigating uncertain futures and giving people hope of what they would not otherwise dare to imagine. I make a point never to use my magic to tell people what they already know."

"But I am so uncertain. I don't know what is to become of me."

"Tell me this troubling vision of your future."

What kind of oracle wanted Cassia to do her work for her? "Has Lio told you anything of what I intend?"

"All Lio has told any of us for the past two nights is that you cannot get away from the embassy. Given the tenuous political situation and the lives that hang in the balance, no one is willing to question that, whatever we may think the real reason is. None of them suspect you plan to go back to Tenebra and take the throne from your father."

A little shock went through Cassia at the words. Kassandra spoke them so matter-of-factly.

"Except Argyros," Kassandra added. "Lio told him everything."

"So you have foreseen my intention."

"You or Lio will tell me about it eventually."

Cassia clutched the robe to her. "Can you tell me if I will succeed?"

"What do you predict is the answer?"

"Yes," Cassia said. "I know I can do it. But what will it cost me?"

"Name your price."

Cassia could not put a cost so high into words. "There is so much I cannot know. I *must know*, Kassandra. Will my policies convince Orthros to keep the border open? Will I live long enough to finish my work and escape Tenebra? Will I survive my reign? Will Orthros be here for me? Will I make it home?"

"On the contrary, Cassia, you are the only one who can know that."

"How can I discern if Konstantina will keep the border closed forever? How can I predict if a fever will waste me away or an apostate mage will cut my life short?"

"Whether those things happen or not, you know what will happen long before."

"I'll die," Cassia whispered. "I'll starve. My body will last and last, but the rest of me will already be gone."

She gasped a breath, if only to prove to herself that time had not come, and there was life left in her yet.

"The cost is me," she said.

"The oracle has spoken, Cassia. What will you do about her prophecy?"

"How can anyone ask this of me?" Cassia pleaded with the only one who was asking—her. "How can I do this?"

"Do not be afraid. You have everything you need for your future within you. Otherwise your future would be different."

"Tell me it is not set in stone. Tell me there is another way."

"You made it, Cassia. It is your work of art. There is nothing to fear in anything of your own making."

"I am afraid. I don't want to live like that, dreading what each new day will bring, with no hope in sight. That is all I have done since I can remember. Such a future looks just like my past."

Kassandra smiled.

"Can I put it in my past?" Cassia asked. "Can I leave it all behind?"

"Are you asking if you can, or if you will?"

"If I should. I have saved many lives. But I could save so many more. How many lives are enough before I'm done?"

"That is a question of conscience, not prophecy. But you have the answer to this as well. Are Argyros and Lyta, Javed and Kadi, Basir and Kumeta enough? Are Bosko and Thenie and Zoe and all the Eriphite children enough?"

"They are more than enough for me."

"Is Lio enough?"

"Lio…he is abundance."

The bells of veil hours sounded, powerful and beautiful and clear with no stone walls to muffle them.

"It's time for you to go," Kassandra told her. "This is the night when you will tell Lio you saved his life. But you already know that."

"Where is he now?"

"Open the bag again. There is one more robe, and it is the one you'll need tonight."

FIRSTGRACE KOMNENA'S PROPOSAL

L**IO LISTENED TO THE** bells toll, but they did not herald deliverance. It was only second veil. The night still stretched on ahead of him.

He cleared his parched throat, but that only made it worse. The Akron's Torch pulsed in time to the glaring pain in Lio's head. But somehow, he drew strength from that light before him.

The bloodborn went down fighting.

Lio pushed the hoarse words out of his mouth. "You have now heard the undeniable evidence that the Departure would have a lasting, grievous impact on Tenebra and Orthros. Sophia Eudokia's research, which I have cited, quantifies what Tenebra will face in the most horrifying clarity. You now know exactly how many exposed children will die each year without Hesperines to Solace them. Will we let our fear sentence children to death? How can we live in a future in which Orthros is safe at the cost of those innocent lives?

"Perhaps it is here I ought to rest my case. But I ask you, is it enough to merely survive, without thriving? As we consider the death toll, is it not worth contemplating the toll upon life? Are we to sacrifice creativity in the name of caution? The opinions of Muse Menodora that I have quoted to you reveal how important the contributions of Sanctuary seekers are to Orthros's music and arts. Like newcomers from the Empire, Tenebrans also bring rich traditions and fresh ideas with them. For every new thought we reject, the beauty of our Sanctuary molders around us a bit more.

"The speires before me on this podium are testament to the Stand's continued willingness to shoulder the burden of violence on behalf of our people and face whatever threats accompany an open border. Are we such cowards that we will not take a stand beside our defenders and shoulder the burdens of what the Goddess calls us to do in this world?

"At its heart, this is not a question of evidence at all. This is a matter of conscience. We face a choice between two paths.

"The Departure is a certain path. It would, without doubt, bring an end to conflict. But at what cost? Are we to sacrifice the very best within us in exchange for certainty? Are you, my fellow Hesperines, really willing to pay this price? The price is nothing short of our consciences. Our hopes. Our love and compassion for others and ourselves.

"An open border is an uncertain path. It brings all manner of risks— but is it not the only way to the greatest rewards? That uncertain path is the one that brought each and every one of us here tonight. Do you regret any of it? Would you not suffer all the consequences again? Are you not willing now, tonight, to find the courage to stay on the Hesperine path, come what may, and face it with both courage and joy?"

"We are."

At the sound of Cassia's voice, Lio spun to face her. His sluggish heart beat with new energy, and he found his breath for the first time in hours.

Cassia stood at the entrance in the highest gallery, holding Zoe's hand.

Lio stared at his Grace. She was here. And she was so beautiful. Her uncovered, unbound hair trailed down over a formal robe of night-black silk. In wide bands of blood-red embroidery, their roses twined around her. Zoe stood with perfect poise in her purple formal robe and favorite mantle, a small, silken heir to vast and ancient power. Knight was their honor guard.

Cassia led Zoe through the crowd, and Knight proceeded with them in his parade gait. As they passed by the Imperial section, Cassia smiled at someone. Lio saw Kassandra had taken her seat. She nodded to Cassia.

As Cassia and Zoe approached Blood Komnena's seats, Mother pressed a hand to her mouth, and Father held Zoe's gaze, beaming. Cassia showed Zoe to her place behind them. Lio watched his sister step into her role as Secondgift Komnena for the first time, with Cassia as her guide.

Then Cassia's eyes met Lio's. She moved to stand before the rightful seat of Firstgrace Komnena.

Lio gripped the podium for support. Was he looking at their future? Or her farewell gift?

"Second Princess Konstantina, I want to speak," Cassia announced in simple, but clear Divine.

"I will give her my place," Lio said.

There was a warning in Konstantina's aura. "I will not see Argyros's third-hand time on the schedule made into a mockery of the Circle."

Cassia faced Konstantina. "Second Princess, everyone is allowed to speak before the Firstblood Circle. Is that not true?"

The challenge now evident on her regal countenance, Konstantina fixed her gaze on Cassia. "Everyone of Orthros. Not members of the Tenebran embassy, except during negotiations. This is a session of the Firstblood Circle, not a Summit event."

"Am I not of Orthros?"

"Are you?"

"You gave me a Sanctuary rose from your own hand at House Annassa. What did that mean?"

That stirred indicative murmurs among the firstbloods.

"It means what you choose," the princess told her.

"I have chosen." Cassia's voice—*her* voice—echoed across the Firstblood Rose.

For the first time. For the last time. She had chosen.

Cassia found Lio's gaze again and did not look away from him. "I am mortal now, but I await my Gifting. When the Tenebrans leave, I will stay here with my people, the Hesperines. I invoke my right to speak."

With those words, she put his world back together again. Lio hardly heard the applause and exclamations of welcome. His heart began to race, and he wondered if it had been beating at all before this moment. The power of her declaration shone out of her, the brightest light in his sky. He could bask in that light forever.

She was going to stay.

When the crowd quieted, there was a faint smile on Konstantina's face and an unmistakable note of triumph in her aura. "No one here can deny that seat is yours by right. From there, you will achieve much and learn much. Take it now, while I take the podium."

Zoe extended her hand in the circle petition.

Lio looked at her little, powerful hand reaching out. He thought his chest wouldn't hold all his pride and affection, and he let it overflow into his Union with his little sister. He felt her smile back at him, but she looked at the Second Princess.

Konstantina's expression softened. The entire crowd went quiet, listening, giving Zoe room to speak.

"Yes, Secondgift Komnena?" Konstantina invited.

Zoe made a beautiful heart bow. "Second Princess, may Cassia and I show our partisanship for my brother?"

Konstantina rested her hands on the railing in front of her, where for centuries, her blood had decided votes and the course of Orthros. Where a scroll now rested, unfurled, on which she had written her version of their immediate future—her proposal for the Departure. "The Goddess hears all of us, from the mightiest firstblood to the smallest child." To those ritual words, she added, "Secondgift Komnena, you are Orthros's future, and so your opinion about our future is most important. By showing your partisanship tonight, you are showing great love for your people and loyalty to your bloodline. We will be proud to see your token on the podium."

Now Zoe's smile showed on her face. "Thank you, Second Princess."

To Lio's astonishment, Zoe did not hand something of hers to Cassia for placement on the podium. She did not let go of Cassia's hand. Together, they went to the nearest stair leading down from the stands and ventured out onto the floor of the amphitheater.

Panic raced across their bloodline's petal of the Firstblood Rose. Zoe's fear tore at Lio's senses. White rimmed her eyes, and she looked to and fro, like a wild thing lost in the emptiness that surrounded her and hung over her. Their parents must seem miles away. The sky must seem enormous. Lio started from the podium, ready to step to her and scoop her into his arms.

But then Zoe's gaze fixed on him. His little sister broke out of her paralysis and marched forward beside his Grace.

As soon as they were in reach, Lio knelt and hugged Zoe close. "You are so brave. I am so proud of you."

"I told you I'd turn into a gargoyle to protect you."

Lio kissed the top of her head, holding her tight. "You have my gratitude."

Zoe's distress must have awoken all Knight's protective instincts, for he sniffed Lio's sister all over, closing her in on her other side with his furry bulk.

Her trembling gave way to an uneasy little laugh. "I'm not done yet."

Reluctantly, Lio released her. Cassia gave Zoe an encouraging nod. Zoe took a deep breath.

Then she lifted her mantle from her head.

Lio gathered his power to conjure an illusion of reassuring stone above them.

Zoe reached up and laid her mantle upon the podium with the Akron's Torch.

Lio released his half-formed spell. Zoe had finally found the courage to face her fears. He would not temper the beauty of her sky.

Konstantina turned her face away. That hand she lifted to her eye... did she wipe away tears?

Zoe gave Lio a smile as he had never seen on her face. Then she turned around and ran all on her own toward Anastasios's statue. Their father was waiting for her and leaned down over the rail to scoop her up in his arms. He settled her on his lap, while their mother, with tears in her eyes, showered her with affection and praise.

Cassia turned and embraced Lio in front of the entire Firstblood Circle.

He enfolded her in his arms, sheltering her, leaning on her. Goddess, it felt so good to hold her. No more secrets. No more doubts.

Not even Konstantina told the crowd to stop cheering.

Cassia looked up at him. "Is this what you needed me to do, Lio?"

"This was exactly what I needed."

The motion of Cassia's hand riveted Lio's attention on her. She lifted the glyph shard from around her neck. Stone clicked softly on stone as she set her pendant on the podium. The sweet, dark power of Sanctuary magic mingled with the sun-warm aura of the Torch.

Surprise and wonder filled the Union. Many Hesperines blinked, shook their heads, and peered at the glyph shard as if seeing it for the first time.

Konstantina's eyes widened, and she opened her mouth to speak. Queen Soteira rested a hand on her daughter's shoulder.

Queen Alea looked around the amphitheater. "Cassia rescued the mage Makaria's ancient Sanctuary ward from Hespera's abandoned shrine at Solorum. That power hides and reveals itself according to need. Behold it now in the Firstblood Circle of Orthros. Will we allow the bearer of the Akron's Torch to speak, but not the bearer of a Sanctuary ward?"

Konstantina shut her eyes, then nodded.

Cassia addressed the crowd, one arm around Lio. "Annassa, Firstbloods, and heirs of the blood, thank you for hearing me under the Goddess's Eyes. By the light you have shined into my life, I shall strive to speak only truth, according to my conscience.

"Fourteen and a half years ago, Pherenike Argyra saved my life. With Alkaios and Nephalea, she gave the Mercy to my sister. I am living proof of how much Tenebra needs Hesperines. My life shows that our people can change the world for the better.

"My love for our people knows no limits. My bond of gratitude with Nike, Alkaios, and Nephalea knows no end. Tonight, I ask you not to dishonor their sacrifices with a hasty decision motivated by fear.

"I of all people am aware of the grave dangers we face. I have lived my life amid the threats that prompt the Circle to consider the Departure.

"That is why tonight, I beseech you to make a compassionate and wise compromise. I do not ask you to rule out the possibility of the Departure. I ask only that you delay the vote until a later time. Know that when that night comes, whatever your decision about the border, I will be on this side of it with you."

Lio hugged her closer, and her arm tightened around him.

"I propose that we delay this vote until the next Autumn Equinox." Cassia cleared her throat. "I am sure you all have questions about why I suggest this date."

Konstantina held out her hand, palm up. "The Autumn Equinox is months from now. It is out of the question for us to do nothing in the meantime and endure whatever disasters may occur."

"We will spend most of that time safe in Orthros Notou," Cassia replied. "When we return to Orthros Boreou at Autumn Equinox, we can assess the new situation in Tenebra and make a better decision about the Departure."

Uncle Argyros made the circle petition next. "What new situation might that be?"

"The reign of the new king I have chosen for my late sister's subjects. I have arranged for a *peaceful* transfer of power. With help from my key allies who remain in Tenebra, Flavian of Segetia will take the throne from Lucis via legal, non-violent means."

Lio could not have felt more relieved or proud to stand beside Cassia amid the crowd's surprise and admiration. There were huffs of disbelief as well. But together, they had overcome those many times before.

"Who are these allies?" Hypatia demanded, her hand thrust out. "How can you attempt a change of government in Tenebra while you sit here in Orthros?"

Cassia looked from one section of the audience to another. "You have all become well acquainted with me since I arrived. I think you know I don't just sit here."

Some good-natured laughter went up.

Cassia smiled and continued. "My allies include handmaidens and seamstresses, household guards and knights errant, noble ladies and free lords. Before coming to Orthros, I laid the groundwork for overthrowing Lucis and putting a better king in his place. My partisans within the embassy will carry my signal back to Tenebra with them. Upon their return, my supporters will spring into action. Come summer, the Council of Free Lords will convene to revoke the mandate they once conferred upon Lucis. They will rally around Flavian, a young, admired figure with broad support among all factions of the nobility."

Aunt Lyta displayed her palm. "I am confident you have taken precautions to prevent civil war. It will benefit the Circle to know the details."

Cassia nodded. "Hadria is the backbone of royal military might, but Free Lord Hadrian's loyalty is to stability, not Lucis. Lord Hadrian pledged himself to a man he hates because he knew only a strong king could control the feuds. Lord Hadrian hates Segetia, too, but when faced with a choice between two enemies, Lord Hadrian will choose the honorable one. When Lord Flavian proves he can keep order, Lord Hadrian will take the opportunity to withdraw his support from Lucis, and many will follow his example.

"All it will take is for him to sheathe his sword, and Lucis will fall. It is true Lucis will not surrender quietly, but with only his personal guard, the forces he led when he was a free lord, and his few remaining supporters, he will be unable to mount sufficient resistance. What violence may occur will be short-lived and limited in scope."

"What do you expect will become of the former king?" Aunt Lyta asked.

"Once he sees that all is lost," Cassia answered, "he will flee to Cordium like the coward he is. But the Mage Orders will not lift a finger to help him, for once he fails them, they will see no benefit in tying their influence in Tenebra to a hated, deposed king. When the Council of Free Lords unites and confers their mandate upon a new king, the Orders will have to acknowledge the legitimate transfer of power. Cordium will have neither motivation nor justification to stand against King Flavian. They will almost certainly begin courting him instead."

Cassia glanced at Lio. "While it rests upon Flavian's shoulders to establish his own policies, I can say with confidence he has neither ambitions of alliance with the Orders nor any extraordinary aversion to Hesperines. His loyalty is to his own people. With the nobility behind him, he will not need foreign mages to secure his position."

"Flavian will not rule Tenebra as a queen would have." For the first time, Cassia's voice wavered. "He is young, and he is flawed. But I hope this Summit has shown you that young people, with all their mistakes, can still do what is right."

Hypatia threw down her hand again. "The Summit is in shambles. The Tenebran embassy cowers. What assurance can you offer us that your supporters will stay the course of such a dramatic rebellion against a feared king?"

"The Summit is not over. The embassy only wants for leadership to bring them to their feet. With Alatheia as our witness, Ambassador

Deukalion and I will wrest the Tenebrans from the influence of the Cordians and deliver them unto our Queens. Before the Festival of the Rose is through, we will swear the Solstice Oath with the nobility of Tenebra, and upon that promise, build a new future for both our lands."

Lio lifted their joined hands into the air. "Will you have faith in us? Will you give us this chance? Will you stay with us on the Hesperine path until we have seen it through?"

Lio waited for the vote, prepared to count the declarations in blood that would appear around him.

Before any firstbloods pricked their fingers, Konstantina stood. "Newgift Cassia, what if your plan fails?"

Cassia did not shy away from the princess's gaze or her question. "Tenebrans wish to be responsible for their own fate, and we must respect their Will. Therefore, I am giving them an opportunity. They can have a king instead of a tyrant. A monarch who will not use Hesperines against them, who will restore the Oath and our rights in Tenebra. So that no more of our Hesperines errant will come home broken for the sake of a victory that can never be won, so no more will die in a kingdom that begrudges their sacrifice.

"The Tenebrans will have the opportunity to stop being silent in the face of King Lucis's lies. To set aside their fear and prejudice. To take back what he has taken from them. I know—*I know*—how much that costs. But I also know what courage sleeps, ready to awaken, even in the hearts of those whom the king has most grievously wronged. Especially in those hearts.

"If Tenebra will not be true, if Tenebra will not be just, if Tenebra will not be brave, they will have to bear the consequences on their own shoulders. If they make the wrong choice, it will be their choice.

"In sixteen hundred years, the power of our Hesperines errant has created lasting change, if not in Tenebra, then in *Tenebrans*. In me. My parting gift to the land of my mortal origins is to set them free."

Lio could scarcely believe what he sensed in Konstantina's aura. Her resolve made him wary of what she had in store for them.

But she was also impressed.

"Your strategy is well developed," Konstantina said, "and principled."

Lio could hear that Cassia was holding her breath.

"For the time being, I am reassured as to the safety of the most vulnerable of our Hesperines errant." The nod Konstantina gave Lio was a subtle, but meaningful acknowledgment between them of his role in helping her protect Ioustin. Rolling up her proposal and holding it before her, she looked at Cassia. "I would like to see Newgift Cassia's effort succeed, or fail, on its own merits. I hereby postpone my proposal until the Autumn Equinox. May the Goddess's Eyes light your path. Orthros will be watching."

AN AKRON'S RANSOM

AUNT LYTA ROSE TO her feet, her hand extended in the circle petition. "Second Princess, now that discussion of the Departure has concluded, I ask that the Circle turn their attention to the hostages."

"Guardian of Orthros," Konstantina acknowledged her, "what is your proposal?"

"The Stand is ready to bring Aithouros's puppy before the Circle so we can give him his sunbound ransom and get my daughter safely home."

"It has yet to be determined," Konstantina pointed out, "whether Firstgift Komnenos's plan should be pursued. However, we must recognize that our hostages can ill afford a lengthy voting process. Furthermore, the decision of whether or not Orthros should offer the Torch to the Aithourian Circle is a matter of Hesperine safety and foreign relations in the purview of the Stand and the diplomatic service. I recommend the Guardian of Orthros be empowered to preside. Let any firstblood who wishes to object do so now."

No objections were to be heard in the amphitheater.

The princess concluded, "Let it enter the annals that I do not rescind my objection to allowing the Akron's Torch to enter the Goddess's Sanctuary, which is an act of desecration. Let us pray that this artifact brings no further destruction upon our people. I hereby yield the floor to the Guardian of Orthros."

"I want to stay for this," Cassia murmured.

"Of course." Lio ran a hand down her back. She was here. She was wearing Orthros silk. "You can watch from your rightful seat with our family, my love, and I shall veil you myself. The Dexion will never know you're here."

She smiled. "Don't imagine I'll run out of your concealment like I did at the fountain. I'm staying put in this seat."

"It has been waiting for you since Orthros was built, and it will always be yours."

She pressed a kiss to the corner of his mouth, then crossed their petal of the Firstblood Rose and ascended the stairs to her place among Blood Komnena and their tributaries. Lio would never take that vision for granted. He wrapped his Grace up in his magic to shield her from mortal eyes while leaving her beauty unveiled for their people to see.

As soon as Konstantina approved the transition from Firstblood Circle to hostage negotiation, Aunt Lyta took charge and dispatched Mak and Lyros to retrieve the Dexion from Kadi at the New Guest House.

"Lio," Aunt Lyta called down to him, "the Stand appoints you Orthros's speaker in the hostage negotiation."

He gave a deep nod. "We will get Nike home."

The whole amphitheater grew quiet while they waited for Mak and Lyros's return. Lio's mother exchanged a veiled word with his father, then stepped away with Zoe. The moments dragged on, and Lio focused on Cassia's nearby aura to bolster his waning strength. He was negotiating for lives after three nights of Craving. *Goddess, give me fortitude.*

At last Mak and Lyros stepped into sight before the podium with Chrysanthos blindfolded between them. A shadowy ward surrounded them on all sides. Mak reached for the Dexion's head, and for a moment, Lio thought his cousin would lose control and deal the mage a blow. But all Mak did was pull the blindfold from Chrysanthos's eyes.

"I don't need to see it to know what it is." The Dexion lifted his head, and the Torch's light bathed his face.

Lio held out his hands. "Come forward and verify its authenticity."

"There can be no doubt." Chrysanthos drew nearer.

Mak and Lyros stood at the ready, their attention and their power focused on the Dexion.

"It burns in me." Chrysanthos put his fist to his chest like a salute. "I have seen it in my dreams."

Lio had never seen the Dexion so affected. It was working. "Your Order has wanted this back for generations."

Chrysanthos looked up at Lio. "So, bloodborn. This is what became of our greatest relic. Prometheus bequeathed you his legacy."

Lio refrained from implicating Kassandra, as she had requested. "Would you, Dexion Chrysanthos, like to be the man who bears the Akron's Torch home to Corona?"

"You will want your hostages in return, I take it."

"This artifact is worth an Akron's ransom. Surely you can spare seven heretics to secure it."

Chrysanthos smiled. Then he laughed. "A worthy effort, Ambassador. But we don't want the Torch as much as we want the torchbearer."

"You flatter me, but I hardly think a young diplomat with light magic is of any use to your Order compared to the Akron's Torch."

Chrysanthos held out his hands to the crowd. "Does a relic leave behind a grieving family? Does a relic satisfy the thirst for justice? How many tears will you shed over the loss of Prometheus's prize? Think how many more you will shed over the loss of your last bloodborn."

Lio leaned his fists on the podium. "You would sacrifice your Order's greatest relic?"

"Oh, no. We will want that, too. We revise our terms. Not only will you and the rest of the Hesperine embassy surrender, but you will also restore the Akron's Torch to us, if you wish your Hesperines errant to live."

"The Queens have spoken. They will not pay in the blood of their people. This is the only offer they will condescend to make. Take the Akron's Torch or nothing at all. What is your choice, Dexion? Will you take your relic in place of the embassy and free the hostages? Or will you sacrifice this chance to regain the Torch?"

"The Queens have heard my Order's terms. Seven lives for seven lives. Return the Akron's sacred relic as well, unless you wish us to exact justice for the theft."

"Hold to those terms, and you will find yourself empty-handed."

"I have nothing more to say, except this, bloodborn. One day you and I will meet with that Torch between us, and not for a negotiation. You will not be so proud of it when I use it to immolate you on the Akron's Altar."

SOLSTICE OATH

AUNT LYTA WAS SUDDENLY standing before the Dexion. "I will take him."

Mak started forward, his fists clenched, but she planted a hand in the middle of his chest. She and the Dexion disappeared.

Everything after that became a blur to Lio. He didn't know how Cassia got from her seat to the podium, only that she slid under his arm so he could lean on her. Her glyph shard was back around her neck. Kassandra closed the Torch inside the silk box.

"We have more than one chance at this," Cassia was saying. "No agreement was ever reached on the first negotiation. We'll try again with Chrysanthos. We may yet persuade him to accept the Torch."

"There's still his secret box." That was Nodora. "We could bargain with whatever power is hidden inside."

"We won't give up trying to open it," Kia promised. "I'll take it around to all the scholarly circles again."

"We need more information about his brother." Xandra was at the podium, too. "Personal information. His weaknesses."

Mak pulled Lio into a hard embrace and whispered, "Next time you ask me to negotiate with my fists while you break his mind, I won't refuse."

Lyros pulled Mak away. "Don't say such things. Especially not when Lio has been starving for three nights."

"We're leaving now," Cassia announced.

"Can you step, Son?" Lio's father asked.

Cassia touched Lio's face and turned him to look at her. "My Winter Solstice gift is waiting for you. Let's go home."

Lio needed no Will to step them to their residence. Home pulled at him. When they arrived, the empty silence he had left was now filled with Cassia's aura. Knight plopped down on his blanket under the window seat.

Lio went still in the middle of the library, all his senses honing to the beacon at the top of the tower. "Cassia…is that…?"

She took his hand and led him to the stairway. "Come to our bedchamber."

They climbed the stairs together, round and round. Lio could not find the strength to carry her or levitate them. They came out in the unfinished loft that occupied the top level of the tower, and Cassia guided Lio to stand in the center of the room.

The two stained glass windows he had already installed cast the room in color, red from his tribute to their roses and violet from the betony flowers that warded off nightmares. But through the six cavernous, empty window frames, no frigid polar air swept in.

She faced him with the full Light Moon behind her and the Eye of Blood's half moon over her shoulder. Not a breath of wind stirred her robe. Sanctuary magic winked at his senses from within her shadow and sent silent echoes up to the vaults of the unfinished roof.

He could scarcely believe it. He reached out and ran his power over the fusion of familiar light magic and elusive warding. The working pulsed silently in his awareness with two different rhythms. As he listened, he realized one beat in time to his heart, the other to hers.

"Cassia, you crafted a Sanctuary ward—here!"

"The magic responded once more in my hour of need. It must have sensed how much I needed to do this for you." She lifted a bundle from the floor and held it in her arms for him to see. "Lio, I've brought a gift. It's for you. And for myself."

He took a step toward her. For the first time, he caught the other odors that lingered in the room beneath the fragrances of living roses and the fresh blood she had shed for her spell.

Old blood, long dried. Horror. Fury. Grief.

Lio closed the distance between them and saw what was in her arms. She had dyed the linen with her blood and emotion. The fabric was rank with flametongue oil. Solia's fabled garments, which Cassia wore in the king's hearth?

Lio reached for her, but halted his hands midair, helpless to stop the flow of blood already spilled. "What made you bleed like this? What happened to you in Tenebra that you have not told me?"

She unfolded the fabric to reveal what she carried. The glyph stone from their shrine. Its magic cried out to his senses. He fitted his hands to the bloody prints of hers.

A forest surrounded her, and a strange, eerie light he had never seen crept nearer and nearer. What was this ochre haze eating the sky, this fleshly pink specter rising? Was that…dawn?

She heaved for breath, pushing her leaden legs onward. Pain tore at her palms as she worked the glyph stone out of the crumbling arch. As a mage sent a cascade of threatening heat over her, she stared Anthros in the face.

Lio relived the morning of the Autumn Equinox in disconnected shards of sight, sound, and smell, until he could no longer bear the boom of war magic upon Hespera's shrine, and he yanked his mind and his hands away.

"I'm so sorry," Cassia said. "I tried so hard. But this is all I could save."

Lio wrapped her in his arms and held her, running his hands over her. The glyph stone throbbed between their bodies. "You're safe. You're safe. Nothing else matters."

"Now you know how I brought the Sanctuary ward with me."

"If you hadn't managed to awaken the ward— If the mages had come upon you a moment sooner— Why didn't you tell me? I almost lost you!"

"I didn't have the heart to break it to you. But I swore that day I would bring this to Orthros to be safe with you. It belongs here, just like me."

She set the glyph stone down in the moonlight, at the head of a makeshift bed. She had spread out their wool blanket and silk pillows from the window seat and scattered them with rose petals. She had even hauled the pots of their roses all the way up from the library. The fledgling vines clung to their stakes, their blooms already turning toward the windows.

"I dishonored your gift." She hung her head. "I tried to refuse the greatest gift anyone has ever offered me. Happiness was within our reach, and I told myself I must not grasp it. I thought I had changed so much since we met, but I haven't. It's more difficult than I imagined."

"I know. It is so hard. But we can do it together."

"My own survival was once the altar where I sacrificed life's sweeter things, but if I put them to the scythe for Tenebra, it amounts to the same. I lived like that for so long, I don't know how to let myself be happy."

"You can learn here, with me. I do not want to follow Bloodborn's Path. I want to chart my own, and I want to do that with you. Will you help me?"

"I have been trying, but some part of me is shaped to the iron rule that something so good cannot be, that this is not how the world works. The rhythm hammers on in my mind even when I think I have shut it out. Lady Cassia cannot. Lady Cassia must not. If Lady Cassia does, someone will die."

"But you can, Cassia. You must. If you do not…"

"*I* will cease to live. I will go back to merely surviving. Since I told you I was leaving, I have been reliving all those nights I endured in Tenebra without you. I can't bear that ever again. I have given my heart to you. I will never again try to live hollow-chested out of your reach. I cannot live without you."

"I was dying without you."

"I am so sorry I hurt you. Can you forgive me for nearly ruining everything?"

"Nothing is ruined, my rose. You have built our shrine anew."

She brought him to stand with her over the glyph stone. "We will treasure Laurentius and Makaria's history, but we will make our own. Our shrine will stand forever. We will not die for it. We will live in it."

"I don't want to be Hylonome, and I don't want you to be Solia. Our stars are sacred to us, and they guide us. But we cannot let them blind us. I will not lose you again. Not for the throne of Tenebra, not for anything or anyone. I will not make that sacrifice. I will not stand by and watch you sacrifice yourself."

"To devote my life to bringing down the king would be the same as letting him take it from me. I refuse to let that happen." Her words carried through the Sanctuary ward, out the windows, and over the gardens of House Komnena. "I refuse. I refuse to be my sister or my mother or one of Tenebra's tragic queens. I refuse to be the next woman who swallows her pain and lays herself down for the kingdom. Good things don't last long in Tenebra. I refuse to be one of them. This is is my promise."

From a pocket of her robes, she pulled out the green fair ribbon. She reached up and separated a strand of her hair from the rest, her fingers sure. He watched her weave a slender braid. When she reached the end, she secured it with the ribbon.

"I will never leave you, Lio. You will never go hungry another night. I love you, and I will love you for so long that I must become a Hesperine to make time for it all."

He felt her decision in her aura and her words and the way she put her arms around him. She held on to him, and he knew she would never let him go. He started at her brow, feathering caresses and kisses over her face, her neck, everywhere he could reach.

"Lio, your hands are shaking. Have you been so hungry these past few nights?"

"I've been so afraid. I have never been so frightened as I was at the prospect of losing you again...losing everything."

"Let go of your fears." She looped her braid around his neck, bringing his face closer to hers. "Our Oath is even more than words now, my love."

She had made her decision and her promise. At last, she had chosen him for all the reasons he had hoped. Nothing more stood in their way.

It was time.

Although he was in the Craving's grip, although it lay ahead of them to rescue the Summit, although their Hesperines errant lay suffering in the Order's custody, he was going to tell her the truth tonight. Now.

Lio lifted Cassia's hand to his own braid. "It is true that far more binds us together. There is something I still need to tell you."

She fingered his braid, bringing it to her lips. "I wondered what words could possibly remain unspoken between us now. Am I to finally discover what promise you meant by this?"

Lio seated her on their blanket and knelt before her, keeping hold of her hands. "There are some truths about Grace that Hesperines cannot reveal, except to the right person at the right time."

Her aura gleamed with anticipation. "Just when I think I have beheld all of Orthros's beautiful secrets, you show me more."

Goddess, let him not shatter Cassia's joy with a word. He must choose just the right way to explain.

But how could he gentle the truth that his life depended on her, and hers would soon hang upon him? How could he tell her that after a lifetime of having no choices, she had no choice in this?

He kissed her hands. "Grace is a powerful bond. Any power so great can sometimes be frightening. I don't want you to feel differently about us once you have learned exactly what it means to be Graced."

"Lio." She shook her head. "My love for you only becomes stronger with each new truth, no matter how difficult."

"I hope that will be the case now. I promise you, I will see to it our life together brings you only pleasure and joy."

"I look forward to everything our future holds."

"By now you have some idea what it is like for two Hesperines who spend eternity together. They do not drink from anyone but each other, and they need no other to sate them. They acknowledge this bond before our people at an avowal ceremony."

"I have often wondered what power makes them able to sustain each other without mortal blood."

"It is Hespera's greatest gift to our people, and all of us long to experience it. But two Graces' need for each other is so powerful that they are wholly reliant on one another. You are surely familiar with plants that, after only one taste, induce an insatiable need to consume them again and again."

Her heart beat faster. "I see. I have never tried such things myself, of course, but it's said that the concoctions smoked in sacred horns in the Temples of Hedon cause fits of ecstasy. Men go mad until they have another draught."

"I have told you Hedon has nothing on Hespera."

She gave him her secret smile. "So Graces are addicted to each other's blood."

"We call it the Craving. Satisfying this need is the most euphoric pleasure of Hesperine existence. But the consequences of going without each other are very dangerous."

Her face fell. "Oh, Lio. That's why Hylonome refused the Drink from others, isn't it?"

Lio wished that tale would cease to haunt them, but he must not shy away from the realities Cassia needed to understand. "She did not wish to prolong her life without her Grace. There is no way to cure the Craving. Other blood could have kept her alive for a time, but the withdrawal only becomes more and more difficult to endure."

"That's what's wrong with Alkaios. He isn't just starving."

"But think of all the Graces who need never be apart. Think how long the Queens or Uncle Argyros and Aunt Lyta have been together. Can you imagine over a millennium and a half of finding all you need in the one you love?"

"I am eager for eternity," she said, as if testing new words, "although it is hard for me to fathom so much time. What is this blood magic that can bind two people together forever? Will you explain the spell to me?"

He looked into her eyes. So much trust there. The most hard-won of all her gifts to him. "No spell is necessary. Grace is not something that must be made, nor can it ever be broken. Grace is as a force of nature or a law of magic that matches two people to one another in defiance of time."

Her face went blank. Fear gathered in her aura, threatening an oncoming storm. Her mental defenses came up with the swiftness and force of survival instinct.

All Lio's fears about her response had been justified.

He leaned closer, wrapping his hands tighter in hers. "No, Cassia, do not be afraid. I promise you have nothing to fear."

"You don't get to *choose*? It just happens…or it doesn't?"

"I can feel your dread, but the Blood Union does not tell me the thoughts that cause it. Hold fast to our Oath, Cassia, for that is more powerful than any mind magic. Tell me why this troubles you, so I can banish your fears."

Her back straightened, and her shoulders went as tense as iron. "Does it happen to everyone?"

"Everyone hopes for it. Some must wait much longer than others, but we have faith that everyone can look forward to Grace. My Ritual father is still searching after nearly sixteen hundred years, but look at my father. My mother has fulfilled all his best hopes."

"How can you be sure it has happened to you?"

"There can be no doubt. Once you've drunk your Grace's blood, the Craving sets in. If you are apart even for a few nights, the symptoms are undeniable."

"I thought Hespera was the goddess of free Will. How can she do this to her children?"

"It is a great blessing," he tried to explain. "Early in our history, our reliance on mortal blood was a cause of great conflict and sorrow. When the Queens were the first to experience Grace, our people felt Hespera had delivered us anew. Some of our philosophers hold that the Goddess bestows Grace in response to our choices. Others believe she crafts Graces for one another, perfectly matching them from the instant of their creation. There is a new treatise in progress—Kia's, in fact—which aims to study Grace as a scientific phenomenon and synthesize the collective evidence of Hesperine experience. Our own nature is sometimes as much a mystery to us as human nature is to mortals."

"I don't want philosophy or science. I just—I just want you."

With that, her mental fortress cracked like the shell of an egg, and her thoughts pounded in Lio's own mind like blows upon an anvil.

Lady Cassia cannot. Lady Cassia must not. If Lady Cassia does...

"Speak the truth, Lio. Just like we promised. Will there be someone else you need more than me? Am I to lose you to this nameless Grace in your future because I am not everything you need?"

That was her greatest fear? Not feeling trapped, but losing him?

"No, no!" He wrapped her thoughts in reassurance and ran his hands over her from her hair to her cheeks to her shoulders. "I did not promise you *time*. I promised you eternity."

Her fears pounded on, but over them, he could sense her defiance shouting. "I already know I'm addicted to you. As soon as you explained the Craving, everything I've felt made sense. But...is that what you feel for me?"

"The Craving is always mutual."

Cassia took a breath. "There is no question you are my Grace. So that means...I must be..."

He took her hand in his and placed her palm over his heart, resting his other hand over her heart. "Cassia. You are my Grace."

Her heartbeat kicked in her chest. Ephemeral joy flashed through her aura, and he saw it on her face for a fleeting instant. Then a shock moved through her. "You could have died."

"You're here now. I'm going to be fine."

"Rudhira said Alkaios had been without Nephalea since the Spring!"

"Yes, Cassia. But—"

She leapt to her feet, her anger a dark echo of the magic she had cast upon the room. "Why didn't you tell me?"

He stayed where he was, leaning an arm over his knee. It seemed his cousin had a point about his preference for hot tempers. Cassia's fury didn't make Lio feel the least contrite. He just wanted to kiss her terrible scowl. "From the moment you arrived in Orthros, I swore to myself I would not tell you that you're my Grace until you chose our love for yourself."

"How could I make the right choice without knowing the consequences it would have for you? How can we decide what's best for *us* if we only talk about what is good for me? I would never have considered going back to Tenebra if I'd known. I've been at Alkaios's bedside. I would never want you to suffer like that."

"Would you really want to stay in Orthros because you felt you must for another's sake?"

"I would never want to leave, only to discover that I—" Her horror crept over the Blood Union. "I would have been the death of you."

"I will not be like the men who try to set your unavoidable destiny before you. I want nothing to limit you. I want no sense of obligation to tarnish the freedom you've found here."

Her lips trembled. "You would place my freedom above your own life?"

"Of course."

"Lio. You are precious beyond measure. The world can't afford to lose you."

A smile came to his mouth, and he stood, gathering her into his arms again. "You're not going to lose me."

"I hope these few moments are the last I ever spend facing that prospect." She tightened her arms around him, pressing their bodies close, her face against his heart.

"I never meant for my explanation of Grace to give you the impression there would be someone else! I was just afraid you would hate the thought of being bound to me and having no choice."

"You are my choice. I want to be necessary to you. I want it to be true."

The last weight Lio had carried all these months lifted from his shoulders. Cassia *wanted* to be his Grace.

"It is all true," he told her.

A TASTE OF ETERNITY

CASSIA LOOKED INTO LIO'S face, studying her future in his ardent blue eyes. In his gentle, sensual smile, she tried to find an explanation for the inexplicable.

"I'm your Grace," she said. "Of all the people in the world—it's me."

"You are the person every Hesperine prays to find. You are the person I have been looking for my whole life. When I realized it's you, it felt so right."

"Then...you're glad it's me."

"Glad? From the first moment I knew the truth, I was overjoyed. Terrified of the distance between us, yes—but it was one of the best moments of my life."

"I wouldn't want you to feel trapped, either."

"Cassia, I do not love you because you're my Grace. I praise the Goddess you're my Grace, because I am so in love with you."

Something fiercer than her dread and even her anger roared to life in her. "Something so good *can* be."

"This is how my world works. Live forever in it with me."

"Now it is my world, too."

"It will be everything your heart desires. *I* am *your* Grace, Cassia. I can make you happy. I will see to it you have all you ever need."

"You have been doing that all along. You were showing me what Grace means, even before you explained it to me." She brushed his braid back from his face.

"That is what my braid meant all along. I always intended to give it to you."

"The same was in my heart tonight when I made my braid and my promise to stay, although I didn't understand everything yet."

"We exchange braids publicly during the avowal ceremony, but now that we've acknowledged our bond to one another, we can trade them privately." He ran his hand down her hair. "I would enjoy wearing your promise where no one else can see it."

She smiled. "Then by all means, I shall not keep you waiting."

Her gardening spade levitated into his hand from where she had left it by the roses. He offered it to her. "No other blade is worthy of this moment."

She caressed his hand, then accepted her battered, steadfast spade. "This shall be its greatest honor yet."

Lio bowed his head, bringing his hair into her reach. A thrill of nervousness went through her. This first heartbeat of their eternity was so important, so priceless. She wanted to mark it with worthy words.

Lio's mouth brushed her neck. "I love you so much, Cassia."

As always, it was easy for them to find the right words together. "And I love you, Lio, with all my heart."

She caressed his head, and the silence that fell between them felt reverent. She separated his braid from the rest of his hair, making sure she would not catch a single extra strand upon her blade. He had started the braid where its loss would not show. But still she felt keenly aware he was gifting her the work of nearly a century, which would take so much time to grow again.

He held very still for her. With great care, she positioned the sharp edge of her spade and sliced through the base of his braid. As it came free into her hand, she gasped. She cradled it, holding the ends, lest it unravel.

"Let me put it on you." With a smile, Lio took her spade from her and tucked it in a pocket of his robe.

Then he disrobed her with leisurely hands and a touch of magic. It was warm here in their Sanctuary ward, but her nipples peaked, and her skin flushed under his touch and his gaze. When she stood nude before him, he took his braid from her and knelt at her feet.

He looped the braid around her ankle, holding the ends together. "How about here?"

"Perfect. No one will see it there...and I love the way it feels on my skin."

She watched him prick his thumb on his fang. He rubbed the ends of his braid between thumb and forefinger, and when he withdrew his hand, she saw the braid was woven together in a single, unending ring.

"It feels so intimate, wearing part of you," she said.

"Just imagine how it will feel to have me inside your veins."

"Oh, Lio, I can hardly wait."

"It won't be long now, my rose."

He got to his feet and ran a hand through her hair. She felt his magic ease through her mind, and she rested her head in his hand.

He retrieved her spade from his pocket. "A touch of mind magic, and this won't pull a bit."

She laughed, and by the time the sound was out of her mouth, her braid slipped free. Her spade levitated away from them and returned to rest in a pot of roses.

Lio stood holding her braid. He ran it through his fingers, caressed it as he did her, with wonder on his face.

"Where would you like to wear mine?" she asked.

He put a hand on his heart. "Right here."

She reached up to lift his medallion of office from around his neck. The silver disk was heavy. Heavier still was the symbol of the Equinox engraved on it, the crescent moons brought together with the shining sun, the impossibly opposed celestial bodies portrayed as if they were one. She dropped the talisman of his highest efforts onto their blanket at their feet. Unfastening his high collar, she freed him from the stiff, embroidered fabric of his outer robe, then from the close-fitting black silk beneath. When he stood before her wearing nothing but her betony charm on a length of twine, she untied the string and let it fall as well.

She threaded the charm onto her braid instead. As she held the ends for him, he pricked his finger once more, then dabbed a drop of blood upon her braid. Before her eyes, the two ends sealed.

He rested his forehead on hers. "Cassia, you have made me immortal tonight."

"Will you do the same for me in return?"

"Right here in this room, in our bed," he whispered to her, punctuating his words with kisses. "I will Gift you, and we will begin our feast that will never end. You can pleasure yourself at my vein till you are sated, then pleasure yourself again."

There was no room in the seductive image for her fears of the transformation. She could think only of what it would be like to experience him as he did her, body and blood. She *would* get to find out what he tasted like. She could have it all—everything she had thought they must give up.

She pressed her body closer to his, running her hands down his chest on either side of her braid. "What does it feel like? You could show me, couldn't you, with your mind magery?"

"Yes…I could give you a foretaste."

"I would treasure it, if you would let me feel what you are feeling right now."

"You need not face the full force of the Craving yet."

"Is it stronger than the desire that comes over me each night?"

"Yes, but so too is the satisfaction. Let me show you that. I'll bring you into Union with me when our feast eases the hunger."

"No, Lio. I want to feel all of it—the pain and the pleasure, the hunger and the satisfaction. I am not afraid."

He hesitated, then slid one arm around her waist. "Very well. Let us face the Craving together, and you will see you need not fear, for we are here to sate each other."

His gaze darkened as his pupils expanded, and the silken shadow of his power descended over her thoughts. Her legs felt unsteady, and she wrapped her arms around his neck. His hand slid under hair and massaged her nape, while his other hand supported her back, pressing her closer to him.

His magic entered deeper than ever before, past the point he had touched her the night they had first made love, surrounding her more completely than in their passion.

She gasped, and scents flooded her nose, powerful and strange. They were so vivid, it took her a moment to recognize them. Moonflowers and cassia, blood and roses. A dual throbbing filled her ears, her head, her body. Their heartbeats.

"Is this what you can smell and hear all the time?" she wondered.

"This is a mere glimpse. There is so much more."

The colors of his windows gleamed around her, as bright as day but far deeper and richer. The aurorae in the night sky were more breathtaking than any rainbow after a storm. The moons outshone the sun. Lio's eyes glittered at her like light through the depths of the sea.

As his magic waxed in her mind, his desire became more evident between their bodies. Her krana tightened painfully in answer.

She moaned in sympathy, rubbing against him. "Are only three nights enough to cause you pain?"

"The first night or two are manageable. The third night is…difficult."

"This"—she gasped—"is 'difficult'?"

"By the fourth night, it becomes excruciating. Beyond that, unbearable."

"I can't bear it now. Lio, I need you. I have to have you."

His hand tightened into a fist at her back. "That night at Rose House, when you could not wait a moment longer for us to feast…you asked me what came over you. I can explain it to you properly now."

Sensation blazed to life under her skin, and she cried out, buckling in his arms. She ached as before a long-awaited tryst and burned as after a tryst interrupted. Her tongue felt as dry as if she had not tasted water in a fortnight.

She gave up on trying to find words and showed him instead, covering his mouth with hers. Oh, yes, at last, a taste of him. She devoured his mouth. So good. But not enough. She wrapped her trembling legs around him.

A quiet laugh rumbled out of his chest, rolling like thunder in her sensitive ears. He kissed her hard, biting a little. She tasted something hot and new on her tongue. The flavor raced through her senses and her body, and she rocked her hips against him, eager for more. Was this what blood really tasted like?

She wasn't sure how, but suddenly they were on the blanket. He lay down on his back and let her straddle him. Yes, at last, she could get to him. His rhabdos awaited, standing tall and ready. She whimpered at the answering tremor inside her krana. This must be what she needed. This must ease the pain.

She came down hard on his rhabdos, filling herself up with him. She let out a moan of pure revelry. He was so good. She propped her hands on his chest and rose up on the balls of her feet, arching her spine and letting her head fall back. Nothing and no one could fulfill her like this.

His answer came in her mind, filling her up under her skin like a second thrust. He was hers for the taking. He knew what she needed. He could sate her.

She rode him fast and hard, wild with need. Her body moved with uncontrollable abandon. She was almost there. So close to curing her hunger.

His hands released their grip on her hips and slid over her skin. She shuddered at the vivid sensation of his warm fingers trailing across her hips, then her lower belly. His thumbs slid through her curls and pressed into the top of her krana. When he touched her kalux, she let out an exultant cry. He massaged her in time to her rhythm. She gripped him tighter inside her, rocking into his caresses as he fed her pleasure. His jeweled gaze held hers, and his fangs flashed white at her.

Her climax flooded through her, filling her with him until she could hold no more, and she came apart. She bucked on him, clutching at him, groaning at the flavor of him in her thoughts, where he made a meal off her pleasure with her.

Although her body still trembled with the last throes of her climax, she tried to speak. "It's not enough. I need more. How can it not be enough? What it is that I need, Lio?"

"You need me. The way I need you." Without parting their bodies, he rolled them over, putting her beneath him on her back. He thrust his rhabdos more securely inside her.

"Oh, yes, Lio, give us what we need." She splayed her legs for him, scrambling to find purchase on their blanket as she thrashed under him, reaching for more.

He penetrated her with one, two, three hard thrusts before he lowered his head and sank his fangs into her throat. She felt her blood rush warm out of her and into his mouth. Sweet, hot pleasure coursed through her veins and pooled in her krana, even as his rhabdos thickened inside her and his presence in her mind weighed upon her like a whole night of strong wine. Words deserted her, her eyes slid shut, and she lay beneath him, drinking down the feast of magic and sensation he wrought inside her.

His climax buried him deep in her and flooded her with his warmth. Waves of pleasure overtook her from her kalux to the depths of her womb, while an even greater euphoria consumed her mind and heart. He was there, closer than he had ever been, to share it with her.

He stilled upon her, still powerful to her enhanced senses. She stroked his body, gazing above them until the brilliant colors faded to velvet shadows again. She caught her breath as the smells around her faded. She suddenly felt she had cloth in her ears. But as he lifted his head from her shoulder, his eyes still glowed at her with their own reflection of the aurorae.

He propped his head on his fist, relaxing over her, and grinned. His energy echoed through her, banishing the blanket of mortal sleep that threatened to claim her. "This is what it is like to feast. Do we not feel ready to take on the world?"

"And so we shall. But the world can wait until tomorrow. Tonight, I want only to take you."

"Mm. And how you give in return."

"If that's what three nights apart do to you, I intend to make up for lost time."

He chuckled. "I think you will have a naturally formidable appetite as a Hesperine."

Her face heated, but she gave him an unrepentant smile.

He settled down beside her on the blanket to hold her close, sighing into her hair. "We are indeed a match."

She lay in their Sanctuary in the darkest reaches of Orthros, utterly naked and entwined with the well-fed Hesperine who would Gift her. "Such good things really do happen in Orthros—and they last forever."

"This, my Grace, is the first night of forever."

THE PETALS OF HESPERA'S ROSE

*Ritual, through which
Hespera first gave us the Gift.*

*The Gift, through which
we overcome death.*

*The Drink, through which
we can thrive without
the death of others.*

*Sanctuary, the Goddess's realm, where
we go if death does find us, and which
we strive to realize in the world.*

*Grace, through which
we experience abundance.*

WINTER SOLSTICE

NOT A DREAM

CASSIA WOKE TO THE bells. She could hear peal after glorious peal all the way down here in the bath. She lifted her head from Lio's shoulder.

The bathwater rippled around them as he settled her more securely on his lap. He fingered his braid around her ankle. "Happy Winter Solstice, my Grace."

The full meaning of that word, Grace, sank into her mind once more, and her heart filled with it. "My Grace. I am staying in Orthros."

"You are staying in Orthros. Last night was not a dream."

"It was too good to be a dream." The mirrors that covered the walls and ceiling of the bath chamber showed her endless reflections of her new reality.

She caressed Lio's throat and ran her hand down her own braid. "Have I succeeded in curing your three nights of Craving so you can fully enjoy the festival?"

With a smile, he displayed how they had tamed his fangs. "You mean that wasn't the festival?"

"Happy Gift Night, my love."

"Needless to say, I am holding the best Gift Night present I have ever dreamed of."

"Shall I give you the same present next year?"

"And the year after that, please. And the year after that..."

"Why wait for a special occasion? You can have your present whenever you wish."

"Now I don't want to leave the bath."

Cassia just smiled, unwilling to acknowledge the world outside their tower. Not yet.

But Lio's good humor faded. He gazed down at her ankle again. "If not for you, I couldn't face this night."

"You did everything you could for our Hesperines errant. Offering the Dexion the Torch was a brilliant idea."

"I wish I had foreseen how it could make matters worse."

"We are not in any worse a position than we were before. The envoys will find our Hesperines errant."

"But now the Order of Anthros knows we have the Akron's Torch. We have not heard the last of this."

"The Dexion has not heard the last of this, either. He threatened you. I will never forget what he said. I will not let him forget."

At last a smile relieved Lio's grim countenance once more. "You will make a fierce Hesperine."

"Of course I will. Just wait until I have fangs of my own."

"You can bring down kings with just a spade. I can't wait to see what you do with fangs."

"The Dexion will get a little preview as he watches the Summit turn against him."

"So he shall. *Your* plan has not failed."

"Our plan. Don't tell me you've given up on your Summit, not after giving so much of your heart to it."

"Given up on the Summit? No. But I have not given it my heart. That is my gift to you."

She put her hand over his heart. "And the Summit is your gift to Orthros and Tenebra. It lies with the embassy not to squander it."

He lifted his eyes to hers again. "You aren't part of the embassy anymore."

"No. I can't achieve my plan without Flavian—but I can do it without me."

"You found a way. For us."

"I started laying the foundations as soon as I received your invitation to Orthros. I told myself I must have preparations in place so my work would not die with me, should Lucis see fit to do away with me between Solorum and Selas."

He opened his mouth, his brows descending.

She preempted him with a kiss. "In truth, my heart was already finding me a way out. I will leave Tenebra's fate in the hands of the Tenebrans. Beyond that, we can only hope they are wise enough to know what to do with it."

"If they are not, they have learned nothing from you."

"We will put my escape plan into action—tomorrow. Tonight is Hespera's sacred festival and my Grace's Gift Night. The world will have to forgive me if I make politics wait for once."

Lio kissed her again, a most expressive thanks. "I wish you could attend your first Solstice Ritual with me tonight."

"That commemorates *the* Ritual, doesn't it?" she asked.

"Yes, when the leaders of Hespera's Great Temples became the first Hesperines. We…reenact our beginning, Cassia, at the sacred hour of midnight. The Queens give of their blood to the elder firstbloods, who give it to their children and tributaries, who give it to their families. I'm afraid no mortal can be present. The flow of magic is too great for anyone who is not a Hesperine to endure."

"You mean it would actually be harmful to me?"

"It would induce the first stage of your transformation, and I would spend this night feeding you my blood to bring you through the rest. Carrying you out of Solstice Ritual for an emergency Gifting isn't really the experience I had in mind for you."

Silence fell between them, and they gazed at each other.

"I wish we could do it tonight, though," she said.

"Goddess knows, so do I."

"I just have to be mortal a little longer." She swallowed. "I have to let them think I'm still Tenebran."

"It won't be long now." He cupped her cheek in his hand.

"Next year, Lio. I will be there."

"We will partake of the sacred Drink together. It is a wondrous experience, when every Hesperine in Orthros is welcome in the Queens' own Ritual hall at House Annassa."

"I just realized you and Annassa Alea have the same Gift Night."

"I feel extraordinarily blessed to share my beginning with her and our kind." Lio sighed. "However, I talked with my parents about canceling my Gift Night celebration. It hardly seems appropriate to hold festivities at a time like this. We finally agreed to go ahead, though, for it would burden our tributaries to delay providing them with the gifts they need for the coming months."

"At a time like this, I think we should do all we can to keep everyone's spirits up. A stranger to happiness such as myself does not say that lightly."

"For a stranger to happiness, you give a great deal to those around you. I have looked forward to my Gift Night since the moment you arrived."

"You mentioned you had something special in mind."

"I want you at my side while I present my gifts to everyone, which will signify to all of Blood Komnena's tributaries what you and I 'cannot say.' Everyone will know we have acknowledged our bond to one another, although we cannot tell anyone else yet. You see, avowal is essentially a verbal profession before our people that we have discovered we are Graced. We have but to say it aloud, and it is legally binding. We want to save that for the ceremony."

She put a hand over her mouth. "I'm so glad you're explaining this to me before we leave the bath."

His grin returned momentarily. "I feel like shouting it from the top of the Observatory, too. But for now, we can only speak of it privately to the immediate family, which doesn't invoke a formal tie. For example, you can call Zoe Grace-sister at home, but you can't call Mak Grace-cousin yet, unfortunately. If anyone asks, just tell them you 'can't say' or we're 'not saying,' and they'll know what you mean."

"We all but shouted it from the podium last night."

"To be sure, last night's Circle will leave no doubt in anyone's mind, but there are certain traditions and formalities to be observed…and the fact is, I want to enjoy every moment of them."

"I will be honored to stand at your side before our bloodline's tributaries tonight. We will revel in it."

"Just wait until you see what the couriers have brought you. I've heard them dropping messages in the entry hall since the moment moon hours began." He cocked his head. "There comes a dozen more."

"Surely you're receiving Gift Night wishes."

"Most people will express those in person. The messages are for you. I'll show you…after another minute in the bath. Just a minute longer."

"It's your Gift Night. You deserve more than just a minute."

They lingered in the bath and washed with each other's soap. At last they trailed puddles over the cerulean-patterned floor tiles on their way to the geomagical drying corner, where they stood fondling one another in the soothing warmth that drifted out from deep in the ground. When they returned to the library, she saw to Knight while Lio made their coffee. So easy to fall into this rhythm. So astonishing to realize every night could begin just like this.

They carried their coffee and breakfast up to the top of the tower again, into the shelter and privacy of their Sanctuary ward. Lio fed her hearty Orthros fare more diligently than ever.

"You fed me all night, but this is nice too." She still felt the vicarious sense of satisfaction she had experienced as he had drunk his fill from her with their minds joined, although her stomach rumbled.

"You cannot live on pleasure," he reminded her, "yet."

"Now I understand your determination to poke me full of cassia pastries."

"I take your nourishment very seriously." All trace of humor was gone from his face. "Providing for you is my responsibility, whether mortal needs or Hesperine ones."

"I love being your Grace. My responsibility to provide for you is such great fun."

When she couldn't hold another bite, they rounded up their scattered clothes. She had never found it so difficult to don a Tenebran gown. But she also wore the secret of his braid, so powerful and yet so light to carry. He knelt before her and slid her enchanted silk shoes onto her feet, teasing her ankle with a finger where his braid was hidden under her stocking.

She carefully folded her new black formal robe. "Would this be appropriate for me to wear to your Gift Night?"

"It would be divine. You conspired with Kassandra, I could see. In fact, I couldn't stop looking. I suppose I must now let you out of my sight—momentarily—so you can put in an appearance at Rose House."

With a sigh, she put the rose-embroidered robe safely in the tapestry bag from Kassandra. "While you go to Ritual, I'll make sure the embassy has no cause for suspicion."

When they went down to the entry hall, Cassia gaped at the table under Lio's Ritual tapestry. It was covered in cups of all kinds, from ceramic mugs to silver goblets to crystal chalices. Piled all around the vessels or tucked inside them were more scrolls than she could count. The library door fell shut. The towers of scrolls collapsed and spilled all over the floor.

At that moment, the front door swung open, and a suckling dashed inside. A garland of red roses decorated with silver stars adorned his courier sash, and there were as many sweets in his satchel as letters.

He dropped another armful of scrolls on top of the heap, arranged half a dozen more cups wherever they would fit, and spoke around a huge candy braid. "Happy Gift Night, Firstgift Komnenos. Welcome to Orthros, Newgift Cassia."

Newgift Cassia. That sounded wonderful.

She beamed at the small, cheerful herald of Solstice and her new life. "Thank you."

Lio reached into his pocket, but his hand came out empty. "When you get back to the Couriers' Circle, spread the word that we'll come by later with tips. Generous Solstice tips."

"Thank you, Firstgift!" The courier bounced back out.

The door popped open three more times, and three more couriers bedecked in festival treats added to the hoard before Lio and Cassia managed to collect the lot of it and restore it to some kind of order on the table.

She picked up a filigreed copper coffee cup she recognized as one of Uncle Argyros's. "What *is* all this?"

"Cups are the traditional gift of congratulations when someone finds their Grace. I can make us some glass cabinets, so we can display them in our residence for years to come."

Cassia found Lio's smile infectious. "What beautiful heirlooms they shall be."

"As for the scrolls…" He searched through the stacks, extricated a particular one, and presented it to her. "Can you read the address?"

She peered at the tidy lines of Divine written on the outside of the scroll, then shook her head. "I still need to work on my reading."

"Interesting. Rapid verbal aptitude and intuitive lip-reading, but no corresponding affinity for the written word. I need to do more research."

"Did you say affinity? You're still convinced I learned Divine quickly because of magic?"

"And so is the rest of Orthros. These scrolls are official affinity reading invitations from various magic circles. It's part of every newcomer's acceptance into Hesperine society. Any circle whose power you might possess reads you for their affinity, so you can find the right mentor for your study of magic, which will in turn help you decide on a service and a craft."

"But I'm not even a Hesperine yet."

"You don't have to wait for that to find out what your affinity is. Since we haven't a clue, every circle in Orthros is drooling to read you first and discover you before the others." Lio tapped the scroll he had handed her. "Including the Circle of Thelemancers. With shameless ulterior motives, I encourage you to accept this invitation from my uncle first."

"I don't have your affinity," she scoffed.

"Do you remember when, at Solorum, we talked about how sites from the Mage King's time feel to you? You accurately described the auras of the palace and the Font of the Changing Queen."

"I'm sure everyone can feel the power in those places."

He shook his head. "Anthrian spells make your hair stand on end."

"That's because I'm a heretic."

"Your blood brings roses and coffee trees and Sanctuary wards back to life."

"It was your blood," she insisted, "and the sacrificial nature of Makaria's magic."

"Cassia." He took her hands. "You *are* a mage."

In the quiet entry hall, she could hear her own heart pounding.

"That's completely impossible," she said. "I'm just good at listening."

He gave her a considering look. "Why does it bother you that you have magic?"

"It doesn't bother me. Of course it would be wonderful. But I don't."

"From the first mention of it, you have been so eager to deny it. If it makes you uncomfortable, I'd like to set your mind at ease."

Sweat broke out between her shoulder blades. She withdrew her hands from his to put the scroll back on the table. "It's almost time for us to go."

He ran a finger between her shoulders. "You don't have to be afraid. It's safe to get your hopes up, because it's not too good to be true. It's safe to want it, and we all want it for you. It's safe to love it. The king can't take it away from you."

Cassia heard a drip and looked down to see her tears falling on a letter sealed with a rose emblem. "Is this an invitation from the Circle of Rosarians?"

"That's addressed in Konstantina's hand. I take it she wants to have you read for garden magic."

"I—I hope it's garden magic." Cassia turned to Lio and wept in his arms.

MY LADY'S LAST SCHEME

HEN CASSIA AND KNIGHT slipped back into her guest room from the courtyard, she found that her bedchamber was not empty.

Perita was waiting for her.

In the silence, Cassia pushed the glass door closed behind her, facing her inquisitor.

Her friend. Her best ally in all of Tenebra.

Cassia pulled off her gloves and tossed them onto the dressing table. "I'm not going to make up any more excuses with you, Perita."

"I'm not going to ask you to."

Cassia held out her hands, and her friend clasped them.

A smile spread over Perita's face. "You've thought of your scheme, haven't you, my lady?"

"I find I have one more in me, and it will be my most spectacular one yet. I am not going to let Chrysanthos ruin everything we have worked for."

"The king isn't here to call me up before him and bully your secrets out of me. Tell me what we're going to do."

Cassia hesitated. "I still want to keep you and Callen safe. Your families depend on you. I will not bring harm upon your loved ones."

"We can see which way the wind is blowing. Before long, we'll all have to choose a side. I can't say either side is safe, whether Cordium's or Tenebra's, when the King of Tenebra sides with the mages against his own people. But I can say which side is right, and I'll not risk my life or theirs for anything less."

Cassia embraced her friend. "I want you to know how much you will always mean to me, no matter what happens."

Perita pulled back, her face falling. "That sounds awfully final. I suppose you're really going to stay with him."

Cassia's mind skipped like a stone on the water over the words she had so carefully planned to say.

Could it be that Perita already knew?

Cassia shook her head, trying to gather her thoughts. "I have always said your insight is not to be underestimated. I thought I was being so careful, the way I speak to him, the way I look at him…"

"Your discretion has never failed you. It's the way *he* behaves with *you*. Not that any mortal can read a thing on that pretty, mysterious face of his. But actions don't lie. I doubt any of the thick-headed lords would know romance from a gas pain if they saw it, but Callen and I haven't taken kindly to the way Ambassador Toothy hovers around you."

Cassia let out a breath of a laugh. Her candid Lio. For all his veils and illusions, she had always warned him he was too honest.

Perita crossed her arms. "When he came down so hard on the necromancer about the smokes, I couldn't ignore it any longer. The Ambassador wasn't worried about his mighty papa's fancy guest house. He was being possessive of you."

"Protective," Cassia amended.

"If you'd been under his influence since he gave you that soap in Tenebra, I figured I was almost too late to save you."

"Rest assured, there were no spells in the soap, and I am not in need of rescue."

"Well, if he bewitched you, how would you know? I had to be sure. And there I was with a pouch full of every remedy my grandmother ever taught me to expose and banish curses, compliments of Ambassador Toothy's own Ritual mother."

"That's what Kassandra gave you?"

Perita nodded. "A kit of all the substances that resist Hesperine magic. She couldn't have possibly tampered with them. So I did what I had to do."

"Is that why you made new bath salts for me?"

"That mix of minerals will turn the water red as blood when it touches the skin of someone touched by Hespera. But if you aren't cursed, the water stays clear. Imagine my relief when you showed no symptoms of being under the thrall of wicked magic!"

"You need not have feared for me. Free Will is sacred to Hesperines, and Lio means every word he says about his reverence for human life. He would never abuse me so."

"It wasn't until the night your betrothal was official that I got really worried. I finally had to admit to myself it wasn't just on his side, and your owl might not be a Tenebran bird at all."

"That's the beauty of him. He's not one of the hawks."

"Hmph. The stars in your eyes would thaw even your heart toward philosophy, I dare say. That's why I've put enough faith in my grandmother's wisdom for both of us. Her concoctions are as old as the Lustra and probably have leftovers of its magic in them. They've satisfied me he's neither magicking you nor forcing you. If only they could satisfy me why my lady's only champion is a fanged heretic."

Perita's protests did not fool Cassia, not after all they had been through together. She could hear the real despair under her friend's words.

Cassia offered the best reassurance she could. "He loves me. *Me*, just as I am. I could ask for no finer champion."

"But what can he offer you? A frozen wasteland!"

"Lio's residence is a finer home than any lady could ask for. I will want for nothing there."

"I suppose his family is quite important," Perita conceded. "Status is one thing he can give you. Luxury doesn't hurt, either. But that's just cold marble and glass. None of that is what makes a home or helps a man's wife feel welcome among his kin."

"Perita, Lio has a sister. She's only seven."

Perita faltered. "The very age you were when you lost Her Highness."

"Yes, and this little girl has suffered a great deal, just as I did. She needs me."

Perita frowned, looking down at her hem.

"Their parents are so kind," Cassia went on. "I've never had parents, not really. They're thrilled to have another daughter in the family."

"His mother isn't the sort who will lord it over you, is she, and treat you like her precious boy's servant?"

Cassia couldn't help laughing. "Far from it! Do you know, she is helping me learn Divine, and she has given me her entire garden to do with as I will, down to the last twig. It's enormous. It will take me the rest of eternity to weed it."

Her friend paled. "As for that, I do my best not to dwell on what Hypnos has in store, but…"

"Yes, Perita. I do intend to become a Hesperine. Do not fear for the fate of my spirit. You have come to know the Hesperine spirit well in our time here, I hope."

There came a hiccup in her friend's throat. "I did think Callen and I would see you on the other side. We'd have followed you to Anthros's Hall."

Cassia swallowed hard. "I was never bound for there anyway, and you need nothing more than your own bravery and honor to win you your place there."

Perita wrapped her arms around Cassia, and they held each other. Cassia felt no shame in their weeping. Parting from such a friend as Perita was worthy of a lady's tears and a warrior's elegy.

SOLSTICE RITUAL

CASSIA STOOD UNDER THE rose window and shut her eyes, listening to the bells ring midnight. As many times as she had heard their beautiful tones, none were so glorious as those that announced Solstice Ritual.

Deep peals invited her down into Hespera's sacred darkness. High chimes seemed to bear her aloft, carrying her up into the gleam of the Harbor Light that shone crimson through the petals of Hespera's Rose.

The bells fell quiet. Cassia held her breath and listened for something even more beautiful, the Queens' magic. When they had called their people home upon Spring Equinox, their spell had awoken Cassia from a sound sleep as far away as Solorum. Standing here in Selas on Winter Solstice, she would surely feel them sharing their power among their people. If Cassia had magic, as everyone seemed to think, that must enable her to sense the Ritual.

The night was silent and still.

Cassia waited. She pressed her eyes shut, reaching out with…what was it? The part of her that could always hear Lio in her mind. The part of her that got angry and grew kinder and loved. The part of her that shuddered at a brush with Anthrian magic and thrilled to the touch of Hesperine power.

The light, the shadows, both seemed to hold their breaths with her. Then the light grew brighter beyond her eyelids. Cassia snapped her eyes open.

The rose window blazed. The harbor beacon beyond grew brighter and brighter. The crimson glass petals flooded the hall with light. Cassia stood and watched the walls, the floor, her own skin turn red as blood.

She stood waiting in that silence of anticipation until the bells rang again in jubilant tones.

Cassia let out a sigh. She ran a hand over the red phantoms upon her arm and watched their light fade.

Whatever secrets went on behind the closed doors of House Annassa, she would be a part of them next year.

As the Harbor Light returned to its wonted brightness, and the shadows in the room shifted, she once more caught sight of the banner under the window.

She smiled at it. That had always been her sister's banner. She lifted her gaze to the window. Hespera's Rose had always been hers.

GIFT NIGHT

LIO FOUND CASSIA STANDING with a meditative aura under the rose
window. Before he fully unveiled himself, she turned to him, her
face alight.

He smiled slowly. "You sensed me."

"Perhaps it's not so hard to believe, after all, that I might have magic."
She took a step toward him. "Your power is different now. I can feel it in
you, Lio. The Ritual."

"The lifeblood of the Goddess flows in me anew. I can scarcely
describe it."

"Next year, you will not have to."

Lio grabbed her up and swung her around. Their laughter echoed
around them.

"I can't wait to spend the rest of the night celebrating you," she said.
"We should get to House Komnena."

"I thought we would have to start without you. How did you get away
before veil hours?"

"Perita and I have reached an understanding. I'll tell you all about it
while you and Knight and I take a long walk across the grounds on the
way home."

By the time they wandered back into the gardens of House Komnena,
Lio felt more hope than he could ever remember. He had his Goddess's
power in his heart, his Queens' blood in his veins, his Grace's hand in his.
All was not lost, and it never would be.

Although the plan they had just discussed during their walk still lay
ahead of them to enact, now that they had agreed upon it, a great weight

seemed to have lifted off of Cassia. She tugged his hand, gesturing to the side of the garden path, where only polar scrub grew at present. "A bed of rimelace right there, I think. What do you say?"

"Of course. The garden must have rimelace."

The moment they arrived at the barn, Zoe dashed out, her goats trotting behind her. Knight bounded forward to greet her.

"Cassia, you're here already! We don't have to wait any longer?"

"I couldn't wait any longer either." Cassia touched the suckling's uncovered head.

Zoe tossed her mantle across her shoulders.

Mother followed Zoe out of the goat barn and put an arm around her and Cassia while they all wished one another Happy Solstice.

"We're going to have so much fun tonight." Mother sounded nearly as excited as Zoe.

Lio bent to give his mother a kiss on the cheek. "Thank you for working so hard on everything."

"I enjoy it so much, I should have another child. Oh wait. I do!" She tickled Zoe.

Zoe giggled and jumped away, only to bump into their father as he stepped into sight.

Father caught her against him. "I hear it's time for your present."

She grinned at their parents. "And yours, too!"

"Ours?" Mother asked. "Oh, Lio, you know we love the window. You don't have to give us anything else."

"My Gift Night may be during the Festival of the Rose, but you know I'm not going to combine your presents." With relish, Lio withdrew a pair of scrolls from his robes and presented them to his parents. "You can take advantage of these as soon as we migrate to Orthros Notou. Through my diplomatic contacts, I secured you invitations to a secluded estate in the Empire."

"The best part is," Cassia added, "he didn't tell anyone where it is."

"Except us," Zoe whispered.

Their father unrolled the scroll with a smile worthy of the Blood Errant. "Thank you, Son. You are a Hesperine after my own heart."

Lio grinned.

Mother smiled too, but concern dimmed her aura. "There are only two invitations."

"I'm afraid Zoe, Cassia, and I can't join you," Lio said. "We'll be too busy touring the western steppes."

Zoe tugged their mother's sleeve. "Lio says it's known as goat country. Did you know there's an entire goat country?"

"There are vast plains of wildflowers," said Cassia, "and great herds of goats who eat them."

Zoe straightened her mantle again. "I can't wait."

Now their mother's enthusiasm was undimmed. "This is lovely. Thank you so much, Lio."

Father pulled her close. "How exciting, my Grace. I get to run away with you."

"Again." She gave him a kiss.

"Are you ready for your present?" Lio asked Zoe.

Her eyes widened. "A tour of goat country isn't my present?"

Lio put his hands on his sister's shoulders. "Your present is waiting for you in the house, upstairs."

"I'm ready!"

The whole family stepped to the upstairs room his parents had long ago reserved as a bedchamber for their future secondgift. Until tonight, Zoe had only set foot here once, and only long enough to grow frightened. Lio turned her to face the wall of windows, whose peaked arches and clear glass panes overlooked her goat barn. All except for the central window, which he had filled with stained glass.

Zoe didn't even glance up at the high, vaulted ceiling or around at the long, spacious room. She ran to his present. "You made me a goat window, too!"

She reached out to stroke the glass portraits of Moonbeam and Aurora. She put one hand on the real Knight, another on the image of him laying down in peace with her goats.

Cassia joined Zoe at the windows. "Lio put a light spell in the stained glass that will make your betony grow better. But only if your plant has more room. It's running out of space in its small pot. If you transplant it, it will start to bloom."

Zoe turned to their parents, her face brilliant with excitement. "Can I move to this room now?"

"This room is right above my workshop," said Father. "I would be so glad to have you closer to me while you sleep."

Mother's aura mirrored Zoe's happiness. "We'll move your things this very night, if you like."

As Lio came to stand by his Grace and little sister, Zoe hugged him around his waist. "Thank you."

He grabbed her and lifted her up. He sensed her surprise, but no fear. He propped her on his hip, so she could see better through her windows.

She wrapped her arms around his neck and looked out at the barn, paddock, and grounds. Her aura lit up just like the moment before when he had revealed his present to her. It seemed the world from his height looked more beautiful to her than either of them had expected.

Together, they all went downstairs to the Ritual hall, to the smells of coffee and cider, savory stews and cassia desserts. Then Lio's mother was everywhere at once, directing the culinary crafters, florists, and ribbon artists.

An ear-splitting whistle echoed across the hall. Laughing, Lio turned to see Mak and Lyros levitate down from the top of the pillar they had been decorating with flowers. Nodora and her Imperial sitarist paused their warm up to wave from the musicians' corner. Xandra and Harkhuf put down the candles they were setting about, and Kia emerged from the library, her mathematician on her arm. Their friends crowded around.

"Look who isn't handing out Gift Night presents alone!" Mak crowed.

Lyros put his arm around Mak's shoulders, tucking a spare rose behind his Grace's ear. "It's a good thing you're here to help, Cassia. One year, when Lio tried to give out gifts by himself—"

"Thorns, please don't tell that story," Lio pleaded.

"This year will be very different," Cassia broke in. "How can I help?"

Lio tucked her under his arm. "Stay right here."

She grinned up at him. "You've assigned me the best task of all."

"Well, there is also that hoard of gifts spanning the length of the Ritual hall. Light items on the table, heavy items under it, and the racks hold scrolls itemizing supplies that will be delivered to our tributaries' homes.

Between the two of us, I think we can manage to give all of them to the right people before the night is through."

Cassia rubbed her hands together. "Ready when you are."

"Let us have a look at the gift list so we'll feel ready when the recipients start to arrive."

"I'm afraid we're early," said Annassa Alea.

Lio turned in the direction of her voice and saw the Queens strolling into the Ritual hall. He put his hand on his heart. "How honored I am that you are the first I may welcome to my Gift Night celebration, Annassa."

Queen Alea's aura gleamed with amusement. "In honor of Anastasios, shall we say, Apollon?"

Father laughed. "I'll never forget the time he waited an hour for his students to appear without realizing we weren't late."

"Annassa, guess what Lio gave me." Zoe began regaling the Queens with a description of her new window.

"A lovely application of our lessons in light magic," said Queen Alea.

Queen Soteira smiled as Zoe clutched at her robes. "You will treasure this night always, I can see."

"I am glad you approve, Annassa," Lio said. "But you have yet to ask me for your gift. I am ready to honor my bond of gratitude with you, as all Hesperines do on our Gift Nights, and grant you your annual boon."

Queen Soteira nodded to him. "We have a great task for you this year. We ask you for a gift beyond price, a contribution to Orthros that will last for centuries to come."

Lio gave the heart bow, torn between trepidation and gratitude that his Queens would entrust such a task to him. What did they have in store for him?

Queen Alea touched a hand to Cassia's head. "Add one new Hesperine to our number before next Winter Solstice."

Lio smiled. "A great task, to be sure, but one I will undertake with joy. She is indeed a precious gift to us all."

"Thank you, Annassa." Cassia's voice was breathy with emotion.

They escorted the Annassa to the place of honor prepared for them at the Ritual circle. Uncle Argyros was already there and offered the Queens the first taste of the coffees he was preparing.

As he dropped a lump of sugar into Queen Alea's cup, he said to Lio and Cassia, "Lyta will be joining us later. She is taking the first watch at Alkaios's bedside. I shall take my turn while she is here. The two of you cannot be spared from House Komnena tonight."

"Thank you, Uncle."

Cassia touched a hand to Uncle Argyros's arm. "It means so much to us that you've made sure Alkaios will not be alone tonight. I also want to thank you for the invitation I received from you. Of course my first affinity reading must be with you."

Uncle Argyros's face lit up. "I shall be delighted, my dear."

"You are not to be read for garden magic first?"

Lio and Cassia stood up straighter. The Second Princess had joined her mothers.

Lio bowed to her. "I'm so glad you could be here tonight, Aunt Kona. I didn't know if we could expect you this year. You have many responsibilities on this important night. It is an honor that you spared the time."

The princess held one of the many glass figurines Lio had cast, with Zoe's input, as presents for any unexpected guests for whom he had not prepared personal gifts. The Second Princess turned the small, milky-white goat over in her hands. "Sixth Fifthgift Konstantina will be quite charmed by this."

"I'm delighted Blood Konstantina's newest suckling will be the recipient of one of my Gift Night favors. But I hope you received my gift for you."

She arched her brows. Apparently she had not expected a gift any more than he had expected her as a guest.

"The glass planter I crafted for you should be at your residence by now."

"That must have arrived when I wasn't at home. Thank you, Lio. I will see it as soon as I return. Speaking of planters, Cassia, how are your roses faring?"

"The first blooms are ready, whenever you'd like to see them."

"Well done. Do you not find them a better reward for your efforts than a crown?"

Lio looked from the princess to his Grace. By the look on Cassia's face, she was as surprised as he was.

Konstantina's mouth curved. "Am I the only one who perceived your ultimate goal?"

"You and Kassandra," Cassia answered. "Flavian will not change Tenebra the way I planned to…but Tenebra will not change him."

"Have no regrets. Your accomplishments in Orthros over the coming centuries will outshine anything you could have achieved from that little throne."

"Thank you for your invitation to an affinity reading with the Circle of Rosarians. I would be honored to accept."

"Hmph," said Konstantina in Uncle Argyros's direction, but she was smiling. "I understand someone else has made a previous claim on you. I might have known you would press your unfair advantage, Argyros."

With a triumphant chuckle, Uncle Argyros put an arm around Cassia's shoulders. "The Circle of Thelemancers has the first claim on her, of course."

"Do not be so quick to think you are the only circle that will vie for her talent. It is entirely possible she has a dual affinity."

"Oh, thorns," said Cassia. "I'm only just getting used to the idea I might have one."

Konstantina unfastened a scroll from her sash and held it out to Cassia. "Allow me to present you with another invitation for after your affinity readings. I think we would work well together."

"I must dissent," Uncle Argyros interjected. "You may not secure the position of service mentor to Cassia before she has even discovered her magic. However impressed you may be with her aptitude for strategy, there is no question that I, as a member of the family, would be most suitable to mentor her in politics. You must forgo the pleasure of grooming her as a magistrate, for I insist she be the next young Hesperine I welcome into diplomatic service."

Cassia looked at him, her aura full. "You wish me to be your next initiate?"

"I sincerely hope you will consider it," Uncle Argyros said, "although I think we must start you out as a full ambassador, in light of your accomplishments."

"What do you say?" Lio asked her. "Shall we partner for a career in diplomacy?"

"I…" Cassia hesitated. "I had thought I might become a gardener."

"That is a craft, not a service." Konstantina handed her scroll to Cassia. "Regardless of what your magic proves to be, you will be most welcome in the Circle of Rosarians, the most prestigious of Orthros's circles dedicated to gardening. I shall not stand by and watch you waste away among Argyros's fruit trees. You must allow me to mentor you in your craft."

Lio recognized the look in Cassia's eye when she was ready for a challenge.

"I accept," she said without hesitation.

"We will begin as soon as the embassy scurries back to their mortal burrows. Expect another scroll from me." With that, Konstantina turned to sample one of Uncle Argyros's coffees.

"Aunt Kona," Lio added, pulling a quick veil around their conversation, "how is Ioustin?"

"He is receiving what he needs. We are confident his situation will improve."

"Would the mind healers allow him to attend tonight?"

"In fact, we are doing our best to encourage him out of his isolation. If you don't see him tonight, however, do not take it to heart. It has nothing to do with you." She put a hand on Lio's arm briefly before proceeding around the coffee table.

"Congratulations on your future in the Circle of Rosarians," Uncle Argyros was saying to Cassia. "A most fitting choice, and certainly a position to be proud of."

"I feel very fortunate in the Second Princess's mentorship."

"Kona is also a most excellent and patient teacher, and I believe you will feel right at home among her students."

"As for my service…" Cassia began.

"Give it some thought. You and Lio deserve a rest from diplomacy tonight, hmm?"

"Thank you for your patience," she said.

"Take your time."

"I will most certainly be lending a hand with your fruit trees, regardless," she said firmly.

"Ah, my coffee sapling can breathe a sigh of relief. Speaking of coffee, I brought a new blend with me tonight, which I hope you will taste."

"It is my favorite coffee in the world," said Lio with anticipation.

"I thought your namesake coffee was your favorite." Cassia accepted a tall mug from Argyros and paused to breathe the fragrance of the creamy, red-brown brew. Comprehension began to dawn on her face. She took a sip, then smiled at Uncle Argyros. "I have been so honored tonight—as a newgift, a new rosarian, and possible new diplomat. But it is a rare honor indeed to be a coffee."

Uncle Argyros had not appeared so sanguine in a very long time.

The night wore on, and the house filled and overflowed with family, friends, and their goodwill, magnified by the power of the Solstice Ritual that had bound them all even closer together tonight. Every new arrival paused to pay their respects to the Annassa before approaching the gift table.

Lio and Cassia stood at the table together while tributaries of all ages came through the gift line. And for the first time in Orthros's history, a liegehound guarded the stash of Gift Night presents. That did not make anyone hesitate to shower Lio and Cassia with well-wishes. His heart filled with gratitude as each and every guest made the same promise.

"We'll visit Alkaios at the Healing Sanctuary on our way home."

"If you'll excuse us after this, we're going to see Alkaios."

"We cannot let this night end without showing Alkaios our gratitude for his role in bringing Newgift Cassia safely to your side, Firstgift Komnenos."

"The entire gift line is going to form up outside Alkaios's door before the night is through!" Cassia marveled.

Lio squeezed her hand. "Have no doubt their power will bring him strength and comfort."

It wasn't long before Aunt Lyta joined the celebration and assured Uncle Argyros he would not fit into Alkaios's room.

Lio heard the congratulations and assurances over and over, but he never got tired of listening to them. It had never been such a pleasure to itemize crafting materials to skilled elders or hand out glass trinkets to the children. It did not surprise him to see Cassia take to the responsibility with confidence and poise.

"You're a natural at this," Lio said between guests. "Did anyone ever tell you that you would make an excellent liege lady…or even queen?"

"I heard that somewhere. What a boring idea. Weaving…taxes…sitting on a throne all day… I think I'll become a heretic instead."

He grinned, flashing his fangs at her. "I can highly recommend it."

Moon hours waned, and the guests' spirits only rose. Sucklings dashed to and fro, engrossed in games of veil and step through the rambling house, while their parents savored the good taste of Blood Komnena. The elder firstbloods sat reminiscing with the Queens. Lio's Trial circle and their companions kept him and Cassia company during lulls in the gift line, and Nodora led the musicians in a few impromptu dances for them all to enjoy.

Everyone traded festive feelings in the Blood Union until together, they were stronger than their fears and worries. Lio took solace in that and in Cassia's nearness. He only wished his Ritual father would take advantage of his rare stay in Orthros and come spend time with them all here at House Komnena. If it had not been Aunt Kona who had assured him otherwise, he would have believed Ioustin truly was unhappy with him.

Not until it was almost veil hours did the gift line give way to a line of those repeating their well-wishes and taking their leave. First veil had rung when exclamations of welcome stirred the remaining guests. There, at last, a noticeable head of blood-red hair was visible amid the crowd. A sigh of relief escaped Lio.

It took Ioustin a long time to make his way through the guests, they were so eager to mark the occasion of him being here. By the time he reached Lio and Cassia, he appeared even less in festival spirits than when he had entered.

Lio clasped his wrist. "I can't tell you how good it is to see you."

Ioustin tugged him closer and turned the wrist clasp into an embrace. "Happy Gift Night, Lio."

"Happy Solstice," Lio replied, standing back.

"Don't look so worried about me."

"I'm sorry you're not enjoying the festivities."

Ioustin sighed. "I shouldn't have come. I knew I would only afflict others with my inability to celebrate."

"No, no, we're so happy you're here," said Cassia. "You don't have to apologize for not feeling like celebrating, not at a time like this. Lio would have called everything off, if his gifts weren't so important to Blood Komnena's Ritual tributaries."

"Thank you, Cassia." Ioustin took a step closer, and a veil rife with royal power rose around them. "I admit to being preoccupied with the latest report from Basir and Kumeta."

Cassia leaned forward. "They managed to deliver news from the Magelands?"

"Now that they have infiltrated Cordium, they cannot risk leaving to make contact with home, but they are relaying through other envoys."

"What can you tell us?" Lio asked.

"Nothing," Ioustin answered. "A remarkable degree of nothing. When an execution is anticipated, it is usually the talk of Cordium. The Order of Anthros makes a point to boast any time Hesperines are in custody. And yet all is silent."

Lio frowned. "Does the Order's secrecy not make sense? They may not know precisely at what moment the Dexion will seize the opportunity to reveal that they have hostages. In the meantime, they wouldn't want word to reach our informers."

Ioustin shook his head. "Even so, there are certain players that respond in situations like this. There are discreet signs we have learned to recognize, which are strangely absent. Orthros is on vigil, but Cordium is not."

"I hope Basir and Kumeta will stay safe," Cassia said.

Lio hesitated. "How are you, Ioustin?"

Ioustin's gaze filled with a fire Lio had seldom seen there. "It will be felt all the way to Corona, now that the eighth bloodborn has taken up Prometheus's torch. Well done. Goddess knows I wish I had been at Circle to see that."

"So do I. But I'm so glad you're here for this." Lio picked up Ioustin's present from the table. "You don't have to open it in this crowd."

Ioustin gave him a curious glance as he accepted the package wrapped in blood-red silk. "Well, I will say thank you now." He cast a mournful glance at the well-wishers lining up behind him.

Before Lio could try to persuade Ioustin not to leave, Zoe slipped out of the crowd and took their Ritual father's hand in both of hers. "Rudhira! You're here! Do you want to see the cave Papa helped me make?"

Her Blood Union might be new, but it was strong. Ioustin smiled as he took his leave of Lio and Cassia and let Zoe lead him away from the crowd toward her hiding place.

Cassia twined her arm in Lio's. "A well-chosen gift."

"I hope Ioustin agrees."

"Stop worrying."

Lio was about to steal a kiss from Cassia, when his Trial brothers' auras drew near again.

If Mak had asked for word of his sister on Ioustin's way in, he gave no sign and began to jest with a vengeance. "Ah, we remember what it was like, don't we, Lyros?"

"Oh, yes." Lyros nodded. "That feeling that comes over us when we find true love for the first time."

Mak put a hand to his heart. "Suddenly we want to pair off everyone around us…arrange romantic vacations for the parents…"

"This from the newly Graced," Lio said, laughing.

"Who went to battle to pair us off," Cassia added.

Mak held out a hand to Lio. "Where's my getaway invitation to use on Lyros?"

"A scroll in the fighting ring?" Lio inquired. "Could be an interesting battle, but I think that would be disqualified as a weapon."

"To use to convince him to leave the ring," Mak clarified, "and take a romantic leave of absence with me."

Lyros looked at him. "I don't need a fancy invitation for that, my Grace. Just tell me you want to do it."

Mak was about to steal a kiss from Lyros, when Lio cleared his throat. "I do have gifts for you, of course."

"After the celebration," Cassia said, "let's all go over to Lio's residence."

Lio wrapped his arms around her. "*Our* residence."

After they had seen the last of their guests to the door, said their good veils, and helped tuck in the sucklings, they retired from the main house with their friends. Talking and laughing, they all sneaked through the garden together, as if they too were playing a game of veil and step, perhaps with the Goddess, who spied them with her half-lidded Eye of Blood.

In the library, Lio put on the coffee he had waiting for them and pulled their gifts from the storage basket underneath the coffee table. He set the five identical silk-wrapped parcels before his Trial circle and watched them unwrap the glass seals he had made for them bearing their private glyphs.

Nodora held hers before her face so the engraved lyre caught the light. "They're beautiful!"

"The thoughts they carry, still more so." Kia smiled at her scroll. "These will mark momentous correspondence between us for many centuries to come."

"Thank you," Xandra said happily of her silk moth seal.

"I don't usually go in for those fiddly scholar gifts," Mak teased, "but these matching speires are all right."

"They don't fit together like two halves of a heart," Lio added, "like those metal ones you made for each other when we were students."

"Thorns." Lyros covered his face. "I'm sorry for trying to tell the story about your sixtieth Gift Night!"

Laughing, Lio reached into the basket for the last gift and set it in front of Cassia. She glanced at it in surprise.

"You thought I wouldn't give you a present tonight?" Lio asked.

"I thought your promise to give me a certain Gift was my present," she answered.

He smiled. "You can have this, too."

She gave him her secret smile in return, then unwrapped her gift. She cradled in both her hands the glass seal engraved with the image of a spade.

"Perfect," everyone agreed.

Cassia finally gave Lio the kiss he'd been wanting. "With this to inspire me, I'll learn to write in record time."

He reached into the basket one last time and pulled out his own seal and a piece of fine paper. Pricking his thumb, he dripped his blood into the grooves of the seal, then stamped his moonflower glyph on the paper.

He extended a hand toward Cassia. "Allow me to do the honors."

She held out her seal, and he pricked his healed thumb once more, covering her seal in his blood, which carried hers. She stamped her glyph on the paper. One by one, their friends followed suit, until their symbols, once six, now seven, marked the page in a circle.

Lio presented the paper to Cassia. "Let this serve as your invitation to our Trial circle."

She looked around at each of them. "I didn't participate in your Trial of Initiation, though."

"For Hesperines who accept the Gift as adults," Kia explained, "the Gifting itself is considered the Trial."

"We'll be here to support you on your Gift Night," Mak promised.

"And when you come through it," Lyros said, "we shall initiate you into our Trial circle, just as we did each other last year."

At last Cassia accepted the bloodstained page from Lio. "I thought this was supposed to be a present for all of you."

"It is," Nodora said without hesitation.

"We've been through so much together already," Cassia said. "Thank you for standing by me. I will always stand by you."

"You've proved that over and over," Lyros told her with a smile.

"There isn't a Hesperine in Orthros who wouldn't be proud to count you a Trial sister," Mak said. "Good thing we got to you first."

Lio kissed Cassia's temple and settled back on their bench with her. Her emotions, fraught from so much recognition, gave way once more to the ease of contentment among friends.

"So, Lio," Kia said as they all settled down to their coffee, "about the Akron's Torch."

Nodora looked from Lio and Cassia to Mak. "Perhaps we should save that topic for another night."

Kia ignored her. "Where was it?"

"Now that you mention it," Xandra interrupted, "why did you even invite me tonight? You could have just lit all these with the Torch." She waved one of the extra decorative tapers that still filled her pockets, and the wick caught on fire.

Kia jumped. "Not in the library!"

"I only made a promise about your mother's library." Xandra waved a second taper, which burst into flame and dripped wax on the coffee table. "Oops."

Lio thought she had saved them from the dire topic of conversation, but Kia was too stubborn. Of course.

Kia turned back to Lio. "I insist you let me be the first to read your treatise on how you rediscovered the artifact."

Lio drummed his fingers on his knee. "What treatise?"

"The one you're going to write, documenting the research that led you to it, of course," Kia replied.

"I'm afraid you'll have to direct all your inquiries to Kassandra," Lio said. "I borrowed it from her."

"That silk box," Lyros said in realization. "The one she put it in at the end of the Circle…"

Mak's eyes widened. "It's the one she keeps under her loom."

"You just noticed?" Xandra laughed. "I recognized it the minute she brought it to the podium. Imagine, it was there all that time, and none of us knew. It's…comforting, actually. I couldn't even sense it. That just goes to show my fire magic doesn't have anything to do with war magic."

What did that say about Lio's ability to hold the artifact without flinching? "Like calls to like, doesn't it?"

Try as he might, Lio could not push away the clamor of the hostage negotiation.

How dare you bring the Akron's Torch within the Firstblood Circle!

…the dreadful consequences of that Torch…youthful recklessness…blind idealism…destruction…

One day you and I will meet with that Torch between us, and not for a negotiation. You will not be so proud of it when I use it to immolate you on the Akron's Altar.

Lio and Cassia looked at each other at the same time.

"If like calls to like…" she repeated.

"…the key to the Dexion's box may be right in our hands," Lio finished.

THE KEY

NODORA SAT UP STRAIGHTER. "Brilliant."

"Why didn't that even occur to any of the scholarly circles?" Xandra asked.

"Because of their little minds," Kia answered. "They don't allow for ideas like using the Torch against the Anthrians."

"Lio," Lyros warned, "we don't have to tell you how dangerous this might be."

"Our wards are ready," Mak said. "If this could help us get my sister back, there's not a moment to lose."

"We should try it now." Cassia gestured toward the main house. "Kassandra's still here. Go ask her."

"I'll be right back." Lio rose from the coffee table. He was about to step, when something arrested his senses and made him pause. He strode toward the door of the library.

"You aren't going to walk through the gardens, are you?" Mak demanded. "Step over there already."

Lio held up a hand. "Wait."

He went out into the entry hall. The silk box was waiting on the table under his Ritual tapestry.

He went to it and made to pick it up. His gaze drifted up to the silk tapestry Kassandra had made for him in honor of his first Ritual. As always, the fine, intricate designs she had woven, painted, and embroidered there befuddled and beguiled his eyes. As soon as he looked at one, it seemed to transform before him, or direct his attention elsewhere.

This time, he found his gaze drawn to a shape on the far left of the tapestry, a tall, golden tower that rose above the small figures of people. Bas reliefs decorated its circumference, and its many-colored windows gleamed. Lio had always taken it for a grand monument, perhaps an architectural wonder he would behold on a diplomatic journey. He peered at it more closely now. It was a pillar of solid gold decorated with filigree and precious gems. He lifted his gaze to the top of it, where a light, like a Summit Beacon or the sun, cast its rays upon the entire tapestry.

Lio shook his head and carried the Akron's Torch into the library.

He could already sense several layers of his Trial brothers' power enclosing the sitting area. Cassia stood ready with the warded bag containing Chrysanthos's box. A hush fell over them all as Lio set the silk box down on the coffee table and opened it to let the Torch's light spill across the library.

"How do we use it?" Cassia asked Lio.

"I am feeling my way, to tell you the truth." He braced himself.

He fastened his hand around the Torch's handle once more, and that sensation of foreign, but exhilarating power shot through him. His friends jumped. Carefully, he lifted the Torch and held it out to Cassia.

She withdrew the Dexion's treasure from the bag. Mak kept a hand on her shoulder, the dark beginnings of a ward at his fingertips. She grasped Chrysanthos's box firmly in both hands and held it over the Torch's light.

They all waited.

In the silence, there came a click.

"It's open!" Cassia cried.

Mak held the bag out. "Give it here, quickly."

She shook her head. "I think it's all right. It's not even hot to the touch."

Lio put a hand on the box, and a rush of power traveled from it, through him, to the Torch. He shuddered. "I can feel their connection, to be sure, but I don't think it's dangerous."

Nodora rubbed her arms. "Would it be all right to put the Torch away now?"

Lio nodded and secured it once more within the container Kassandra had crafted for it. Cassia sat down with the Dexion's box before her, and everyone huddled around.

She lifted the lid. Lio peered inside.

"Papers!" she exclaimed with satisfaction.

"Perfect," Lio said.

"Not an artifact?" Mak shook his head.

"Better, Cousin. I promise." Lio reached for the first sheet on top. "No telling what we can find in his documents that we can use against him."

Kia held a hand out. "If we all start reading now, we may find a way to free the hostages by moon hours."

Lio and Cassia passed the papers around. Silence fell between them all, punctuated only by Lio's murmurs as he read sections aloud to Cassia.

Cassia was the first to say it. "They aren't just documents. They're his letters."

"His *private* letters," Mak said in disgust. "To a woman."

"Look here." Lyros pointed to a section of the letter he held. "Not just any woman."

Lio nodded. "His brother's widow, the mother of his nephew."

Xandra tossed down the note she had just gone through. "This is it? He hauled this all the way from Cordium…for what?"

"Love," Cassia said.

She reached into the bottom of the box and pulled out the last of the papers. One by one, she laid them out on the coffee table. One drawing after another, the simple, colorful works of a child.

Lio looked over Cassia's shoulder at the artwork. "I can't use this against any man, not even the Dexion."

Cassia studied a blobby green shape that might be a dog. "I think he actually loves his nephew."

Lio rubbed his face. "Chrysanthos carried his nephew's drawings all the way to Orthros with him, along with all the detailed letters the boy's mother writes describing their daily lives. If that isn't love, I don't know what is."

"Chrysanthos, whom I believed heartless." Cassia shook her head.

Kia stacked a series of papers on the table. "These are inventories and budgets. Based on these figures, Chrysanthos is running a modest estate for them. He's thought of everything. A spending allowance, salaries for servants, an ample larder, women's and children's clothes, even toys and primers for the boy."

"This is one of his unfinished replies." Nodora held up an already lengthy letter. "He devotes an entire page to persuading her not to hesitate to summon a healer, and he includes a reference to one of his colleagues in the Order of Akesios."

Lio stared at the pile of evidence before him. "Whatever else Chrysanthos is, I have to acknowledge he takes good care of the women and children in his life."

"As long as they aren't the wrong kind of women or the children of heretics." Cassia looked away, then frowned at one of the woman's letters. "Read this part to me again."

Lio picked it up. "'Since the day your brother first made it known to me I was his choice and elevated me to the most fortunate woman in the world, I have remained ever sensible of the great distinction conferred upon me, but so too of the great responsibility. Consider me the cherisher of your brother's secrets, for who would hold them closer than she who carried his dearest one?'"

"His dearest one..." Cassia murmured.

"His child," Lio said.

"Or his dearest one, as in his dearest secret?" Cassia looked around at everyone. "Does she say anywhere in these letters that she was actually his brother's wife? Does the word 'widow' appear once?"

Everyone returned to their respective piles, looking again at what they had read.

"I don't believe so," Lio said at last.

Their friends shook their heads in agreement.

Cassia sat back on their bench, as if wishing for greater distance between her and the letters. "I knew there was something familiar about the way she talks around it...her bold requests disguised in self-deprecating persuasion... I should have acknowledged it sooner. It's just...a surprise."

"Do you mean she was his brother's..." Lio trailed off.

Cassia nodded. "These are the letters of a powerful man's concubine, fearful for her child's future. If she were his widow, their child wouldn't be a secret, and as the mother of a Cordian prince's son and heir, she would never want for anything."

"We trust your insight on the matter, Cassia," said Kia.

"Certainly," Lio said. "What do you make of it? Why would it concern a powerful man for anyone to know he has a child outside of marriage?"

"It is hardly a scandal, to be sure," Cassia answered. "It is a matter of course that a man in the brother's position would keep a concubine, and accidental children do happen. However, the child is a boy. Bastard sons have a way of turning up later and causing inheritance trouble. The brother was probably trying to spare his dynasty the worry, or spare his bastard son a knife in the back."

Lio shuddered. "I hate that you ever lived in that world."

"It's still hard to believe I don't anymore," Cassia said.

"Look at this." Lyros held up a note in one hand and in the other, a gaudy gold ring covered in sapphires and engraved with peacock feathers.

Mak took the note from him. "'From your loving mother, Her Serene Highness Princess Piles-of-Names-and-Titles, on the occasion of your ascension to the office of Dexion.'"

Lyros studied the detailed lettering on the ring. "It bears his mage name, office, circle, and order, but also his birth name. The jeweler must have cried trying to fit all this on here."

"What is his birth name, then?" Cassia asked.

"Florian Pavonis, it looks like," Lyros answered.

Cassia let out a low whistle. Knight lifted his head from his paws where he lay on her feet.

She stroked the top of his head. "I'm hardly an expert on the intricacies of power in the Cordian principalities, but anyone with an ear to politics hears about the Pavones. They are one of the two greatest dynasties of Corona and the bitter rivals of the other, the Tauri."

Lio nodded. "Uncle Argyros gave me lessons in what we know about the Pavones and Tauri."

"You think Hadria and Segetia have a feud?" Cassia shook her head. "From what I hear, more than one Pavo has paid with his life for looking wrong at a Taurus."

Mak frowned at the letters. "So Chrysanthos may be all that stands between this child and assassination by a jealous Pavo or a feuding Taurus."

"I could come up with all kinds of explanations for why Chrysanthos might find the woman and child useful for his own gain." Cassia hesitated.

"But you don't really believe them," Lio said.

"No," Cassia replied. "A man who wants to use his brother's bastard in a contest for power does not cherish the baby's nonsense drawings in a box so covered in spells, it took the Akron's Torch to open it."

"'I miss the boy every moment,'" Lio read. "'Tell him I keep his drawings with me always. I count the days until I can see him again and in him, glimpse my brother for one moment more.'"

"Goddess," Xandra said. "I actually feel sorry for the Dexion."

"So do I." Cassia sucked in a breath. "That man, who called me the worst kind of woman. He *does* have a heart in his chest. He's taking care of his dead brother's concubine and her orphan…"

She didn't finish, but Lio knew what she was thinking. The king had been far crueler to his own concubine and child. A loving sibling had been all that stood between her and death. Lio put an arm around Cassia.

"It sounds like his brother is sorely missed." Mak read, "'Our father carries on with fortitude, but I see the toll my brother's death has taken on him. Pray for our father. His position does not permit pain or allow time for mourning.'"

"By the sound of the woman's letters," Lio added, "she and the brother were devoted to one another."

Cassia pursed her lips. "She would certainly say so to secure Chrysanthos's favor."

"But you don't really believe that, either," Lio said.

"No." Cassia sighed. "Do you notice they never mention any names? They are clearly taking care, in case their correspondence is intercepted. They're protecting his brother's memory and each other, and especially the child."

"Another woman like all those in the history scrolls who are never named." Kia shook her head.

Lio studied the woman's handwriting. "At least we have these letters, through which she may speak for herself."

Another moment of silence fell.

"I think we should leave these off the Summit record," Lio said.

Mak sighed, then nodded. Lyros took his hand.

"Certainly we should," Nodora agreed.

Xandra and Kia slid their piles of correspondence across the table to Lio.

He looked at Cassia, who was silent. "I cannot in good conscience use a woman and child to manipulate or threaten him. I know you can't, either."

"No," she said firmly. "There was a time when I would have, but that was another life. I won't see a woman like my mother and a child like me become tokens in a political game, not even our own."

FESTIVAL OF THE
GIFT

1 Night After Winter Solstice

TRIAL BY COMBAT

FROM BEHIND HIS VEIL, Lio assessed the New Guest House with all his senses, careful not to alert any of the resident mages that the ambassador was paying them a visit. "Have the Cordians stirred at all within the wards?"

Lyros smirked, leaning in the doorway of the gallery. "Skleros, Chrysanthos, and Tychon haven't twitched an eyebrow."

"Wise choice." Cassia gazed at the door of the common room with the eye of a field commander preparing for a siege.

"I'm disappointed." Mak bared his fangs. "I hope they give us an excuse."

"Grace-Mother is in the corridor," said Lyros, "to ensure we behave ourselves. She's maintaining individual wards around each of the mages. They are not permitted contact with one another."

Mak's lip curled. "What an adjustment for the Flower of Cordium to do without his shoe-shiner. Do you suppose he knows how to put on his clothes without Tychon to serve him?"

"He knows how to clothe his nephew," Lyros reminded his Grace.

Mak gritted his teeth.

"What about Eudias?" Cassia asked.

Mak huffed. "He's the only twitchy one."

Lyros nodded, his brow furrowed. "One moment he's pacing and fidgeting all about his room, the next he's listless in bed as if he's ill."

Cassia frowned. "I hope he's all right. As glad as I am to be relieved of his constant presence, I am sorry for his situation."

"As am I," Lio agreed. "Although we must include him in his masters' house arrest, he has done nothing to deserve it."

"Except be a war mage," Mak said.

"He didn't have a choice about that," Cassia pointed out.

Lio shook his head. "Anthros excels at violating the Will of everyone, including his own worshipers."

Lyros sighed. "Unfortunately, that makes it necessary for the Stand to restrict Eudias as well."

"Mother's orders," said Mak, "and that's that."

"Kadi is on border patrol again," Lyros informed them. "Tonight and tomorrow, Grace-Mother has tasked Mak and me with the lords. We are ready for anything. Nothing will interfere with your shadow summit."

"How glad I am we are facing the end of this Summit together," Cassia said. "I think we're ready."

"Our first negotiation at Rose House awaits." Lio offered her his arm.

She accepted, standing an intimate, but discreet distance from him. "Thank you for doing this."

"It is a wise political move. It is also my pleasure."

"I wish we could offer you some advice," said Lyros, "but we have no experience asking for a mortal family's blessing."

"Lyros couldn't help you anyway," Mak added, "for he never had to ask. I thought Father was going to beg him to braid me up."

"Grace-Father thinks my 'considered approach to life' is a 'moderating influence' on Mak." Lyros flashed a very immoderate grin.

"Good luck," Mak wished them.

As Lio and Cassia proceeded into the gallery, his cousin clapped him on the shoulder.

"Goddess bless," Lio heard his Trial brothers say behind them.

"I think the celebration for your parents this moon went well," Cassia mused, "even though you and I didn't get any sleep between yours and theirs."

"I have to say," Lio replied, "I've seldom seen Zoe so excited."

"She explained the Festival of the Gift to me three times while we were getting everything ready. She could hardly wait to give your parents a present to thank them for making her a Hesperine."

"She's thrilled you were there to help."

"I wouldn't have missed the installation of their goat window for the world. But it still bothers me that I—"

Lio shook his head, smiling at her. "Don't say you didn't bring a gift."

He realized they were in the courtyard of Rose House, and Cassia had made him forget his apprehensions for a moment. Cup and thorns, he loved his Grace.

"Do you have any final words of counsel?" he asked.

She glanced at her hound, who stood at attention beside them. "Knight approves. The hardest battle is behind you."

"Alas, I cannot convince your human guardians of my good intentions with treats."

"You are one of Orthros's foremost experts on Tenebran custom. No one is more qualified for this than you."

He rubbed his mouth. "I fear these leave me hopelessly disqualified."

"Nonsense. All my other suitors lacked an essential feature. Fangs. I insist on fangs." She gave him a quick kiss on the mouth before she turned to her curtained door.

Lio smiled, but he could sense his challengers waiting within. Cassia opened the door and pushed the curtain back, and he escorted her into her quarters on his arm.

Perita halted in the act of tidying the already spotless room. She froze, staring at them. The color was gone from her face. She cast one glance at Knight, and disbelief flashed in her aura. It pained Lio to listen to the way her heart raced.

In the awkward silence, he heard it. The other heartbeat in the room, soft and quiet but strong, beating within Perita.

Lio tried not to smile or stare, lest he alarm her further. He stood there and listened, trying to grasp it. She had two hearts. She was carrying a little body inside of hers, crafting it like a spell without even trying.

He bowed deeply to her.

"Perita," Cassia said, "I'd like you to meet Lio."

"Ambassador." Perita's fear did not make her voice waver. She swept a deep curtsy.

"It is an honor," he told her.

As if the sound of Lio's voice were an alarm, Callen burst through the door. He charged in front of his wife, sweeping her behind him.

"Callen, at ease," Cassia said. "There is no danger."

His hand clenched on the handle of his scythe. He gaped at Cassia arm in arm with Lio and at her vicious liegehound unconcerned in the company of a Hesperine.

Lio held up his hands. "You are safe with me. First, because I am a Hesperine called to cause no suffering. Second, because I am a diplomat and have devoted my life to peace. Most importantly, because you are under Cassia's protection, and she is under mine. None of her own will come to harm while my heart beats."

Callen relaxed his grip, but did not budge from in front of Perita. "My lady is still under my protection. My wife assures me there is no foul magic at work here, but do not think I have surrendered my watch."

This was what courage smelled like—like honor coated in fear coated in bravery. Lio wished he could convince Callen how much he admired him. "I am here to thank you for your roles in stopping Dalos. I owe you and Perita my life, as does every member of the Hesperine embassy. On behalf of Orthros, allow me to tell you that you have our deepest gratitude. We shall not fail to honor what you have done for us."

Perita stepped out from behind Callen, and he let her, although he put an arm around her shoulders and held her close to him.

"I'd like to ask a boon," said Perita. "Will you honor how we helped you by granting a request?"

Cassia's aura brightened with hopeful surprise. But Callen's face darkened, and he gave Lio no time to reply.

"With all due respect," Callen all but growled, "I'll not allow my wife to accept anything from Hesperines."

Perita faced him. "I'm not going to accept it. You are. You're going to let me honor what you did for me."

He shook his head. "You're everything to me, Pet. I'd give up far more to take care of you."

"I know. But what kind of wife would I be if I didn't take care of you right back?" Perita turned to Lio. "I would ask that your healers see to my husband's leg."

Callen stiffened beside her.

"I can say without hesitation," Lio answered, "our healers would spare no effort in reversing the effects of your husband's injury."

"Now see here—" Callen protested.

Perita persisted, "Do you know how much they might be able to do for him? Can your Queen really do for a mortal what we saw her do for that Hesperine? Answer me honest."

Lio nodded. "Mine is not the most qualified opinion. However, I can tell you that Queen Soteira has treated Imperial soldiers with limbs so damaged that mortal healers' only recourse would be amputation."

Callen took a step back.

Lio met his gaze. "Every one of those soldiers has returned to march in the Imperial army."

Perita clutched her husband's hand. For the first time, the hostile armor in his aura cracked, and Lio caught a hint of longing.

Cassia went to her bodyguard. "Before we left Tenebra, I secured Lord Hadrian's promise that you and Perita will always have a place in his service, come what may. You know how well he keeps his oaths to his people. But think how much better he could keep it if you accept Perita's gift to you."

Perita looked up at her husband, her eyes pleading, her chin stubborn. Callen was indeed fortunate in love, and Lio suspected the man knew it better than anyone.

"I'm grateful to you, my lady, and to his lordship." Callen hesitated.

"I know you," said Perita. "You'll not live on his charity thanks to some empty position he invents to keep you in his pay. You'll not accept anything less than real work."

"Lord Hadrian will need you," Cassia urged. "You are too good a man and too fine a warrior to waste. Will you deprive him of your sword on the field?"

Lio weighed in. "It is perhaps pretentious of me to comment on the business of warriors, but there is one thing I can say without doubt. You are a man who protects women at any cost. I have the utmost respect for how you have guarded Cassia, and I can see how fortunate your wife is in her husband. It is also my understanding that your mother is a widow, and you the only son among several daughters."

He had Callen's attention now, although the stoic warrior gave Lio no clue whether he was making progress.

"I take that to heart," Lio said, "as the eldest and only son of my family. I think my sister is the same age as your youngest. My thoughts are troubled by keeping her safe from the threat of Cordium's rising aggression. What an astonishing time, when the same threat hangs over your own family as over mine."

"Aye," Callen said at last. "I never thought a Hesperine and I would find ourselves on the same side of the battlefield."

Lio stepped nearer. "I will gladly do anything I can to help you care for your family through the coming trouble. It is the least I can do, when you have so faithfully protected mine."

Lio rested his hand on Cassia's arm just above the elbow. It felt uncomfortable to make a Tenebran male gesture of claim, but Lio reminded himself what it meant between them. He was just touching Cassia's freckled elbow.

"You drive a hard bargain," said Callen. "It may not be my place to arrange my lady's future, but her father isn't here. So I'll say it's not his place, either, and he showed that by bartering her off to Segetia." The way he said the name, the king might have betrothed Cassia to Hedon's privy-sweeper. "In Lord Hadrian's absence, it falls to me to make sure she's treated as she ought to be."

Lio bowed again. "That is precisely why I have come tonight to petition you for her hand."

Callen drew himself up. Perita exchanged glances with Cassia.

Of course, Cassia had already decided where her hand and the rest of her would remain for eternity. She and Lio had agreed, however, that it would strengthen their political position if they secured Callen and Perita's support.

They had also admitted to each other it mattered to have her friends' blessing. The spirit of it would not get lost in translation between Tenebran and Hesperine custom.

Cassia gestured toward the sitting room. "Why don't we all take a seat and discuss this together?"

They went into the next room, and Lio seated Cassia on a couch. Callen showed Perita to a chair as if he expected spikes were hiding in the silk padding. Then Lio sat down beside Cassia at a respectful distance. Callen stood at attention beside his wife.

Lio embarked on the speech he and Cassia had rehearsed together. "The first matter of concern is, I believe, a betrothal promise recently finalized under Tenebran law. Although that agreement has no legality in Orthros, I want you to be satisfied Cassia and I shall not live in violation of sacred oaths."

"Well, if there isn't a way to break that promise after all," said Callen. "If tiptoeing over a border is enough to bring Segetia's claim on her to naught, I am satisfied as to that."

"I am happy to free your lady from such an unworthy match. I know, however, it will be difficult for me to demonstrate my worthiness. Ask me anything you will, and I will strive to reassure you. She will want for nothing. I will never betray her by so much as looking upon another. I will do everything in my power to keep her safe and happy."

Callen crossed his arms over his chest. "You're a diplomat, quick with words. At the risk of offending my lady, I'll speak the plain truth. You're also a heretic and a sorcerer. It's not our way in Tenebra to take such a character's word for anything."

"How would you have me prove my intentions to you? Only name it."

"I ask no more and no less of you than of myself. You must be willing to die for her. There is only one proper bride price for any woman, and that is her husband's life."

Lio met Callen's gaze and looked into the unflinching eye of judgment. "In this, our creed is the same. My life is already hers. I live for her, and I would die for her. Let my deeds speak for me."

Callen's answer was a single nod. "Aye, and so they do."

Cassia let out the breath she'd been holding, so quietly only Lio could hear.

"Thank you, Callen," Lio said. "From a man of your deeds, that means a great deal to me."

Callen looked on, grave, but without censure. "You'd little enough reason to face off with a war mage for the sake of Tenebra's Council. You could have fled the Equinox Summit to save your own hide, like mages say slippery Hesperines always do. But you stayed. That's more than many men would have done. While I was flat on my back, you saved my lady's life, and from a foe who would have laughed at my sword. The oldest law is trial by combat, older than your ways or mine. By that ancient test, you have proved yourself worthy and won her hand in all fairness."

"No man has ever honored me with such words. I take your judgment to heart. I will not disappoint you."

"Thank you," Cassia told Callen. "This means so much to both of us." She turned to Perita.

"You know you already have my blessing." Perita eyed Lio. "My lady has high standards, and she says you've met them. She's the frostiest in the kingdom. I suppose it would take a Hesperine to get through the ice."

Cassia laughed and rose to her feet. Lio followed suit, watching her go to her friend. She and Perita held each other for a moment. It was that gesture of love that dimmed Lio's mood for the first time. He hated that he must part Cassia from the few people she cared about. She could look forward to countless friends here, but none were a substitute for the first and dearest one she had won for herself.

"I want to thank you both," Lio said, "for everything you have done for Cassia. Know that I and my bloodline consider ourselves bound to you in gratitude. If there is anything we can do for you, you have but to ask."

Perita pulled back, taking her husband's arm again. "Imagine having one of Orthros's oldest families in debt to us. Are we so well off that we can afford to scorn such an advantage? We may have Lady Valentia's purse, but no amount of gold can buy your health. Even an Akesian healer from Cordium can't do what Hesperines can."

"You've shown great respect for our traditions in this, for my lady's sake." Callen looked at Perita. "For my wife, I'll try to find it in myself to endure the touch of magic, even if it is Hesperine. I ask only that the Semna take part in the healing. Maybe that'll save my chances at Anthros's Hall. With two good knees, I can kneel in the Sun Temple for the rest of my life praying for forgiveness."

Tears glittered in Perita's eyes. "All the gods be praised!"

Her aura was so felicitous, Lio fancied she might really mean all the gods, Hespera included. But just in case, he offered up his own silent prayer of thanks.

"You'll need two good knees," Cassia predicted, "to keep up with a child of your union."

Lio folded his hands behind his back, if only to emphasize he was not one to snatch pregnant women to foster Hespera's dark brood. "Would you accept a Hesperine's congratulations on the forthcoming addition to your family?"

"No, sir," Perita replied. "But we'll accept congratulations from my lady's intended."

"You have them, from my heart."

"Now then," said Perita, "you know a lady can't join her new family till the knot's tied."

Callen nodded. "My lady must remain with us in her own household until the embassy is over. There can be no negotiation on this matter."

"I know her work here is not done," Lio answered.

Cassia looked from Callen to Perita. "Will you help Lio and me wrest this embassy from Cordium's hands?"

WHEN BRAVERY CALLS

ASSIA COULD NOT HAVE asked for a better force for her final confrontation with Tenebra. She entered the New Guest House from the courtyard with Callen and Perita at her back and Knight at her side. She was glad they were together now, here at the end of the journey they had begun together in the king's prison.

At the sight of her and her retinue, the lords assembled in the common room fell silent. Benedict, Lord Severin, and a few others got to their feet.

Cassia held the list of terms they had worked on together and looked at the sparse, subdued gathering in challenge. Most looked away, while others continued to gnaw on their provisions in stubborn silence.

Benedict came to her side. "Your Ladyship. Your handmaiden has given us the direst tidings of your health these past few nights. How glad we are to see you are improved."

"I am perfectly well, after discovering that the cause of my malady was my conscience and heeding it the cure. Judging by the ill looks in this room, we could all do with a dose of the same tonic."

"Who better to administer it than the ladies of our company?" Lord Gaius came in through the opposite doorway.

The Semna entered on his arm, and the younger Kyrians and Cherans were close behind. The Semna shuffled to her seat and let Lord Gaius lower her into the chair. The toll this journey had taken on her was clear, not least in her attendants' diligent hovering, but she leaned on her walking stick with great dignity. The Cherans sat down with the Kyrians in a silent but undeniable statement of alliance.

"How glad I was to sense you coming, my dear," the Semna said to

Cassia. "Perhaps these cocks will heed our thrush's singing, although they turn a deaf ear to the biddy who hatched them."

Benedict bowed. "Forgive us, Semna, but I fear there is nothing more we can do. I would gladly rise to the occasion, were it possible."

Lord Gaius shook his head. "It is a sad day when defeat puts Hadria and Segetia on the same side. All our ancestors are rolling over in their graves while we sit swordless and watch the mages set fire to the Free Charter."

"They've yet to burn what Lady Cassia carries in her hands," the Semna said. "She does not appear to have surrendered."

"How can I," Cassia answered, "when Cordium jeopardizes everything Tenebra has worked for? How can I let the Orders decide our kingdom's fate? My lords, it is neither Hadrian nor Segetian to accept defeat—indeed, it is not Tenebran. I do not believe triumph is out of reach. With the Cordian mages under house arrest, there is no one to stop us from pressing forward with the Solstice Summit. We, not they, are the rightful negotiators in Tenebra's dealings with Orthros, and I fully intend to present our terms in the hopes of reaching a truce. We have no excuse to sit idle when we could storm the gates."

Lord Adrogan used an embroidered Hesperine handkerchief to pry a bit of dessicated Tenebran jerky from between his teeth. He cast the silk and gristle onto his plate. "You shall find no army here to take the moral high ground, 'Your Ladyship.' What use are trade agreements with Hesperines, when Cordium will confiscate any wealth gained from treating with heretics?"

One of his rivals agreed with him. "Aye, what use is wealth if the inquisitors send you to Anthros's pyre? You can't take coin with you to Hypnos's realm."

Lord Severin shook his head. "What good if Hesperine aid ensures a good harvest, only for the forces of Cordium to trample the fields?"

The Semna folded her hands over the top of her walking stick. "I took a vow to practice my goddess's mercy. Compassion is the only way to save anyone from the pyre. The gods have never before given us a chance like this to bring light into the darkness of Orthros, and it would grieve me to see it ruined."

"I pray only that I can be free to serve," said Pakhne. "We make our vows to the gods, and yet men would keep us from being fully obedient to the divine. If the Orders gain greater sway in Tenebra, we will meet the same fate as our Cordian sisters."

Ariadne nodded. "Their every prayer must pass before the scribes of Anthros to receive the Order's seal!"

"Thank you for your support," Cassia said to the mages. "This is indeed a sad day. Every feuding lord in Tenebra rallies around a white flag. Meanwhile your women are braver than you. As Anthros holds the power of a husband over his wife, his order holds the power of life and death over Kyria's. As Anthros cast Chera's husband Demergos from the pantheon, so too can his order give her handmaidens cause to mourn. And yet these mages are ready to risk everything to keep their sacred vows and pursue peace. What will you risk?"

Lord Severin stiffened where he stood. "A great many lives depend on us. We must not bring Cordium's ire down upon our people."

"Enough with your noble excuses," Lord Adrogan retorted. "You can feel the heat of war magic on your own skin already, and it's enough to make any man piss his breeches."

"Watch your tongue," Benedict cut in. "There are ladies present."

"And that's more than enough from you," Lord Adrogan shot back. "Stop hiding behind that amulet. You're just as much a coward as the rest of us."

Benedict took a step toward Lord Adrogan. "Had I my sword in hand, I'd not let such an insult go unchallenged. If we live to see Tenebra again, don't think I'll forget your words."

"If it's the truth, it isn't an insult. I don't see you hurrying to risk your hide for Her Ladyship's hopeless campaign."

"Enough!"

Cassia's tone silenced every man in the room and fetched their gazes to her.

"For shame!" she cried. "The warriors of Tenebra bicker like children while the fate of the kingdom is in their hands. And yet I know you are not cowards. You proved that when you willingly set foot in Orthros. Prove it again! Treat with the Hesperines in spite of Dexion Chrysanthos! And when Cordium retaliates? Prove it again! Stand fast and do not allow them to set foot upon your fields. When you feel the heat of Cordian magefire, rely on the strength of our Tenebran mages' wards."

"What is this disturbance?" came a voice from the doorway. Master Gorgos marched in.

Cassia turned upon him. "Will you let the likes of Dexion Chrysanthos march through *your* temple? Will you tolerate his insults to the ancient skills of Tenebra's mages? Will you, who sets the example of Tenebran discipline and virtue, let that perfumed drunkard from Corona lead Anthros's obedient astray?"

The mage hesitated. "I cannot see how treating with heretics will win our god's favor."

"I am but a woman. Far be it from me to take it upon myself to speak for Anthros. I can only repeat the teachings I have received in his temple since I was but a tiny child. Cowardice is not pleasing to the god of war. He demands that we face any foe and defend the godly from the godsforsaken. When our bravery calls us to face the Hesperines, is not peace a mighty sword?"

She could see it in the mage's eyes. By throwing his own principles back at him, she had stirred him. All around her, she could feel the men's strings at her fingertips, and she knew how best to pull them.

But she must pull carefully. If they felt the tug from a woman and a bastard, they would tear away.

"What will you risk?" Lord Adrogan sneered. "You'll go home to Tenebra to sit in the weaving room where the king puts you. You'll go on wearing your fine gowns, which men of noble birth cannot afford for their wives. You'll pamper your purebred liegehound with better meat than Severin's peasants will ever see in their lives."

Cassia's fury came to her hand, its edge sharp and ready, and she turned it upon Lord Adrogan with a precise stroke. "If you would like to see the price I risk paying, visit my sister's crypt when next you are in Tenebra."

The room fell silent.

"Do you wonder why I have never set foot there?" she asked. "Because the king forbade me. He denies me the most basic opportunity to honor the memory of my sister, who was the only mother I ever had. Our princess, who nurtured us, her people."

"Kyria bless her," murmured the Semna.

"And Anthros laud her in his Hall," said Lord Gaius.

No one asked Cassia why the king banned her from her sister's sacred place of burial. They must all believe it was because of her shameful birth.

"You might well ask why I am here, such as I am," Cassia said to them all. "As the Dexion has done, you might demand to know what I have to gain from the Summit. I could give you the same answer I gave him. I want only the best for Tenebra. That is true. But men of the world such as yourselves will be just as unsatisfied as the Dexion if I wax poetic about the common good.

"So I will give you another answer, which is even truer, a reality no man here can deny. I owe my sister my life. She persuaded my father not to expose me, his castoff out of his concubine. For seven years, she treated her bastard half-sister as tenderly as her own child. Even the most hardened among you understand life debts. You know one season of brave deeds in her memory is worth more than a lifetime of kneeling in a crypt."

"No man here can deny she would be proud of you," Lord Gaius said.

"Thank you, my lord. I take Hadria's testimony on this matter to heart."

"But she would be ashamed of the rest of us," said Benedict.

All the eyes in the room went to him. Standing beside him, Cassia could see the tide of censure rising around him. How well she knew it.

He faced down their stares. "Princess Solia was worthy of the throne. A fine future awaited all of us under her reign. She cared for the common folk and respected the rights of the lords. And see how those very lords repaid her. They squandered her. They bickered for her hand and coveted a place at her side until they destroyed her. My father gave the order, but who among us has no blood on his hands?"

Lord Adrogan let out a huff. "Yes, yes, the sad story of our sweet little princess. She's just bones now, in case you hadn't noticed. What does she have to do with this Summit?"

At the sound of Lord Gaius's footfall behind his chair, Lord Adrogan jumped. Lord Gaius grasped Lord Adrogan's arm and hauled him out of the chair with such force that the young lord let out a howl.

The old warrior spun Lord Adrogan to face him. "The moment we set foot over the border, have your sword ready. I shall not allow Sir Benedict the first crack at you. I will give you a lesson in respect."

Lord Adrogan's only reply was a wheeze.

"If you sit again while Lady Cassia is still on her feet, I will help you stand once more." Lord Gaius twisted the young man's arm one more time for emphasis, then released Lord Adrogan and turned his back.

The young lord stumbled and caught himself on his chair with one hand, his face ashen, his other arm hanging from his shoulder at an unnatural angle.

The Semna clucked her tongue. "I'd best put a slow healing spell on that, my boy. I do hope everyone will be more careful after this."

Lord Gaius bowed to the Semna, then turned to Cassia. "Our princess's memory has everything to do with this Summit, it is clear."

"If we want the future she would have given us," said Cassia, "we must make it. You do not need me to tell you the king will not make it for us."

No one protested that she had just spoken treason.

Lord Gaius wore a hard smile. "The king is not here to make anything."

Benedict thumped a fist to his chest and saluted the paper in Cassia's hands. "Let my deeds be the first to honor Her Highness. I will stand with you in support of peace."

He had come through for her. "Thank you, Benedict. Tenebra is fortunate to have you on her side."

"I will not let Tenebra's traditions die with our princess. I will not fail to defend her people's safety—even from their own king. I am not a free lord with a duty to the Council. I am a knight, and my sword is bound by my honor. By Andragathos, if the lords of Tenebra are to invoke the Free Charter tonight, I will be their conscience and see to it we challenge royal authority for the common good."

"For the common good," said Lord Gaius, "I will stand with you, Sir Benedict."

"Thank you, my lord," Cassia told him. "Hadria's support brings great strength and honor to our cause."

Lord Adrogan found his voice, although pain twisted his face. "It takes more than one knight and one lord to swear the Oath. Neither of you are even free lords."

Lord Gaius shot him a warning glance. "It is true we have neither Charter rights nor seats on the Council, but our liege lords do. We are fully empowered to act on behalf of Free Lord Hadrian and Free Lord Titus here in Orthros, thus we are within our rights to invoke the Charter in their names tonight."

Lord Severin looked pale. "As my father's heir and representative in this embassy, I also can invoke his Charter rights, but if I do so in the name of peace with Hesperines, I may not be his heir much longer. I must be sure this is best for my people, before I risk my position as their last line of defense against their liege."

"We mustn't do anything rash," agreed Lord Adrogan's rival with sweat on his brow. "There's a fine line between invoking the Charter and committing treason."

It was time. Cassia must tell them now. "Let the truth free you from your fears of committing treason. I have here a witness who will testify before the gods that the king has betrayed us and is no longer worthy of our loyalty. He has violated his responsibilities toward us, thus we are no longer bound by our oaths of fealty."

At that, the gathering rumbled with surprise and unrest.

"All the worst rumors about the Equinox Summit are true," Cassia told them. "Callen, will you tell us what you learned of Dalos when you were in prison?"

Callen stepped forward. "Aye, my lady. I will testify before the gods that the king conspired with the mage Dalos and his Order to assassinate not only the Hesperine embassy, but also the Council of Free Lords."

The other men leapt to their feet. Fists pounded the table, and outcries went up.

Callen faced them with the same matter-of-fact dignity he had shown to Cassia the first day they had met. As he had for her then, he now bore witness before the lords that he had seen Dalos use his war magic upon the king's prisoners. But this time, he worked into his tale all the details of the conspiracy that Cassia had later discovered. He hadn't asked Cassia how she had learned the rest, and he had agreed the lords didn't need to know either.

The end of his testimony was nearly lost in the embassy's uproar.

Cassia spoke over the lords. "Some of you were sitting at the Summit table when Dalos unleashed his spell. Every man here had a father, brother, or liege lord under that pavilion. The king has already given Cordium leave to destroy our nobility and lay waste to Tenebra."

THE APPLICATION OF REASON

Lio stood with Mak outside Eudias's rooms. "Of all times for Eudias to request an audience with Cassia."

"Mother won't approve it, of course, but she wants you to have a word with him."

"I told Cassia I would watch her back while she confronts the lords."

Mak clapped him on the shoulder. "She'll be fine for a few minutes. Lyros will keep guarding her and the embassy while you and I find out what Eudias wants. This is a task for a diplomat, and your insight as a mind mage could help us learn the apprentice's real intentions. Mother will keep her full attention on the other mages in case Eudias is trying to create a diversion."

Lio could sense Aunt Lyta a couple of corridors over, her aura powerful at the heart of her wards around Chrysanthos, Tychon, and Skleros's lodgings. "I wonder if asking to see Cassia was what Eudias was deliberating over when he seemed so ill."

"It does appear he came to some kind of decision. Since he approached Mother about his request, he has been uncharacteristically calm. Almost confident."

What would make the poor mouse confident? Hope of earning his masters' favor? Or finding the courage to defy them for the first time? "I may be very foolish to want to believe better of him, but I cannot help hoping he will not do anything that will make him our enemy. I even dare believe his request could somehow prove advantageous for us."

"I can't forget that when Dalos tried to murder all of you at the Equinox Summit, Eudias was his channel."

"Eudias's late master used him."

"You go ahead and give him the benefit of the doubt. I'll think ill of him for you, and between the two of us, we'll find the truth." Mak rapped his knuckles on the door, which hummed with his wards. "Apprentice Eudias, Ambassador Deukalion would like a word with you about your request." After so warning the mage, Mak opened the door and brought Lio inside.

Mak was right about the apprentice's unusual confidence. Eudias waited with his hands in his sleeves, not even fidgeting. He would not meet Lio's eyes, but he stood up straight. No longer slouching, he proved himself to be as tall as Tychon.

Eudias's tidily arranged possessions looked surprisingly familiar to Lio. An admirable collection of scrolls and writing supplies were organized on the desk, one spare robe hung upon the stand by the dressing screen, and a rarely touched shaving kit occupied the wash stand next to a basic but well-used bar of soap.

"Apprentice Eudias," Lio greeted him, "it is my understanding you have requested to speak with Lady Cassia."

"Yes, Ambassador." He was soft spoken as always, but did not stammer. "It is imperative that I be allowed to speak to Basilis."

"Under the terms of your house arrest," Mak reminded him, "you are not permitted contact with any of your fellow Cordians or the Tenebrans. The Guardian of Orthros will not approve your request unless the ambassador deems it of importance to the Summit."

Eudias gave a deep nod. "I will meet with Basilis wherever and with whatever escort the Stand requires. Ambassador, what must I do to earn your permission?"

Lio opened his mind to Eudias's, although he made no intrusion into the young man's thoughts. "May I ask why you wish to speak with her?"

"With all due respect, Ambassador, this is not a matter of diplomacy with Orthros." Eudias's thoughts and tone were equally courteous. "It is a conversation between two members of the mortal embassy to your lands."

"I am afraid I must remind you that it is the Tenebran embassy. Unfortunately, under the present circumstances, any discussion that occurs between Tenebra and Cordium here is indeed the affair of Orthros's diplomats."

"I understand. I make no objection to you being present for the encounter. I only ask that I be allowed to speak with her."

"Perhaps if you explain your reasons for this request, we can come to an arrangement. What is it you wish to discuss with Lady Cassia?"

A sense of conviction stirred in Eudias's aura. "You say 'Cordium' as if it is the name of a single entity, but Cordium is not one mind, and that mind is not the Akron's."

"I beg your pardon," Lio said, to encourage Eudias to continue.

"Did you know that war magic is the least common affinity among the mages of Anthros? The vast majority of our Order are warders, geomancers...weather mages. The Aithourian Circle is small enough for me to know each of them by name. Yet they wield a disproportionate amount of power over all the ranks of our cult and, indeed, the world. The Akron is an administrator who always rises to power from among mages who rarely set foot outside the temples of Corona. It is the Synthikos who drives policy within the Order, although his priorities are even more distant from the concerns of most worshipers of Anthros."

"I am sincere when I say that I appreciate your insight into the inner workings of your Order. It was never my intention for this Summit to be a one-sided exchange, and I value the opportunity to learn from you, as we have tried to demystify our own people in your eyes."

"Yet you must be wondering what this has to do with my request."

"I think if I wish to find answers to my questions, it behooves me to listen."

"Thank you." Eudias hesitated. "Critical analysis is a time-honored philosophical pursuit in my Order, although the application of reason to magic and magical institutions is much more dangerous now than it was in the past. I am not afraid to speak of facts with you, however."

Lio spread his hands. "As a heretic, I am not one to report you to the inquisitors. Dare I hope you are convinced of my people's love for the free investigation of ideas?"

"Sophia Eudokia's time with me in your libraries has given me great food for thought, as did Princess Alexandra's demonstration and my conversations about magic with Muse Menodora. I hope I have also convinced you of my priorities as a mage."

"It is clear to me you are a dedicated and well-read scholar with a keen awareness of your Order's history."

"Magic is the pursuit of truth, not ambition. Not all of us are like the Dexion. That is what I wish to say to Basilis."

"I see. It would not satisfy you for us to carry a message to her?"

Mak nodded. "A message, at most, is what the Stand can allow."

Eudias shook his head. "This must be said in person." He hesitated again. "I was sent here with two tasks. To serve the interests of my Order and to protect Basilis from magical dangers. Those two imperatives have proved to be opposing ones. I wish to offer my regrets to her that the magical dangers my masters pose have imperiled her cause."

How well Lio understood opposing duties, especially regarding Cassia. "I am certain she will appreciate your concern. However…"

Eudias's aura gave a throb of protectiveness, an echo of what he had felt when he had told them of his village, which he had once safeguarded from bad weather and famine. "Basilis has dealt fairly with me, and I regret that I have not been in a position to reciprocate."

Incredible. Eudias still had honor within him, which had not been pounded out of him by his ordeals in Corona. His opportunity to act as Cassia's defender seemed to have tapped into the role he had once played for his own people at home, at a happier time in his life.

But Eudias's sudden attack of conscience, however considerate, was more likely to inconvenience Cassia's cause at the moment.

Lio bit back a sigh. "I understand."

"I remain convinced a message would be sufficient," Mak said.

Lio nodded. "I would gladly convey your thoughts to her in a message. If you are not confident in us to deliver your words on your behalf, you could write a letter to her yourself, and we could bring you her reply."

Eudias swallowed and moistened his lips, his first betrayal of nerves since their conversation had begun. "I dare not commit what I have to tell her to paper. Please do not take offense when I say she would not trust my words, should she hear them from a Hesperine."

Lio frowned. "Apprentice Eudias, it sounds to me as if you have more to say to her than an apology."

"It is in your best interests to deal straightly with us," Mak said.

"Well." The young mage took a deep breath. "Where is the harm in confessing apostasy to heretics? Ambassador Deukalion and Steward Telemakhos, would you like to help me throw away my career in the Aithourian Circle, which most mages would kill for—and have killed for?"

Lio took a step closer. "Apprentice Eudias, are you…defecting?"

Mak crossed his arms over his chest, but he studied Eudias with consideration.

Eudias looked from Lio to Mak. "I hardly know what will become of me after tonight, but I am going to tell the truth, nothing more and nothing less, about the corruption in my order. I will tell Basilis what really happened at the Equinox Summit this winter past. I believe your people already have a suspicion of the truth, as do some Tenebrans. All they need is for someone to confirm the rumors flying about. I can do that."

"What do you know?" Lio asked.

Eudias's aura chilled with apprehension even as it heated with anger. "I was privy to all Master Dalos's conversations with Basileus. I know the Tenebrans' king conspired with my order to murder most of the nobility and your embassy."

Eudias was ready to stand witness to Cassia's truth.

"We did know," Lio said, "but Tenebrans are more hesitant to believe such a thing of their mages and their king."

"They deserve to know the truth." Eudias had never sounded so vehement. "I think they will believe me, because it is not in my best interests to say this. I think you will help me because it is in your interests for them to hear it. Why would I lie about something that will…well. End my career."

Or get him executed by his order.

"Eudias," said Lio, "we appreciate the risk you are taking. The sacrifice you are making."

"Yes, I suppose you do."

Lio looked to his Trial brother.

Mak nodded. "On behalf of the Stand, I can assure you release from house arrest—into our protection."

"Whatever happens," Lio promised, "we will see to it you come to no harm on Orthros's shores."

Eudias took another deep breath, as if he had cleared a hurdle. "I will worry about my future later. Please take me to see Basilis so I can tell her the truth. The other Tenebrans will listen to her."

"Let me tell the Guardian of Orthros the new facts of the situation." Mak stepped out of sight.

A moment later, he reappeared in Eudias's guest room. Lio felt Mak's wards come down, and Eudias must have as well, for his eyes widened.

Mak gave him a short bow. "The Guardian of Orthros has approved your request and thanks you for your courage and honor in the face of danger. The ambassador and I will take you to Lady Cassia right away."

"In fact, now is a perfect time. It appears she is in council with the lords here in the common room." Lio added innocently, "I cannot imagine what they are discussing, but perhaps it will prove an opportune setting for your revelations."

Eudias gave a nod. "I am ready."

Lio offered him a hand. "I don't know if it means very much coming from a Hesperine, but you have my utmost respect."

Eudias gazed at his hand. He said nothing for a long moment. Then he clasped Lio's wrist.

When the three of them entered the corridor that led to the common room, Lyros manifested before them. Mak must have already told his Grace what had transpired, for Lyros gave Eudias a bow. "We are ready. You can rely on our protection."

Eudias only nodded by way of thanks. It seemed he must now save all his words for what he was about to do. Lio walked beside him, and Mak and Lyros guarded them. As they drew near the open doorway of the common room, the uproar inside spilled out ever more loudly.

Lord Adrogan's voice rose over the rest. "Benedict would take sides against the king. Like father, like son."

"Lady Cassia has nothing to gain by this," Benedict shot back, "and everything to lose. Think what it costs her to speak out against her own father for our good."

When Lio appeared in the doorway, Cassia's gaze fixed on him. She stood at the opposite side of the round table, hands braced before her, the moonlight streaming in from the courtyard behind her. Lio bolstered her mind with encouragement.

He bowed to her. "Forgive our interruption, Lady Cassia. It is clear this is not a discussion for Hesperine ears, and I regret that we must intrude. But we have come to deliver to your side a true ally. Apprentice Eudias has requested an audience with you."

All eyes in the room went to Eudias. Lio could smell the sweat breaking out on the mage's skin.

"After hearing his purpose," Lio said, "I am confident you will welcome him at this table."

In Cassia's mind, he sensed her surprise, but also her trust in his verdict. She straightened, and then she stepped to the side, making a place for Eudias at the table, a place such as she had once gained at the Equinox Summit.

She gestured to invite the mage to stand beside her. "Please join us, Apprentice Eudias. What is it that you wish to say?"

"Your Ladyship?" Benedict queried. "Are you certain this is wise?"

Master Gorgos glared at Eudias. "He is an impostor who has occupied my temple under false pretenses!"

Lord Gaius warned, "With all due respect to the ambassador, we have no other witness as to Eudias's intentions."

Lio gave another bow, this time to Lord Gaius. "Please consider I have no reason to aid Cordium and every reason to support your embassy."

Mak cleared his throat. "The Stand will ensure the other Cordian mages have no contact with Apprentice Eudias—for his own safety."

"As a result," said Lyros, "it will also be impossible for them to get any information out of him about what transpires tonight."

Cassia raised her brows. "What could cause an Aithourian apprentice to need Hesperines to protect him from his fellow war mages? It sounds to me as if Eudias is taking a risk as dangerous as our own this night, and I for one wish to know what it is."

"Let us hear the boy out," said the Semna.

"What harm could come from simply listening to him?" Lord Gaius conceded.

"Very well," said Benedict. "Let us decide by his words whether we will make him privy to our own."

Eudias, still speechless, looked everywhere but at the place Cassia had made for him at the table.

Ariadne caught and held his gaze. They exchanged a long look.

Eudias walked forward. His shoes padded softly on the carpets. At last he reached Cassia's side and slowly stepped up to the table, glancing around him at each of the Tenebrans.

Lio Willed the young man to sense his support. "We will excuse ourselves from your conference."

"Stay," said Eudias. "That is, with your permission, Basilis. I think Hesperines, Tenebrans and myself, as a Cordian, should all be aware of what I have to say."

At his own open mention of his origin, a start went through the gathering, as if some imperceptible thin ice had broken.

Cassia studied Eudias, then she nodded. "Very well. Our gracious hosts, please do us the honor of joining us for this council."

"We thank you, Lady Cassia," Lio replied. "We shall join you at the table, representing the diplomatic service of Orthros and Hippolyta's Stand."

The Tenebrans on the side of the table nearest Lio and his Trial brothers slid quickly apart to make room for them. But the berth they gave was not nearly so wide as the one at the Equinox Summit had been. Lio stood across the table from Cassia, grateful for her before him and his Trial brothers on either side, and the hope of an ally in a thin, hesitant young man in yellow apprentice robes.

Eudias cleared his throat. Then he stood up straight once more. "I can no longer in good conscience support the intentions of my circle. I pray you will not take me for a traitor to my masters, but a devoted servant of my god." He paused to take a breath. His throat worked as he swallowed. "As Honored Master Dalos's apprentice, then as the Aithourian Circle's only emissary at Solorum, and finally while serving under Dexion Chrysanthos, I have heard with my own ears how the highest officials within the Order of Anthros conspire with your king. This treachery is driven by the Synthikos of the Aithourian Circle, but with the full knowledge and support of the Akron. Master Dalos was sent to Tenebra not to protect you from the Hesperine embassy, but to assassinate you along with them. He fully intended to catch the entire Council of Free Lords in his fire spell."

Gasps and outcries went up throughout the room.

"You see?" Benedict challenged the lords. "Everything Her Ladyship has told you is true. Eudias has verified Callen's story."

Lord Severin shook his head. "I can scarcely believe it. The king is forsworn."

"Thank you, Eudias," said Cassia.

He looked at her, his eyes wide. "You knew, Basilis?"

She nodded, gesturing to Callen. "When my bodyguard was falsely imprisoned, he saw and heard everything Dalos did in the king's dungeon. Dalos did not hide his true purposes, for he believed Callen to be dying."

Callen gave Eudias a nod that bespoke respect. "I thank you for standing witness with me."

Eudias hung his head. "I knew before Dalos unleashed his spell, and yet I said nothing. If he had succeeded, all of you... I...I can only pray what I have said tonight will make me worthy of your forgiveness."

"You have risked your life to tell us the truth," Cassia replied. "For that, you have my admiration."

Eudias met her gaze. "Thank you."

"Dalos did not succeed," Benedict reminded them all. His gaze rested on Lio, Mak, and Lyros.

"Of course not," Mak replied. "The Guardian of Orthros fought Aithouros himself."

"It was my privilege to stand against Dalos at her side," Lio said. "Thankfully, given our long experience dealing with war mages, we were well prepared for the assault and ready to counter his spell when he unleashed it."

Suddenly Eudias was no longer the subject of the shocked discussion around the table, and Lio heard his and the embassy's names on all the lips in the room.

"You stayed," Perita declared. "To protect *us*. If you'd wanted to protect yourselves, well, you would have just left us, now, wouldn't you?"

"Aye," said Callen, "we owe the Hesperines our thanks for protecting us from our own king."

BEARERS OF TRUTH

Lord Gaius called for silence, and the noise died down a measure. "It is a great deal to ask that we believe such a thing of our king."

Cassia searched his gaze. Did any of Lord Hadrian's close comrades know the whole truth? "It would be easy for you to believe it of the king if you had been at your lord's side at the Siege of Sovereigns. Lord Hadrian was there. He can speak to what the king is capable of. So can I. I know better than anyone."

Questions about the siege joined the volley the lords hurled by turns at Cassia's and Lio's sides of the table. Lio's presence reached easily across that insignificant divide, filling the room with his light and shadow so that Cassia felt surrounded not by opposition, but her dearest ally. How right that he should get to be here with her, as he had been the first night she had found words to describe what had happened the night she had lost her sister.

Benedict stood close to her and spoke low. "Are you sure you wish to do this?"

"Yes. The time has finally come."

"Then know that I stand beside you and bear the truth with you."

"Thank you, Ben."

A chill went down Cassia's spine, even as she felt a great weight trembling upon her chest, ready to lift. She had waited so long. She had never imagined speaking these words publicly.

Cassia looked to the Semna. "Will our Mother of the Harvest hear my vow?"

The mage replied with the ritual words. "Kyria listens. Do not injure your mother's ears with lies. Speak only truth before your goddess."

"With Kyria as my witness, I shall speak only truth," Cassia promised.

She looked from one person to the next, willing them to see the truth in her eyes. The pain. The horror. "It is so wrong, I could not invent such a tale."

In that instant, the years of strain came to a head. The dam broke. The words rushed out of her.

"My father murdered my sister."

A fatal hush fell over the room.

Cassia slammed her hand onto the table. "He didn't meet her captors' ransom demands. Without even a moment's hesitation, he refused their terms. They told him he sentenced his own heir to death. And do you know what he said?"

They waited, watching her. Solia's people, strong and weak, honorable and selfish. Each one listened.

"He said he would get him another." Cassia didn't weep. The truth made her strong, and she kept speaking. "As if there could ever be another Solia. This was how he threw away our princess, who can never be replaced."

Lord Gaius was the first to break the silence. "I do not doubt your words. One of my sons died at Castra Roborra in the name of avenging our princess. But I have never understood why the king wasted his best men, reducing them to bodies to be thrown against the walls of that fortress."

"I am so sorry for your loss," Cassia answered. "The king sent those men, your son among them, to their graves in order to bury the truth."

For an instant, the old warrior's face showed all his wounds. Then his armor was in place again. "I have always wondered if there was more to the grief my lord harbored since that night."

"He carries the truth in silence, for he knows he must, for the good of us all. But that time is over. The truth must free all good men from their service to the tyrant king."

"We're to take your word for this?" Master Gorgos demanded. "Women can't even testify in court."

The Semna struck the floor with her walking stick. "Every mortal can swear oaths before the gods. That predates the king's magistrates."

"I can tell you where to find all the proof you need," said Cassia. "When you return to Tenebra, all you need do is open her crypt. You will find it empty, for my father did not even bother to recover her body."

Lord Gaius's face paled.

Cassia nodded. "There is one more truth your son took to his grave. Like him, I listened to the catapults that fired the bodies of my sister, her servants, and her guards over the walls of Castra Roborra. As they lay without dignity on the field below, Lord Hadrian's men begged the king to let them retrieve her and those who had served her faithfully. Again, he refused."

Lord Severin signed a glyph of Hypnos. "That is ungodly."

Eudias stared at her with a startled gaze. "Basilis, I'm so sorry."

"Kyria have mercy," said the Semna. "Shame upon any man for denying the godly a mage of Hypnos's prayers."

"Only one deity did not forget her," said Cassia. "One goddess's servants gave her the honor Anthros's champion denied her."

"Who?" Lord Gaius asked.

"What mages were there who defied the king?" Lord Severin wanted to know.

Now at last Cassia could fully honor the one who lay in agony in the healers' hall, the one who languished in the Order's custody, the one whose likeness stood guard at Victory Point while she and her comrades faced defeat at the war mages' hands. Now at last Cassia could tell other Tenebrans the truth that had changed her life. Would that moment mean anything to them? Would it prove to them the true nature of Hesperines, as it had to her?

Cassia looked at Lio, who held her with his magic, Lyros, from whose gaze she drew strength, and finally Nike's brother. Mak gave a nod.

"You have but to look around you," she said, "and you will see them. You have come to know them these many nights that we have dwelt in their goddess's temple. The Hesperines gave Solia her sacred rites. Hespera escorted our princess to Anthros's Hall."

"Impossible!" Master Gorgos pointed a finger at the three Hesperines. "Lies. Poison they have dripped in your ear. They have taken advantage of your grief and told you this tale to seduce you into their treaties."

"No one told me, for I was there. I went to find my sister's body when no one else would. I, a defenseless girl of seven, frightened, grief-stricken. I would have died, if the Hesperines had not saved me from the archers on the walls of the fortress. They asked my permission to give Solia her rites. Then they took me back to my father."

"No Hesperines would ever do such a thing!" Master Gorgos protested. "Surrender a child?"

Cassia looked at him calmly. "On the evidence of my own experience, I was forced to conclude Hesperines errant do indeed adhere to the Oath. When I explained I was not an orphan, they returned me to camp. And here I am."

Cassia could scarcely believe it. She had just laid all her dearest secrets on the table.

All except one. Cassia parceled out secrets as necessary, and no one yet needed to know she had been spying on the king or by what means. Was that why she was not ready to reveal the dagger up her sleeve? Or was it because she couldn't quite make herself believe she didn't need it anymore?

The ivy pendant, which was even now in Alkaios's hand, had been Solia's legacy. She had bequeathed Cassia the hidden passages inside Solorum. She had instructed Cassia it was the "women's secret" of the Tenebran royal line, and so it must remain. The hush into which Cassia had spoken Ebah's name prevailed upon her heart, and she would not break that silence.

"Lords of Tenebra!" Master Gorgos pointed to Cassia. "You see before you the first of us to fall to the Hesperines' influence. Clearly their wiles and insidious magic have robbed Lady Cassia of her senses. They have implanted in her mind their perverted vision of her past and made her believe it."

"That is an insult and an injustice to Lady Cassia," Lio said. "You ought to give her strength of Will far greater credit, if you cannot bring yourself to trust our intentions."

Mak stared Master Gorgos down. "One of the Hesperines who saved her life that night was a Master Steward of the Stand. Do we appear to need 'wiles' to achieve our goals?"

Lyros cast a staying glance upon Mak and Lio. "Our Hesperines errant risk their lives to uphold the Equinox Oath. None of us would ever taint their sacred purpose by lying about it."

"See here," Perita spoke up, "I'll swear before Kyria there's no foul magic at work on my lady."

She proceeded to make her oath of truth before the goddess, then recited her grandmother's recipes for discovering whether malign spells were at work. "I used every single one on my lady to be certain the Hesperines haven't harmed her."

"This hedge witchery is not enough to satisfy Anthros," Master Gorgos replied.

The Semna drew herself up. "You call Kyria's own beneficent plants witchcraft?"

Lord Severin skewered Master Gorgos with a gaze. "Can you cast a revealing spell and prove otherwise?"

"Well," the mage puffed, "that is, with all the thick layers of Hesperine spells about, such a test would be inconclusive in any case…"

"But not beyond your skills, of course!" Lord Severin replied, the mockery obvious in his voice. "Shall we take the lady before your brothers from Cordium so they may wave their hands over her?"

"Nonsense," Master Gorgos said, "I need no Cordian mage to prove me right."

"I can cast revealing spells," Eudias spoke up.

Attention returned to him, as if most had forgotten he was there.

Cassia had not, and while she placed her trust in her Sanctuary ward, she also trusted the apprentice's intentions. "I will gladly submit to any test to which you put me, Apprentice Eudias. I would appreciate your help reassuring everyone."

"I can," Eudias repeated, "but I shall not. For what my confidence is worth, I trust you, Basilis, and so too should your countrymen."

"Your trust is worth a great deal to me," Cassia said. "Know that you have mine in return."

He looked away, clearly uncertain how to respond to such a declaration. "My order has meddled in Tenebra's affairs enough. You should put no more faith in our revealing spells or anything else."

"I agree with the apprentice," said Lord Gaius. "Let us not give the uninvited guests a chance to discredit our songbird and prevent Tenebra from treating with Orthros, as is the purpose of this Summit."

Lord Adrogan grimaced. "I think you'd all best surface from your nostalgia for a queen who never was and think about the reality of rebellion. If there's a lesson in Solia's death, it's that revolts against Lucis end well for no one."

"Revolt?" Cassia poured outrage into her voice. "Who has said anything about revolt? I see no rebels here, only the protectors of Tenebra, who will not stand by while any man violates his oaths to his people. We must have recourse to the law, not break it."

Benedict laid his notebook on the table before him. "Aye. Rebellion was the mistake my father made. Violence will accomplish nothing except bringing innocent lives to harm. Here is a cautionary tale, my lords. I lived through it, but I did not understand what it meant until the Hesperines shed light on it for me."

Cassia looked from the journal to him. "Your notes on the Summit?"

"No. My detailed account of the Siege of Sovereigns, which I have researched in the libraries of Orthros, complete with sketches of the catapults." He opened the leather cover on a drawing.

Cassia bent over the page with him. "This is what you have used Kassandra's drawing tools for."

"I needed an engineer's drawing tools to reproduce the diagrams from Hephaestion's written descriptions. So I could be sure."

Lyros rounded the table. "Sir Benedict, may I?"

Benedict turned the journal so Lyros could see it.

Lyros studied the drawings. "Incredible. As many times as I've read the descriptions, I could only imagine what they looked like. Sir Benedict, your work deserves to be studied in its own right. Thanks to you, we are the first people to see Hephaestion's inventions in over sixteen hundred years."

"On the contrary," Benedict replied, "someone has built them within the last sixteen years."

Cassia touched a hand to Benedict's arm. "I watched them roll into the king's camp. They are the catapults he used to bring down Castra Roborra faster than any siege in history. But how did you recognize them?"

"When I was a boy, the king required Lord Titus to take me to look at the siege engines that killed my father. For instructional purposes, you understand. To make sure I never grew up to emulate his treason."

Lyros bowed his head. "I carry your grief in my veins, Sir Benedict."

"No one mourns a traitor, Steward Lysandros," said Benedict.

"Hesperines mourn everyone," Lyros said.

"Mourn that night, then." Benedict held up the diagram for the whole embassy to see. "Here I have proof of how long the king has conspired with the Order of Anthros, and how thoroughly they have violated the very laws they demand we obey. These siege engines are ancient innovations by the Aithourian war mage Hephaestion, which never saw use in battle, for his own Order forbade men to live by both magic and war. Mages are to cast spells. Kings are to build catapults. So how are we to explain that at the Siege of Sovereigns, Hephaestion's catapults, built from the king's lumber, hurled fire spells that ate through the mundane walls of Castra Roborra?"

"That I should live to see such times." The Semna put a hand to her chest. "Master Gorgos, you must agree the temples of Tenebra cannot turn a blind eye to this."

The mage of Anthros hesitated. "I don't see what a lot of scrolls from a Hesperine library prove."

Eudias turned the page of Benedict's journal and studied the next diagram. "These are blatantly against the Order's own prohibitions. The laws don't stop at men who wield swords and spells; there is an entire article that itemizes the exact limitations on siege weaponry. Worse still, when the Aithourian Circle aided the king in a political struggle in this manner, they violated war mage neutrality laws. How eager they are to forget the founding principles of our order. One of the original, key purposes of establishing the Orders was to address the chaos and harm caused by mercenary war mages who hired on with every feuding noble."

The Semna looked at Master Gorgos. "What are we to do when the gods' mouthpieces disobey the gods?"

Benedict signed a glyph of Andragathos. "We must indeed trust in the strength of our Tenebran mages, Semna, and your virtue. We will need all your strength to stand against a king who has Cordium at his back."

Cassia thumped Benedict's journal. "This is what you can expect to meet in battle, if you take up arms against the king. But the Orders cannot fight peace with catapults. They can break the law with fire, but they cannot destroy it."

"Hadria and Segetia must stand together in this," Lord Gaius said at last. "Our divisions will leave us vulnerable, but if all the lords of Tenebra join forces, we will be strong enough to unmake the king and keep his foreign allies out of our lands. We will need no revolt, only the Free Charter."

Lord Severin spoke, his brow furrowed. "I believe my father and I are of one mind in this, if nothing else. Regardless of his stance against Hesperines, once he learns his king tried to murder him, he will not try to stop me from invoking the Charter."

Cassia spread their terms out on the table before her. "We must take the high ground of the council table and uphold the law as laid down in the Free Charter, which empowers every free lord in Tenebra to make treaties and contracts for the safety and prosperity of his own people."

Benedict shoved his journal to the center of the table. "The law is on our side."

"The power is in our hands," said Lord Gaius.

"We are not without foreign allies, either." Cassia looked to Lio.

"We are here to serve," Lio replied, "and lend all our power to upholding peace."

"You can rely on our strength," Mak promised.

Lyros saluted the warriors. "We will stand as Tenebra's allies against Cordium, if you will stand with us."

Once more, Cassia challenged each man in the room with her gaze. This time they did not look away, and she saw in their eyes anger and resolve, indignation and courage.

She had done it. They were ready for her to cut their strings.

"I have armed you with the truth, my lords," Cassia said. "You must find the courage to take it up and wield it in defense of all you hold dear."

FESTIVAL OF THE
DRINK

2 Nights After Winter Solstice

CASSIA'S SANCTUARY

WHEN MOON HOURS CAME, the mortals' emotions crested through the streets of Selas. Their auras were afire after a sleepless night of deliberating over the terms they would propose to the Queens. Lio had seldom felt more exhilarated about a negotiation himself.

But they formed an orderly column of dignified emissaries, whom Cassia led to House Annassa with Lio, Mak, and Lyros as their escorts. Bearing the historical Tenebran banner, the embassy followed in the footsteps of generations of Hesperines to make their pilgrimage up the steps of the Queens' Terrace.

Annassa Alea's eyes gleamed as she watched them approach, and her Grace squeezed her hand. The firstbloods in attendance shared a collective wave of amazement in the Union.

"Guests from Tenebra, how we rejoice to see you here on our terrace." Annassa Soteira gestured around them, where platters of food grew cold. "We have prepared a banquet for you to celebrate the Festival of the Drink, when we thank all mortals for their generosity to us, but we had begun to fear our guests of honor would not attend."

"To what do we owe this wonderful surprise?" Queen Alea asked.

Lio made the heart bow before his Queens. "Annassa, imagine our own surprise when the Tenebran embassy expressed their wish to petition you for an audience this very night."

Cassia sank into a deep curtsy before the Queens, while Lord Gaius and Benedict bowed, and Eudias lowered his head with his hands tucked in his sleeves.

"Annassa," Cassia addressed them, "we have come to offer Tenebra's formal apology for Dexion Chrysanthos's actions against Orthros."

"Speaking for all those who are loyal to Hadria," said Lord Gaius, "we beg your forgiveness for not warning you of the mage's true nature. We regret being the means by which Cordium's agent has trespassed in your lands."

"Speaking for all those who rally to Segetia's banner," Benedict continued, "let it be known that we had no knowledge his circle is keeping Hesperines errant prisoner, and we share in your sorrow for the hostages' plight."

Lio could see Eudias trembling. It seemed the young mage's great deed at the guest house had used up all the confidence he had mustered, and he now stood before the Queens on the last of his courage. Feeling the excruciating trepidation in Eudias's aura, Lio could imagine what an ordeal it was to speak before this circle when you were shy in the first place.

"Eudias," Queen Soteira coaxed, "do not allow your masters to make you feel ashamed of your goodness."

He startled where he stood, his eyes downcast. But he answered. "Annassa. I have asked the Tenebrans' forgiveness for—for my complicity in my masters' misdeeds. I—I will have no more part in the Circle's— abuses. Not all mages in the Order—even in Cordium—agree with this— this aggression. Many of us only...only want to use our, our magic...for the good of our people, too."

Cassia unrolled the document she carried. "Allow us to make amends for the misconduct of the Aithourian Circle and the Gift Collector. We are resolved not to let Cordium undermine the peace for which Orthros and Tenebra have labored. Would Orthros hear the terms the Dexion prevented us from proposing at the Firstblood Circle?"

Could the embassy see the expression on Queen Alea's face for what it was? Lio knew it well, for he had seen that same gaze of love turned upon him and all her children countless times.

"Hespera never turns a deaf ear to any plea," Queen Alea assured them. "So too shall we hear your terms."

"Rise." Queen Soteira lifted her hand. "You are welcome here."

Queen Alea beckoned to Lio. "Ambassador Deukalion, you may resume negotiations on our behalf."

"It will be my honor, Annassa."

Across the negligible distance that separated the Hesperines from their mortal petitioners, Lio faced Cassia. Their gazes and minds met, and they shared a moment of sweet triumph.

"Lady Cassia, you may at last present your terms without interruption."

"Thank you, Ambassador. Allow me to give an overview of the matters the assembled lords, knights and mages would like to discuss with you tonight. First, the free lords of Hadria and Segetia propose the restoration of all the traditional protections of the Equinox Oath, within all the lands under their authority and that of their vassals, which comprises the majority of Tenebra."

Lord Gaius and Benedict each gave a deep nod.

Cassia continued, "The Tenebran mages of Anthros are prepared to uphold these protections and act as enforcers of the Oath's traditional restrictions upon Hesperines to ensure no conflicts arise."

Master Gorgos's glare promised they would be watching Lio's people like hawks, but he was here, and he did not protest.

With a smile in her eyes, Cassia glanced at the Semna. "The Tenebran mages of Kyria wish to discuss modifications to the original tenets of the Oath regarding children, namely the possibility of Hesperines providing direct aid to Tenebra's orphanages in the form of provisions, clothes, and other necessities."

Lio bowed to the Semna, struggling not to beam at her and show her his fangs.

The venerable mage rested on one elbow upon her litter. "We can't accomplish anything if we ban you from our only common ground."

"Lord Severinus the Younger," said Cassia, "is prepared to lead an effort to reform and restrict the heart hunters in exchange for famine relief."

"I will do everything in my power," Lord Severin promised. "I am not without my own supporters, who will stand with me to moderate my father."

Cassia went on, "Several other lords wish to seal the trade agreements they have been discussing with Orthros's bloodlines during our time here."

Lio would have to ask Cassia later why Lord Adrogan had fashioned Kassandra's gift of silk into a sling.

Whatever had befallen the young lord, it was not him, but Callen to whom Cassia looked as she concluded. "Finally, there are some among us who wish to accept Annassa Soteira's generous offer of healing, and the Semna is prepared once more to assist. Let this stand as a bond of gratitude between our peoples."

Anxiety bestirred Callen's aura, but he offered a bow in Annassa Soteira's direction. When their gazes met, his emotions steadied into confidence.

"I will see to the healing myself," Queen Soteira said.

Cassia rolled up her paper. "We must thank Orthros for Hesperines' deeds on our behalf."

Lord Gaius stepped nearer. "As you know, we are now aware that the Council of Free Lords and all who attended the Equinox Summit owe their lives to the Hesperine embassy. Ambassador Deukalion, Master Ambassador Argyros, allow us to convey the gratitude of those men and their families."

"Please accept our gratitude," Benedict echoed.

"We are glad we were able to prevent such catastrophic loss of life," Lio replied.

"I will convey your message to the rest of my family and our colleagues who were there," Uncle Argyros said.

Lord Gaius's heavy heart weighed on the Blood Union. "You have seen the ugly truth of events in our lands. The king has betrayed his people and the Oath, with the aid of the Cordian Orders."

Benedict's aura was resolute. "This embassy's commitment to peace with Orthros rather than an alliance with Cordium is a break with the king and the highest religious authorities. The consequences of that schism remain to be seen."

Lord Severin nodded. "We will endeavor to fulfill the commitments we make tonight, despite the opposition we may face."

"We ask only that you try," said Lio. "We appreciate how much you all risk in defying the king and the Orders. Know that you have Orthros at your backs, come what may."

Cassia's eyes shone. "Those of us whose lives you have touched know the depth and breadth of all you are willing to do for us. Before your people and mine, I give you our gratitude for the Mercy you showed Solia, our beloved princess. I thank you, too, for the gift of my life. I hope to make those Hesperines errant glad they saved me."

Lio joined Cassia in their final act, replying as they had planned together. "Their deeds are well known among us. I only wish they could hear your words, which they would treasure."

"I know that one of them is here in Orthros, where I may thank him. I recognized his name when we saw him arrive in the Healing Sanctuary. Alkaios."

"Lady Cassia, it grieves me to break the news to you that Alkaios is not expected to live. The lasting effects of what he suffered Abroad are beyond even our power to heal."

Cassia gasped, touching a hand to her chest. "After all he has done for us? What about my other two rescuers? Please tell me nothing has befallen them."

Lio bowed his head. "They are among the Aithourian Circle's prisoners."

A murmur of shock passed through the onlooking humans. A tear slid down Cassia's face for all to see. Lio knew it was as genuine as all the blood, sweat, and tears she had shed for Orthros.

"This cannot stand," she cried, "not after everything you have done for my sister and me."

"Hesperines do not practice debts," said Lio. "Only bonds of gratitude."

"And yet your laws demand a life for a life. A rescue for a murder. Is that not so?"

Lio paused for effect, looking upon Cassia with an expression of caution and concern. "There is no murder on your conscience."

"And yet eight Hesperine lives hang in the balance, among them my rescuers. I cannot begin to even the scales, yet there is one thing I can do."

Worry rose in Benedict's aura, and Lord Gaius frowned. Eudias appeared more startled than usual. Even the Semna looked puzzled.

Cassia turned, taking in first the Hesperines, then the Tenebrans with a glance. "My fellow mortals, you surely see what virtue demands of me, in the spirit of Hesperine and human law. I must do this for our people. For our honor. For our princess." She turned once more to the Queens.

"Let this be the royal family's thanks and Tenebra's promise of peace. This life your people have saved now belongs to you. I hereby offer myself to Orthros."

Perita rushed forward to play her part. She had promised she need not put on an act. Her tears and pleading with her lady tore at Lio's heart. With gentle firmness, Cassia murmured reassurances to her friend.

Benedict took Cassia's arm, his face flushed with outrage. "Your Ladyship, this is not right. You should not be the one to pay for the hostage's lives—for the king's crimes! You least of all!"

"I must honor what the Hesperines did at the Siege of Sovereigns. You understand, don't you?"

"No! I do not. How can you even consider this? Did the words you told me mean nothing? 'My life is no use laid down, nor is yours.'"

"Orthros does not demand my death. This is not a sacrifice, but a dedication. It does not grieve me to do this for Solia's people."

"Her people need you in Tenebra!"

Lio clenched his hands, but he made himself wait out the storm. They must see their act through. He must do his part and let Cassia do hers.

He must not give into fear. She had made her promise.

She took Benedict's hands. "My work there is done. It is up to you to carry on her work there now. Flavian will need your wisdom and strength in the coming days."

"What of your betrothal promise to him? Does it mean nothing?"

From her gardening satchel, Cassia drew a bundle of papers. The green wax that secured them bore no seal. No one would guess how much power the author of those documents wielded.

But Lio knew Cassia was holding a throne, a kingdom, an entire people's future in her hands.

She wrapped Benedict's hands around the documents. "This is my repayment to my lord Flavian. He will find himself well compensated for my bride price. I need you to give it to him for me."

Benedict looked down at the papers, speechless. When his liege lord opened them, they would realize Cassia had presented Flavian with the plan for his peaceful takeover, spelled out to the last detail.

Cassia added the list of the embassy's terms to the papers in Benedict's hands. "I know it is a great deal to ask of him, but I believe he will rise to the occasion. You must promise me you will deliver these safely to him, and him alone."

Benedict was silent a long moment before he answered. "I swear on your life. So you'd best not lose it."

"I will be safe and well," she assured him.

Callen spoke up as planned. "Segetia may surrender you that easily, but Hadria will not!"

"My lord charged me with bringing you safely home, and I shall." Lord Gaius turned to the Hesperines. "You cannot ask this of her."

"We are not asking," Queen Alea replied. "She has offered."

Queen Soteira gave a nod. "It is entirely her choice."

"Will you have me?" Cassia asked.

"With joy," said Queen Alea, "we will welcome you as one of our own."

"Orthros is open to all who wish to remain." Queen Soteira swept a gaze over the rest of the embassy, and many eyes did not shy away.

"In so doing," Cassia asked, "will I satisfy Hesperine law?"

"Let us consult Princess Konstantina on this matter," Lio said.

The princess actually looked pleased to take part in their display. "There are indeed considerable legal precedents to support Lady Cassia's offer. As codified in the Law of Sanctuary, we must provide a home in Orthros to any who ask. This law is often invoked in conjunction with the Law of Atonement. Justice may be served by offenders delivering lives to safety in Orthros—but never by force. Lady Cassia's choice is in accordance with the Law of Will."

"I am but one life for eight," said Cassia.

"Your very willingness holds great legal weight. It is not merely the count, but the magnitude of the rescue which must be taken into consideration. You do great good for both our peoples by your choice."

"How much choice does she have?" Lord Severin demanded. "It is in your power to release her from this burden of honor."

"No," the Semna spoke up, "that power lies only in her conscience."

The mage held out a hand, and Cassia went to her, kneeling beside her. Lio bowed his head as the Semna made a blessing of Kyria over Cassia.

"No man must stop you from heeding the goddess's call," the Semna said at last. "You answer her with wonderful courage. Undertake this mission of mercy with her blessings."

"Thank you, Semna. Please give my farewells to the Prisma and everyone at the temple."

"They will hear of your deeds!"

No man there raised another protest.

Except one. When Cassia rose and moved away from the Semna, she found herself face-to-face with Eudias. Lio's heart went out to the young mage, as surely as to Cassia's other defenders.

Eudias ducked his head, looking into Cassia's face. "Basilis, I promised to protect you."

She smiled at him. "You have gone above and beyond your promise. Your duty to me is done, and you have freed yourself from the Aithourian Circle. What will you do now?"

He looked around him at the gathering of Hesperines, warriors, and mages. "I shall finish what I've started."

Benedict held Cassia's documents aloft. "We will not waste our princess's death or our lady's life. We will see the truce decided before we leave Orthros."

"We will return home the champions of peace," Lord Gaius called out, "and the protectors of freedom."

The embassy met their words with a chorus of "ayes." The few who seemed unmoved received ungentle nudges until they too voiced their support. Master Gorgos, not to be outdone by the Semna, hastened to intone an Anthrian prayer for Cassia's safety, praising her courage to the heavens. Lio thought Laurentius would appreciate that.

At last Cassia turned to Lio. "Ambassador, my offer stands."

He wore a diplomat's face for the embassy, but as he spoke, he touched Cassia's mind with all his love for her. "On behalf of Orthros, it is my honor and my pleasure to accept you among our people for all time. In Hespera's name, we grant you Sanctuary."

FESTIVAL OF
SANCTUARY

3 Nights After Winter Solstice

TIME TO ACT

THE REMNANTS OF CASSIA and Lio's ruse lingered between them in the form of half an arm's length of dock.

She leaned a little closer to him and stood on tiptoe in an attempt to speak quietly with him. "Ambassador, may I ask who had the honor of planning this event?"

He stooped, leaning still closer to her. "Every Festival of Sanctuary, the first ceremony of the night, the Commemoration of the Founders, is overseen by the Second Princess and a committee she appoints the night after last year's event."

"Ah." Cassia nodded. "I see her eye for detail and appreciation for history at work."

Lio gave a slight bow, the corners of his mouth twitching.

From behind her, Cassia heard Callen clear his throat. Lio eased aside to increase his distance from her.

Cassia bit back a sigh and tried to pay attention to the podium on the central dock.

Yet another elder official whose name she had forgotten was giving yet another long speech. Something about the lasting, worldwide historical impact of a five-minute conference between the Queens and the elder firstbloods at a particular spot on the beach in the third hour after their arrival at Harbor.

If Cassia's role hadn't warranted a place at the front of the huge audience at the Commemoration, she would never have been able to see over all the tall Hesperines. In a stand of festival seats covered in miles of stately draperies, the Queens and the elder firstbloods sat at Hespera's feet. Somehow, the real founders did not look small, even while they sat facing their massive statues.

"I'm looking forward to the lightworks," Lio murmured. "Later tonight, our master light mages will hold a display of spell lights and illusions over the harbor."

"When can we look forward to that?" Cassia asked.

"After the Commemoration, there's another ceremony at the ward. Then the founders return across the Sea of Komne and land in Harbor. That's when the real festival starts."

Cassia swallowed a yawn. "Will there be coffee?"

When the dispersal of the audience restored her to some alertness, she wasn't sure if she had actually napped on her feet or not. The cozy tiredness in her limbs reassured her she really was experiencing the benign effects of too little sleep. Never mind. She could Slumber when she was a Hesperine.

"I will escort you all back to Rose House now, honored guests," Lio said. "Please accept the founders' regrets that you cannot join them for the next ceremony at the Queens' ward. The festival is on a tight schedule, which requires that all attendees step between events, a demand to which we would not subject you."

"Ah, sailing over would take too long, of course." Eudias sounded disappointed.

"That's perfectly all right, Ambassador." The diminutive Semna, reclining on her litter on the shoulders of the knights, was on eye level with Lio.

"I don't fancy another trip on the choppy waves," Perita muttered, "to say nothing of this stepping sorcery."

"A considerate decision," Lord Gaius said.

Benedict nodded. "Especially on behalf of our ladies."

Cassia and Lio exchanged a glance. They need not fend off any untoward curiosity after all, for the Tenebrans had accepted his justification for their exclusion. The embassy seemed content to be free of the obligation to attend, blissfully ignorant that the founders' visit to the ward upon the Festival of Sanctuary was more than a mere formality.

Lio took his leave in the entry hall of Rose House and disappeared into the gallery to the New Guest House. Knowing her seafarer would remain on this shore, Cassia could not have felt safer. It was highly unlikely the mages, unaware of tonight's events, would try anything in the few hours the entire Stand was at the ward with the founders, but Lio would make sure.

The lords and knights drifted into the main hall. Cassia was about to follow them, when a draft drew her attention to the door. It was still open, just wide enough for thin Eudias to linger there. He gazed out to sea, and the polar wind tugged his hair out from under his cap. His brow gleamed with sweat.

"Perita," Cassia said, "be so kind as to pour me a goblet of Notian red, would you?"

Perita glanced from her to Eudias. "Certainly, my lady."

Cassia ran her hand over Knight's shoulders to remind her bodyguard she was not without protection.

"At your leisure, my lady." Callen gestured to their seats in the main hall, which were visible from the entryway. "We'll be just inside."

As their footsteps receded, Cassia approached the young mage. "Apprentice Eudias? Are you all right?"

Without a twitch or a tremble, his hand closed over the handle of the door. He thrust the heavy panel shut. The thud echoed, and the cold air was gone.

Standing tall, Eudias turned to Cassia. She had to tilt her head back to look at him.

"I am all right, perhaps for the first time in my life." His voice, devoid of timid tones, was almost unrecognizable. "It is time to act."

"I am glad you do not regret coming forward."

"I have barely begun. You cannot imagine all I have seen and heard in my time studying magic." A flicker of distress reappeared in his gaze, and his voice faltered. "I wish I'd realized sooner. I really should have understood what it meant. But then, how could I, until I knew what I know now? Oh, no time to look backward now, time is of the essence. I must tell you, in case it is significant."

"I'm sure you know a great deal that can be of aid."

"I may be able to help the hostages, Basilis."

"I beg of you, tell me!"

"Bear with me." Eudias took a deep breath. "Master Skleros has been working with certain members of the Aithourian Circle for some time. Not officially, you understand, for the elite war mages would never let on there is anything they cannot accomplish, much less that they condescended to ask a Gift Collector for help."

"I have often wondered at Skleros and Chrysanthos's rapport. It is clear they have a history."

"The Synthikos holds himself above the rules that he and the Akron enforce upon their subordinates. Dalos and Chrysanthos have always done the same. They did not hesitate to employ a Gift Collector when it suited them. In their vicious competition for the position of Dexion, they resorted to the most extreme means at their disposal. Master Skleros is the best at what he does."

"You mean he assisted them against one another?"

"He did what he was hired to do, whichever it was who hired him. Now, however, he is no longer the occasional associate of two Honored Masters of the Aithourian Circle. It is the Dexion himself who encourages the all-seeing Order of Hypnos to turn a blind eye to Master Skleros's activities."

"What do you know about the nature of the work Master Skleros does for the Dexion?"

"Why, his work. Don't you see?"

"Oh, I do see. How could I not have seen? You are brilliant."

He flushed. "Well, now you know why I am in agony that I did not realize sooner. What else would a Gift Collector be doing for anyone, but..."

"...collecting Hesperines. The Dexion may have boasted before the Firstblood Circle, but I would stake my life Skleros has been doing his dirty work for him."

Eudias nodded. "I daresay the Gift Collector seized the Hesperine hostages for the Aithourian Circle."

"The question now remains, where did he deliver them?"

"There's something else." He took a step forward. "Master Skleros has not set foot in Cordium for over a year. His bounties are piling up uncollected. Before the Equinox Summit, Dalos had to arrange to meet

with him in Namenti for—for—in preparation for our arrival at Solorum."
Eudias looked away.

That must have been when Skleros had performed the essential
displacement on Dalos, which had been a harrowing experience for
Eudias. An invaluable informant on essential displacement stood before
her. She found herself as unwilling to press him about what he had suffered
as Dalos's channel as to use a woman and child against the Dexion. "I was
given to understand that this autumn, Master Skleros joined the Dexion
at Solorum directly from Corona, with the sanction of the Inner Eyes in
his hand."

"Oh, that scroll he brought? No, no, the Dexion wrote it. He sent
me to deliver it on the road. I put it in Master Skleros's hand myself, so
he could enter Solorum with it, as if he'd had it all along." Sweat broke
out on Eudias's brow anew. "I didn't know what was in it—I—the other
necromancers, the ones Corona really did send…"

Cassia recalled the sight of their lifeless bodies, and her chest
tightened. She did her best to feign ignorance. "The Order sent Cordian
necromancers to join the embassy?"

"You see, you didn't even know. It's as if they never existed. A whole
hex of them. I didn't know I was sentencing them to—to—"

"I know life under a tyrant," Cassia said. "You witness deeds. You even
commit deeds. You tell yourself you had no choice, while you wonder how
you could have done better. It is important to realize you suffered, too."

"I'm not a weakling, as everyone accuses me." Eudias's voice rose.

"Of course not. Everyone here has seen you face their abuses with
strength and courage. We survived, Eudias. Gratitude makes us strong."

Eudias swallowed hard. "I'm going to make it right. A rescue for a life,
yes? Seven isn't enough, but it's a start."

"I understand. Let us go save their lives."

LOYALTIES

MAK CROSSED HIS ARMS at the Dexion's door. "The wards will last till well past our return. As soon as we're back from the border, we'll relieve you."

"Mak, I'll be fine." Lio posted himself between Chrysanthos's and Skleros's respective guest rooms.

Lyros, his aura flaring with power, paused in front of the Gift Collector's chambers. "The wards will admit only you. The blood shackles Grace-Mother cast on each mage will prevent them from trying anything if you need to go inside—and you shouldn't. Give them no opportunities to lay traps for you."

"Unless there's fire or blood," Mak instructed, "all contact with the mages should wait until the Stand is in Selas again."

"What about screams?" Lio asked.

"Eh, you can ignore those." Lyros waved a hand at Tychon's door. "It's probably the apprentice crying for his master."

Mak laughed darkly. "All right, we shouldn't wait any longer. If we're late for the Libation of Renewal, I dare say Mother will delay our mastery for a century."

"Go, Stewards of the ward," Lio said. "This is the most important night of the year for the Stand and Orthros's safety. I will not allow the Summit to interfere."

Lyros strolled over and halted before him. Mak stood shoulder to shoulder with his Grace.

"Don't worry," Lio told them. "Aunt Lyta has taken every precaution. It's perfectly safe for the entire Stand and all the elder firstbloods to devote undivided attention to the Queens' spell. If the Guardian of Orthros is satisfied the mages aren't a danger, you can attend to the Renewal without concern."

"We're not concerned about the mages," Mak replied.

"Lio," Lyros said, "don't have a chat with the Dexion. Don't offer the Torch to the Dexion."

Mak leaned closer to Lio. "Don't raid the Dexion's mind for information on the hostages."

Lyros's eyes gleamed. "If you feel tempted, remember the powerful motivation to stay safe who stood next to you at your Gift Night celebration."

Lio gripped each of their shoulders. "You have no cause for worry."

Mak sighed and lifted a hand. "It still feels like we're marching naked into Corona. I don't like us giving all our concentration to a spell that can't be interrupted while there are mages at our backs."

"And at my mercy?" Lio quirked a brow.

"I wish we could postpone the Renewal till the embassy is gone," Lyros said. "The Queens decided against it, though. They were concerned it might diminish the ward's preservation of the vacant city while we're in Orthros Notou. Architectural repairs would be a small price to pay, but they don't want the gardens and the wildlife to suffer."

"That's out of the question," Lio said. "I would be aghast if the Summit made anyone think otherwise. The Annassa must give the ward an infusion of their magic for the coming year, and all the elder firstbloods must lend their power to the working. It's an honor for the Stewards to get to participate and strengthen your connection with the ward. I can only imagine what that must feel like."

"We promised to tell Bosko all about it at bedtime," Mak said. "Why don't you and Cassia bring Zoe over?"

Lio smiled. "We'll do that."

Lyros pulled him a little closer. "I mean it, Glasstongue. Don't get any ideas about talking to the mages."

Lio signed Alathea's constellation over his heart. "My lips are sealed. I don't need to talk to gouge their eyes out with blinding light or break their minds into little pieces, should they cause trouble."

Mak grinned. "Are you sure you don't need a couple of Chargers to hold them down for you?"

Lyros released Lio with some reluctance. "The Chargers need to be on alert at the border in case the envoys send word of the hostages while we're engrossed in the casting."

"I managed hundreds of heart hunters all right," Lio reminded them, "without killing them. You can trust me with two mages and an apprentice."

His Trial brothers saluted him and stepped away.

Lio let out a sigh. He focused his thoughts on Cassia's aura in the next building. Like the Harbor Light guiding him home, she kept him from straying into dire thoughts of the hostages and the envoys who were searching for them.

The beacon of her aura gleamed brighter with surprise, then hope so fierce, Lio could taste it. He shut his eyes. No one else in either guest house was astir, except…was that spirit afire Eudias? It was indeed.

Lio was still debating whether this justified leaving his post when he heard footsteps in the gallery. In a moment, Cassia strode into the corridor and approached with Eudias, Callen, and Perita. Knight's hackles rose as they neared the mages' doors.

Cassia spoke first. "Apprentice Eudias has new information about the hostages, which could help us discover where the mages are holding them."

"Thank the Goddess." Lio turned to the young mage.

"Is it safe to do this here, now?" Eudias peered up and down the hall. "You're the only guard tonight, Ambassador?"

"Yes."

"But—but—you're a light mage."

"I am." Lio left him to imagine the dangerous mystery skills Hesperines possessed, which he now had on his side.

"We must do this now," Cassia said, "regardless of the risk. There is no time to lose."

Lio hesitated, a hand on his breast where he had just signed Alathea's constellation. "I know you would not suggest anything risky unless it were necessary."

Eudias gestured to Cassia. "Go ahead, Basilis."

Cassia spoke quickly. Lio listened in silence as she described what they had learned about the Gift Collector's work for the war mages and his whereabouts during the past year.

"So you see," she finished, "we have reason to believe that Skleros captured the seven Hesperines errant for the Dexion. We also know the Gift Collector has not been in Cordium for a year. Do you have any reason to believe the hostages were taken before that time?"

Lio thought back to what Ioustin had told him about the disappearances Abroad. "I am certain they were not. I have it on the best authority they went missing between the Spring and Autumn Equinoxes."

"That must mean Skleros delivered the hostages somewhere in Tenebra."

"We have to find out where."

"I'm afraid we must take into consideration that the mages may have moved them since then."

"Even so, from their last known location, our search parties would have a hope of picking up their trail. Skleros may even know where they are being held now and which 'colleagues' of the Dexion's are keeping them."

Cassia stood with her courtly poise, but the sound of her heart hammering filled the quiet hallway. She looked into his eyes, her own pleading. "A Gift Collector will not surrender what he knows easily. We must try to negotiate."

This was their chance to save the hostages from the Akron's Altar. Lio could not hold to the promise he had just made his Trial brothers, but they would be the first to understand. "A Gift Collector will not listen to reason."

"I must agree with Basilis," Eudias said with conviction. "If she negotiates with Master Skleros, she could surely accomplish great things, as she did with the members of the embassy."

"I have the utmost respect for Lady Cassia's accomplishments as a negotiator, but how can any diplomat change a Gift Collector's mind? We have nothing to offer him that he wants. We have no secrets to use against him. If there is a shred of goodness in his heart to which we can appeal, I am not aware."

"And yet negotiation is our only recourse," Cassia insisted.

He met her gaze. "Is it?"

"It must be," she entreated him. "How can any diplomat consider the alternative?"

"Gift Collectors truly are the archenemy, Lady Cassia. They are immune to the greatest weapon of Hesperine diplomats. Words. What would you have me do?"

"Remain on the path of peace. Don't endanger yourself or your people by engaging your archenemy."

Eudias was watching the exchange between Lio and Cassia. "Oh, Ambassador, are you thinking of enlisting one of your people's renowned thelemancers? Could such a formidable master break through a Gift Collector's mental defenses? What a duel that would be."

Cassia turned toward the apprentice. "What mental defenses?"

"It is not only Gift Collectors' tolerance for physical pain that is legendary. They have specialized, secret strategies for withstanding mental attacks." The apprentice whispered, "Dream wards."

She faced Lio. "A dangerous mage duel will not help the Summit."

"Basilis is right. We cannot afford to antagonize the Gift Collector. At least let her attempt to negotiate with him before trying any…contentious alternatives."

"Out of the question," Lio replied. "A dangerous negotiation will not help the Summit, either. I would fear for Lady Cassia's safety in the presence of the Gift Collector."

Cassia took a step closer to him. "We would fear for the safety of the Hesperine thelemancer who would engage with Skleros. You must not take all the risk upon your—people. This is a crisis that concerns all of us. We are talking about a Hesperine rescue party on Tenebran soil taking action against Cordian mages."

Lio shook his head. "The more people we involve in this, the longer it will take."

"Combined pressure from Orthros and Tenebra will be more effective than either of our lands acting alone," Cassia argued. "If we announce our new agreement, the mages will realize they are at a disadvantage. We should negotiate with Cordium with the Tenebran embassy present."

"Cordium?" Lio asked. "You suggest we involve the Dexion in this as well?"

"Yes. We won't need to get the information from Skleros if we can persuade Chrysanthos to get it from him for us."

"Oh, Basilis," Eudias interjected, "are you sure you do not wish to go directly to Master Skleros for information? Can the hostages afford for us to negotiate with the Dexion first? It could take a great deal of time. He and Master Skleros have everything to gain and nothing to lose by staying allied against us."

"I am certain," Cassia answered. "Chrysanthos will fall to our persuasion much faster, for he is not immune to words."

Lio could smell Cassia's fear for him, but also sense the workings of her mind that he trusted so well. "How do you intend to convince him to help us?"

"Skleros aided both sides of the battle for the position of Dexion," Cassia said. "No matter who won, he would have the victor's favor. What if he went a step further to secure his advantage and handed victory to the side he preferred?"

Fire blazed in Lio's memory, and he smelled the burnt corpse of the mage who had wielded it. "That is entirely possible."

"I have absolutely no evidence to suggest that is the case," Eudias objected.

"I do." Lio looked at the apprentice. "I think you are aware the necromancy that allowed the Dexion to enter Orthros in disguise is the same that enabled Dalos to hide his identity at Solorum, and Skleros performed it for both of them."

Eudias averted his gaze.

Cassia tried to catch his eye. "Gratitude makes us strong."

"This will not avail us, Basilis."

"The necromancy served Chrysanthos well," Lio said. "We all witnessed the moment at the Firstblood Circle when he threw off the spell and revealed his true power. How can we forget how differently it went for Dalos when he did the same at the Equinox Summit?"

"Do you understand what happened that night?" Cassia asked Eudias.

The young mage sounded hoarse. "This has nothing to do with the hostages."

"It could help," Cassia said gently.

"We who dueled with Dalos sensed the turmoil in his aura," Lio explained. "It took even my battle-tested elders by surprise. It was clear the necromancy had a strange and dangerous effect on his power. It is entirely possible the Gift Collector sabotaged Dalos."

"But not Chrysanthos," Cassia said. "Could he not have hired the necromancer to remove his rival for the office of Dexion? He was born a Pavo. It is family tradition."

Eudias didn't have a rebuttal this time.

Cassia gave him a questioning look. "Do you know anything that could confirm or deny this?"

Eudias sighed. "Dalos was born a Taurus."

Surprise and satisfaction came together in Cassia's aura. "What more need I say?"

"I am convinced," Lio answered.

"Apprentice Eudias, you have said the leaders of the Aithourian Circle hold themselves above the rules. Would it trouble the Synthikos to learn his Dexion stole the position through conspiracy and assassination?"

His throat worked. "The Circle are your brothers. The Synthikos is Father. No matter who you were before you donned the robes, you leave all other loyalties on the steps of the Hagion. You stand together and betray the world, but not each other. That is the one rule you do not break."

"The Dexion will beg for our silence," Lio vowed.

"We will threaten to reveal his betrayal to the Aithourian Circle." Cassia smiled. "Let us see how quickly he finds out from Skleros where the hostages are."

THE CRUEL INQUISITOR
AND THE KIND INQUISITOR

LIO GATHERED SHADOWS AROUND the edges of the main hall. Gloom descended over the chamber, leaving their makeshift Summit table spotlighted in the beacon's rays that shone through the rose window.

Crimson light bathed the faces of the mortals seated there and caressed Cassia's shoulders where she sat with her back to the window. Perita smoothed the white silk tablecloth, while Callen cut an ominous figure, sitting in the darkness behind Cassia.

Lord Gaius took the chair at her right hand. "We may consider this the first test of the Council's new agreement with Orthros. If we carry this out with honor, we can send a strong message to Cordium and spare needless bloodshed."

"I could not agree more." Lio stood at the place to Cassia's left.

Benedict sat down on Lord Gaius's right. "Apprentice Eudias, you don't have to appear among us before the Dexion. You could preserve the secret that you have changed sides."

Eudias pulled out the chair beside Benedict and joined them at the table. "I have chosen my side. I will have everyone know it."

Benedict and Lord Severin clapped him on the shoulders. A hesitant smile came to his face.

Cassia turned to Lio. "We thank you for your insight, which will aid us in the coming confrontation."

"The Blood Union does convey a certain advantage during negotiations. Whenever I sense a strong emotional response in the Dexion, I will give you this signal." Lio touched a hand to his medallion of office. "When he is most vulnerable, I will indicate his breaking point thus." With a smile, Lio put his hands behind his back.

Cassia returned his smile. "We are ready."

"I will retrieve the mage," Lio said.

He stepped to the corridor outside Chrysanthos's door.

"Nothing is amiss." Xandra chuckled, teasing a flame under Skleros's metal door handle.

Nodora frowned over Xandra's shoulder. "Except that Skleros has fashioned a makeshift weapon of some sort. You can hear him throwing it at the wall over and over."

Lio shook his head. "He must know that's no use against the Guardian of Orthros's wards."

Xandra smirked as the door handle blazed red. "Come now, Master Skleros. Just be a little bit stupid. Try the door."

"I think he's just fending off boredom." Kia bent an ear to Tychon's chambers. "This one's doing *another* set of push-ups."

"Thank you all for keeping an eye on them for me," Lio said.

"Our pleasure," Kia replied.

Nodora put a hand on his arm. "Be careful, Lio."

"I will," he promised.

Lio lifted a hand and knocked on Chrysanthos's door. "Dexion Chrysanthos, I am here to deliver an invitation."

"Didn't you get yours from Hypnos, Ambassador?" the mage called.

Having given fair warning, Lio waited a moment longer, then let himself into the room, passing through the familiar embrace of his relatives' warding magic. His Trial sisters closed the door behind him.

Chrysanthos gave Lio a sardonic look. The mage lounged on his back on the perfectly made bed. He had burned the outline of a kings and mages board on the ceiling over his head and conjured little flames for tokens.

"Really, Dexion?" Lio raised his eyebrows. "Such a petty act of revenge upon my father's architecture. I'm sure we could have provided you with paper and ink to keep your mind occupied."

"You didn't hear? The Stand thought I might write something of a magical nature or commit suicide with a quill. Mama Steward has swaddled me in her wards so I cannot come to harm, even from my own spells. For the sake of the prisoners, you know."

"When you made their survival contingent upon yours, I am sure you were prepared for such consequences. I am aware she also cast the blood shackles on you to prevent you from harming others. Fortunately, this unpleasant experience could be over for you very soon. If you will come with me, the Tenebran embassy would like a word with you."

"I am not interested in anything those bumpkins have to say. However, as I have nothing better to do, I will humor them." Chrysanthos sighed and got to his feet, smoothing his robes.

"Bear in mind the blood shackles upon your person. Our stroll over to Rose House is not an opportunity for you to repeat the tantrum you threw before the Firstblood Circle."

The Dexion retrieved his mantle from the back of his desk chair and arranged it upon his shoulders. "Rose House? Without me to discipline them, have that witless lot returned to eat out of Basilis's hand?"

"They know the gentle, steady hand of good leadership from an abusive grasp."

"They'll regret biting the hand that's been feeding them."

Lio opened the door for him. The Dexion proceeded through the gauntlet of Lio's Trial sisters as if making a formal procession down the aisle of the Sun Temple.

Lio shadowed the mage in his blind spot, his senses straining to the highest alertness.

They were halfway down the gallery when Chrysanthos halted in his tracks.

Lio held his magic at the ready. "Kindly remember my warnings."

Chrysanthos made no sudden moves, only turned slowly to face Lio, but his aura was vicious. "There is nothing I despise more than a hypocrite. Your sanctimonious diplomacy sickens me. I want you to know that no matter what you say, no matter what you do, no matter how this Summit ends, I regard you only with contempt."

"Peace does not require us to like one another, only to choose to act according to the common good, rather than our own passions."

"Ambassador Deukalion, the bottomless jug of cloying principles.

Nothing could be a more insidious veil with which to cover your ruthless promotion of Orthros's interests."

"I see I have graduated in your estimation from a wordy novice to a merciless politician. Our round in the gymnasium must have left an impression on you. I genuinely wish I could convince you both assessments of me are wrong, now that I have discovered my own assumptions about you to be just as misguided."

"All you need to understand about me is that I will bring you to justice. It may not be this winter, but you are marked, and every mage from here to Corona knows you are mine."

Lio could not allow this personal grudge Chrysanthos had developed during the Summit to stand in the way now. The hostages' lives were at stake. Lio would not let them die because of Chrysanthos's petty thirst for revenge for an embarrassment in the fighting ring. "I urge you to set aside your desire to settle matters between us, at least for tonight. Rather, look to your own affairs. Your future is in the Tenebrans' hands. I suggest we do not keep them waiting."

Chrysanthos stood where he was, seething. Would he make this difficult after all?

At last the Dexion continued down the gallery. "You and I are not done here."

When they entered the main hall, a table full of watchful gazes and hostile auras greeted the Dexion. Lio hounded him to the seat they had prepared for him across from Cassia, flanked on either side by the Tenebran mages. Lio remained standing in the Dexion's blind spot. Chrysanthos lowered himself into the seat with great dignity, but he squinted and grimaced when the beacon shone in his eyes.

Cassia got to her feet, silhouetted against the window. "Welcome, Dexion Chrysanthos, to Cordium's first and only negotiation with Orthros and Tenebra's Acting Council of Free Lords."

Chrysanthos laughed. "What is this self-important nonsense?"

Cassia held up the document in front of her. "Here is the written attestation of the treaty between Orthros and Tenebra, which bears the blood of the Annassa and the elder firstbloods."

Benedict glared at the Dexion. "I am sure you will easily recognize the seals of Hadria, Segetia, and every free domain in Tenebra represented in this embassy."

"As well as the glyphs of the Tenebran mages of Anthros, Kyria, and Chera," Master Gorgos boomed.

"*This* is your attempt at a winning move, Basilis?" The Dexion gestured at the document. "You are as foolish as I first believed, after all. How long do you think your pretty piece of paper will last when you are once more in your father's domain?"

Cassia smiled. "It won't be his domain after the free lords revoke their mandate from him."

"Oh, I see now. It turns out you are merely another bitter, ungrateful bastard out for vengeance like all the rest. Shame. You could have been someone more interesting—and lived longer."

"I am going to outlive you, unless you let us help you."

"I need not remind you the king has cleaned up rebellions before."

"With the help of Aithourian siege engines," Benedict said. "We know how long your circle has been violating the Law of Neutrality and the Law of Sword and Spell."

Chrysanthos drummed his fingers on the table. "I see you learned something from your study of Hephaestion, Sir Benedict."

"You don't even deny it?" Benedict shot back.

"It will not stand!" Master Gorgos shook a finger at the Dexion. "Apostasy within Corona itself!"

"The good mages of Tenebra will not tolerate such treatment of the people under our care," the Semna said.

"You have pushed Tenebra too far," Lord Gaius warned. "Prepare yourself, for Anthros's Aegis shall push back."

"Dexion." Cassia's hushed tone echoed through the shadows, and even Lio, who knew her voice so well, shivered in surprise. "Have you heard the Tale of the Cruel Inquisitor and the Kind Inquisitor?"

Chrysanthos turned his head in Lio's direction. "There is no cruel Hesperine in the tale."

Cassia's laughter could have seduced Hypnos into his own realm. "Ambassador Deukalion is the kind one."

Lio smiled. "Before we begin, I will explain the rules of this negotiation.

Noncombatants have immunity. Regardless of tonight's outcome, no innocent women or children will be involved."

Cassia withdrew Chrysanthos's letter box from her gardening satchel and set it on the table.

Fury erupted in the man's aura. "How dare you!"

Lio levitated the box across the table. "Do not regret that your letters came into my hands and made a testament to your character. Against all odds, I no longer believe you to be a man without honor. I shall even go so far as to rest my hopes on an appeal to your conscience."

As soon as the box came within Chrysanthos's reach, he snatched it to him and snapped it shut. "You are wasting your breath."

"Recall that Hesperines don't need to breathe." Lio began to pace behind Chrysanthos. "I could do this all night, and I will, if that's what it takes to reach an agreement."

"My terms will not change."

"The Order of Anthros's terms won't, I am sure, but what about yours? I can secure for you a life you cherish, if only you will restore the lives I cherish."

Chrysanthos's hand tightened on the letter box. "Whose life?"

"Yours. I don't mean your survival. I mean the life to which you are accustomed."

Cassia gestured at the mage's chest. "Was it hard to leave the Dexion's medallion behind when you came, after all you did to earn it?"

"I'll live," the Dexion snapped.

"You are clearly fond of the finer comforts of life." Cassia lifted her goblet of Notian red from the table. "Your position certainly affords the best."

"I can see the robes you wear mean more to you than luxury, though," Lio said. "You wear them with pride."

Cassia toasted the mage. "Surely nothing is more satisfying than to experience the gazes of those around you and know they look upon the third most powerful man in Corona. The future Synthikos. Perhaps even the future Akron."

Chrysanthos bowed in his seat. "I see you have an appreciation for how dangerous a person you are toying with. Don't forget it."

"But what is left," Cassia mused, "when the medallion and the robes and the admiring stares are taken away?"

"Magic, certainly," Lio said, "but also the strictures that make it useless without the authority to use it. A man who has lost everything he thrives on. Hungry mouths to feed."

Chrysanthos drew the box still closer. "You agreed to leave them out of this."

Lio halted behind him. "But you didn't. Every risk you take, you risk them. Every mistake you make, you hurt them. If you fall, they fall with you."

"Do not lecture me on my responsibilities."

"I understand responsibilities to your dependents. The rigor of duty. Obligations you must fulfill to secure your future and theirs."

Cassia took a sip of her wine. "How much does admittance into the Aithourian Circle cost, really? A sum comfortable for your family to manage, I am sure."

"But what about the cost you have continued to pay in the years since?" Lio asked. "How many promotions did you pay for in blood?"

They let a hush fall over the chamber.

Lio braced a hand on the table, leaning over the Dexion. "Hesperine blood. Your entries in the Order's register of kills must be impressive indeed to have brought the medallion within your reach."

Strange that the Dexion did not take this opportunity to boast. Had they struck a nerve? Lio touched his own medallion of office.

Cassia set her goblet down, and red wine splashed onto the white tablecloth. "When you began, did you know you would pay in human blood, as well?"

The Dexion did not reply.

"I understand weights on the conscience," Lio said.

"There are those who stand in your way." Now Cassia began to prowl on her side of the hall. "Something must be done about them. You may not have the luxury of time or knowing whether they deserve to die. It is you, or them, and you must make a choice."

Lio paced in the shadows that ringed the table. "But did you imagine whose death you would one day carry on your heart?"

"Someone most worthy among your peers." Cassia paused.

"Someone on the right side of the gods." Lio drew alongside her.

Next to him, she faced Chrysanthos. "Someone who trusted you."

"A brother," Lio declared.

He felt the tremor that went through Chrysanthos's aura, although the mage was still and silent without. Anger lashed out of the man's heart, the kind that hid pain. Lio put his hands behind his back.

"We know you murdered Dalos," Cassia said.

The mage showed them his impassive, ruined face.

"You might not have done the deed by your own hand," Cassia went on, "but you were undoubtedly responsible."

In the silence, Lio heard Chrysanthos's heart laboring.

"Please, be honest about your role in his death." Lio gave a slight bow. "I am the last person who will judge you. I am partially responsible for it myself, after all."

"Whatever my failures," Chrysanthos spat, "I am nothing like you."

"Failure?" Lio echoed. "Far from it, Dexion. Allow me to thank you for protecting countless people from him."

"A number of us were sitting in the path of his flames at the Equinox Summit," Cassia said. "None of us around this table will lose any sleep over his demise."

"Go to Hypnos," Chrysanthos hissed.

Lio grimaced. "I am afraid that may, in fact, be *your* destination if your circle finds out. They may not take it as well as we have when they discover how your infamous rivalry with Dalos concluded."

"I understand you war mages thrive on competition," Cassia said, "but betraying your own brother? That is unforgivable."

A drop of sweat trembled on Chrysanthos's brow.

Cassia planted her hands on the table and leaned forward. "You can bid your medallion goodbye when the world learns you hired an assassin to rid you of Dalos's competition and clear your way to the office of Dexion."

Chrysanthos let out a breath that sounded like a scoff. Then he smiled. Then he tilted back his head and laughed.

"Oh, Ambassador." Chrysanthos lounged back in his chair, still chuckling. "The thorn has fallen far from the thicket, indeed. This is your grand maneuver? You and these pretenders have nothing to say to me. Take me back to my rooms."

Lio veiled his face so his expression would not betray his surprise. Where had they gone wrong?

Cassia's frustration and dismay mingled with his own. "I am sure you wish it were so easy, but you are not leaving this table until we reach an agreement about the hostages."

"That won't happen unless the ambassador leaves with me."

The abrupt change they had just witnessed in Chrysanthos was far more than a mere recovery of composure. Lio had sensed the mage's deep response to their accusations. The answers were right in front of them, Lio was sure, but they hadn't learned them yet. They must keep probing his weaknesses.

Lio circled back toward the Dexion. "Did you know what else Dalos was doing in Tenebra?"

"I suspect so." Cassia paced in the opposite direction. "You know all the Aithourian Circle's ugly secrets, don't you?"

"I'm afraid you do me too much credit." Chrysanthos looked at his letter box, not at Lio over his shoulder. "I have no idea what Dalos might have been up to on the side. Care to tattle? Since we're sharing secrets."

Lio paused right next to the mage. "You really didn't know he was planning to consign two-dozen children to the pyre for heresy?"

Chrysanthos shifted in his chair, putting distance between them. "I will not listen to Hesperines make such malicious accusations against my circle."

"I think your conscience gave you pause," Lio said, "although Dalos's did not trouble him. I heard your response to Princess Alexandra's relation of her past. I have also seen the evidence of your love for your nephew. You value the lives of children more than Dalos ever did."

"Any children rescued from heretical parents are given into the care of Kyrian orphanages for proper teaching. Aithourians do not stoop to murdering children."

Lio brought his face closer. "Even Eriphite children?"

"You must think me a fool. The bandits the Tenebran mages of Anthros were hunting were anything but children."

Cassia stood by the Semna. "So you were aware Dalos intended to apprehend the Eriphites in return for the Temple of Namenti's cooperation."

"Solorum Temple knew nothing about this!" Master Gorgos's jowls shook.

Chrysanthos shot him a glance. "A mage of Anthros from the royal temple colluding with a Hesperine. I never thought I would see the day. The Akron will ensure we never see such a day again."

"The transgressions be upon your head, you traitor to Anthros! Your blatant sacrilege against the god of war's virtues will cost you his Hall!"

"Well, Ambassador, I see you have made a convert of Master Gorgos, here. The resolve of Cordian mages is considerably greater, I'm afraid. You may skip the sordid tales of child murder and tell me what you want."

"No, I think you will be interested in this." Lio leaned against the edge of the table, crossing his arms. "You may have received word the Eriphites disappeared from Tenebra around the same time as the Hesperine embassy returned home."

Chrysanthos straightened in his chair. "We are sharing secrets, indeed, heretic. Are you confessing before the Dexion that Eriphites begged you for Sanctuary and came to Orthros with the aid of the Hesperine embassy?"

"No," Lio answered. "The adult Eriphites were long gone by the time Dalos arrived in Tenebra. All that remained of a once-thriving cult were twenty-four children between the ages of two and ten. We Solaced them so Dalos wouldn't burn them to death."

"Is this an attempt to twist my thoughts against my own circle?" Chrysanthos demanded.

The horror in his aura told Lio he had succeeded, although the Dexion might never admit it. "I am only trying to impress upon you that there are those who sympathize with your motivations for putting an end to Dalos's cruelty."

"Unfortunately," said Cassia, "I don't think the Synthikos is one of them."

"Is that a threat?" Chrysanthos asked.

"To be sure," Cassia purred.

"Imagine." Lio laughed. "Hesperines reporting a transgression to the inquisitors."

Chrysanthos lifted his gaze to the ceiling. "As if they will credit it."

"Indeed," Cassia said, "they would hardly take the ambassador's word for it. They may, however, credit sworn testimony by Dalos's former apprentice, a member in good standing of the Aithourian Circle; an Anthrian master of Solorum and future royal mage; the Prisma of the oldest Temple of Kyria north of Cordium; and any number of Tenebran nobles who were present at the Equinox Summit. If all these people come forward and instigate an inquiry in Corona, it could cause you some trouble."

"Be my guest." Chrysanthos bowed again. "The Synthikos will not believe a word of it."

"You have him wrapped so securely around your finger?" Lio lifted his brows. "Impressive. Whether or not he believes it, however, the news all over Cordium will surely create an unwelcome scandal for your order. It's difficult being the paragon of virtue for the entire world, isn't it? When you transgress, those who are supposed to follow your example question your moral authority. Those who wish to preserve that authority have little choice but to make an example out of you."

"What happens to a Dexion in disgrace?" Cassia asked. "A slap on the wrist while the inquisitors investigate? A luxurious carriage for your ride to your trial? An opulent place of exile, I am sure, when the Synthikos realizes he was deceived as to your worthiness. When Dalos's illustrious family sends an assassin to avenge him, I'm sure they will use a bejeweled dagger."

"The Synthikos knows I would never betray one of our own," Chrysanthos maintained.

"How convinced is he as to Skleros's good character?" Lio inquired.

"Now this is almost as bold as stealing the Akron's Torch, Bloodborn." Chrysanthos's mouth twisted. "A Hesperine trying to frame two high-ranking Order mages for crimes they didn't commit. Do you really expect to succeed? Do you think your little threats here in Selas will ever have a hearing in Corona? What do you really think you can do against the spell my circle holds over the world?"

"Is the necromancer you hired to tamper with Dalos's magic really worth defending?" Cassia asked.

Chrysanthos hesitated. "Your invented conspiracy only grows more fantastical."

But he had hesitated.

Lio touched his medallion, gliding through the dark behind the mage again. "We are prepared to make you a compelling offer. You will use your influence with Master Skleros to discover where he delivered the Hesperine hostages, then reveal their location to us."

"In return," Cassia said, "we will turn a blind eye to the assassination Skleros committed for you on Tenebran soil."

Chrysanthos laughed again. "I thought you were going to try to make me believe Skleros told you about this alleged plot."

"He didn't have to," Lio said. "We felt what happened to Dalos at the Equinox Summit."

Chrysanthos's jaw clenched. "Did you enjoy your duel with my… erstwhile colleague? Did it make you feel powerful to kill a mage of my circle, Ambassador?"

"Like every Hesperine there, I vicariously experienced Dalos's death with him. I assure you, none of us relished it."

"There are plenty of mages who thrive on the experience of death."

"Like you?"

"I am a warrior, not an assassin."

"You are friends with one."

"Gift Collectors do not have friends."

"They have associates," Cassia said. "How much do you really know about what Skleros does when he is out of your sight? Although you are his colleague, I am certain he keeps you in the dark as much as possible."

Lio followed Cassia's insightful change of course. "Then again, he has been doing, shall we say, unsavory work on your behalf. You must have had to do something for him in return. You know at least a few of one another's secrets."

Chrysanthos shot Lio a glance. "Wouldn't you love for me to answer such questions?"

Cassia gestured around her. "All of us here are expert players at the game board. We all know a token that changes hands once could do so again."

"Perhaps I am prejudiced, as a Hesperine," said Lio, "but I would not put it past a Gift Collector who turned on one high-ranking member of the Aithourian Circle to turn on another, as it suits him."

"Throw him to the liegehounds," Cassia urged. "You won't miss him. But you will miss the sun, if the move Skleros made for you comes to the temple's attention."

"All my dealings with Skleros are in writing in the Synthikos's office— next to the records of the Gift Collector's dealings with Dalos and the Synthikos himself, I might add. I am one of the Synthikos's mentorees. I do not need to deal under the table to accomplish my ends, and I certainly don't need to commit murder to attain a promotion. I will without hesitation disclose before this half-baked rebellion and you, upstart Ambassador, that the Aithourian Circle has contracted with a well-qualified Gift Collector of the Order of Hypnos in the name of cooperating against Hesperine aggression."

That Chrysanthos disclosed anything showed he was on the defensive. Lio touched his medallion. "Was it Hesperine aggression that nearly cost the Council of Free Lords their lives? Is it Hesperine aggression that has sabotaged Tenebra's every effort at peace with Orthros?"

A chorus of "nays" around the table supported him.

"Really?" Chrysanthos demanded. "You have convinced the Tenebrans *you* are protecting *them* from their own gods?"

"You, young man, are not the gods," the Semna said.

Benedict stamped his feet. The shadowy room filled with the rhythm of Tenebran applause. Cassia joined in on her side of the table, while Lio clapped his hands just out of the Dexion's sight. Chrysanthos's heart pounded faster.

Callen laid his scythe on the table with a clang, and the applause hushed. "My lady could have died at the Equinox Summit."

Benedict leaned forward. "You'd best make it clear whether you were in favor of Dalos's assassination—or the man who killed him and stopped it."

"We now know everything about your circle's plan to destroy the nobility," Lord Gaius said. "Now would be a wise time for you to abandon it."

"You believe these Hesperine lies?" Chrysanthos demanded.

Eudias spoke for the first time. "They're not Hesperine lies."

Chrysanthos's gaze swiveled to him. "I told Dalos he never should have wasted his time on you."

"I told them everything," Eudias shot back. "Basilis, Callen, Perita—all the Tenebrans who witnessed Dalos's activities at Solorum confirmed it."

"We believe their statements given under oath before the gods," said Lord Gaius, "and yes, we believe the ambassador's account, too."

Lord Severin joined in. "We also believe you were standing unharmed while we nearly died in an avalanche and subsequent heart hunter attack. It was the Hesperines who saved us then, too."

"Thank you for your trust, allies from Tenebra," Lio said. "You see, Dexion, I have explained the precise details of the Hesperine embassy's duel with Dalos to the Tenebrans. I have withheld nothing. I have offered them evidence that Dalos tried to assassinate everyone there with a massive fire spell and that we tried to stop him with a ward."

"Your ward spell made his power rebound on him," Chrysanthos said. "You killed him."

"Our ward spell prevented his power from harming the Summit attendees. However, we were not the cause of his death."

"You may twist those events in the minds of the Tenebrans, but such wiles will not work on me."

"During our duel with him," Lio went on, "the evidence of his condition was dramatic. You revealed your true affinity before the Firstblood Circle in a deliberate reclamation of your power, which summoned your magic to its natural place within you. When Dalos attempted the same, it was as if a break occurred inside him, and uncontrolled power was unleashed. His magic was fearsome in its power—unnaturally so. Unstable spells raged forth from him and struck our senses in disparate barrages."

Chrysanthos sat very still, his breathing quiet. He was actually listening.

Lio touched his medallion and prayed they were approaching victory. "Our embassy consisted of powerful elders and battle-hardened Hesperines errant. They all attested to me they had never encountered anything like that duel. His own magic destroyed him. As a forest fire consumes a tree, his power ate him from within and expended him."

The anger lashed out of Chrysanthos, as raw as a fire spell itself.

"I would not wish that on any fellow mage." Lio drew near the Dexion once more. "It was a horrific way to die. Did you see his body when they sent it back to Cordium?"

Chrysanthos's knuckles were white where he clutched the letter box.

Cassia emerged from the shadows on his other side, flanking him. "Did you look upon the consequences of your choices? Were you proud of how you secured your position? Do you ever get a whiff of his burnt-out flesh when you smell your fine wine or see his blank eyes staring back at you from among the admiring gazes?"

Chrysanthos covered his face in his hands. A long groan grated out of him. "You know nothing!" he screamed across the table. He stumbled to his feet, rounding on Lio.

The man disappeared in a blast of fire magic. Lio could only watch as the ward around Chrysanthos pulsed with red light and black shadow. The fire spell fizzled and revealed him once more. Tears streaked his face.

"I did see his body," he roared. "My own flesh and blood. Our father and I lit the funerary pyre together. Gods doom you for what you did to my brother."

Lio faced him, speechless. On his other side, Cassia was a silent flare of shock in the darkness.

Chrysanthos hammered a fist against his chest. "He should have had that medallion! He should have had the chance to watch his son grow." His face contorted. "I should have been there. I should never have let him go alone. I *am* to blame. I, who was not at his side in battle, as I swore I always would be."

The Dexion sank into his chair, and his hand curled into a fist on the lid of his letter box. His body shook, and then his sobs filled the hall.

RESTITUTION

ATREMBLING HAND WAS THE only mask the Dexion of the Aithourian Circle had to hide his face from the room full of onlookers. He was out of clever words. Cassia watched the grief she recognized break him.

His shoulders convulsed, and uncontrolled, wretched sobs poured out of him. Had he ever cried until this moment?

She reached out a hand to the suffering man before her, then pulled it back. It was not safe to touch this fellow mourner. It was not possible to give the enemy comfort.

She waited until he spent himself, and his weeping quieted to rasping breaths.

"I am so sorry," she said softly.

Lio pulled out the chair next to Chrysanthos and sat down beside him. "I carry your grief in my veins."

"Your pity is a sacrilege against his memory," Chrysanthos hissed.

"It is not pity," Lio said. "With Hespera as my witness, I wish you knew what I feel for you."

Lio met Cassia's eyes over the Dexion's head, then both their gazes fell to the inlaid box. In the man who had been ready to send Zoe, Bosko, and Thenie to the pyre, they could not see the doting father described in those letters. They had never considered that the man who had nearly destroyed families with one spell at the Summit could leave behind a grieving lover, son, brother, and father.

"Dalos is still the mage who tried to assassinate everyone at the Equinox Summit," Lord Adrogan reminded them.

"Whoever he was," Benedict returned, "whatever he did, he was Chrysanthos's kin."

"Like your father was your kin?" Lord Adrogan challenged.

"Yes," Benedict answered.

Lord Gaius came round to Chrysanthos carrying a flask that smelled of strong spirits and held it out to the mage. "Enemy warriors mourn their fallen the same as we do."

Chrysanthos took the flask and put it to his mouth, throwing his head back. Then he took a breath, growled, and handed the flask back to Lord Gaius.

"Go ahead," Chrysanthos dared. "Try to use this against me. Scandal may spread like wildfire, but the Synthikos will douse it as easily as a candle flame."

"He is your father," Cassia said, "in more than name."

"Try to tell the Pavones I'm the Synthikos's bastard, if you like. Mother is above reproach. Her own husband died believing I was his."

Master Gorgos was aghast. "This is exactly the kind of perversion the vows of celibacy were established to prevent."

"Actually they were to appease the Cordian princes, who feared the consequences of hereditary inheritance of high positions in the Orders. Consider that the result is dilution of magic in all mortal bloodlines over time." Chrysanthos put on one of his mocking smiles, and for the first time, Cassia realized he was mocking himself. "I was bred for the benefit of humanity."

"War mages fornicating to breed their own apprentices!" Master Gorgos exclaimed.

"Producing an apprentice for the Synthikos is quite the distinction among the princesses of Corona, you know. Mother will never cease to congratulate herself for being one of only two women to secure the honor."

"How she must revile the Tauri princess who is the other," Cassia guessed. "It was prudent for you and Dalos to pay lip service to your families' feud, while you grew up together as brothers under the tutelage of your father."

"Is that your nephew's destiny?" Lio asked.

"I resent your implication he is a tool to be used," Chrysanthos shot back. "But what would a Hesperine know about protecting a child from schemes?"

Trust Lio to respond only with a diplomatic answer. "Your loyalty to your brother and the loved ones he left behind does you great credit."

Chrysanthos rose to his feet, looking down upon Lio. "This changes nothing, Ambassador. Our circle's war upon Hesperines errant was my brother's life's work, and I will go to my grave striving to finish it. I will see you burn on the Akron's Altar, followed by every other member of the Hesperine embassy who faced Dalos that day. I will not fail him twice."

Lio remained in his chair. "I know my words mean nothing to you. But we have real reason to believe the essential displacement Skleros performed on Dalos had an adverse effect on your brother's magic. It is no deception that the Gift Collector is to blame for Dalos's death."

"Those are the only words that have ever come out of your mouth that have a shred of worth. I credit them only because they confirm my own concerns about my brother. The warning sign confronted me the day I arrived at Solorum—the remains of a shrine of Hespera."

Lio did not look at Cassia. She resisted the irrational urge to straighten her gloves. She had to remind herself they had allowed Chrysanthos to believe she was out to depose her father. They had given him no reason to suspect her of being a Hesperite.

"My brother was supposed to have full access to his power," Chrysanthos said. "I have confirmed Skleros's assertions in that regard during my own experience with essential displacement. And yet Dalos spent fortnights at Solorum without even mentioning that shrine of Hespera to me in his letters. I can only conclude that he, the greatest Aithourian mage of our generation, was unable to even sense it was there."

Lio's face was so impassive, Cassia was sure he had veiled himself again.

"I, on the other hand," Chrysanthos told him, "detected the stench of your goddess's refuse the moment I set foot on the grounds. Needless to say, I cleaned up after her."

Cassia came to Lio's side. "Tonight, we cannot afford feuds. Skleros is the worst criminal among us. We will never succeed in discovering his grand design against us unless we act together."

Lio got to his feet, standing almost close enough to touch her, with an eye on the Dexion. "You have done everything in your power to cost me what is most precious. I dueled your brother. I will do my best to forget that for one night, if you will."

"You still expect me to get information out of Skleros about your hostages?" Chrysanthos asked.

"He still believes you are his ally," Cassia said. "You could simply ask him where they are, and he would tell you."

Chrysanthos all but rolled his eyes at Cassia. "He would be suspicious about any change in our plans. He has a vested interest in the hostage situation proceeding precisely as he and my circle agreed. He has dedicated most of his career to inciting war between Hesperines and the Orders on Tenebran soil so his prey will go errant in greater numbers."

Lio responded before Cassia had a chance. "It sounds as if he and your brother had the same life goal. Why would he betray Dalos? You want to know. You want to confront him about your brother's death. But as soon as you do, he will know he has lost your favor. The moment you leave Orthros, he will slip from your grasp and return to the shadows whence he came, and you will be left empty-handed, thirsting for revenge."

"You doubt my ability, as the Dexion, to reach anyone, anywhere?"

"What use is fire against a shadow? Can you shine a light spell into Hypnos's realm? You cannot deny Skleros will prove a challenge, even for you. But tonight, here he is, a fish in a barrel of Hesperine magic."

Cassia knew what Lio was about to propose. Unless she tried to stop him, her mind mage would challenge his true nemesis. If she did not speak now, Lio would duel a Gift Collector.

"But as the Dexion," Cassia tried, "you surely have influence over Skleros. You ensure the Inner Eyes do not interfere in his activities. If you threaten to revoke your protection and leave him at the mercy of his superiors, he will tell you anything you want to know."

"I'm afraid the ambassador's assessment is correct," Chrysanthos replied. "My threats will mean nothing to Skleros. I have been influential in keeping the robes from trying his patience, to be sure. But if he wishes to avoid their discipline, he can do so without my help."

With each beat of her heart, Alkaios and Nephalea suffered a heartbeat longer. Nike was apart from her family a heartbeat longer. Five other bloodlines' loved ones were a heartbeat closer to the Akron's Altar.

Cassia tried to keep the desperation out of her voice. "You have worked with him these many years. Surely you know his secrets."

"I'm a pyromagus, not a mind mage."

Lio met Cassia's gaze. "Will Tenebra's representative hear a new recommendation from Orthros's ambassador?"

Her neck popped with the tension in her. "Under protest."

"Understood." Lio turned to the embassy. "Lord Gaius, have you ever had in your custody one of the enemy's men who knew where your own were imprisoned?"

"To be sure," he answered.

"What did you do to the enemy you had captured?"

"One time we gave him bread, and he told us everything, and we sent him on his way. Another time, it took a fair bit of coin. Sometimes it's enough to get his wife and children to safety, and then he doesn't care how his liege punishes him for talking."

"I hope you know I would give the Gift Collector all the provisions and wealth in Orthros, if he would accept. But those things matter little to him, and family even less."

Lord Gaius eyed Lio. "No one here is going to regret the Gift Collector, Ambassador."

"If you'd had a thelemancer with you in the wars, would that have made your interrogations easier?" Lio asked.

Cassia held her breath.

Lord Gaius's eyebrows shot up. "I wouldn't trust a mage of dreams. But if he spared me having to torture a man, I'd thank him."

"I am not a mage of dreams," Lio said. "I am a Hesperine mind mage."

Perita clapped a hand over her mouth. Callen held her a little closer. Cassia was grateful Lio had won their trust before this moment. Murmurs of dismay swept around the table, but so did exclamations of triumph at securing a formidable ally.

"Gods." Chrysanthos took another swig of Lord Gaius's flask. "Next you'll tell me you're as powerful as Argyros."

"I stopped the heart hunters in Martyr's Pass," Lio replied.

Chrysanthos wheezed a humorless laugh and leaned on the table.

"Is that what you call diplomacy?" Benedict demanded, his face ashen.

"I call it a last resort," Lio answered. "Ask yourself if I would bother using diplomacy to persuade you, if my scruples would allow me to simply change your mind for you with thelemancy. If you are familiar with my Uncle Argyros's history, you will not find it surprising that he trained me in both."

"Oh, my," said Eudias. "When the combined forces of the Orders of Anthros and Hypnos and the alliance of Cordian princes came to raze Hagia Anatela, Argyros held them off—with his mind."

"He has also led every embassy from Orthros for the last sixteen hundred years," Cassia told them, "risking his life to show Tenebrans that Hesperines mean no harm."

"Tonight," Lio said, "it falls to me to take any risk necessary to discover the hostages' location from the Gift Collector. I will return to all of you when I have the information we seek."

He turned away from the table. It took all Cassia's Will not to reach out and hold him back. Was she to just stand here and let him go, alone, into what might well be the worst danger he had ever faced?

No, they must do this together. Her Sanctuary ward could not safeguard his mind, but could at least protect his body while he dueled Skleros. She must convince him to let her go with him. Now.

As she was wracking her mind for a means of persuasion, Eudias spoke. "Ambassador?"

He turned to them again. "Yes, Apprentice Eudias?"

"Would it not be best to bring the Gift Collector here, before us all? Let it be a sign of trust between our peoples, unlike the secret conspiracies against one another that have done so much harm."

"I am eager to demonstrate Orthros's trustworthiness to Tenebra. However, my foremost duty is to ensure our guests' safety. The Gift Collector is a very dangerous man. He will not submit to my magic quietly."

"You'll need help," Chrysanthos said.

Lio raised his brows at the Dexion.

The war mage managed to smile and to make it appear insulting. "I'm familiar with your combat abilities. You won't be able to fend off a Gift Collector's attacks while you work to bring down his dream wards."

"I had intended to seek Hesperine assistance."

Eudias cleared his throat. "We appreciate your dedication to our safety, Ambassador, but we must all work together to free the hostages. You have here a room full of capable mages and warriors."

There was a chorus of agreement from all the Tenebrans.

Eudias gave a satisfied nod. "We are more than enough to keep Master Skleros from doing any harm while you employ your affinity."

"This will be a proud night," Lio said, "when we work together against a rogue necromancer who has brought great harm upon all of us."

Cassia blinked hard. Lio would be protected. Eudias and the Tenebrans were rallying in defense of her Hesperine.

"I would lend my battle wards to the cause," the Dexion drawled, "but alas, the Guardian of Orthros has shackled me so thoroughly that I cannot hurl fire at a Gift Collector trying to turn her nephew into mincemeat."

"And yet we find ourselves working together." Lio offered Chrysanthos his hand. "When I bring Skleros before this gathering, we will also help you find out what he really did to your brother and why. Let it be a demonstration of Orthros's condolences for your family's loss."

"I will not forgive you." The Dexion turned his back on Lio. "But I will forget, if only for tonight, while I watch you teach the hunter to fear his own prey. I can think of no sweeter vengeance upon Skleros. Bring him here."

BROTHER GODS

SKLEROS HAD FASHIONED HIMSELF a game of darts from the wrought iron thorns that had decorated the footboard of his guest bed. Lio watched the Gift Collector hurl one broken spike after another into the silk wallpaper. Leisurely, Skleros swung his feet off the dresser and got up from his chair to retrieve his collection of shivs.

"The Dexion has asked to meet with you," Lio repeated.

Skleros stuck one of the shivs between his lips, where his smoke usually hung. "He must have bartered his bollocks to Hespera for you to permit this."

"I will be present, as will the entire Tenebran embassy. Neither of you will be able to take advantage of the situation."

"Huh."

Lio pointed at the vandalized thorns. "You will not bring those."

Skleros chuckled and dropped them on the dresser on his way toward the door.

Lio rapped on the door to signal his Trial sisters, then moved aside to let Skleros past him, keeping an arm's length between himself and the Gift Collector. The door opened, and latent fire and water magic hung heavy in the air. Lio was surprised no sweat beaded on Skleros's skin as he passed through the cauldron of Hesperine power in the corridor.

Lio saluted his Trial sisters. Kia and Xandra returned the gesture, their auras full of triumph. Nodora emanated wariness and cautioned him through the Union.

Skleros strolled to Rose House in silence as if there were nowhere else he would rather be. Lio did not so much as stir his magic. He must give Skleros no warning about what was to come.

Now that Lio had made up his mind, a surprising calmness had come over him. There was a certain confidence that came from knowing you were past the point of no return.

Lio had just promised to a war mage he would extract a confession out of necromancer.

Lio thought back upon all the twisted paths that had brought him to this point and asked himself if his conscience was satisfied.

He could not see another way to rescue the hostages. He could not see himself shying from a duel with a monster, when it would give Alkaios back his Grace, Mak back his sister, and Ioustin back his hope. Lio could see himself resting easier at night while he watched Cassia sleep, knowing he had not let Skleros live to threaten her again.

Did a carcass so rotten as Skleros even warrant a consultation with the conscience?

Did this man, too, have a nephew somewhere?

All Lio knew was that Skleros's choices, not his own, had made this duel necessary. Whatever had motivated those choices and however Skleros had felt about them, Lio knew what he must do in response.

His conscience would be satisfied, as long as he broke Skleros because he must, not because he wanted to.

They had made it to the entryway. Lio directed his wrath at the doors of the main hall, and they slammed open. "I will do my best not to enjoy this."

"Suit yourself." The Gift Collector cast a smile over his shoulder. "I'm going to enjoy every moment of it."

Lio felt the doors plucked from the grasp of his Will as if sheets of paper had fluttered from his hands. The massive iron panels slammed, barring him from the hall, locking Cassia and the mortals in with a Gift Collector.

AN OLD FRIEND

T HE BOOM OF THE doors reverberated around Cassia. Mere doors couldn't stop Lio. How could this be happening?

Nothing stood between her and the Gift Collector who prowled toward her. Nothing stood between the Gift Collector and the embassy but her.

She put a hand on the glyph shard and faced Skleros with Knight at her side.

Beyond the panes of the window, shadows gathered and roiled. Storm clouds. The beacon's light shrank. The rose's red petals turned a deathly shade, and the room plunged into shadow.

Cassia held fast to her pendant and listened to her own breaths. No one stirred around her.

"Cassia." A deep, articulate voice spoke in the gloom. "We meet again at last."

Her chest tightened. She knew that voice.

"You will not remember me, but I am an old friend of your father's." His words reached for her in the emptiness.

She had heard that voice in the king's solar out of the mouth of a man who was now dead.

"One question, as an old friend." The mage's voice deepened. Without an invitation from the king, he took the chair on his side of the desk and sat in the royal presence.

From his decanter of wine, the king filled the empty goblet beside his own and slid it across the desk. "What would you like to discuss?"

Dalos took a sip of the wine and savored it in his mouth for a moment.

When he spoke again, all trace of his nasal tone was gone. His voice was rich and smooth, his words articulate. "Have you reached a decision on what you wish me to do regarding Cassia?"

The king shook his head. "Not yet."

"I need to know so that I have sufficient time to prepare before my working." The mage's tone had never been so clear and cold before.

She listened to Dalos's voice, the voice of the man who might be the one who killed her. A realization thawed her frozen thoughts.

She had heard that voice before.

The mage had spoken to her that way when the king had ordered her to his solar to humiliate her. It had not been her imagination.

The king went on, as if nothing had changed. "I will inform you before the hour comes... She has forgotten she must ask my leave before she breathes, eats, or shits. I must make sure her restless aspirations will not be an inconvenience."

"The hour draws near," the mage warned. "Do not wait too long."

"Indeed. I have waited too long already for the day when I have expended her usefulness and can finally be rid of her."

"I look forward to taking care of her for you."

A deep instinct made Cassia back away. She stumbled against her chair and caught hold of it to steady herself. Light returned, brilliant as a lightning strike, and glared without ceasing into every corner of the hall. She could see Knight barking so fiercely his body jolted with each bellow, but the room was silent. Skleros stood beneath the window, his head bowed and his hands folded before him. Cassia dared take her eyes off him to glance at Chrysanthos across the table.

The war mage did not rise from his seat. Not a single person around the table moved.

The rustle of fabric startled Cassia. She stared in the direction of the sound.

Eudias rose gracefully to his feet. He gave her a dignified smile and strolled toward her. As if she were a hare and he the hunter, she stood paralyzed where she was and watched him approach.

He drifted to a halt within arm's reach. Then he picked up Cassia's goblet of Notian red. Cupping it in his palm with the stem between his fingers, he lifted it to his nose and took a deep breath. Savoring a sip of the wine, he turned, his robes sweeping around him, and joined Skleros under the window.

Skleros fell to one knee and put a fist to his chest in salute. "Master."

"Skleros, my greatest Overseer. It is good to speak to you with my voice." Eudias extended a hand and rested it on the Gift Collector's head.

Cassia sensed a disruption of the Hesperine magic in the room, as if something shattered in her very veins.

Skleros shuddered and rasped a breath. "Thank you for freeing me from the Guardian's shackles, Master."

No, that was not Eudias. That was not Dalos, either.

Hespera help her. Was this Hypnos himself?

Man or god, he would have to get through Cassia to hurt anyone in this room.

She hoped Sanctuary magic would withstand his unnatural power. Ready to awaken the glyph shard at any moment, she dropped to a crouch behind Knight and extended a hand toward him.

The Master made a scolding noise. A spark of lightning danced across her fingertips. She swallowed a yelp and snatched her arm back.

Knight lunged at the Master. She caught a glimpse of brilliant tendrils in the air when his body slammed against them. He fell to the floor.

"No!" Cassia drove her hand into the shocks of magic, gritting her teeth against the pain. She could not reach Knight.

He shook himself, then leapt to his feet again. He tried his jaws next, only to recoil again from a web of lightning magic.

Cassia's arm dropped at her side, numb to the shoulder. If she drove the glyph shard into the magic, could she free Knight? Or would the shrine's ward refuse to be a weapon?

"Please don't do that again, Cassia," the Master requested.

"Shall I constrain her, Master?" Skleros asked, still kneeling.

"Patience, my eager Overseer. The less we disrupt such fragile material, the better."

They thought her fragile? Surprise was a powerful advantage. She must not let them know she had magic at her disposal until the moment came to use it. She made no further motion toward her pendant.

The Master beckoned to Skleros. "Rise. Let us finish our work."

The Gift Collector got to his feet.

Cassia walked toward the mages with her best posture and spoke in her most courtly tones. "As you are a friend of the king's, shall we not have a proper introduction? To whom do I have the honor of speaking?"

"Address the Master with respect," Skleros warned.

Cassia quirked a brow at him. "This uncouth knave works for you?"

"Indeed, he is one of my Gift Collectors. At ease, Overseer. Cassia has waited for this moment for so long." The Master paced in a circle around her, looking her up and down.

She stood where she was and let him walk behind her. She would not show that she feared him. "So the bounty hunters work for you. What does that make you? A bored exchequer from Corona out for a little adventure?"

"You may think of me as *the* Collector."

"Hm. No, didn't leave much of an impression on me. Do refresh my memory."

"I certainly shall, in time. We will become intimately reacquainted." He halted in front of her. He met her gaze through Eudias's eyes. The Master, strange and yet familiar, intelligent and heartless, looked out at her from within the apprentice. "Orthros is not the place for our reunion. However, since you have appointed yourself a novice in my field of expertise, I shall condescend to provide you with a brief explanation of what is transpiring."

"What is your field of expertise?"

"I will characterize it for you in terms the mortal mind can comprehend. I am a legendary player of Kings and Mages. I have been playing since long before the Hesperines devised this little modification called Prince and Diplomat." He swept a hand at the table of Cassia's motionless allies and friends, antagonists, and enemies. "Everyone is my token."

"I am no one's token," Cassia told him.

The Collector drew nearer. Bile rose in her throat.

"You don't understand," he explained patiently. "I designed the paths and the plane. I built the board. I made the tokens—including you. You were born because I require you. You continue to exist at my pleasure."

"Let me guess. I'll die when you're done with me."

"That depends on you. You have shown yourself to be much more than a mere liegehound, Cassia. You jumped the plane during the Equinox

Summit and have vanquished the paths ever since. You are the sort of token I love to unleash upon the board while I sit back and watch. You could clear your way to become one of my Overseers."

"I have chosen my path, and it is Hespera's, and so it shall remain for eternity."

"It is immortality that you want? I can give you that as no one else can. Magic? I can put impossible amounts at your fingertips. Power?" He laughed. "I am power."

"I don't want the power I see before me."

"You will learn to appreciate the offer. I make it to very few, Cassia. Fewer accept, and fewer still survive to become this magnificent weapon you see before you." The Collector held out a hand, gesturing from Skleros's scarred face to his spurred boots. "What do you think, Skleros? Will she last?"

Skleros smirked. "Let me play a few rounds with her and find out."

"I will," the Collector promised, "if she survives my current match."

"Against whom?" Cassia asked. "If you call all of us in this room tokens, who is your opponent?"

"In time, you will see the broader board and realize every move you have made has brought me closer to victory."

"You will not win. The Hesperines will not allow you to harm anyone."

"The Hesperines have tampered with my delicate instrument. It is high time you returned to Tenebra with me, where I can readjust you." He traced a finger in the air over her breastbone.

She flinched away before she could stop herself, then hated that she had given him the satisfaction. "You will never take me back to Tenebra. I am staying in Orthros."

"That is an illegal move," the Collector informed her. "I am correcting you."

"If you're a friend of the king's, you should know I don't respond to correction. Ready yourself. I shall be disobedient."

"Ah, yes, you are quite fond of being disobedient in the arms of the ambassador. Such petty rebellions make you feel free. The fact remains, however, that you belong to me."

"If you have any idea what I mean to him, you know he will break in here any moment with most of Orthros for reinforcements."

"I have given the ambassador a mental exercise to entertain him."

Cassia laughed. "We'll see how long that keeps a mind mage of his skill busy."

"His display in Martyr's Pass served only to give me an accurate impression of his power. I have adjusted the exercise to his level."

"We have our orders. She belongs to the boss. No hands, no darts, nothing— right to the boss, untouched."

"He could at least let us have her when he's done," the swordsman complained.

"Not on your life. She's to die after he's gotten his use out of her—if she survives it. That's what the boss and the king agreed on."

Cassia put on the stone face she wore before the king, when she showed no fear, and looked into the eyes of the heart hunters' leader. "Very well. Take me to your 'boss.' We shall see if he survives me."

A chorus of whistles and catcalls went up around her.

"The boss has his work cut out for him," said the swordsman.

"But he always has his way, in the end."

"You are the heart hunter's 'boss,'" Cassia realized. "You are the mage of dreams."

"I have invested great effort in keeping you secured in Tenebra. You should never have crossed the border into Orthros." Eudias's face hardened into malevolence that could never come from him. "The Ambassador committed the most illegal move of all. He tried to claim my token."

Lio, Cassia called in her thoughts. *Can your mind magery reach across his game? If you can hear me, I want you to know. We are not going to lose tonight.*

Cassia lifted her chin. "I'll tell you what I told your mongrels. We'll see if you survive me."

MAGE OF DREAMS

LIO IGNORED THE BARRED doors and stepped into the main hall.

He froze in his tracks. The chamber was deserted. Not a single aura lit the Union. No spell light illuminated the leaden shadows. Dust motes fluttered in the beams of sickly light that fell through the window.

"*Cassia!*" Lio bellowed.

Only the echoes of his own voice answered him.

No time to rally his Trial sisters. He must light the distress signal now. He turned on his heel, ready to step to the Harbor Light.

The doors hung open on their hinges. All that remained of his window were broken, jagged pieces of glass. He could not see the beacon's light.

"No!"

He raced through the entry hall and out of Rose House. The sky above him was flat black, devoid of stars. He almost stumbled on the broken front steps. He took a leap down to the road and lifted his eyes to the statue of Hespera.

Lio slid to his knees. There was no beacon to tune. The Harbor Light was gone. The Goddess's hands had broken off at the wrists and fallen away. Perhaps they lay at the bottom of the harbor even now. Crevasses and cracks marred her beautiful hair and body.

Something in the water arrested his attention. A broken plank in the pale color of the hulls of Hesperine ships.

Lio stumbled to his feet and went out onto the nearest dock. Up and down the harbor, bits and pieces of the fleet bobbed in the water, sails and rigging, broken masts and shattered hulls. Lio stared down at the figurehead of his Ritual mother's flagship. The gargoyle snarled up at him, missing her wings.

He would go to the ward himself and get help. Lio covered his face in his hands and reached out with his senses for the Queens' ward, every Hesperine's anchor.

He couldn't sense the ward.

"It can't be," Lio cried. "No one is that powerful."

"Except me," a voice answered.

The voice was everywhere. And nowhere. He was part of the still air and the fetid water and the crumbling stone under Lio's feet. Yet Lio could not think his name. He could not envision his face. He was an iron rule and a whisper on the edge of Lio's senses. Lio could almost hear him in his own thoughts.

"The Hesperine path is outside my board," the voice said. "I do not permit such paths to exist."

"Mage of dreams!" Lio bellowed at the sky. "You are but a man! You cannot break the Goddess's path!"

"What is left of your goddess now but broken stones?"

"This." Lio sank his fangs into his hand and scattered his own blood across the water.

The water dissolved. The sea itself began to evaporate, revealing nothingness beneath. The dock was gone from under Lio's feet, and he fell into the void.

BLOOD SACRIFICE

THE COLLECTOR SPUN AND lifted his hands in front of his face so fast Cassia jumped. A horrible groaning filled the chamber. The iron tables rose from the floor, their silk cloths fluttering. Not a single wine goblet spilled. The treaty signed in blood rose out of Cassia's reach before she could grab for it.

She backed away and took a running leap. Her fingers caught the edge of the table. Clawing at the silk, she heard cups and wine bottles clash against each other. She dragged the tablecloth and the treaty over the edge.

With the paper in her grasp, she let go. She landed hard in a crouch and caught herself on one hand to a flare of pain in her wrist.

"That was not up to your usual standards of subtlety," the Collector critiqued, "but a satisfying reminder of my own. I shall excuse you."

Cassia darted under the levitating tables. She positioned herself in the empty center of the ring of chairs and faced the necromancers. The embassy gazed at her with unseeing eyes, all of them eerily still. Perhaps from here she could make her ward reach everyone.

Skleros sneered and laughed. "You have done fine work on her, Master. All she has to battle us with is a piece of paper."

"She tried her gardening spade on me last time."

The Collector spread his arms with a flourish, then lowered them. The sideboards flew apart and shuddered down to their positions along the edges of the hall. The Collector flicked a hand again, as if dusting something off the air. Knight flopped onto his side and skidded across the floor, between two chairs, and landed at Cassia's feet.

Should she awaken the shard now, or would that waste her advantage?

While she debated with herself, Knight lay there struggling to get up, and she could give him not one comforting touch.

The Collector paused at a sideboard to refill his goblet. "The treaty is brilliant, though, Cassia. You have lured the free lords into a rebellion that will give the king a reason to crush them. The Hesperines will of course come to their rescue. You have succeeded where Dalos and Chrysanthos both failed. You have given Orthros a compelling reason to go to war in Tenebra."

It couldn't be true. All their plots behind the king's back...all their hard-won successes...it couldn't all be for nothing. They had been trying to heal the world, not twist it into the shape the Collector envisioned.

Sweat broke out all over Cassia's body. Had the Collector been in *her* mind?

Skleros tilted his head back, and his nostrils flared. "Ahh, the smell of fear."

"Sweeter than the most ancient vintage." The Collector toasted him.

No, the mage of dreams couldn't possibly have tampered with her. Lio would have driven him out of her thoughts, just as he had driven him out of the heart hunters. Annassa Soteira, when she had rescued Cassia from the sickroom of her mind, would have saved her from the mage of dreams, too.

Cassia tucked the treaty safely in her gardening satchel and tightened it on her shoulder. "We are not your tokens. You cannot arrange our hearts to your satisfaction. These men and women believe in something. The teachings of their gods, the good of their people, the honor of battle— Solia's memory. In the face of our conviction, the king is just one small man. We will crush him."

With a sigh, the Collector took two wine bottles from a rack. He tossed one to Skleros, who caught it deftly. Twin pops sounded, and the corks flew from the bottles. The Collector tipped his bottle and spilled more of the Notian red on the pale floor.

He walked around the outside of the chairs, marking a semicircle on the floor in wine, Skleros following suit on the opposite side. Their lines met at a point behind Chrysanthos, and Skleros stood still again, as if waiting for orders. The two lines of wine surrounded the embassy, as if enclosing them in a great eye.

They were going to set a fire, Cassia guessed. Was that all? Ha. Her Sanctuary ward had withstood much worse.

The Collector paused in front of her again. How strange Eudias's face looked when the proud, malicious Collector wore it. The Collector snapped Eudias's fingers, and little darts of lightning skittered along his hands.

Cassia's hands were halfway to her pendant, when a bolt of lightning arced toward one of the sideboards. She squeezed her eyes shut, and when she opened them, the only casualty was the silk tablecloth she had disturbed. What had been a rumpled pile of fabric was now a pile of ash.

The Collector went to the sideboard and thrust his hands in the ashes, caressing them. Then with speed and agility, he retraced the semicircle of wine in ash. When he reached Skleros, he straightened and clasped his Overseer's hand, smearing ash on the other man's fingers. Skleros completed the other half of the oval.

"Not up to your usual standards of subtlety," Cassia said. "The display positively screams necromancy. What next? Little eyelashes like a glyph of Hypnos?"

Without flinching, Skleros snapped off one of his own fingers with his bare hand. Cassia fell silent. When he began to pry the finger bone out of his detached digit, she looked away.

There came a soft grinding noise like a mortar and pestle. Was Skleros turning his own bone to meal in one of the drinking cups?

The Collector's throaty laughter taunted her. "You always did have a weak stomach, Cassia."

This wasn't the king's solar. This wasn't that tent fourteen and a half years ago.

This might be the worst enemy she had ever faced. More powerful and more insidious even than the king.

"My strength is in my heart," she said, "which Hespera gave me."

The necromancers circled her at the edges of her vision. Flesh and bone emboldened the line of wine and ash. As the smears of pink and beige neared one another, Cassia lifted her hands.

"I am strong in magic and the will to survive. You have no choice but to relinquish me. You cannot hold those of Hespera's blood." She grasped her pendant firmly in one hand and, aiming for the unseen scar of all her past blood rituals, drove the glyph shard into her palm.

Her heart jolted. Light and strength burst from her and flashed outward.

The spell marks met. A great, silent scream of magic tore at her flesh and grated in her bones. The lines on the floor cracked and split. They did not form an eye. It was a mouth, and it began to open. It was a void, waiting to consume them. Bit by bit, the floor of Rose House chipped away and disappeared into it.

A shining veil passed over the faces and bodies of the embassy. Cassia's Sanctuary ward halted and hung poised between the backs of the chairs and the necromancers' spell. The tear in the world slammed into her weaving of light and halted.

"What?" Skleros snarled. "Master—!"

Cassia met the Collector's gaze through the shining light of her ward.

His smile was a grimace of bared teeth. "*You* are no Sanctuary mage."

"Tonight I am." Cassia focused all her thoughts on the ward, squeezing her hand. She didn't feel any pain. More blood spilled out around the glyph shard, and tendrils of light spread under the surface of her skin.

"Using magic that isn't your own is an acquired skill," the Collector warned.

"She won't last," Skleros predicted.

"Let us take her for a few rounds."

Skleros knotted a silk table napkin around his bleeding hand. "I am ready, Master."

With an expression of savage exultation, the Collector lifted Eudias's hands. Lightning lanced downward at Cassia's Sanctuary ward.

WORST FEAR

LIO CRASHED THROUGH PANES of glass. Slivers dug into his skin. He landed hard on sharp, jagged stones and caught himself on his hands and knees. A groan escaped him. The pain felt so real. Yet he knew better.

This was a mind game.

He stayed where he was and checked his mental protections from the inside out, racing through every self-defense exercise his uncle had taught him for just this kind of duel. He found no breach in his own mind. A superior mind mage could gain the upper hand against a lesser one, while still making the lesser mage believe his defenses were intact. Neither Lio nor the mage of dreams were lesser thelemancers.

Lio was made for this, but it could be the worst battle of his life.

He rolled onto his side with a wince, touching a hand to his bleeding knees. They weren't healing. He reached for the nearest support. His hand met the lip of a fountain. He pulled himself to his feet, shaking off pieces of broken glass. His blood spattered the ground.

He looked around at a desolated version of the courtyard at Rose House. The fountain was dry, and potholes riddled the floor. There were only dead, frostbitten stalks where the Sanctuary roses had been. Everything lay in the grip of ice. When Lio took a step, the remains of the last glass roof panel came crashing down at his feet.

"You've already worn out this trick," Lio said. "It won't fool me twice."

He was trapped in a waking dream. The only way to Cassia was to find his way out of this fortress the mage of dreams had built.

Lio would destroy it from the inside out.

He considered the fragments of his medium that surrounded him. He would perform a test upon the mage's world. He listened, attuning his senses to the voice of each piece of glass. Just like playing with a project in his workshop, he applied his Will to the fragments and summoned them together.

They shattered into finer slivers. Lio coughed the glass dust out of his lungs.

"That confirms this world isn't real," he choked. "My own craft turns against me."

Lio sniffed the air. He could smell ice and sea. The illusion around him was astonishingly complete. How had the mage constructed such a consuming experience without invading Lio's mind to make him believe he was seeing, feeling, and smelling all of this?

Lio eyed the lightless sky. Light magic. He ran a hand over the back of a stone bench, and frost came off on his skin. A polar wind cut through the torpid air and blew the rime from his fingertips. Elemental magic.

"The novice studies my technique," said the mage of dreams. "I am flattered."

Mind magic, of course.

It should take a coordinated effort by several mages to construct an artificial environment such as this. Skleros, Chrysanthos, and Tychon could not account for the various affinities Lio saw at work here. He had enough faith that the rules of magic still applied to conclude that the Queens' ward was still in place, and no other enemy mages could possibly be in Orthros.

Except the mage of dreams. How had he gotten in?

"Evil," Lio said.

"Such a simplistic word." The mage's disdain filled the air.

"The truth is often simple. Did you forget I am the son of a mind healer and the devoted servant of her mentor, the Great Healer of the Empire? I am not ignorant of the particular necromancy Imperial theramancers keep at bay in their communities. Alas, Tenebra and Cordium have no such protection. The Order of Hypnos claims to guard against such violations, but we both know how corrupt they are. You must be able to run rampant in this part of the world."

"The world is mine."

The mage's aura filled the realm where he had trapped Lio. The walls of this prison were built of the pleasure the mage took in control. His arrogance held up the sky. His lust for power was the foundation on which all of it stood.

"Yours is the purest form of evil," Lio snarled. "Possession."

"Anyone," the mage whispered. "Look into any pair of eyes, and you might be looking at me. Confess to any ear, and you might be baring your heart to me. Feel the caress of any hand, and you might be mistaking my grasp for love."

"I could never mistake evil for love."

Lio had been in the depths of Cassia's mind. No evil had breached her there. If his Union with her had not been enough to reassure him, Queen Soteira's healing was. The Annassa had thoroughly examined her after Skleros had drugged her. If the mage of dreams had dared touch Cassia, Annassa Soteira would have found him and driven him out.

"You have come to an inhospitable land for one of your expertise," Lio said. "You are aware that Hesperines cannot be possessed?"

"Your unnatural union of flesh and spirit defies the laws of magic. It cannot be allowed."

"Nothing could be more unnatural than your defiance of each person's innate free Will. I know you care nothing for right and wrong, for nature and law. I begin to think you enjoy this fantasy of Orthros's destruction because you know Hesperines are the beings you cannot control."

There came a crack, and fire sprang up in the dry bed of the fountain. The bonfire rushed across the courtyard at Lio. He felt the heat bathe his face.

"Do not think you can teach me a lesson in domination." Lio braced himself.

The fire caught the hem of his robes.

"Will you stand their like a fool and live out your worst fear?" the mage of dreams asked. "Or will you admit I am in control?"

"You show the limits of your power over me. You are wrong. This is not my worst fear."

"Not terrifying enough for you? So be it."

The ground bucked under Lio's feet and hurled him through the open door of Cassia's guest room. He staggered, barely catching his balance.

"This is no fantasy," the Collector said. "It is a demonstration of the future I have in store for you. Everything will turn against you, before I am done with you. Especially Cassia."

Her room was deserted. The potted roses were dying, and the dressing table was rusted. Shreds of paper lay strewn amid the moth-eaten bedclothes upon the moldering mattress. The treaty.

"Lady Cassia?" Lio shrugged. "I worked with her to pen the treaty, yes, but what is she to me beyond a diplomatic associate?"

"You think your intimate secrets so secure behind the bastions of your mind. Yet human error can topple the most secure fortress. I heard how tenderly she pleaded with you not to duel Skleros. Her urgency that you try diplomacy was not the response of an 'associate.' She was protecting you."

"It took you that long to understand? I thought my demonstration in Martyr's Pass made it clear I am protecting her."

"You cannot hope to protect her from me."

"Underestimating Cassia and me will be your last mistake."

Lio turned his back on the ruined chamber and went out to the courtyard once more. He pierced his hand with his fangs again and circled the courtyard, making a libation of their blood upon the Sanctuary roses. They revived, just as the rose vines at their shrine had returned to life. He focused on the auras of their roses growing in their residence and stepped.

THE HESPERITE SORCERESS

THE WARD WAS NOT just around Cassia. It was part of her. She felt each lightning bolt strike it. She braced herself against the pain, and the ward hardened. Thunder rocked the hall. Rain lashed against the ward, and sweat rolled down her skin.

"This is rather dramatic for our taste, is it not?" the Collector mused. "You and I do not favor brute force. I am certain you will appreciate my strategy."

Cassia heard a footstep behind her and turned halfway. On the other side of the circle, Callen left Perita's side.

"I'll protect you, my lady!" He charged past her, drawing his scythe.

"Callen, no! Do you understand me?" She clutched the glyph shard in her bleeding hand and reached for him with her other.

He shook her off and headed toward Chrysanthos.

The Collector stood watching, a hand on his chin. "I wonder how Callen will enjoy the inquisitors' prison after he assassinates a high-ranking member of the Aithourian Circle? I don't think you can afford the Dexion's life price, Cassia."

No time to try reaching Callen through the Collector's control. Her ward was her only hope. Cassia held out her hands, digging the glyph shard into her palm harder. The light in her veins spread to her elbows.

Callen raised his scythe over Chrysanthos.

Cassia felt for the ward with that strange new sense she had never believed she had. The dome around them all brightened, blocking the necromancers from view. No use.

Callen brought the scythe down.

"What a shame," the Collector said. "There's the hostages' death sentence."

Cassia focused all her Will on that blade, on the trusted arm that held it, on what the mage in the chair represented. Light flashed on steel. The front of the Dexion's robes parted, sliced in two. Cassia's blood dripped onto the floor as Chrysanthos's colored Callen's blade.

Light flashed over the Dexion's heart and bloomed on the air. Too late. Her ward threw Callen back, and his scythe fell to the ground and slid out of his reach. Chrysanthos slumped in his seat, covered in his own blood.

"No, no, no!" Cassia raced to the mage's side.

She half-caught him as he slid from his chair. She did her best to lay his heavy, muscular body gently on the floor. The blood was everywhere. Would he live?

She pressed her hands to the open wound, gathering his robes to staunch the bleeding. "Don't you dare die! Not until the hostages are safe!"

He did not even flinch, and he uttered not a single sound of pain.

Cassia leaned her weight on her arms. "Dexion Chrysanthos! Listen to me! Don't give in!"

He lay limply, staring at her with blank eyes. The gaze of the Collector, or of death? Was there a difference?

A Sanctuary ward could stop spells and magic. Could it stop bleeding?

She focused her Will again, this time upon the mess that covered the mage's chest. Light glimmered over his blood. The blood disappeared into the light, and there was only the glow of Sanctuary magic upon his wound. Cassia heaved a sigh and dared lift her hands. No blood rushed out.

She felt of the mage's body, trying to assess the damage. "Do you hear me, Florian? There's a little boy who can't lose his uncle. There's a grieving mother who needs your next letter."

His eyes unglazed and focused on her. He started, then let out a cry of pain.

Carefully, she held him down. "Easy. I don't know how bad the wound is. The ward will stop the bleeding, but I'm not a healer."

He lifted his head, his gaze roaming over her, then over himself. He matched one of his hands to her bloody hand print over his heart. "It's you. You—at the shrine. You all along. Helping the treaty, the Hesperines."

"Yes. I am a traitor and a heretic, and I'll risk my life for everything Hespera stands for. Are you going to lie there and think about burning me at the stake, or are you going to give all your strength to staying alive for your nephew and his mother?"

"You only want the hostages."

The chairs scraped over the floor. Footsteps sounded. The hairs on Cassia's arms stood on end.

"I want everyone to be treated with dignity. I want children to be safe. I want peace. Keep your eyes open till this is over, and you might learn what heresy really means."

She jumped to her feet and turned around. Every member of the embassy stood glaring at one another.

Benedict reached for Lord Gaius's collar, while Lord Gaius raised his fist. Every Segetian ally stood poised to charge across the circle at the Hadrian supporters. The stone under Master Gorgos's feet shuddered and broke out of the floor, levitating to meet the shards of ice shooting from the Semna's hands.

"Peace!" Cassia screamed.

The Sanctuary ward around them bucked, twisted, and then shot down in vines of light to wrap each and every member of the embassy. Master Gorgos's rocks turned to dust against the light around the Semna, and her ice shattered. Benedict and Lord Gaius's fists bumped harmlessly against warding magic. The other men struggled to move toward each other as if wading through a swamp.

Cassia fell to her knees, veins of light glowing through her clothes up to her shoulders. "No one will die tonight!"

The storm crashed against her ward again. She flexed her hands, feeding more blood to her spell.

She tossed her head to get her damp hair out of her eyes and looked around her at all the people whose lives depended on her. "Do you hear me, Collector? You aren't going to take a single one of them!"

Lio, I know your mind can always reach mine. You can hear me. We are not going to lose anyone tonight.

BATTLEGROUND

LIO WAS NOT SURPRISED to find his ritual tapestry in shreds in the entry hall or the library covered in the ashes of his scrolls. He could not read the words on his windows through the soot.

None of the embassy had ever been in here. Through whose eyes could the mage of dreams have beheld this place? Lio could only conclude the enemy thelemancer had not brought him here. He had brought himself.

Lio smiled. He was not a helpless bystander in the other mind mage's world. They were building and destroying it together. This waking dream was not merely their battleground—it was the battle.

"Is this where you bring her?" the mage of dreams asked. "The lair you tempt her into, where she imagines she is free? I know you will kill to possess her."

"I didn't kill the heart hunters. You did."

"I could not allow you to make my acquaintance until the appointed time. I had to wait until the right opportunity to make you regret interfering with my work in the pass. You did not chase down one stray mortal in the snow out of Hesperine altruism. You wanted her. Tonight you were ready to destroy my Gift Collector for her sake."

"*Your* Gift Collector?"

"My Overseer."

The words sent a chill down Lio's spine, but his reason saw him through. The mage was fearsomely powerful, but he was a mere mortal. Wasn't he? "Do you fancy yourself a god of death in your petty kingdom?"

"Mortals have worshiped me for ages, but those are not the rules of the game in this era. This tournament is all about subtlety. *This* is *my* element.

This is my epoch. You never know I am there, but you all meet me. The Unseen Hand. The All-Seeing Eyes. The Voice behind your voice. I am the Collector, Deukalion. I collect people. Once someone is in my collection, they remain there. Thieves face punishment."

"I don't have to steal to win people over, Collector. I don't lay claim to anyone's Will. I strive to earn their loyalty and their trust, to inspire them to choose my side. When they do, they remain there, because there is no magic that binds people together more powerfully than choice."

"You are a thief. You tried to steal Cassia from me. I will punish you."

"Do your worst, and know that I will do my worst to keep her free."

"Lio," she called.

"Cassia!" He turned all around, searching for the source of her voice.

"Lio, can your mind magery reach across his game?"

"Your worst?" The Collector spoke over her. "What do you think your worst is to me? I, who have watched greater mages than you live and die?"

"I am not just another mage." Lio shook his fist. "You have yet to see the worst Cassia and I can do together."

"Where is she now, she you marked for your mate? Does it enrage you to imagine what I am doing to her while you are trapped here?"

"If you can hear me, I want you to know." Her beloved voice was everywhere, whispering in with the scents of the garden, creeping through the windows with a hint of moonlight, thundering down from the top of the tower. "We are not going to lose tonight."

"I can hear you!" Lio raced for the stairwell and began to climb.

"Flee from me," the Collector said. "Run as far as you can. You cannot escape me."

He didn't know Lio was not running away, but toward Cassia. He didn't realize she was here. The Collector couldn't hear her or what Lio said to her.

"Lio, I know your mind can always reach mine."

Lio spiraled upward and upward toward their Sanctuary. The joy of recognition burst upon his heart, too great for the necromancer's world to hold. "This is Grace Union! This is what it feels like."

"You can hear me. We are not going to lose anyone tonight."

"No we aren't, my love."

He reached their bedchamber. The roses had overflowed their pots to cover the floor and climbed past their spindly stakes to entwine the window frames and rafters. The sky above was full of stars, and on the horizon, the Light Moon shone through a crimson aurora. The glyph stone rested in the center of the chamber, pulsing. The Sanctuary ward throbbed around him, invisibly shining.

Although he could not see Cassia, he felt her as near as his own heart. Stepping to her was returning home from the place he did not belong. The Sanctuary ward manifested to his sight, and a glorious flash of light consumed the world around him.

When he could see again, he beheld the Harbor Light shining through the crimson window. The ceiling was lost in storm clouds, and thunder boomed through the hall. The void he had fallen into in the waking dream surrounded him, a great swath of nothingness.

But it could not reach him. The voracious emptiness and the rain lashing down halted at the Sanctuary ward that throbbed in a dome around him. Within the spell, a small but powerful heart beat.

Lio smelled Cassia's blood and turned to see her kneeling at the center of the ward. The embassy surrounded her, staring at her with mad eyes, but her light wrapped each of them and held them in place.

Lio went down on his knees behind her. He felt no pain. He wasn't wounded. This was reality.

He laid open both of his hands with his fangs and wrapped his arms around her. He cupped her bleeding hands in his. The glyph shard glowed bright, and that gleam raced up Cassia's arms, tracing the paths of her veins in light. Magic shot through Lio, as if the flow of their blood had become one, and he could not have released her if he'd tried.

You're here! Her voice filled his mind.

He held her mind as he held her body. *We'll do this together.*

Lio fed more of his magic to her spell. The madness faded from the eyes of the mortals around them.

How did we just do that? she asked.

Your Sanctuary magic in Union with my mind magic will keep him beyond the threshold of the ward.

She breathed a sigh of relief. The tendrils of light lay the mortals gently on the ground, then withdrew into the dome around them. The vines of her spell expanded and melded with the dome, brightening the barrier.

A silent howl of rage battered their auric senses. A new storm of lightning struck the ward all at once.

He has too much magic. Cassia shook in Lio's arms.

Lio shuddered with her. *He stopped me from signaling for help. I'm not sure anyone in Orthros knows we're under attack.*

It's up to us, then.

My Grace tells me we aren't going to lose tonight.

He felt her smile in her aura, even as she gasped aloud. *I will* hold the ward. *If I protect us from his war magic, can you battle his mind magic?*

I will try to drive him out. But who brought him in?

Even as Lio asked, one volley of lightning faded. In the moment of darkness before the next, he beheld whom they dueled. Eudias stood at the eye of the storm with Skleros for a shadow.

The Collector had appointed the apprentice's mind their next dueling ground. The Collector had reduced a human being to this, a weapon for them to fight over, a field to be trampled in their battle.

Eudias needed someone to rescue him.

Lio's magic was ready, answering to the call of Cassia's blood ritual. Another break in the lightning revealed the tendons in Eudias's neck as his possessor braced himself. The Collector was ready for a bombardment.

Lio approached Eudias's mind as slowly as he would a startled deer and touched a gentle brush of power to the young man's mind.

The storm of the Collector's magic batted him away like a butterfly in a strong wind.

Lio tried again. He hovered on the edges of Eudias's aura, studying the obstacles between them.

The Collector opened the apprentice's mind and dragged Lio in.

THE GREATEST MAGE

LIO STOOD IN A long corridor of sandstone. The sun glared in through rounded arches, casting swaths of light at intervals. The shadows between were the only respite from the heat of the day.

"No, please!" came Eudias's voice.

"Listen to him beg!" Tychon laughed, and a chorus of other young men joined him.

Lio stalked through the shadows in their direction. Figures were silhouetted in a patch of sun, bent over something—or someone. Lio glided past Tychon and the two youths in apprentice robes who flanked him. In the shadows, Eudias lay cowering amid a pile of scattered books and scrolls. On his other side, four more apprentices stood in the light, blocking his retreat. An entire war circle of apprentices against one.

Lio made a quick immobilizing strike at the war circle's minds. His senses could not fix on any of them. All he could feel were Eudias's terror and humiliation.

"There is only one mind here—the one in which we battle." The Collector spoke from among the war circle.

Lio glanced at each of them, but could not tell who had spoken.

"I am here." Now the necromancer's voice came from the shadows on the ground by Eudias. "I can give you the strength to teach them a lesson."

"No!" Eudias's voice broke. "No, please!"

Lio would use what he'd learned from Mak and Lyros on the war circle, then. He made a lunge at Tychon. The closer he came to him, the farther away the apprentice seemed to be.

"Memories require precision," the Collector said. "You wouldn't know anything about that. You lack my lifetimes of experience."

The war circle hoisted Eudias between them, dangling him from his arms and legs. His head snapped back, and he whimpered.

"I've done everything you asked!" Eudias's bleeding tongue slurred his words.

"Where is your influence now?" Lio demanded. "Where is the strength you promised him? You're just going to let them take him?"

"He is learning a valuable lesson," the Collector replied.

Tychon laughed again. "You really think you can ever prove yourself?"

"What have all the tests been for?" Eudias cried. "I haven't failed a single one."

Tychon grabbed Eudias by the hair and shouted in his face. "You'll never be good enough! To the bathhouse with this pathetic excuse for an Aithourian."

As the war circle carried Eudias off, he said not another word. Lio could scarcely bear to hear another of Eudias's piteous pleas, but his resigned silence was worse.

Lio followed them through a blur of misery to the next scene of the memory. The war circle carried Eudias into a muggy bathhouse. Eudias's personal torture chamber was appointed with towels, warming bricks, and jars that smelled of therapeutic oils. Steaming benches where comrades could relax surrounded a bathing pool in the center of the room. The war circle dropped him to the tiled floor and wrestled him onto his belly.

"Eudias," Lio said. "I'm here to help. Will you let me?"

Eudias didn't acknowledge Lio's presence. What would Lio's appeals even mean? He must sound just like the Collector to Eudias's embattled mind. Lio watched helplessly as Tychon and his war circle stripped Eudias naked.

"You must enjoy this part," one apprentice taunted.

"Do you sleep on your belly?" another mocked.

Eudias didn't make a sound except for his stifled breathing.

"Why don't you reach for your magic?" the Collector asked. "Now is your chance to strike."

Sweat trickled down Eudias's body, and he began to shiver. The world around Lio trembled with Eudias. The young mage's mind and body were under far too much strain to muster the concentration and Will to formulate a spell.

The war circle hurled Eudias over the side of the pool. Anthrian warding magic chased him into the water and filled him with a sense of inevitable terror. Glyphs of Anthros gleamed around his wrists and ankles. The apprentice warders' spells shackled him in the pool on his belly with his arms and legs stretched out, facing away from them. He craned his neck to keep his head above water.

"Don't try any lightning now, Eudias," one warder warned.

"That wouldn't go very well for you, would it?" the other warder sneered.

It was going to happen again, and there was nothing he could do to stop it.

"Water, your element." The Collector roamed the edges of the bathhouse, just out of sight. "They transform it into your prison. Don't let them get away with it. Strike now!"

Lio wished Eudias would lash out with his water magic, just to spare himself from what he was about to suffer.

"Imagine your water spells dragging *them* down," the Collector said. "What must it feel like to listen to *them* beg?"

Anger roared through the bathhouse. All of Eudias's rage, bred and born in this room, trapped here.

"Imagine the way they will writhe as *they* struggle for breath," the Collector went on.

Lio gave his head a shake. "No. We can't give in, Eudias. He wants to turn you into a monster like himself. You don't need him in order to be strong." Lio threw himself down beside the pool and stretched out his arm as far as he could reach. Almost far enough. "Take my hand. I'll help you free yourself."

"Can't you taste their fear?" the Collector asked. "Can't you taste your power?"

Eudias's anger shrank and concentrated within him. He was so afraid. He wasn't powerful enough.

"Don't you see what you're doing?" Lio cried. "You're pushing his anger too far. He's turning it on himself. Do you want to destroy him?"

"If he isn't strong enough, he will be destroyed."

Eudias's mind could escape, even if his body couldn't. He seized on the *Meditations of a Great Temple Mage*.

"Yes," Lio said, "the *Meditations* are powerful words, Eudias. Hold fast to the founding principles we share."

The *Meditations* had so captured Eudias's imagination when he had first begun studying magic. They had made him feel part of something greater than himself.

"I'll recite them with you," Lio promised.

Eudias focused on the beloved words. *A Great Temple is as a deity's glyph, to which worshipers may turn their eyes with hope.*

"A Great Temple is as a deity's glyph," Lio said aloud, "to which worshipers may turn their eyes with hope."

The war circle lined up in threes on either side of Tychon. Chrysanthos's apprentice lifted his hands.

The words of the second meditation went through Eudias's mind. *A Great Temple mage must be as a deity's hand, which worshipers can reach for.*

Fire billowed across the water. Over the roar, Lio shouted the second meditation.

The war magic stopped short at Eudias's feet.

Tychon traced his fingers in an intricate spell pattern. "Wouldn't want to leave a mark where anyone can see it, would I? That might mislead them to think you've actually been brave enough to use real war magic in battle—and survive."

Lio stared at the bottoms of Eudias's feet. Many old burn scars already marred them.

Tychon's fire spell inched closer. Eudias shut his eyes and grimaced, hissing through his teeth.

Great magic is not a gift from the gods, but the mark of the gods upon the mage, who is their greatest gift to this world.

"Great magic is not a gift from the gods," Lio recited with Eudias, "but the mark of the gods upon the mage, who is their greatest gift to this world."

"I don't think he properly appreciates your spell, Tychon," said one apprentice. "Compliment Tychon's advanced fire spell, Eudias."

A Great Temple's mages are worshipers, who must never set themselves above those they serve.

"A Great Temple's mages are worshipers," Lio said, "who must never set themselves above those they serve."

"I'll teach him some manners for you, Tychon." The apprentice commenced a set of deliberate casting gestures.

From an opposite corner of the bath, a warming brick rose and sailed toward Eudias.

"Every spell is a brick of the Great Temple that will stand for ages," Lio called out. "Say it with me, Eudias."

"Every spell is a brick of the Great Temple that will stand for ages," Eudias chanted under his breath.

"What was that, Eudias?" the geomagus called. "I couldn't hear you."

As the brick neared Eudias's face, he flinched. All the war circle howled with laughter. The brick slowed, passed over Eudias, then came to rest on the back of his head.

"Praise Tychon's spell," the geomagus said again.

Endeavor ever to be praiseworthy, and never to be praised.

"Endeavor ever to be praiseworthy, and never to be praised."

The brick pressed against Eudias's head. His neck strained. Lio focused his Will on the brick, but it was as if it were not there. His power could not alter the course of Eudias's memories.

At last the brick forced Eudias's head down. He gulped a breath before his mouth went under the water. Tychon's fire spell flared brighter. Eudias writhed against his magical shackles.

Lio's chest burned. Primal panic seized him. This was a mortal's fear of drowning. He heaved a breath for Eudias and said the next Meditation for him. "Fear not your power, only the misuse of it."

Moments dragged by. Lio kept his arm stretched out, straining, although it was useless. He could not bear to watch and do nothing.

The water in front of Eudias's face bubbled. He began to gurgle.

"Eudias," Lio called again. "'Magic is your sacred name and your divine inheritance, and all its heirs your brothers and sisters.' You are not alone. I am with you."

"What is the meaning of this?" Dalos demanded.

Lio jumped at the sound of the dead man's voice.

The fire went out. The brick sank. The war circle scrambled into a tidy line. Eudias floundered in the water, choking. As he struggled to the side of the pool, his master did not go to help him. Lio tried to grab hold of him, but Eudias always slid out of reach.

Steam plastered Dalos's dark hair to his head and made sweat gleam on his olive skin. With his medium height and plain features, he bore no resemblance to his glamorous brother. But as he patrolled before the war circle, he scrutinized each apprentice with fearsome authority in his brown eyes. He halted in front of Tychon. "Tell Honored Master Chrysanthos he is a petty coward for pursuing our rivalry through a boy. If your master wants to send me a message, he can do so himself in the dueling court."

"I will deliver your invitation to him, Honored Master Dalos." Tychon put his hands in his sleeves and gave a slight bow, but his tone was anything but respectful.

"Back to your masters, all of you," Dalos ordered.

Six of the apprentices hurried out, but Tychon disappeared, showing off his traversal skills.

Dalos stood and waited. Avoiding his gaze, Eudias dragged himself out of the water and huddled on the side of the pool. He strained to reach his clothes without standing on his burned feet. Finally he managed to snatch one of his robes and pulled it over his wet, shaking body.

Dalos watched him. "You will learn many important lessons in the Aithourian Circle. This is one of them. Only through the most brutal challenges can we harden ourselves and attain true strength."

It made Lio sick to listen to him.

"Yes, Master," Eudias whispered.

"Every famous war mage here once faced the same tests of his mettle. The battles you fight as an apprentice are some of the most important of your career. Reading does not prepare you for war. Get your nose out of your scrolls and learn from experience. Within these walls is where you first encounter the realities of life."

"Yes, Master."

"I am still waiting for you to prove me wrong about you." Dalos turned his back on Eudias and headed for the door.

"Master?"

"Make it quick."

"Why did you bother with me?"

Dalos let out a short sigh. "Your magic cannot be allowed to fester among the general populace. Someone had to teach you not to kill yourself or other people."

"Why didn't you leave me to one of the lesser masters?"

Dalos looked over his shoulder at Eudias. "Apprenticeship is a pragmatic institution designed to furnish me with a useful subordinate to perform menial tasks. Unlike Honored Master Chrysanthos, I do not entertain emotional notions of trust, camaraderie, and mentorship. Those tend to backfire later. You are suitably unambitious not to cause trouble for me in future. I simply require you to do as I command when I command it, stay out of my way the rest of the time, and not ask too many questions. You're very good at the first two."

Dalos slammed the door on his way out.

The Collector remained. "What a hypocrite. He was not so high and mighty when he lay dead beside you."

Eudias hugged himself. "I don't want to remember that night."

"Everyone has always underestimated you. Except me. I alone recognize your true potential and can help you fulfill it. That is why I chose you after Dalos failed me."

"In the moment when your magics destroyed him, I was the only option you had if you wanted to remain at Solorum. You accepted me because you had to, just like the Aithourian Circle."

"Dalos was weak. He could not withstand the fullness of my power. But look what great things you and I are already doing together. You are a very powerful young mage. With me, you can be even more powerful."

"I don't want to be powerful," Eudias whispered, as if it were the most shameful of confessions.

"Imagine if you could strike Tychon to the ground with your own advanced spells. You know them all, Eudias. You have the power to perform them. You only need the confidence I can give you. Imagine the look on his face when you turn the tables on him."

"I just want it to stop," Eudias said to himself.

"Coward," the Collector accused. "Be a man. Be a master mage. The mage you always dreamed of being. A man others will fear."

"What *I* wanted was…" Eudias looked at his hands. "…a dream all along. Nothing more." He looked down at his feet still dangling in the water.

Lio heard the words go through Eudias's mind again. *Don't try any lightning now, Eudias. That wouldn't go very well for you, would it?*

"Eudias." Lio knelt beside him. "Everything you want is still possible. Don't give up."

The chaos in Eudias's mind collected into resolve. All the Will that had deserted him when he tried to harm others now came to him when the enemy was himself.

"Eudias," Lio pleaded. "'Every mage who draws breath within its sacred walls is necessary to keep a Great Temple alive.'"

For the first time, Eudias looked right at him. *"Ambassador?"*

"I'm here to help," Lio said.

"You're surrounded by enemies," the Collector declared. "Here is another taunting you, making demands. Do not give in."

"I know it's hard for you to believe anyone," Lio said, "but I want you to know I am your ally. How can I prove my worth to you?"

"I recognize your voice." Eudias leaned closer. "You were the one saying the *Meditations* with me. You tried to make it easier."

"I am so sorry for what you've endured."

"He pities you," the Collector scoffed, "just like everyone else. Do not tolerate his condescension."

"I don't pity you, I—"

"You feel for me." Eudias's voice was full of astonishment.

"And I know you have the Will to drive him out of your mind."

"You would never give me up," the Collector said. "All this power, right at your fingertips. Men have killed to become what you are."

"I've been trying to banish him for months," Eudias lamented. "Everyone's right about me. I'm too weak."

"You are nothing without me."

Lio shook his head. "You have survived his tyranny all this time. You are one of the strongest people I have ever met."

"Not strong enough." Eudias looked at the water again.

It did no good for Lio to berate Eudias with his truth. Eudias had to discover his own answers for himself. "What is the final meditation?"

Eudias hesitated. "'Carry the one who stumbles today, for you will stumble tomorrow.'"

"Every single one of us needs help from others at times. There is no shame in it. In fact, it is a sign of strength." Lio offered his hand.

"What will he demand of you tomorrow?" the Collector asked.

"You carried me yesterday," Lio told Eudias. "Now it's my turn."

"The help I gave the Summit was atonement," Eudias protested.

"Wasn't it Kheimerios who wrote about what makes a great mage?" Lio asked.

"'A great mage is seldom wrong.'" Eudias hesitated again. "'The greatest mage knows he is wrong all the time.'"

"Rise beyond the foibles of mortal mages," the Collector invited. "Endure with me through the ages."

"Who is the mage and the man *you* want to be, Eudias?" Lio asked.

Eudias uncurled his hand. He held a rough-hewn wooden charm in the shape of a lightning bolt. Lio sensed the Collector's retort, but the words were indistinguishable.

"That's a storm charm," Lio said. "Farmers carry them to petition the gods for fertile fields and rain, is that right?"

Eudias nodded. "I don't know where Kassandra found one just like we used to carve in my village, but it was kind of her to replace the one I lost when I came to Corona. It was a gift from...from a grateful family, the day I discovered my affinity for lightning. I thought I was just a rain mage, you see. Their farm was barren, and I was trying to tempt a storm to drop some water on their fields. It was a most incredible moment. I still have difficulty describing it. I rode a lightning bolt down from the sky and into the soil. Oh, that probably sounds foolish."

"Not at all. It is a challenge to describe the indescribable, to put words to magic, but it is a time-honored tradition to try."

Eudias turned the charm over in his hands. "Their fields produced more that year than they had in a generation. I got to celebrate harvest with them before I had to leave."

"What happened to your original storm charm?"

"Tychon burned it."

"Leave behind the boy you were," the Collector commanded. "Only then can you become the man you are meant to be."

"I don't want anything from you," Lio said. "I only want to help you achieve what you want for yourself."

Eudias looked at Lio. "Why bother with me?"

"Your magic must be allowed to benefit the general populace. Your example has to teach them not to harm themselves and each other. I entertain notions of trust and camaraderie. You have already shown how they backfire on those who care only about themselves. I know you are ambitious enough to bring a storm down upon your order—the kind that cleanses and leaves the fields prosperous. Someone who is good at asking questions, even the difficult ones, can find real answers."

When Eudias reached out to Lio, the distance between them shrank. "I'll try to find the answers. If you'll help me."

Lio put an arm around the young mage's shoulders, another under his knees, and lifted him from the pool. Water dripped from Eudias's swollen, blistered feet. Tears fell from his eyes. He did not apologize for them.

Lightning danced across the water where Eudias had sat only a moment before. The Collector's voice crashed down upon them. *"Thief!"*

"You are the thief!" Eudias shouted. "I will not let you take from me any longer. You will not have my magic. You will not use my power for the atrocities you commit."

Lio channeled the strength of Eudias's conviction into a mental defense around them. Water and lightning lashed around them, but did not reach them through their combined Will.

"I can hear my own thoughts." Eudias slumped in Lio's arms. "How did you do that?"

Lio held Eudias. His life. The thin young man was so light to carry, a precious, but by no means fragile burden. "You did it. I only helped you."

"I...I don't think he can hear me." Eudias breathed a sigh, almost a sob. "I haven't had a moment of peace like this since the Equinox Summit."

"All your moments will be like this once we've freed you from him."

"You are a powerful mind mage, and I know his secrets. Together, I think...I actually think we might be able to do that."

"I have some understanding of the evil of possession, but you have surely learned much more during this experience. What knowledge can you grant me?"

"Possession and essential displacement are one and the same. Possession is displacing your essence into someone else. It is the same principle as displacing a person's essence into you."

"Then we must drive his essence from your own."

"We cannot know the true extent of his magic. He has claimed too many other mages' power. If you free my mind from him and he departs, he will try to take my magic with him, as he has done to all the others. He will attempt to tear my affinity from my mind, every last trace of my magic."

No mage could survive that. "We won't let him have it."

Eudias looked out over the pool. The storm raged down, and the water churned. Dozens of lightning bolts roamed between the clouds and the pool, lashing out here, then there, as if hunting for their target.

"I must tell you something now...in case," Eudias said. "The Collector knows everything his Overseers do. I've seen where they took the hostages. Skleros delivered them to Solorum. The rest of Chrysanthos's war circle is keeping them in the catacombs of the Sun Temple."

"Hespera and Anthros bless you. You have saved beloved lives with those words. You have our gratitude."

"I have one request of you, not for myself, but on Ariadne's behalf. If I don't get a chance, tell her I...how much I admire her. She doesn't know. I dared not return her...kindness. I couldn't let *him* anywhere near her."

"You were protecting her."

"She deserves the highest appreciation. She must think I have not shown it to her."

"You will get the chance to tell her yourself."

All around them, Eudias's mind steadied with concentration. He closed his eyes and went still, his hand tightening on his charm. He made no elaborate gestures and muttered no incantations. His Will focused.

The Collector closed in around them. He was everywhere. He went on forever. There was nowhere to hide. The past was full of him. He ruled the future.

"Not our future," Lio said.

Lio devoted all his Will to the mental defenses around him and Eudias. Their spells aligned, resonated, and grew louder than the storm. The lightning began to inch away from the boundaries of the pool and hover closer to the center.

The Collector was countless minds and countless magics. He was an army in one person. He was vast. The two of them were so small.

"I've fought your army before," Lio reminded him.

Lio reached within himself for the power that had brought the heart hunters to their knees and the control that had kept them alive. Holding Eudias within his protections, he unleashed his thelemanteia upon the Collector.

His magic echoed out of him, deep into the void that clouded Eudias's mind. Was there any end to it? But even as that echo died away, more magic came to Lio's Will, and he shouted their defiance again.

Eudias shouted with him, and the many lightning bolts on the water snapped together into only a few.

The Collector did not shout back. He opened his maw.

"Try to take our magic!" Lio challenged. "You'll bite off more than you can chew!"

Eudias clutched his chest, his face contorting in pain. But the lightning bolts hovered nearer and nearer each other, closer to the center of the pool.

Lio tried to brace himself for the Collector's grasp. "I dare you to try to rip the Gift from me. Hespera's path is beyond your reach."

The assault on his essence never came. He kept pouring his magic out against that vast emptiness, and he found neither the other side of the chasm, nor the end of his own power.

The water rose up out of its pool, battering their defenses. As the rest of the room was submerged, Lio stood with Eudias in an island of dry ground. The futile attack subsided.

The stone benches shattered. Boulders, bricks, and slivers of stone launched at them. They were a hand's breadth away when the perimeter of Lio's defenses flashed bright. There came an instant of heat and tremendous pressure. Then the streaks of lightning faded from his vision, and he saw the refuse of scorched, shattered rocks all around them. He realized his arms were at his sides. Eudias stood on his own feet, his arms outstretched, one clenched into a fist around his charm.

A roar behind them made Lio turn. Flames blasted through the doorway, as if all of Corona poured itself into this one room. The rocks turned molten around them, and the floor ran with liquid fire. The current parted around them and flowed into the water, gradually filling the pool.

Lio felt the Collector in every lick of flame, in every rivulet of magma, in each bubble of the boiling water, in each clap of thunder from the clouds above. But he did not feel him in the half-dozen bolts that leapt together into one great column of lightning.

"You're winning, Eudias! You're almost there! We can do this."

Eudias bowed his head. The lightning reversed itself and rose upward into the storm.

Light crackled through the dark storm clouds. The water evaporated. The magma stilled and cooled. The fire died to embers.

Lio heard the sound of glass breaking, the Collector's final protest. Then the clouds cleared.

MARBLE DUST

THE CLARITY OF THE Union told Lio he was alone in his own mind. Cassia's aura told him his Grace lived. The distant presence of the Queens' ward told him Orthros still stood.

The Collector was gone.

Lio held Cassia close and opened his eyes. Eudias had made it inside the Sanctuary ward and lay unconscious nearby, his heart beating slowly, but steadily. All around them, the Tenebrans cowered and cried out in fear.

Shards of crimson glass lanced down through the air on the other side of the gauze of Sanctuary magic. Chairs and tables tumbled, and silk tablecloths whipped about. A white pillar collapsed with a tremendous crash. Chunks of red and black granite hurtled. Rose House was crumbling, falling into the necromancer's portal.

Skleros stood on a shaking crag of floor tile and shouted over the noise, shaking his fist at Lio. "Yours will be the next head I deliver to my Master!" The Gift Collector leapt from his perch and dove into the portal.

In his wake, the void collapsed. Released from its pull, the debris crashed down upon Lio, Cassia, and the mortals.

A heap of rubble landed on the ward and enclosed them all in stone and broken glass.

Sanctuary magic still emanated from Cassia, but the intimate Union their spell had fostered had faded. Lio took a breath to say her name. The odor of scorched stone assailed him, twisted around the sweet fragrance of her blood.

Lio coughed. "Cassia?"

She didn't answer. He realized he was holding her up. Knight lay still against them, his fur soaked. The pool of blood under them was Cassia's.

"Cassia!" Lio lay her back in his arms. For the first time, the sight of her blood turned his stomach. Where the light of her spell had permeated the veins of her wrists and arms, her skin was broken. Blood ran in rivulets down her body.

"Stay with me! We won. Don't give up now."

So much blood. So many wounds to heal. No time. Lio put his mouth to one of her wrists, pressing his tongue to her major veins.

"He's killing her!" Benedict shouted.

There came the sound of a scuffle, then Callen's growl. "Stay out of the way."

"He's saving her life." Perita crowded near with the Semna's attendants.

"Ariadne," the Semna instructed, "a tourniquet on her other wrist. Pakhne, join my healing spell."

Cassia's skin was not closing under Lio's tongue. Why wasn't the wound healing?

"Semna, why isn't her body responding?" Pakhne asked.

"She's far gone," the Semna answered, "but we won't give up until she does."

Lio touched Cassia's mind with his weary power. That short reach frightened him more than a long fall into the Collector's void. She felt farther away from Lio than she had even a moment ago.

Cassia, I know you can hear me. We are not going to lose tonight, remember? You're going to stay in Orthros with me. You're going to stay!

Lio heard the groan of rock. Another cry of panic went up among the mortals.

"Brace it up!" Lord Gaius commanded. "On your feet, men. Use those chairs for supports."

Lio sensed the ward dim. The bundle of light in his arms grew fainter. *Goddess, please. Goddess, please—!*

Novas exploded in the Union, and the deep, dark sky wrapped around them, full of stars. The Sanctuary ward blazed back to life with Queen Alea's magic. The Union shook with Father's wrath as the rocks were tossed away.

Queen Soteira's power filled the night. "I've got her, Lio."

Only her voice could have persuaded Lio to lift his mouth from Cassia's wrist and let go. "Annassa. Will she—?"

Queen Soteira took Cassia in her arms. "She will come through this safe and sound, with my healing. How well I know the wounds of Sanctuary magic."

The world spun around Lio. They were perched on a solid island of rock, surrounded by a ditch full of rubble. Beyond the gulch, Rose House lay in ruins. Only the skeleton of the facade still stood. His rose window was no more, but through the empty frame shone the Harbor Light, undimmed.

The Queens, the elder firstbloods, and the Stand had arrived. In their wake came Chargers, healers, most of the royal firstbloods, and Lio's Trial sisters, blessedly unharmed. Lio's father knelt beside him, holding him upright. His mother supported him on his other side, and he felt her magic make a gentle examination of his mind.

Lio's uncle knelt down in front of him and touched a hand to his face. For a long moment, Uncle Argyros said nothing, his aura furious. "I am proud of you."

In spite of everything, Lio smiled briefly. "Thank you, Uncle."

Aunt Lyta joined them. "We need you to tell us what happened, as you are able."

"Eudias needs a mind healer," Lio blurted. "He found out where our hostages are. Chrysanthos's war circle is keeping them in the crypt beneath the Sun Temple at Solorum."

"We're on our way." Ioustin gripped Lio's shoulder.

After a moment of veiled conference with the Queens, he and the Chargers stepped away.

Lio's mother turned his face toward her and looked into his eyes. Her own gleamed with tears, but her voice was calm and steady. "You are going to be all right."

He nodded. She kissed his brow, then went to Eudias's side.

Queen Soteira's power already touched the young mage. Lio could feel her at work upon all the mortals. Chrysanthos gasped and pushed himself to a sitting position.

He felt of his chest, then stared at Queen Soteira. "You already know where the hostages are. You don't need me."

She met his gaze.

He looked into her eyes for a long moment. Then he turned his face away with a grimace and a whimper. "Why did you bother?"

"Because your heart could still be saved," Queen Soteira answered.

Callen still held Benedict by the collar. The knight was staring at Lio's mouth.

"Don't you understand what just happened?" Perita demanded of Benedict, pointing at Lio. "He protected our lady!"

"And she protected all of us." Lio looked away.

His father gave him a handkerchief. Lio wiped his mouth and beard. But the truth sat there in his hand, a bloodstained square of silk. He did not put it away.

Cassia's eyes fluttered open. Lio heaved a sigh and caressed her head. Her gaze met his. "Is he gone?"

"I believe so," Lio answered.

"He fled," Queen Soteira said. "His presence lurks nowhere in Hespera's temple."

The ward around them shifted, and the presence of Sanctuary magic faded from the ruins. But it was not gone. Lio could still sense it... somewhere.

Queen Alea joined them at Cassia's side. She turned over Cassia's hand. There was nothing there but marble dust.

"A warding artifact?" the Semna marveled. "It was ancient and powerful, by the feel of it. Astonishing that she could use it without any training."

"She told me she rescued it from an abandoned Tenebran shrine." Queen Alea smiled at Cassia.

Cassia's eyes slid shut, and her breathing eased into the rhythm of sleep.

Benedict stepped back from Callen and straightened his tunic. "That's our Tenebran thrush."

Queen Soteira put Cassia in Lio's arms again. The wounds and blood were gone. Lio ignored the stares and rocked his Grace, listening to the strength of her heartbeat.

THE CENTER OF HESPERA'S ROSE

Hespera herself,
who binds us together,
and from whom everything grows.

sometime after

WINTER SOLSTICE

FAMILY

S HE WAS ON HER back. She couldn't move. Where was she?
Had the Collector taken her from Orthros?

Even as the fear struck Cassia, Lio was there in her mind, reassuring her. The Collector was gone. All was well.

She tried to move again, then groaned. Her body felt so heavy. His arms felt so good.

"She wakes," said a voice she had not heard in over fourteen years.

Cassia gasped and opened her eyes.

Nephalea looked exhausted and emaciated, but the gentle compassion on her face had not changed. Alkaios's face hovered next to hers. For the first time, Cassia saw him smile. Her hand tightened on something, and she recognized the feel of Solia's pendant.

"You're safe," Cassia croaked.

"Thanks in large part to you two," said Alkaios.

Nephalea smiled. "Well met, Cassia."

"It's so good to see you. I can't find the words…to say thank you."

Nephalea touched a hand to Cassia's, where she held the ivy talisman Alkaios must have returned to her. "Your actions have spoken for you."

Cassia gave up trying to budge from Lio's arms and took in her surroundings. She was neither in the sickroom of her nightmares nor in the all-too-real nightmare at Rose House. This appeared to be a room at the Healing Sanctuary. Lio reclined on the bed beside her, while Alkaios and Nephalea had pulled chairs near. There were flowers everywhere.

Lio held her with the greatest gentleness. "Eudias escaped his ordeal with some secrets. One of them was the hostages' location."

"The Sun Temple at Solorum," Nephalea said, "a place steeped in more Anthrian magic than anywhere else in Tenebra. They hid us in the crypt."

"You were right there all along?" Cassia cried. "I went to temple right above you! If only I'd realized—"

"You were my talisman the whole time, Cassia. There before me in the crypt, I beheld an astonishing monument to hope—the tomb of Solia, which I knew to be empty. Then I sensed your aura in the temple. Not even layers of Anthrian spells could prevent me from recognizing you in Union. Feeling how powerful and kind you had grown in the years since we met, I never lost sight of what all Hesperines errant are fighting for. The real good we are able to do in this world."

"I was doing everything I could," Cassia explained, "to prevent war, to keep all our Hesperines errant safe. Especially the three of you."

Nephalea's eyes shone. "Alkaios and I have now heard a great deal about your deeds. You have done us all proud."

Cassia swallowed. "Is Nike—?"

"She was not one of the Hesperines errant in custody," Lio answered.

Nephalea laughed. "Not in the wildest dreams of that green crop of Aithourians. She was leading our efforts to free the prisoners. The three of us decided I would allow myself to be captured, while Iskhyra and Alkaios remained on the outside. It led me right to the missing Hesperines errant, leaving Iskhyra and Alkaios in position to rescue us all. It was a good plan. Until it took longer than we intended. The Aithourians had secured the temple more effectively than we thought. We soon realized a Gift Collector had assisted them." She looked at Alkaios, gripping his hand.

"When I agreed to remain with Ishkyra, I accepted the risks. Our Grace Union was the best way for you to pass us information. I only wish I could have gone in your place."

"We needed a warder on the inside. I only wish you had sought healing in Orthros sooner."

"I led two members of the Dexion's war circle on a merry chase, though."

"You cut my work in half. I only had the other two to dispatch from within. Ishkyra made sure their replacements never arrived. The Tenebran mages were of no concern when she infiltrated the temple and freed us. The Charge arrived just in time to escort us home safely."

Cassia smiled. "Time and experience usually break the spell of our imaginations and reveal those we admired are mere mortals. But you three are every bit the immortals of my childhood memories. Where is Nike? Can I see her?"

Lio sighed. "She is still Abroad."

Nephalea nodded. "When she realized the Charge was coming for us, it spared her a return to Orthros to deliver us."

"I don't understand," Cassia protested. "Doesn't she want to come home?"

"Her work is not done," Nephalea replied.

"What is she working on?" Cassia asked.

Alkaios looked at his Grace. "The day I met Nephalea, I came to her family's keep to collect my brother's life price from hers."

"My brother refused," Nephalea said, "as I'd known he would. He was bred, born, and raised to carry on the feud. I was made to mourn. Most of all for Alkaios."

"After Nephalea's brother was done with me, Iskhyra found me on the battlefield. She asked me if I wanted revenge. I told her I wanted Nephalea. Ishkyra saved me, and armed with the Gift, I was able to save Nephalea from her family."

"Iskhyra gave us more than the life we thought we could never have. She gave us eternity."

Alkaios smiled at Cassia. "That is what she is always working on. Alkaioses and Nephaleas. Cassias and Solias."

Cassia bit back her disappointment. "I should not have needed to ask."

"But I have to wonder," said Lio, "is her work ever done?"

"No," Cassia answered, "but perhaps one night, she'll decide it is enough."

Alkaios wrapped her hand more securely around the pendant. "Rest now. We'd best do the same. We aren't supposed to stay out of bed too long. Annassa Soteira's orders."

Nephalea blushed. "We'll never live down the healers having to feed us each other's blood. Certainly not the reunion I had in mind."

Alkaios grinned, getting slowly to his feet. "We'll soon enjoy our first Grace Dance here in Orthros. We'll make it a real celebration."

"That's right," Lio said. "The Queens have postponed the Festival of Grace until everyone is well enough to dance."

"I shall be so proud to dance with my Grace." Nephalea stood and ran a hand over Alkaios's lock of hair. "This is very dashing, you know. You may start a fashion."

"Will you be staying after you recover?" Cassia asked. "Or will you be rejoining Nike in the field?"

"Iskhyra has done so much for us," Nephalea answered, "and we have learned her lessons well. We think she is ready to follow the next stretch of her path on her own, and that we are ready to do the same."

"Orthros is fairer than we ever imagined," Alkaios said. "We've decided it's time we get to know our homeland, and there seems to be a need here."

Nephalea nodded. "Hippolyta needs more Stewards. The changing political situation is running the Stand ragged. We've talked with her about serving, and she's offered to put us on patrol with full rank, since we've already had years of training with a Master Steward."

"That's wonderful news," Cassia said. "I know Nike would appreciate that."

"Cassia's awake!" Zoe squealed from the corridor. The goats bleated.

"Alkaios and Nephalea are here, too?" Bosko had never sounded so excited.

The sucklings dashed through the door curtain. Cassia swallowed a laugh. Bosko had used his speires to separate and tie a section of his hair to match all that remained on Alkaios's head. Alkaios looked rather startled, but Nephalea made over the suckling's new hairstyle.

Zoe and the goats climbed in bed with Cassia and Lio. Zoe's only admission of distress was how close she cuddled to Cassia. Cassia wasn't sure how much Lio had told his sister about what had happened, but she held Zoe tight, while Lio held her.

Moonbeam tasted Cassia's bedclothes. Aurora looked interested in the flowers on the nightstand, before Zoe hauled the kid onto her lap. Cassia's throat tightened, and she tried to fight off tears long enough to ask the question.

"Lio...where is Knight?"

Lio pointed at the door. Bosko's parents followed the sucklings inside. Knight walked in at Kadi's side, heeling perfectly.

Kadi grinned at Cassia. "The animal healers were terrified to try bringing him to you. He seemed glad to see me, though."

Cassia held out her arms, leaden though they were. Knight bounded onto the bed, shaking the frame, scattering goats and rousing a peal of laughter from everyone. He fit himself onto the bunk by sprawling all over Lio and Cassia's legs.

Cassia yawned, rubbing Knight's ears. "How long was I asleep? It feels like I've been in bed for a month."

Lio scratched Knight's chin. "Annassa Soteira put a slow healing on you and said you needed absolute rest. It's only been three nights, though."

"Three nights?" Cassia shot him a frantic glance when Zoe wasn't looking.

He angled his head toward his parents, who were walking through the door. "I'm fine."

Zoe giggled. "Lio's a suckling again."

Lio reached over and ruffled her hair.

Bosko didn't seem to realize his attempts at conversation with Alkaios and Nephalea were keeping his heroes from their rest, until Apollon and Komnena gently mentioned Queen Soteira's instructions. When Alkaios and Nephalea invited Bosko to visit them in their room later and offered to answer all his questions about his Aunt Nike, he let them leave at last.

"Bring Cassia's get-well present over here, Bosko," Zoe urged.

Bosko approached Cassia. He held out a handful of rimelace. "We picked these wildflowers for you. I'm glad you're all right."

Cassia took the profusion of tiny, white flowers from him and held them to her nose. They smelled like spring and freshly fallen snow all at once. Like home. Like Orthros, where medicine that saved children's lives grew as wildflowers.

She gestured around her at the room full of gifts. "Don't tell anyone who gave me all these lovely things, but your flowers are my favorite."

Bosko gave Cassia a real smile.

"You like ours even better than that huge one?" Zoe asked.

Cassia eyed the gaudy statement of grandeur in the far corner of the room. The vase was too tall for a table, and the spiky, vibrant flowers were bigger than Knight's paws. "Well, it's not roses, so it can't be from Konstantina. Let me guess. Hypatia?"

"Of course," Lio answered.

Javed's healing magic swept over Cassia, while Kadi commandeered a vase for the rimelace, and Apollon and Komnena took the chairs. No sooner had they sat down, than the rest of the Stand and Uncle Argyros all came into the room, bringing more chairs in with them. Cassia found herself surrounded by Lio's family.

Her family.

"I'm sorry about Nike," Cassia said.

"It's all right," Aunt Lyta replied.

"Aunt Nike's on an adventure," Bosko said enviously.

Kadi smiled. "She still has work to do."

"We miss her every moment," said Uncle Argyros, "but we understand."

"I'm still trying to," Mak admitted. "I want to meet my sister. Now that Alkaios and Nephalea are joining the Stand, I've half a mind to go find her and see if she needs a hand."

Lyros spared Mak's family having to utter the horror written on their faces. He pushed Mak into a chair and sat on his lap. "You're not going anywhere."

Mak laughed and wrapped his arms around his Grace.

After that, they talked about everything and nothing. Everyone laughed and smiled, and when the children were loud, no one scolded them. No one mentioned politics, and Cassia could not find it in herself to ask.

"We won't wear you out, Cassia," Mak promised.

Lyros crossed his arms. "We won't allow the embassy to tire you, either. They're all but beating down the door of the Healing Sanctuary to visit their Tenebran thrush."

"Please bar the door a little longer," Cassia said. "I don't feel like singing. I need...some time. With my people."

THE OLD MASTERS

W
HEN JAVED TOOK THE sucklings home, and the elder
firstbloods and the Stand remained, Cassia knew politics
were about to find her again. She began to feel a council of
war was gathering around her.

Lio pulled the covers further over her. "We have to keep this brief."

"Very brief." Komnena reached over to pat both their hands. "Cassia
and Lio's minds need time to process what happened before we pressure
them into important decisions."

"No one will be allowed to pressure them," Apollon threatened.

Aunt Lyta tugged the door curtain more securely closed before
returning to her chair. "I have informed the other half of the elders they
are not invited. We'll start when the Queens and Kassandra arrive."

Cassia ran her hand through Knight's ruff. "I have questions about
what happened."

Uncle Argyros sighed. "We have more questions than answers,
I'm afraid."

The Queens entered, Annassa Alea carrying a pot full of soil. There
appeared to be no plant in it. She set it on Cassia's nightstand next to the
rimelace. "A gift from our daughter Konstantina. She sends her regrets."

"From the Second Princess?" Cassia asked. "Then...I think it must
be a rose."

"She excavated the courtyard of Rose House herself and assures me
this is the only surviving root system. She said you would know what to
do with it."

Cassia put a hand to the soil. "Please tell her I sincerely appreciate her gift, and…I may have two entries for the Circle of Rosarians' gathering next season."

Annassa Soteira came to Cassia's side and sat down on the edge of the bed. She looked into Cassia's eyes, and Cassia felt magic fill her veins, as when she was casting a spell. But this magic took nothing from her, only restored everything in its path.

"How are you feeling?" Queen Soteira asked.

"Tired," Cassia admitted. "A small price to pay. Thank you, Annassa."

"Don't forget to thank Lio for saving your life, too."

Cassia wrapped her hands around one of his. "Again."

His eyes filled with his familiar, tender warmth. "You'll get your chance to thank me."

"Be patient with yourself, Cassia," Queen Soteira advised. "Sanctuary magic is profoundly draining as other affinities and mundane blood loss are not, especially for a mortal using it through an artifact. You will need rest, at least until the end of the week."

Queen Alea took a chair at the foot of Cassia's bed. "You worked a beautiful spell. I could not bear to end it, even once the danger was past. I channeled it back into the glyph stone so you may keep it forever. Although the glyph shard's power is spent, the mother stone endures. If you take care not to break any more shards from it, it should last as long as Orthros."

Lio brushed Cassia's hair back from her face. "I'm sorry about your pendant. I know how important it was to you to carry its protection with you."

"It's all right. I don't need it anymore. I'm ready to discover my own magic."

A smile lifted his exhausted expression. "I'm glad to hear that."

"I will find out what my affinity is, and I will become a master in my own right."

"You are well on your way," Queen Alea said.

The curtain flipped back, and Kassandra strode in. "I brought you something from Rose House." She held up her prize and unfurled it before them. The historical Tenebran banner now had new burns, stains, and tatters as well as old ones, but the Mage King's emblem endured.

"How did it survive the attack?" Cassia wondered.

Kassandra hung the banner over the bouquets. "I have a feeling this is only the latest of this artifact's many adventures."

"It stands testament to the true queen." Cassia turned Solia's pendant over in her hands. "Will the embassy bear it back to Tenebra as the banner of their cause against the king?"

"I gave it to you, not the embassy. Flavian may come up with an emblem of his own." Kassandra took her seat next to the Queens.

Lio gestured at Cassia's gardening satchel on a side table. "I did take the liberty of turning the treaty over to Lord Gaius and Sir Benedict."

Cassia looked around her at the elders. "Chrysanthos knows I was at the shrine. By now he must have told the Tenebrans I was a heretic all along. He'll say I was never acting in Tenebra's best interests, only to further the interests of Hespera worship. I'm so sorry. The secret is out, and it will destroy the embassy's trust in me and in the treaty I championed."

"As a matter of fact," Queen Soteira replied, "Chrysanthos has not mentioned the matter to anyone."

"Not even during his long discussion with the embassy regarding his own future," Queen Alea added.

Lio rubbed Cassia's palm. "The Tenebrans believe you discovered an abandoned shrine on the palace grounds that was so ruined, you could not distinguish its origins. You found a warding artifact there that you brought with you to Orthros for their protection."

"They didn't recognize the spell as Sanctuary magic?" Cassia asked.

Queen Alea folded her hands. "My magic hasn't been seen in Tenebra since the Last War. It is not only extinct, but was the specialty of mages now considered heretics. Even a mage of the Semna's expertise wouldn't recognize it."

"Everyone assumed it was a Kyrian shrine," Lio explained, "since feminine warding magic is associated with the Harvest Mother. The Semna has done nothing but praise your rescue of a sacred relic from the king's neglect. Master Gorgos seems willing to forgive your unauthorized use of magic, as it is the reason his heart still beats."

Queen Alea's eyes twinkled. "I see no reason to correct that assumption, do you?"

"Then…" Cassia took a breath. "The treaty stands?"

Lio looked into her eyes. "The Tenebrans have framed the paper stained with your blood in a place of honor in their new lodgings. We won your fight."

She gazed back at him. "Our fight."

"The embassy is eager to return to Tenebra to enact the changes we agreed on. As soon as everyone has time to recover from the attack, we will see to their safe return. Hesperine magic will make it possible for them to leave Orthros before the spring thaw."

"What is to become of the Dexion?"

"After considerable negotiation, Orthros is surrendering him to the custody of Tenebra's Acting Council of Free Lords. They have assured us he will be held responsible only for his own deeds and suffer no vengeance for his half brother's crimes. He will be allowed to correspond with his dependents in Cordium while the Council negotiates with the Aithourian Circle."

"So the Dexion is going back to Tenebra as their hostage. Incredible."

"They will offer to return him to his father in exchange for a treaty. They want guarantees that the Orders will not take a side in the struggle for the throne or in any way attempt to weaken Tenebra's sovereignty."

Uncle Arygros sat back in his chair, a faint smile on his lips. "Orthros has a treaty with Tenebra, and Cordium shall be forbidden to interfere. We have lived long enough to see a new age."

Cassia did not want to dim the elder diplomat's good spirits. But the Collector's threats whispered in her mind, wearing away at her hopes.

Had they really furthered his plan without realizing it? Was all of this really just another twist in his game, another move toward his inevitable victory?

Cassia shook her head. "What about Skleros?"

Apollon rumbled, "The Gift Collector escaped through the portal before I could call him to account."

Worry furrowed Komnena's brow. "The embassy remembers when Skleros entered the hall and when he fled, but nothing in between."

A chill skittered over Cassia. "They don't even know the Collector was ever here."

"No," Lio said tightly.

"They blame Skleros and, by extension, the Order of Hypnos for what took place," Uncle Argyros explained. "They recognize that the Gift Collector acted against the Order of Anthros, as well, but they still hold the Aithourian Circle responsible for involving the Order of Hypnos, which gave Skleros the opportunity to pursue the necromancers' feud with Hesperines. The whole event has further weakened the Tenebrans' faith in the Orders—and once more painted Orthros as their saviors."

"Then we are not planning to correct that assumption either?" Cassia asked.

"That is our recommendation." Queen Soteira put a hand over her Grace's.

"Given the nature of Tenebran superstitions," Komnena put in, "if they had any idea Eudias had been possessed, it would destroy all the trust he worked so hard to earn. He would be, at best, an outcast."

"At worst, they would cast an exorcism on him." Queen Soteira looked disgusted. "The spells Tenebrans call exorcism are barbaric and usually fatal."

"Eudias has been through quite enough," Komnena agreed.

Lio nodded. "I did not fight the Collector alone. We fought him together. Eudias could have surrendered, but instead he found the Will to turn on the Collector and make a stand."

"He deserves to be lauded as a hero for all he has done," Cassia said, "and the Council's trust in him is essential to the success of the treaty."

"We'll do what we must to protect him," said Lio.

"Do they know what you did for us, Lio?" Cassia demanded.

He half smiled. "Actually, they credit me with the light magic they sensed intertwined with your warding magic. They thanked me for lending my power to your spell and bodily shielding you from harm."

Cassia's jaw dropped. "But they know you're a mind mage."

"They congratulated me on my clever bluff to get the mages to cooperate."

"You fought the hardest battle of your life! They should recognize your deeds."

He rubbed the inside of her wrist. "I am content to be known as your protector."

She frowned at him. "Are you certain?"

"Yes. Not because of politics. Because it's true."

"If you're sure that's what you want, I will say nothing."

His half-smile widened a bit. "Perita and Callen defended my good intentions to the others. It was quite gratifying."

"The end of the battle is a blur to me…what exactly happened?"

Aunt Lyta's hand curled into a fist upon the arm of her chair. "What happened should never have been possible."

Uncle Argyros looked haunted. "He veiled his casting, if you can even call such a foul concealment a veil. Acts of magic that catastrophic. Concealed from *us*. He could have—" Uncle Argyros rubbed a hand over his face. "And we never would have known."

"Our young ones, left to fight alone." Queen Alea's voice ached with regret. "We are so sorry."

"Annassa," Cassia said, "you need never apologize."

"We, most of all, must apologize when it is due," Queen Alea replied.

"This mage of dreams," said Queen Soteira, "who calls himself the Collector, took advantage of our concentration upon our own casting at the ward and used his multiple affinities to conceal his attack at Rose House. We did not sense the disturbance until we felt his evil flee through a tear in the world. When Lio helped Eudias free himself, all the Collector's spells failed. We sensed everything, but the danger had also passed."

"We barely arrived in time." Apollon sounded murderous. "Skleros should be with his god, not on the loose."

Komnena gripped his hand.

"We had far too little time to assess the nature of that portal," Uncle Arygros lamented. "It is unlike any magic we have ever seen. It appeared to operate on the same principles as a spirit gate, but—"

Queen Soteira shook her head. "It was a stationary portal between two fixed locations, but that is the only resemblance it bears to an Imperial spirit gate. The underlying principles were entirely different and far more destructive. It felt as if he had ripped a piece of our land from its natural place and banished it elsewhere. As if he had performed essential displacement on the world itself."

"A displacement gate?" Uncle Argyros suggested.

Apollon crossed his arms. "There's no telling where the other end was. He could have brought an army into Orthros if he had wanted to."

"It's astonishing he didn't try," Aunt Lyta said.

"But he didn't want to bring anyone in," Cassia murmured. "He wanted Skleros to get away. With me."

"Yes." Lio's voice was strained. "He said as much to me. You were his target."

"I *am* a mage." Cassia's words failed her. But she had learned she must not let the most horrific moments of her life fester in memory. She must not allow her enemies to lurk where she did not want to look. She made herself speak, because she knew it robbed power from him. "The Collector told me I'm not a Sanctuary mage, as if he were an authority. I think he knows what kind of magic I have, and he wants it."

Lio's jaw clenched. "That would explain everything."

"It sounded like he was planning to take me somewhere where he could perform an essential displacement on me. Is that possible? Can he steal someone's magic against their Will and take it for himself?"

Lio nodded. "After the Collector is finished with someone, he takes their magic. He tried to take Eudias's power with him when he left, as he did Dalos's."

"The Collector is out there somewhere, projecting his mind through his victims and stealing their magic?"

"That's why he has so many affinities. It seems his supply of magic is virtually endless, limited only by the endurance of the mage through whom he wields his power. He would have pushed more types of magic through Eudias until it killed him. That's what he did to Dalos in the effort to defeat us at the Equinox Summit."

Was that what he might have done to Cassia?

"Skleros never could have escaped with you through our ward." Queen Alea's voice, her very presence, were deeply reassuring. "That's why the Collector had to resort to a dramatic, unstable portal spell."

"I know you must wonder how he ever got into Orthros," said Queen Soteira, "how such an entity could ever cross our ward."

"It will never happen again," Queen Alea said simply.

"He played a game with me." Cassia had never heard Queen Soteira sound so dangerous. "He knew what it would require to avoid my detection. Every time I focused on Eudias, the Collector must have receded from the young man's mind and deeper into Skleros's. When I scrutinized Skleros, the Collector was free to increase his influence upon Eudias. He used the young mage's good heart and the necromancer's heartlessness as disguises. When Eudias passed through the ward, all I sensed were his good intentions. Knowing what Skleros is, when I felt the death in him, I had no cause to be surprised."

"You mean the Collector possessed Eudias and Skleros?" Cassia asked.

"Not in the same way. There seems to be a distinction between those he abusively controls and those he relies on as his 'Overseers.'"

"He called Skleros one of *his* Gift Collectors. Does that mean all of them are Overseers? Did he found them? Why does he want to harm Hesperines?"

"If only we knew. What we have seen of the Unseen Hand is…" Uncle Argyros held up his little finger, measuring its tip with his thumb.

"I've told you everything I learned during my encounter with him," Lio said. "Perhaps Cassia has something to add that will help us understand him better."

Queen Soteira shook her head. "Not tonight. In time."

Cassia sat up further in bed. "You might learn something. I must try."

"Not tonight," Queen Soteira repeated.

"As you say, Annassa." Cassia leaned on Lio.

Apollon studied his brother. "Can we be certain of this?"

"No," Uncle Argyros answered, "we are not certain of anything. That is why I believe our theory is correct."

"You have a theory?" Lio asked.

Komnena reached out and touched Lio's hair, as if on impulse.

When Aunt Lyta put her face in her hands, the dread took hold of Cassia.

"I can't believe this is happening in our lifetime." The Guardian of Orthros quit her chair and began to pace.

"What's happening?" Cassia breathed.

"It is the only explanation," Queen Alea said. "No one else could test our power in this way."

"Who could possibly test your power, Annassa?" Cassia shook her head.

"Very few," Queen Alea answered. "Only six, to be exact."

The color drained from Lio's face.

Cassia touched his cheek. "Who are they?"

"The Old Masters," Uncle Argyros answered.

Silence fell.

Lio broke it. "That's impossible! They're a hypothesis. If one is generous. They are more legend than anything else. We don't even know if they exist, much less if they really have the kind of power the sources, such as they are, claim."

"They are real," Kassandra said.

Everyone attended to her.

Orthros's oracle spoke. "They are in and out of the past, present, and future. They move as fast as lightning, and if I blink, I miss them. They move at the pace of the mountains rising, and I cannot detect their progress. I will tell everything I can to assist against the Collector, but act upon what I see with great caution."

"What do you see now?" Queen Soteira asked.

"Cassia and Lio are the first to surprise him since before Orthros was founded. He will not make the same mistake twice."

"An Old Master was in Orthros. I—" Lio's hand was shaking in Cassia's. "Goddess. He tried to take you, Cassia."

"You speak as if we faced Hypnos himself," Cassia protested. "I admit, when he showed himself, I fancied we might be battling a god, he seemed so powerful. But we defeated him. He was just a man."

"The Old Masters are neither divine nor mortal," Uncle Argyros said, "as far as we know from legends and scraps of ancient writings. Lio is correct that the evidence is scant. Name any of the catastrophic events of the past few millennia, and a source about the Old Masters was destroyed in it. Our cult's best research on them went up in flames with Hagia Notia. Other scrolls simply disappear."

Cassia tried not to see a game board in her mind. She willed herself not to try to make connections, not to analyze the moves.

"According to what information survives," Uncle Argyros went on, "the Old Masters are the oldest known hex of necromancers mentioned in the writings of what are now Tenebra and Cordium. They are said to have extended their lives and amassed great power through necromantic arts. These figures appear and reappear in different accounts and esoteric writings. Sometimes there is a mere mention, a fearful allusion, other times worshipful incantations or mad ravings. Extracting a coherent account of each Master from this is impossible. Even determining which figures are the same, which are two different figures, and how many there are is a challenge. Six is the prevailing hypothesis due to some slight consistency between the sources referring to them as a hex."

Cassia must keep trying to shrink the Collector down to size. She must not let him loom so large in her thoughts and fears. "So they're just necromancers. Old, powerful ones, but—just mages of Hypnos."

"They predate the Order of Hypnos. They may have founded it, or they may use it when it suits them, but they do not serve it."

"Well, they can't be older than Hesperines."

"We are ancient," Queen Alea said, "and the bearers of wisdom even more ancient. But the Great Temples stood for thousands of years before Hespera saw fit to create us. We are not the oldest beings in the world."

Uncle Argyros nodded. "The earliest known texts on the Old Masters are not originals. They are believed to be tertiary sources based on writings from an earlier time, however, we can attain a degree of certainty, given references to concurrent historical events that place them in context."

"How old are the Old Masters, really?" Cassia had to know.

Uncle Argyros leaned toward her. "They were active at the *beginning* of the Great Temple Epoch, some six thousand years ago."

"One of the earliest fragments…" Lio licked his lips, as if his mouth had gone dry. "It's a plea to the Master of Dreams for release from a nightmare of his making."

"Well, he can't be as mighty as the scrolls make him out to be, can he?" Cassia declared. "A mortal woman and the youngest Hesperine in Orthros's diplomatic service sent him running and lived to be nibbled on by Zoe's goats afterward."

Lio let out a strained laugh, then rested his head against hers. "Thank the Goddess for you, Cassia."

"I don't care who he is. He'll get no respect from me. He's just another man with too much magic or too many swords trying to take what he wants. That *is* as old as the world, and they're all the same."

Queen Alea smiled. "Ah, the courage of youth. There is indeed no shame in being young."

"He called himself an old friend of the king's," Cassia said. "I wonder if Lucis realizes he's just a tiny spider in a bigger spider's web. Whatever the Collector's goals or motives, the Council will have to face him, if they want to depose Lucis."

Aunt Lyta paused behind her chair, gripping the back of it. "I still vote we should warn the Tenebrans about the severity of the threat they face. We can mitigate the consequences of telling them the truth, but the consequences of keeping the truth from them are unknown and potentially devastating."

Queen Soteira turned to her. "The way the Tenebrans would interpret the truth would have devastating consequences as well."

Queen Alea's face was grave. "It is not our way to conceal knowledge. When we Ritual firstbloods waited to share the Gift, thinking to protect others from our untested discovery, we caused consequences the world still lives with now. In this case, however, I suggest we defer to my Grace's expertise on evil."

"Only temple scholars are aware of the Old Masters," said Queen Soteira. "Imagine if we tried to explain to the Tenebrans that a powerful mage of dreams is at work in their lands. He has a king in the palm of his hand and an army of Gift Collectors at his back. He can possess any mortal. You will not perceive the sign—his voice—until it is already too late."

Cassia shuddered. "And I thought Chrysanthos's witch hunt would be devastating. The panic would spread everywhere. Anyone who hinted at sympathy with the king would be suspected of possession."

Lio nodded. "Eudias would only be the first of many innocent victims to be brutalized by spells. Neighbors would drive out neighbors, relatives would beat their own kin to death…"

"We have experienced it," said Queen Alea.

"Would the Orders be any defense against the Old Masters," Cassia asked, "or would they make the persecution worse?"

"I would expect the Order of Hypnos to assist any Old Master at his pleasure," Queen Alea answered, "or at the very least, scurry out of his way. The other Orders' relationship with the Old Masters is more difficult to assess, since so few temple mages become Hesperines and bring us insight into the current workings of the Orders."

Uncle Argyros spread his hands. "The Order of Hypnos most likely knows as much as can be known about the Old Masters, but those are secrets no one outside the Inner Eyes will ever learn, not even their so-called brethren in the Order of Anthros. We cannot know the state of the other Orders' research into the Old Masters, but based on the temple scholarship available to them, I reason their knowledge is similar to our own."

"The Order of Anthros prizes their supremacy," Queen Alea said. "They will not tolerate any mage who holds himself above the Akron's authority. If we informed them about the Old Master, they might refuse to believe us and see it as a ploy to sew discord between the Orders and deflect their aggression from Orthros. Even if we could persuade the Dexion and his colleagues an Old Master really is at work, the world could not afford their effort to defeat the Collector. We would have a war between Aithourians and an Old Master from which to defend innocent bystanders. The Order of Kyria would act as protectors, only to bear the brunt of their brothers' attacks. We must handle this information with the utmost care, lest we incite more violence than necessary."

"Now Cassia needs rest," Queen Soteira announced, "and Lio needs to speak with her without elders hovering."

Komnena embraced Cassia and Lio, her worry and her love evident in her touch. Apollon stood near, just outside Cassia's vision. He was making it easy for her. She realized how comforting his presence was.

Before Cassia knew it, she and Lio were alone.

ENOUGH

Lio's kiss was so gentle, Cassia felt like the most treasured person in the world, and so desperate, he need not say how close he had come to losing her. She stroked his face, reassuring him, tasting him to reassure herself. He pulled away well before she was ready, and he rested her against him.

"Are we all right?" she wondered aloud.

"I'm not sure."

"I'm not either."

They held each other without speaking for a long moment.

"Is your Craving all right?" she asked.

"You nearly bled to death. I will not take a sip from you until you are entirely ready."

"I didn't want you to go hungry ever again."

"Let me take this opportunity to make something clear. Although you are my Grace, you are never obligated to feast with me, and I am never entitled to expect it. When you are not willing or able, I will take responsibility for my own needs."

"I love you, Lio."

"I love you, too." He stroked her hair.

"Tell me it was only a nightmare that he broke your window."

"You are safe. That's all that matters."

Cassia squeezed her eyes shut. "It was a beautiful work of art. You made it with your own hands. I will never forgive him."

"It was just a window."

"It was more than just a window."

He fell silent. Then, "I know."

"I'm so sorry."

"Cassia." He took a breath. "I invited an Old Master into Orthros."

"Don't you dare blame yourself that a legend turned out to be real and took advantage of your Summit."

"I don't blame myself. But I must own the unintentional consequences of my actions."

"He told me the treaty helped his plans. That everything we've worked for was exactly what he wanted. He praised me for being his token. Lio, he invited me to become an Overseer."

"*What?*"

"He said I could become like Skleros. It made me sick. I've done things I'm not proud of, but I've chosen not to do many things I would have been ashamed of. How could I be so heinous as to gain the Collector's attention?"

"Put his poison out of your mind. He would say anything to torment and manipulate us. He trapped me in a waking dream. That's why I couldn't get to you at first. He showed me a vision of Orthros in ruins. It was so real. At first, I actually believed it."

"How did you escape?"

"I heard your voice."

"You're right. If we allow ourselves to believe even one thing he said or did, we let him in. We have to reject him with all our strength. I'm just... so tired."

"So am I. I'm not sure what I'm doing anymore."

"My rebellion has become something larger than me. It isn't really mine now. It is a thing of its own."

"So too did my Summit grow beyond my control."

"What are we going to do?"

"I don't want you to have to face any difficult decisions tonight, but the embassy is leaving as soon as the Festival of Grace is over, and I want you to have plenty of time to think about some things."

"I'm bearing up under the burden of secrecy so far."

"I know. I thought we were done with secrets. But I can see the surest way to undermine our treaty is to reveal to the Tenebrans they are facing an enemy too powerful for them to fight."

"He *is* too powerful." Cassia finally admitted it. "They won't win against him."

"Not alone."

The way he said it struck Cassia.

"Lio?" she asked.

"My actions during the attack came across well, I suppose," he said. "The Acting Council invited me to return to Tenebra with them in a long-term capacity as Orthros's diplomatic representative during the transfer of power."

Cassia sat up again, although her head spun. "Lio…that's…incredible. Just think of the night you left Tenebra. We could never have imagined something like this could be possible. This is what you've dreamed of and worked for your whole career. Tenebra doesn't just want a Summit. They don't want to lock Orthros's diplomats in a fortress. They want a Hesperine ambassador to join them."

"You know they would be thrilled for their Tenebran thrush to change her mind and return with them to work toward her sister's vision of Tenebra."

The future Cassia had felt certain of turned on its head. She did not recognize it, and she did not know what to make of it.

"Well," Cassia began, "it's clear what we must do."

"Cassia, aren't you tired of doing what we must?"

"Of course. But this is better. We could do what we must together. I think I could bear that, as long as I'm not apart from you."

"We need to talk about whether this is what we want."

Tenebra. Again. Another tent in another camp full of soldiers. Another rebellion.

No, it would be different this time. She could see her sister vindicated. This would not bring fear and grief, but victory and peace.

She would be with Lio. In Tenebra. But with Lio.

"We would have to keep us a secret," Cassia realized. "Still."

"My display after the attack made it obvious to the embassy what I feel for you."

A memory flashed in Cassia's mind, and she touched a hand to Lio's lips. "You put your mouth to my wrist to heal me. Did they see?"

Lio looked away. "Benedict watched your blood drip down my chin."

Cassia stroked Lio's beard. "Then we don't have to lie anymore."

"It's not that simple. Callen and Perita tell me the embassy is busy gossiping about my unrequited love for you. Apparently, I'm eligible to share in their admiration of you, but not to act on it. Since I saved your life, most of the Tenebrans are tolerant enough, as long as my devotion to you does not stray beyond the boundaries of a minstrel ballad of courtly love."

"Oh." Cassia's heart sank. "Then they don't know what I feel for you."

"We have succeeded in preventing accusations of Hesperite heresy against you from undermining the treaty. We ought to consider what political impact it would have if they knew you were not only planning to stay in Orthros, but planning to stay with the ambassador."

It was all right for Lio to love her, Hesperine though he was. It would never be all right for a whore's bastard to love anyone, especially a heretic. A whore's bastard who violated her betrothal promise to Tenebra's beloved Flavian, no less. Cassia would fall from her Kyrian pedestal so fast, she would break when she landed.

"So we would have to keep on as we have during the embassy," Cassia said.

Lio didn't answer right away. "I can't see any other solution."

She would be with him for stolen hours at night. Come sunrise, she would have to miss him all day. No polar night. No slow starts under stained glass windows over coffee. No breakfast with Zoe and the goats.

When they were in front of other people, she would miss him, although he stood a pace away. No kissing in front of their friends. No dancing together before their people.

Lio's body was tense against her. "We would have to go to some lengths to break your betrothal to Flavian."

"We would find a way," she said firmly, even as the thought of it all filled her with frustration she could scarcely bear.

She would be a woman who fought tooth and nail for every sliver of influence. She would go back to being all those masks she wore to others and all the masks they put on her. The bastard daughter of the king soon to be deposed. The virtuous Kyrian devotee. The schemer.

No affinity readings. No choice of a service. No roses. The garden at House Komnena would lay choked in weeds for...

"How long?" Cassia asked. "Did they say how long they want you to stay?"

"They suggested the standard tenure of Tenebran emissaries to Cordium. Three years to start, extended to five, depending on events."

Three to five years.

"I'd have to wait to become a Hesperine."

"We would have to make a decision about that, yes."

"Lio, is this what *you* want?"

He hesitated.

"You waited months to tell me the truth," Cassia said. "You risked your life to give me time to decide I want to spend eternity with you. No one has ever made that kind of sacrifice for me, and you know I love and respect you for it."

"I swore I would protect your freedom."

"You will not compromise that if you answer my question. We're only talking about it. We have to talk, just like always." She put a hand on his neck to remind him of her braid and all their promises to each other. "When I tried to go back to Tenebra without you, I threw my plan in your face without asking how you felt about it. I will never do that again. This time, you should tell me what you want."

Lio let out a sigh. "What I want has changed, Cassia. I have found something better than what I always dreamed of. I am living it with you every night here in Orthros."

Cassia held her breath.

"Can we agree we've done our part?" Lio asked. "Could we let Tenebra go?"

A smile overtook Cassia, and suddenly tears were streaming down her cheeks. "I never want to set foot in Tenebra again. I want to stay home."

Another sigh escaped him, almost a laugh. "Then we want the same thing."

She rested her face on his chest. "No matter how many times I face the threat of losing Orthros, my answer will always be the same. Never."

"In that case, I will go ahead and apply to Uncle Argyros for a leave of absence from my duties. A *long* leave of absence."

Cassia's smile widened. "How long?"

"As long as we need. I want you to have plenty of time to recover from your Gifting and become comfortable with your new nature. Then we'll want to take our time planning our avowal. These things happen once in an immortal lifetime, so be prepared for no one to know when to stop celebrating. Eventually we'll get away from them all for our Gracemoon. A whole month all to ourselves, anywhere you like. By the time we get back, Zoe will be excited for a visit to goat country, and you and I will have no trouble providing for her while we're away from our parents."

"Travel in the Empire sounds wonderful."

"If you find you like it, well, I have a rough draft ready of my petition for permanent reassignment to Imperial affairs. We don't have to travel at all, though. Uncle tells me he's in need of home diplomats to discuss cultural affairs with visiting administrators the Empress sends to Orthros. He has two openings, to be exact."

"Joining the diplomatic service looks better to me all the time."

"Would it be terribly selfish of me to try to persuade you?" He breathed into her hair. "I don't know if I'll ever shake up politics again. But I know I want to be with you all the time."

Cassia's spirits fell as quickly as they had lifted. "But who will protect Tenebra from the Old Master? They need a mind mage."

"They shall have many, now that Hesperines errant are permitted in Tenebra again, thanks to the treaty. What's more, Annassa Soteira has mandated that every errant circle travel with at least one mind healer. Hesperine theramancers trained in her techniques will protect mortals from the Collector's evil."

"The Tenebrans won't need us."

"It's time to leave this in the hands of our Hesperines errant, don't you think?" Lio asked. "Haven't you been errant long enough?"

Cassia tried to swallow her tears. Could it really be that easy?

"Cassia, think of what the Collector did to try to capture you. If you're necessary to his plans, depriving him of you is the surest way to foil his ambitions. You're safe behind the ward of Orthros or traveling anywhere in the Empire. But the moment you enter Tenebra, you're vulnerable to him. Staying out of his reach is the safest course for both you and Tenebra."

For once, what was good for her was good for others, too.

"I'll never try to take your weapons out of your hands," Lio promised. "I'll never condescend to you and say you should sit at home where it's safe. Only you can decide if you're ready to lay down your work. But Orthros is ready for you, if you are ready for it."

Cassia looked at Lio. "I am ready."

FESTIVAL OF
GRACE

WITHIN REACH

$\mathcal{P}$ ERITA'S LAUGHTER FILLED THE rooms at the New Guest House that were now Cassia's lodgings. Cassia had never heard her friend make such a free and happy sound.

Callen danced his beloved wife from one end of the sitting room to the next. With the giddiness of children and the gazes of newlyweds, they leapt, clapped, and spun together in a country reel.

Cassia would never have been able to give them up, if she hadn't known she had helped secure them this future.

Callen picked Perita up off her feet and swung her around, turning in a circle on two good legs. "I thought I'd spend weeks in a sickbed! But here I am, ready for a dance."

Cassia watched them from a couch with Knight on her feet. "You're a fine dancer, Callen."

Perita's eyes twinkled at her over Callen's shoulder. "Oh aye, that he is."

"Well," Cassia teased, "I am sure the two of you have exciting plans for tonight. You must go into the city as the Hesperines have invited us to do and get the most out of the festival."

Callen came to a halt, setting Perita on her feet and holding her close. "What do you say, Pet? Shall we dance our way across Selas?"

She grinned, but glanced uncertainly between him and Cassia. "Are you sure it's all right, my lady? Master Gorgos was very firm about none of the embassy participating in the Hesperines' courtship festival. I don't want to get my Callen in trouble."

Cassia looked at Callen. "Are you planning to engage in any 'orgiastic rituals that will rob you of your mental faculties and ready your body for corruption' with my handmaiden?"

Perita snickered.

"Hmph," said Callen. "If Master Gorgos hasn't sent me to the pyre for letting Queen Soteira fix my leg, he can't hold a few dances against us. We don't know any Hesperine dances, in any case. There's no heresy in a Hadrian carole."

"I'm sure there will be plenty of songs suited to Tenebran dances. The city is full of music tonight." Cassia could hardly wait to join Lio in the Hesperine dances. Tonight would not be a celebration of the Summit. This night was a celebration of them. Of love.

Perita eyed her with a knowing look. "Yes, why don't we just be going."

Callen took her hand, and they escaped across the courtyard through mint and junipers, murmuring and laughing together.

Now Cassia could ready herself for Grace Dance. She pulled her feet out from under her hound and stood up, smoothing the skirt of her dear old gardening dress. It was a good thing she had forgotten it at Lio's tower the night Rose House had been destroyed. She found she didn't regret that the rest of her Tenebran gowns hadn't survived the attack. Neither she nor Solia needed them anymore.

Now it was time to don her silk festival robes.

Cassia went to pull the green velvet curtains, but a figure in the courtyard caught her eye. She stepped outside. "Ben?"

He halted his steady pace across the courtyard and stood at attention under a set of wind chimes. "Evening, Your Ladyship."

She approached him. "You know, you can call me Cassia."

"You'll always be Your Ladyship to me."

She would not rub salt in his wounds by protesting. "Aren't you on your way to enjoy the festival?"

"I thought to make myself more useful tonight."

One of the Prince's Charge walked through the light spilling from the common room. "Sir Benedict was kind enough to offer his assistance on our patrol. He is helping us keep the guest house secure."

"I'm sorry you shall miss the festivities," she said, "but that is a fine thing to undertake, indeed."

Benedict gave a nod. "The danger is mostly passed, but the Dexion and his apprentice are still under house arrest. Orthros and Tenebra must keep an eye on Cordium together."

"Thank you, Ben. You know how much your support means to me."

He didn't smile, and she could see on his face how heavy his heart was. "You aren't taking part in the festival tonight, are you?"

The Charger's patrol took him under another archway and out of sight.

In the silence, Cassia drew closer to Ben. "Yes, I plan to participate in the celebrations to the fullest."

"You were only well enough to leave the Healing Sanctuary last night. Shouldn't you stay in your new guest room and get some rest, Your Ladyship?"

"I'm feeling well rested, thank you."

"I don't know how you find it in yourself to be a good guest tonight. This festival isn't like the others we've been to."

"I must make a life for myself here in my adopted land."

"Your Ladyship." Benedict's voice all but broke. "What kind of future can you have here, really? What occupations can there be for you? What companions?"

"I will have the future I make for myself. I intend to be happy."

"The ambassador's untoward admiration for you concerns me. You must take care he does not misunderstand your choice to remain here to do Kyria's work. Do you need me to set him straight?"

"Not at all, Ben. I have made my intentions very clear to the ambassador. Why don't you lay down your worries for just an hour or so and stroll through the festival?"

He shook his head. "I don't feel like celebrating tonight."

"Not even celebrating the victory of the truth?"

He looked away. "This Autumn Greeting seemed like a victory over the past for some of us."

"Ben."

That fetched his gaze back to her.

She gave him a look. "Can you deny there is another who is much more suited to partner Flavian in that dance?"

"Segetia needs a lady such as you."

"But what about your friend? What does Flavian need?"

"Needing what's out of reach never brought any man happiness."

"Nothing is ever out of reach, Ben. That is the lesson of this Summit. Tell Flavian I said so."

"I'll do as you ask, Your Ladyship." He bowed, then turned away and strode into the darkness after the Charger.

GRACE DANCE

NO ONE DRESSED CASSIA for Grace Dance, and no one anointed her in scents dictated by tradition. Alone in her guest chambers, she bathed herself in cassia soap and perfumed herself with rosewater. It took her but a moment to slip into her new silk festival attire. The cassia blossom robe was as easy to wear as her own skin. The yellow silk shoes were as sturdy as they were beautiful, and the red-brown trousers would be so comfortable to dance in. She looked at herself in the dressing room's luxurious, full-length glass mirror.

She gasped. "I'm not Cassia Basilis anymore. I'm just Cassia now."

Knight sniffed her, investigating her unfamiliar clothes, then sat on her feet.

She scratched his ears until his tail wagged. "No one shall lock you in a cage tonight, my brave Knight. Let's wait on the front balcony for Lio. He said the sight of the harbor during the Festival of Grace is not to be missed."

She tossed her bespelled silk cloak around herself and left her lodgings carrying nothing but his braid upon her ankle. It took her a few moments to navigate the unfamiliar halls of the New Guest House. Finally she and Knight padded through a wide, deserted sitting room, past a lute and vases of ferns. She pushed open double doors of glass and wrought iron and stepped out onto the front balcony.

Rose petals of every color swirled around Cassia on the cold sea wind. She reached out and let them flutter through her silk-gloved fingers. Tonight the Harbor Light shone crimson in the goddess's hands, casting a glow like the Blood Moon's upon the crowd below.

The street that ran in front of the guest houses was packed with celebrants. Hesperines in robes, mortals in cloaks and garments of every origin, people of every color and every age. All danced or strolled arm in arm along the docks. Couples slipped off into the dark alleys between the guest houses or idled together eating food out of their hands before groups of musicians. A cacophony of songs both familiar and new rose up to Cassia.

She could not stop her gaze from straying to where Rose House had stood. Festival planners had cast wards and veils over the unsafe ruin so that no one would venture inside and an illusory festival pavilion hid it from sight. Amid the beautiful noise of the festival, Cassia observed a moment of silence for Lio's lost work of art, for their memories there, for everything the Collector had broken.

Motion in the crowd called her back to the festival. A figure with dark hair and strong shoulders rode through the celebrants upon a tall white horse with neither a saddle nor reins. She leaned out over the railing and watched her champion halt his steed below her balcony.

Lio's robe of deep crimson, split in front to reveal loose trousers in the Imperial style, suited a world-traveling diplomat. But with his windblown hair and his unshaven face, he looked every bit the part of a Hesperine errant.

His gaze traveled over her, then traveled over her again. He gave her no flowery flattery, as a certain Tenebran lord had once done before a different dance. The effect the sight of Cassia had on Lio was written on his face. He looked half stunned, half delighted, and entirely as if he wished to eat her up.

Cassia grinned down at him, resolving to thank Kassandra again. "Only festival attire of true Orthros silk is worthy of tonight's occasion."

"It is worthy of your beauty." Lio lifted his hand, and for the first time she noticed what he carried. A flower crown of their roses.

She put a hand to her mouth. "Oh, Lio. Thank you."

He held his gift up to her in offering. "Will you join me in the Goddess's eternal dance?"

"I shall have no other partner, and I shall never leave you to dance alone."

He tossed the wreath up to her, and it came into her hands with the graceful precision of Hesperine levitation. He had removed all the thorns.

The pain of autumn eased, becoming as distant as Solorum itself, and Cassia's heart lifted. She looked at Lio, letting him see all the love in her eyes, and crowned herself in Hespera's roses.

Then suddenly Lio was there with her on the balcony. He tucked a strand of her hair under the wreath, and she shivered, relishing his touch. He slid two fingers under her chin, lifting her face nearer his. His first kiss of the night was a gentle, heated promise.

She licked her lips. "You are extraordinarily well equipped to storm damsels' balconies, my champion."

"I promise only to use my powers for your good." His voice was low and ardent and a little rough. His hand drifted down one line of embroidery on her robe, then paused to trace the petals of a cassia flower right over her heart. "Cassia. Seeing you dressed like this makes it seem real to me somehow."

"It's really happening, my love."

He scooped her up in his arms. When he levitated them over the railing of the balcony, she couldn't help laughing, too. He descended with her slowly. Before they made it to the ground, applause rose up from the crowd. They landed amid the congratulatory calls of the onlookers.

It was so easy to smile tonight. Cassia could not seem to stop. She gave her true smile to all the kind faces around them. She didn't even know most of their names, but they all had the most important thing in common. They loved under Hespera's gaze.

But the friendly faces at the very front of the crowd were all familiar and dear. Mak and Lyros called out loudest of all, and Nodora, Kia, and Xandra waved, hand-in-hand with their Imperial shares. Waving back at their friends, Cassia had seldom felt more honored.

Lyros gestured at Cassia's attire. "Look at you, all dressed like a Hesperine ready to dance wildly under the moon."

Kia grinned wickedly. "We have succeeded in corrupting her."

Lio gave a dark laugh.

"Incoming." Mak shooed the crowd back.

Knight made a great leap and landed among them. The onlookers suddenly gave them plenty of room, although Mak had stopped trying to direct them.

Lyros stared at Cassia's hound. "Now we've seen for ourselves that liegehounds can indeed make jumps to snatch a levitating Hesperine out of the air."

"But not this liegehound." Cassia smiled. "You've succeeded in corrupting him, too."

Lio lifted Cassia up onto his horse. She tucked her dangling feet close to the giant creature's sides, wrapping her fingers in its long, flowing mane. It stood steady beneath her, not so much as twitching its feathered feet.

"Who is this noble beast aiding you in my capture?" Cassia asked.

Lio chuckled. "Moonflower."

She patted Moonflower's neck. "What a fine name for a Hesperine horse! Has Lio told you how much I love moonflowers?"

"He is a very fine horse." Lio gave Moonflower's nose an affectionate pat. "Aunt Lyta bred him for me from Prometheus's familiar."

"That does not surprise me. How else could she get a horse tall enough for you?"

Lio swung up behind her, and Cassia leaned back against him, relishing the strength of his body against hers, chest to back, thigh to thigh. She felt him flex his knees. His horse walked forward, and the crowd parted to let them through.

"We'll see you at the dance!" Nodora said as they passed.

"If they make it." Mak snickered.

Lio leaned down and took a playful swing at his cousin, which Mak dodged without effort.

"I'll make sure my lady arrives on time to her first Grace Dance so she can enjoy it to the fullest," Lio said indignantly, but he grinned. "We just have a stop to make first."

"Better make it a few stops," Lyros called after them. "You've been starving all week."

Cassia spoke quietly to Lio. "As if we didn't make plenty of 'stops' last night, as soon as I got out of the Healing Sanctuary. I wasn't about to let you come to Grace Dance on an empty stomach."

He nibbled her collar. "After last night, I can definitely enjoy our first Grace Dance to the fullest, too."

They rode through the music and light, the swelling crowd, and the fragrance of sea and roses, past the train of Hespera's hair.

"Where are we headed?" Cassia asked.

"Well, would you mind going home for a few minutes? Zoe said she wanted to see us on my horse in our festival attire."

"Of course I don't mind. She must be anxious about us not being home much tonight, especially after I've been at the Healing Sanctuary all week."

"Thank you, Cassia." He nuzzled her shoulder. "Bosko and Thenie are spending the night at House Komnena, so I think Zoe won't worry if we take the scenic way."

Lio's horse carried them at a leisurely pace along the full length of the docks. When Cassia spotted Lord Adrogan under a lamppost, she tensed. But all his attention was on the Imperial beauty before him. He gestured to his arm, speaking with great animation.

Cassia raised her eyebrows. "Is he allowed to be speaking with her?"

"The Empress has graciously agreed that for tonight only, she will not object to her people and Tenebrans attending the same festival. Apparently Harkhuf put in a good word for us after we proved ourselves against the Collector."

"I'll have to thank him."

"Why is Lord Adrogan still wearing his sling?" Lio asked. "Queen Soteira healed everyone."

Cassia snorted. "Bragging rights."

The Imperial guest did not look impressed. As Cassia and Lio rode past, she glanced at them, but Lord Adrogan did not.

Lio spoke close to Cassia's ear. "It's very easy to deflect unwanted attention in a crowd like this. So many relaxed minds and interesting distractions."

"I hate pretending, even for one more night."

"The embassy is leaving tomorrow. We're almost done."

"But they leave without knowing I return your love."

"You may return my love all night long," he purred in her ear. "We needn't watch our backs tonight. We will spend most of our time among our friends, from whom we need not hide."

As they followed the curve of the bay, they passed the Semna and

Lord Gaius sitting together on a bench, looking out to sea together. Lord Gaius leaned closer to her, saying something Cassia did not hear. The mage nodded and smiled, tapping her foot in time to the music. Pakhne was some distance down the docks with the Cheran mages. The three women laughed together, slipping morsels of food under their veils.

"Where are Ariadne and Eudias?" Cassia wondered.

"He took her to the library. Without an escort."

Cassia smiled. "Spending the Festival of Grace in the library sounds like just what Ariadne will enjoy."

"He had something important to tell her."

Cassia patted Lio's hand. "You're going to miss him."

Lio sighed. "We could have been great friends."

"You are great friends. I'm just sorry you have to be that on opposite sides of the border."

"Perhaps I understand how you feel."

"Yes. But Perita has Callen."

"I think Eudias has Ariadne, however they express their devotion to each other, according to their devotion to their gods."

The guest houses, coffee shops, and shipyards gave way to gardens, then grounds, then bare coast. Moonflower left enormous hoofprints in the snow amid Knight's paw prints. The music drifted after them, mingling with the soughing of the waves and the wind. They rode beneath the aurorae along the meeting point of land and sea. Warmth rose from the horse's body under them.

"I understand horseback riding was a favorite pastime of a particular suitor of yours," Lio mused.

Was. They could talk about Flavian as someone who was in her past. "He galloped on race horses, jousted on war horses, and made daring jumps on hunting horses. He invited me to watch him from the back of a docile palfrey, who would not go faster than a safe and ladylike pace."

Lio slid his hand under her cloak, caressing her thigh. "That's no way to show a lady a good time. His feats in the saddle were not impressive enough for you?"

"No one is as graceful on horseback as a Hesperine." She flexed back against him. "And your horse is the largest I've ever seen."

Lio's chuckle was halfway to a growl. His horse leapt beneath them, and suddenly they were flying along the beach. The gallop brought tears to Cassia's eyes. Her hood fell back, and her hair whipped behind her around Lio as they leaned together over his horse's neck. The icy air swept around her, but Lio's body sheltered hers in silk and strength. The ground seemed to fall away. She thought they might race right up into the sky.

The arm of the bay curved far out to sea, and Lio raced them to the very end of it. On a long finger of land, he brought them to a halt. But he turned their mount away from the surrounding sea to face the way they had come. To one side, the harbor glittered and to the other, the cliffs of House Komnena rose toward the moons.

As they took in the view, Lio feathered warm kisses along Cassia's neck. She let her head fall back and slid her hand along his leg, caressing him through his trousers. He brought his mouth to hers. They sat there tasting and touching each other until their breaths steamed the air around them, and Moonflower twitched.

Lio pulled his mouth away, grinning with all his fangs. "One course of the feast at a time."

"How many courses do I have to look forward to?"

"As many as you want."

He nudged Moonflower into motion again, and they headed for the cliffs that marked home. Despite his size, Moonflower navigated the rising terrain with ease, carrying them along a path up through the hilly grounds. As they emerged from the trees and approached the house, Cassia spotted Lio's parents on the terrace outside Komnena's study.

Apollon and Komnena danced together to some music only they could hear. He stood behind her, holding her to him with his face nestled against hers as they swayed and turned. The first Hesperine to receive the Gift from a Ritual firstblood appeared entirely focused on his young Grace in his arms and utterly content.

Cassia shifted on the horse. Should they stop before they interrupted a private moment? But Lio rode Moonflower right up to the edge of the terrace.

His parents looked up, not even halting in their dance. They made a playful two-step sideways along the terrace, and Cassia suddenly recognized the pattern of the timeless couple dance, although no Tenebrans ever dared dance it holding each other in such intimacy. Lio must have learned the Tenebran dances he performed so effortlessly from his parents. Of course his mother would know them, and some of them must even date from his father's time as a mortal.

"Oh," Komnena exclaimed, "look at our son. All grown up and riding to Grace Dance with his sweetheart."

Apollon smiled. "And at a fine time of life."

"You look lovely tonight, Cassia," Komnena crooned. "Are those gifts from Kassandra?"

"Thank you. Yes they are." Cassia blushed. "I understand the children are staying here tonight. Will you miss much of the festivities, after working so hard to help prepare them?"

"We have arranged everything so our students and tributaries will have no trouble carrying off the event. The initiates especially like to have their chance to shine. As for us, we are not missing anything." As she stepped away from Apollon and let him twirl her, she cast a contented glance at the barn.

He pulled her close again. "The tireless ladies of the Stand have had all too little time with their Graces lately. Argyros and Javed are both mightily in need of a night of dancing. But Komnena and I both remember far too many winters spent without any children around us."

Zoe bounced out of the barn with her goats at her heels. Bosko lingered behind her in the doorway, holding Thenie. Zoe climbed over the fence and came to Lio and Cassia's side. Knight twined around the suckling, greeting her with a wagging tail.

Zoe held up a basket full of betony flowers. "Happy Festival of Grace and welcome to our family."

"Those are for me?" Cassia leaned down to caress the child's head. "They're beautiful. Thank you so much."

Apollon and Komnena left off their dance and drifted closer. He picked Zoe up and lifted her to Cassia's eye level, then held her while the child wove the purple flowers into Moonflower's mane.

"Now Moonflower is truly ready for the festival," said Lio. "What a lovely idea, Zoe."

She smiled, but her fingers were tense as she worked the flowers into the horse's hair. When she was done with her decorations, her father set her down, and her mother relieved her of her basket. But Zoe stood there hesitating beside Lio's big horse. The tumultuous conclusion of the Summit had shaken her fragile sense of safety.

Cassia glanced at Knight. He looked up at her with his adoring brown eyes, as eager as ever to please her.

"We're going to be gone awhile tonight," Cassia said to Zoe. "Would you like to keep Knight with you until we get back?"

Zoe gasped. "Your liegehound? But he is sworn to remain at your side."

"He knows it's all right to leave me alone with Lio. Don't you, Knight?" He sniffed Lio's silk shoe.

"*Ckuundat,* Knight. *Barda kaetlii. Barda loma.*"

Knight wagged his tail again and sat on Zoe's feet. She looked down at him with her hands clutched together. Slowly she unknotted her fingers and wrapped her arms around his furry neck.

Lio gave Cassia a squeeze. "There's nothing better than a good dog to keep you company."

"Thank you!" Zoe smiled at Cassia over Knight's head.

Cassia leaned down, giving Knight's chin a good scratch. "*Oedann.* Such a good dog deserves to have fun with his *kaetlii* on a festival night."

The family waved to them as Lio guided Moonflower away from the terrace and toward the grounds again. Just before they rode under the trees and out of sight, she saw Knight bound after Zoe and her goats into the paddock.

"That was a wonderful thing for you to do," said Lio. "I hope it was not hard for you."

"Actually, it makes me feel better knowing he and Zoe are at home together." She hesitated. "I think it would be good for him to learn how to be a companion instead of a bodyguard. Letting me out of his sight is the first step."

"Well, you could not be safer tonight. The entire population of Selas is the embassy's bodyguards, and I am yours."

"You know how I love it when you personally guard my body."

He tickled her behind her knee. "I will be thorough in my patrols, I assure you."

Cassia glanced around them at the trees that had stood the test of time. "I can't wait to be a Hesperine. I will be able to fully enjoy myself in the cold weather without fear of catching a chill."

"Mm. I have many, many uniquely Hesperine enjoyments in mind for us, my love. We will start at a particular tree that will always live large in my memory, thanks to you."

"That occasion lives very large in my memory, too. Very large indeed."

"We'd better hurry to the dance. Otherwise I fear we will become distracted and never make it."

He guided Moonflower into a faster pace once more. The Warmblood navigated between the trees and through the underbrush at breathtaking speed. A fallen log loomed ahead, and Cassia's heart leapt into her throat, even as a thrill of recklessness made her pulse pound. Moonflower surged beneath them. For an instant, they were airborne. Then the horse landed, and the impact echoed through the trees.

"Can Hesperine horses levitate too?"

"What magic Aunt Lyta gives them is a mystery. Moonflower is half as old as I am and surprises me more every night."

The horse carried them through the woods as if dancing on air, over frozen creeks and under low-hanging boughs. At last, music and light beckoned through the trees ahead.

The sounds of celebration welcomed them out of the woods onto the shore of a broad, frozen lake. Couples crowded the banks, but none as yet set foot on the ice. The lake gleamed under the moonlight as far as Cassia could see, the opposite shore lost in darkness. Upon the water's frozen surface glowed a Rose of Hespera graven on the ice and marked with spell light.

"No bonfire dances for those who pledge their love under Hespera's gaze," Lio murmured to her.

"Her Sanctuary of ice warms me as no fire ever could."

All around Lio and Cassia, other celebrants rode up to the lake or arrived in sleighs pulled by boreian deer jingling with bells. Hesperines who appeared a little older than Bosko gathered around to take Lio's horse. Lio dismounted and handed Cassia down, then let the youths lead Moonflower away to a roped-off area where other horses milled about in warm blankets with feed bags on their noses.

Lio took her hand and led her down toward the ice. They walked through clouds of smells: coffee and cider, roasted almonds and fresh pies, evergreens and snow. Some of the Imperial guests sat nearby in their enchanted cloaks, laughing as they wrestled out of their snowshoes in order to strap metal blades onto the bottoms of their boots.

"What are those?" Cassia asked.

"Ice skates, a Hesperine invention for the benefit of our mortal guests. They enable you to glide across the ice."

"They look like they take some practice."

"You can certainly try them if you like, but you won't need them, for you shall dance every dance with me. I won't let you slip on the ice anymore than I would let you sink into a snow bank." He caught her up and swung her around on the spot.

From her higher vantage point, she caught sight of a lone figure standing under a tree some distance from the crowd. She wouldn't have noticed him if not for his red hair. "Rudhira is back."

Lio set her down and stared in the direction she pointed. "He never comes to Grace Dance."

"Let's go find out if this has anything to do with your Gift Night present."

They made their way out of the gathering. As they approached him, Rudhira lifted a hand in greeting and smiled faintly. He lounged against the tree as if he were tired, although Cassia knew an immortal Hesperine's weariness was deeper than the body. In one hand, Rudhira dawdled the package wrapped in blood-red silk that Lio had given him on Winter Solstice.

Lio clasped his Ritual father's wrist. "Have you opened it yet?"

"Yes. Point taken. And thank you."

Smiling, Lio gave a nod.

Cassia clasped Rudhira's wrist in turn. "Thank you for bringing Nephalea and the hostages home safely."

"Nike carried the night, as always." Rudhira's voice thickened. "Our victory star, Methu called her."

"Are you all right?" Lio asked.

Rudhira huffed. "She didn't stay in one place long enough for me to wave at her on her way out."

"It must be hard to understand why."

Rudhira sighed. "No. I understand perfectly. I think I'll let some concerned parties do a little more than wave at me tonight." He straightened and took a step away from the tree, then pulled them to him briefly, one under each arm. "Congratulations. I'll enjoy watching your dance tonight."

He let them go and stepped out of sight. His red head reappeared a short distance around the lake, amid Konstantina's Trial circle. His sister started and swiveled to face him. Watching the siblings embrace, Lio and Cassia exchanged a smile.

They caught sight of Mak waving to them. They waved back and made their way to their friends. Mak and Lyros stood holding each other, already swaying on their feet as if impatient to dance. Xandra, Nodora, and Kia stood waiting for their companions. Harkhuf, Nodora's sitarist, and Kia's mathematician sat in the snow in their Imperial festival attire, strapping on the ice skates. They laughed and talked amongst each other with the good cheer of men who had already availed themselves of some festival drinks.

"Rudhira's here!" Xandra squealed. "I can't believe it."

"We just saw him," Cassia said.

Xandra narrowed her eyes at Lio. "Just what did you give him in that present he's carrying around?"

"A congratulatory cup," Lio answered.

"What?" Xandra demanded. "Do you know something we don't?"

Cassia knew Lio would leave it to Rudhira to decide how much to tell his family regarding Kassandra's prophecy about his Grace.

Lio just smiled. "I thought he needed a reminder of what he has to look forward to. What all of us believe in for him, even when he doesn't."

"Oh, Lio." Nodora clasped her hands. "That's so thoughtful."

Mak wiggled his eyebrows. "My guess was a copy of the *Discourses on Love.*"

Xandra snickered. "Rudhira doesn't need a book on that."

"Maybe," Kia suggested, "he is the anonymous author of the most recent addition to the canon."

"That's…awkward." Mak made a face.

Lyros laughed. "This from the one who hunted through Laskara's vaults with me, trying to find her sculpture of our accomplished prince."

"If you ever find it," Kia teased, "Nodora wants to see."

Nodora put her hands to her cheeks. "Don't you dare say that loud enough for anyone to hear."

"Oh, I see," said Cassia. "It's *that* kind of statue of the First Prince."

Lyros lowered his voice. "It's my sister's private portrait of him. After they stopped sharing, she locked it away. She does her best not to acknowledge its existence."

"Rudhira prefers not to acknowledge that entire century of his life," Xandra said. "He was devastated when he realized they weren't a match, and unlike Laskara, he hasn't met his Grace since."

Cassia watched Rudhira sip a festival drink while he talked with Konstantina and her Trial circle. "Now I think I have at least some sympathy for why Laskara was willing to support Konstantina's plans."

Lyros nodded. "My sister was worried about Rudhira, too."

"Well," Cassia said, "now I have to know. Who was Nike's first love? Please tell me it wasn't Epodos."

Nodora was the first to burst into laughter. "Definitely not."

"By all accounts," said Mak, "Nike's heart is not easily won. She likes to have fun, though. She's admired for her exploits in both love and war."

Lyros rested his hand on Mak's chest. "You passionate Argyroi. I had to beat a long list of admirers off Mak to get to him first. My Stand training served me well."

Mak ran his hand down Lyros's back. "I made my list a long time ago. There was only one person on it."

"You know," Xandra said, "it's worth remembering Methu was Kona's first love."

"Konstantina and Prometheus?" Cassia paused, her mouth open. "I can definitely see that, actually."

She could not bring herself to disrupt their pleasant talk by voicing her sorrow that Methu had never met his Grace. Perhaps they were together in Sanctuary.

Lio, of course, sensed her thoughts. "Methu was blessed to find love, if not Grace, more than once over the centuries."

"Konstantina has her Grace now," said Xandra. "She got over not being Methu's match, but no one in Orthros ever got over losing him."

"Bloodborn's path is hard to get over." Cassia slid her arm around Lio's waist.

He pulled her close. "But it can be overcome."

The others looked expectantly at Lio and Cassia.

She cast him a questioning glance. He returned a stoic expression.

"Well?" Mak prompted.

Lyros crossed his arms. "In between wrecking the plans of Cordian mages and hauling negotiations with Tenebra into a new era, did you get a chance to…"

Kia coughed. "…invite Cassia to the second dance of the evening?"

"The 'second dance?'" Cassia arched a brow at Lio. "Why, that sounds like we're all going to have great fun tonight after the public dance is over."

Lio lowered his voice. "I won't tell them I had some dessert first."

"She stood beside him at his Gift Night celebration," Nodora said. "Most of Orthros has already given them cups. That must mean they've talked things over."

"That's certainly indicative," Kia agreed, "but it's not official till they dance the dance."

Nodora frowned at Cassia. "Based on your expression, Lio still has some explaining to do."

"Do you know about the order of events tonight?" Xandra asked a little too brightly. "My mothers, as the first Graces, open the evening, then after them, anyone who is Graced may join in the first dance."

"As for the second dance…" Nodora cleared her throat. "…it is open to couples who haven't avowed but, ah, know something important they'd like everyone else to know, too."

"Lio?" Cassia asked innocently. "Do we know something everyone else doesn't?"

He stroked his chin. "Let me think. There may be some inside information about the embassy we've been keeping under our hats."

"Sir Benedict is in love with Lady Eugenia of Segetia," Cassia offered.

Lio nodded. "But I think that's obvious to anyone who's heard him mention her."

"Hmm," Cassia went on, "Lord Adrogan needed a clean pair of breeches after Lord Gaius dislocated his shoulder."

Lio held up a finger. "Ah. Tychon's affinity is all that saved him from following in the footsteps of his entire family tree and becoming a pig farmer."

Cassia blinked at Lio. "Really?"

"Eudias is a fountain of gossip from Corona."

Cassia looked around. "Oh dear. Everyone is looking rather exasperated or worried. I don't think political secrets are what they meant."

Lio stood behind her and wrapped his arms around her. "Maybe they mean what we're *not saying*."

"Ohhh! You mean what you said to me the other night, after the Firstblood Circle?" She tilted her face up toward him. "What you said over and over again, after I told you I was staying in Orthros?"

Mak let out a whoop, Lyros a whistle.

Lio's cheeks flushed, but he gave Cassia a squeeze and his friends an unrepentant grin.

"Of course I know," Cassia announced. "I am here tonight to dance the second dance with Lio and reassure all of Orthros he will never be alone again."

Lio rested his chin on the top of Cassia's head. "I am here to enjoy being the most fortunate person in the world."

With sighs of relief and smiles and laughter, their friends showered them in congratulations. The men rejoined them, teetering on their skates, and lifted steaming mugs in a toast to Cassia and Lio.

"Well," Nodora interrupted, "I'd best take my place among the Muses. I get to play during the first two dances, unavowed daughter of Blood Kitharos that I am." She and her sitarist shared a glance that suggested they were enjoying her freedom very much indeed.

"And I get an exclusive seat closest to the Muses, where I can hear every divine note." The sitarist departed with her.

"Speaking of exclusive seats, come with me and stand closer to the shore so we can see when Mama and *Bamaayo* arrive." Xandra led them to the bank of the lake, and the crowd parted for her in deference to her relation to the Queens. "They aren't dramatic by nature, but they oblige us with a spectacle at Grace Dance, to keep our traditions strong and inspire the young ones, they say. It's so romantic!"

A pipe let out one long, aching note that sang across the lake. Then a lyre joined in, its notes running fluid and sweet. Beneath the dance of wind and strings, a drum took up a beat that fluttered, then began to throb.

On opposite sides of the lake, there came two shimmers of light, one white and one red, as if the moons had touched the ice. When the gleams cleared, Queen Alea and Queen Soteira stood where the two lights had been.

Alea extended both her hands toward Soteira, as if reaching for her. Soteira held out her hands, beckoning. They hardly seemed to walk as they closed the distance between them with weightless Hesperine steps. When they met, they joined their hands, holding fast to each other.

From here, Cassia could see the expressions on the Queens' faces. They exchanged a smile as if enjoying a private jest. Alea's gaze sparkled with delight like a young lover's, and Soteira's warmed with devotion.

The song's luring strains plunged into a powerful, passionate melody unlike anything Cassia had ever heard, and the drums beat a compelling rhythm that must make anyone within earshot long to move. She caught her breath as the Queens began to dance.

They were indeed the image of Hesperine Grace. Beauty in motion, darkness and light playing together and worshiping each other. In Alea's movements, Cassia caught glimpses of familiar Tenebran dance steps, which blended fluidly into motions that could only be Hesperine. Soteira seemed to set the drums' pace, rather than follow it, with her feather-light footwork. She swept her hands gracefully out at her sides as she moved her hips in a swift, nimble rhythm. She must bring her own ancient Imperial traditions into this creation of hers and her Grace's. Hesperines must wonder to behold the timeless steps year after year, and yet each time, the Queens' dance must be unique, as they improvised it anew for every Grace Dance.

The Queens' dance brought them body-to-body once more, and they rested their faces upon one another's necks. The Hesperines waiting on shore responded as if to a well-known signal. Graces both ancient and young joined the Queens upon the ice.

But every couple stood around the edges of the lake, not yet joining the dance. They parted their circle to make way for someone. Alkaios escorted Nephalea out onto the ice. Cassia and Lio joined everyone in a cheer and a round of applause.

The Graces of Orthros waited for Alkaios and Nephalea to begin their dance first, before commencing their own patterns upon the lake. Mak and Lyros levitated out onto the ice together and charged into the dance. They moved with the power and elegance of warriors, as if each knew how the other would move before he did so, with their hands or shoulders or bodies always touching. Kadi and Javed sailed past, laughing, looking as much like newlyweds as new parents. Konstantina had never appeared so relaxed as she did now, swaying in Adwene's arms.

"Hmm," Cassia observed, "I don't see any sign of your aunt and uncle."

Lio's chest shook with laughter against her shoulders. "It looks like Uncle Argyros and Aunt Lyta really were mightily in need of a night without the children. I think they skipped to the private dance."

As they watched the dancers, the music seemed to wrap closer around Cassia and sink under her skin, and she realized it was Lio's magic. Their friends standing within arms' reach seemed far away. She felt she and Lio were enfolded in their own little world, alone in the crowd.

He swayed on his feet, rocking her in his arms. "Next year, my love, we too shall craft our own dance to that music."

"And the year after that."

"And the year after that." He placed a kiss on her neck.

"When I think of how much time we have ahead of us, the time we spent apart does not seem so terribly long after all." She took a deep breath, drinking in his scent and the smells of Orthros. "My whole mortal life will begin to feel like the blink of an eye."

"And all of this trouble will keep fading into our past until it seems like nothing more than a bad dream."

"How quickly you have transformed everything, my Hesperine. When I think about how different our lives were only a year ago..."

He huffed a laugh. "I stayed only until the second dance to watch Mak and Lyros share their good news. Xandra and I stood on opposite sides of the lake. Then I went home and spent the rest of the night packing my bags for Tenebra. In hindsight, an entirely appropriate activity for Grace Dance."

"I lay awake the night before Winter Solstice debating with myself whether or not I should risk manipulating the king into taking me to court during the Equinox Summit. My temptation to meet a Hesperine proved too powerful, and I spent your Gift Night on a few little machinations to make sure I would be at Solorum when you arrived." How frightened she had been then. How unknowing that her reward for risking the king's retribution would be the Hesperine who now held her.

Lio wrapped his arms closer around her. "From now on, there will be no room in your thoughts for a shred of worry, only for pleasure, and no room in your heart for fear."

"Only love," she answered.

The first song came at last to an end. The Graces on the ice drifted to a halt, and applause went up all around and across the lake once more. Cassia felt Lio's magic release her.

He moved to stand beside her and took her hand, gazing down into her eyes. "The next dance is for us."

She touched a hand to his chest, feeling her braid and the betony charm beneath his robes. "I am so proud to pledge myself to you before our people."

He kissed the palms of her hands. "This is one of the best nights of my life. I would say *the* best, but there is the night we met…and the night we first made love…and the night you told me you love me…"

Happy laughter bubbled out of her, and then the music began again, catching hold of her spirits and lifting them still higher. The drums set the pace for the second song, faster than the first, full of possibilities. The pipes and horns announced the dance with a thrilling flourish, and the lyres and harps, as if braiding their notes together, interwove the sensuous melody and harmony.

The Graces on the lake retreated, leaving plenty of room on the ice for new dancers to join them. The onlookers upon the shores waited, murmuring. Out on the ice, Mak and Lyros appeared to be battling the urge to come over and drag Lio and Cassia onto the lake.

She glanced around and asked him quietly, "Aren't there other couples sharing their happy news?"

"Grace is just that precious. We may be the only ones who have discovered it this year."

"This really is our dance."

Lio pulled her close, wrapping one arm around her waist while he twined his other hand in hers. "Do you, my darling Cassia, wish for a dance?"

"With all my heart, my love."

Her feet never touched the ground as he slid out onto the surface of the ice. His shoes soughing, he guided them in a graceful pirouette. Ahhs and cheers and applause erupted from the crowd. Lio spun her all around, giving her a complete view of everyone who watched them.

"What a different audience we have tonight," she marveled.

"Months ago in Tenebra, the night of Caelum's temple day, I had never been so furious in my life, watching you present his gift while the heartless court looked on. It was all I could do not to touch you as you walked past me. But I've got you now." He lifted her in his arms, holding her fast. "I wanted you to look at me, so you could see that one person in that crowd cared for you. But see how many eyes now gaze upon you with goodwill."

She wrapped her arms around his neck, looking out over the crowd once more. All the weights on her heart became an ache in her throat, but then fled altogether, carried away on the music and the currents of kindness she could almost feel around her like magic. She felt light and free, twirling in Lio's arms. She leaned into his turn and lifted her feet behind her. The wind made her robe swirl around her and snatched her impetuous laughter from her lips.

"This is how Hesperines dance," he said.

In Tenebra she had partnered with him, watching him dance across from her, coming near but still moving too far away, getting to enjoy him only in brief touches of his hand. But now he danced with her body-to-body, letting her feel all the power and grace in him. Silk was no barrier, only a luxurious seduction between his skin and hers.

This was even more than the Tenebran court dance they had shared in their residence. There were no steps except the ones they chose. There was no pattern but the one they made. They danced as it pleased them from one end of the lake to the other.

"Can you tell what they are saying about us?" Lio asked her.

She shook her head, trying to catch her breath. "We're moving too fast. But don't slow down."

He laughed with relish. "Let me help."

His magic swept into her mind once more, unfolding within her, and she felt she herself was opening up. The music soared, and the distant murmurs of the crowd became personal greetings in her ears.

"Firstgift Komnenos, Graced so young! How Apollon must rejoice that his son will not wait as long as he…"

"…two new daughters in one year! Deukalion has brought such joy to his mother…"

"…our Cassia errant, safely among us…"

"…can finally escape that wretched land and enjoy the life she deserves…"

"…destined for great things, to be sure, as accomplished as they already are at such a young age…"

"What a beautiful couple they make…"

"…never seen Lio or Cassia look so happy…they've earned it, after all they've been through…"

Time seemed to ease to a halt, while the voices lauded them and the music played on. The third dance brought the rest of the crowd out onto the lake, swelling the tide of magic around them. But it was Lio's magic that made her skin shiver and her heart pound. His power caressed her like his hands did and played in her mind like the music, deepening the Union of their dance.

Each dance was a new thrill and a different pleasure. And every dance was theirs. Cassia tried to capture every one in her memory, to fully experience each step and each beat of their hearts. But she need not hoard each crumb of time to survive on when this was over. She could dance and dance with him, as long as she wanted. The feast would never end.

HEARTS' DESIRE

L IO DIDN'T KNOW WHAT the hour was when they stumbled, kissing and laughing, back up to their bedchamber. Was this what mortals felt like after a night of drinking? Lio was buoyant and intoxicated from dancing and thirst and magic.

Keeping his power close at hand all night, keeping thoughts and sensations and sound flowing between them, had his magic coursing, his senses singing, and his hunger mounting. Their Sanctuary ward seemed to echo it all back to him. The glyph stone's heartbeat was more powerful than ever since it had absorbed the shard's spell.

Cassia unfastened his collar, pressing her body against his. "I've been watching you and feeling you move all night. I can't keep my hands off of you any longer."

He walked her backward into the room, sliding her cloak off of her as they went. "All that dancing worked up my appetite."

"I can feel it." She mouthed a kiss over his throat.

It was becoming instinctive to feed more power into their mental connection. He gave her a fresh taste of his hunger, and she moaned, nipping at his neck.

The sensation of her lips and tongue and teeth made him shudder. "This connection between us, this is what it will be like all the time, when you're a Hesperine—only deeper."

"Thank you for showing me what Blood Union can be like. Thank you for everything. Tonight has been—better than perfect."

"It's about to get even better." He turned her so she was facing what had recently been an empty window frame. "Happy Festival of Grace, my rose."

She gasped. "You added a new window while I was in the Healing Sanctuary!"

"My first two attempts to present you with a Sanctuary Rose were unsuccessful."

"So you crafted one in stained glass, a perfect white rosebud, eternally on the verge of opening into a magnificent bloom."

"I hope you will accept this one."

She pulled him into her arms. "I will keep this one forever."

He smiled around his fangs and stole a kiss from her lips. She opened her mouth to him and urged his hands to the collar of her own robe. Her pulse pattered under his palms.

He pulled back from their kiss long enough to speak. "No, I don't want to take it off of you. I want to make love to you while you're wearing this. Are you feeling adventurous?"

"Oh, yes."

"Not all worn out from dancing?"

"I feel like I could run a mile. I think it's your fault for kissing me so much and bewildering me with your mind magery. I heard somewhere Hesperine properties have an energizing effect on mortals."

He took both her hands in his. "Are you sure you're feeling entirely well?"

"I am entirely ready for whatever you have in mind tonight."

He backed her further into the room, past the bedclothes on the floor. "Tonight is a very special night. We should do something we've never gotten to do before. Something we've always wanted to do."

When her back came up against one of the chamber's supporting pillars, she gasped. "Oh, Lio. That column in our shrine..."

He nuzzled her throat where he had taken his first drink from her. "That night, when I got to taste you for the first time..."

Her breath teased his ear. "That was the first time I ever imagined having you inside me."

He lifted his head, looking at her lovely, flushed face. "So it wasn't just me."

She gave her real, hiccuping laughter, grinning. "It took me some time to admit it to myself, of course. But oh, how I wanted more."

He ran his hands up her thighs and eased them apart, grinding gently against her so she could feel his rhabdos through their robes. "You could feel how much more I wanted that night."

She rubbed against him in return. "I envisioned you turning me around and pushing me against that pillar and thrusting inside me then and there."

He groaned, jerking his hips and trapping her more securely between him and the stone.

She twined her arms around his neck. "I was so wet. Just like I am now."

"I know."

He covered her lips with his again and slid his tongue deep into her mouth, caressing, thrusting. She went limp against him, clinging to his neck. He swept his hands under her robe and slipped her trousers down, running his hands over her buttocks as he did so. The trousers fell to the floor, and he caressed her bare legs beneath her robe.

She seemed to find her feet, and her hands roamed down his chest, then his belly. His fingers dug into her hips of their own accord as she unfastened the front of his trousers. With a touch of levitation, he lifted her higher in his embrace. She ran her hands through his hair as she wrapped her legs around him.

Entwined against the pillar, they stood poised between the stained glass rosebud on one side and on the other, the open space that awaited a future flower. She didn't cast a single nervous glance at the gaping window frame or the drop below. She trusted him and the spell she had cast upon this room.

He held her hips in both his hands and looked into her eyes as he thrust his rhabdos inside her. Her lips parting, she gave a sigh. The sound of her pulse pounded in his ears with the rhythm of the dances. He sucked in a breath and flexed his hips. Her eyelids dipped, and she tightened her legs around him.

He looked at where their bodies joined, feasting his gaze on the petite bundle of silk in which he was wrapped and her bare freckled legs tangled around his waist. Her quick breaths made her chest rise and fall under her brilliant robe. Supporting her with his magic, he put both hands on her breasts and stroked their contours through the silk, letting her feel the caress of the fabric and his hands.

"I've decided..." She swallowed. "...there is nothing else like making love in silk. It makes me feel...beautiful."

"You make it beautiful."

"I do love your glass tongue, Sir Diplomat."

"It's at your service." He licked her neck in one long, slow stroke.

She tilted her head back, baring her throat as eagerly as ever. He tongued and licked and teased her there, adoring her skin and the vein beneath, which she shared with him so generously. To think, this was to be his eternity. No more doubts. No more fear of losing each other. They began that eternity tonight. Cassia baring her throat, night after night, him losing himself inside her. Until at last the night would come when he too could bare his throat for her and feel her bite.

"I love you," he vowed against her throat.

"Lio," she gasped, "I love you so much."

Lio sank his fangs into his Grace, knowing it would not be the last time, and it thrilled him just like the first time. The taste of her blood was a stunning revelation. Everything their first drink had made him dare long for was now theirs.

He let his hunger move him. Need drove him to devour her. He braced his feet on the floor and thrust inside her, satisfying the urge her every smile and step and touch had built and built during their long night of dancing.

Her exultation slammed through the Union, levitating him off the floor, until it was his own magic that gave him the leverage to move their bodies. She held him to her with her legs, tilting her hips to make her krana open to him, and let him set the pace.

Her mind cried out her thoughts, and he drank them down through the constant rivulets of Union they had nurtured all night long. Their Union sucked him deeper in, down under its current. Yes, he needed to get deeper inside her. To fill himself up even more with her.

Her thoughts throbbed through his veins. She was living her wildest imaginings. She didn't want it to end.

He fed her the certainty, filling her up with it in return. It would never end.

It will never end, Cassia.

Lio!

He gasped aloud. She—her voice—her words—echoed within his heart.

Lio! I can hear you inside me.

She was pure music. A heated caress. A dose of blood right to his spirit. He groaned aloud, digging his fingers into her hips with the effort not to climax. His head fell back, and her blood slid down his throat. *Cassia. You're so beautiful.*

Oh, Lio, your voice. It's incredible.

He didn't know how to try to speak inside her. He didn't have to try. *Cassia. My love, my Grace. You are astonishing.*

Don't stop.

He sank his fangs into her neck again to drink her blood and her voice. She let out a cry, and then her krana gripped around him. Her climax resounded through him as her voice had. Waves of pleasure pounded his body, and he spilled into her in wild thrusts. His jaw locked on her throat, and his throat kept swallowing her blood, feeding his Craving again and again.

When the pleasure ceased to carry them, his feet hit the floor. He stumbled a little and groped for the pillar to steady himself. Cassia clung to him, her thighs trembling.

He eased out of her and gathered her into his arms. He carried her over to their bed and sank down onto the blanket with her. They lay there holding each other, she catching her breath.

He let out an elated laugh. "It happened again."

She swallowed. "I was afraid only danger could push our minds that close. That Union we felt during the battle seemed to shatter with your window."

"No, Cassia. What we tasted that night was Grace Union, the Blood Union only Graces share."

"When I am Hesperine and experience the Blood Union, will we be able to speak in each other's minds all the time?"

"Without effort. I've heard that's what it's like. Graces talk all around it, as if it's difficult to describe. But we're told Grace Union is something deeper and more powerful than any Blood Union or mind magery can achieve."

"I'm so glad we felt it tonight. This redeems that moment during the battle. Our Union does not belong to that night."

"It transcends time, danger, and distance. Do you remember when I once told you I have seen the world through your eyes?"

A smile crossed her face. "Yes. I remember thinking that no one had ever seen things from my point of view before."

"I did—literally. I'm afraid you weren't aware of it at the time. It was not intentional, you understand. It took hold of me, the way this connection overtook us tonight." He tried to gather his thoughts to explain it to her. "In Tenebra, at Caelum's temple day feast, all I could think about was you sitting across the room from me. I was trying to understand you through the Blood Union. Then suddenly, I was seeing the room through your eyes. I could look down at my feet and see Knight there. I felt myself trying not to look at the king. When I looked across the room and saw Initiate Ambassador Deukalion sitting at table, it startled me back into my own thoughts. Entering your mind so intimately went against all my convictions not to abuse my mind magery. But I did not even try to do it."

There came no anger in her aura. "You must have gotten an eyeful of yourself. I couldn't stop staring at you."

He couldn't hold back a grin. "It was the first hope I had that I had earned your notice."

"I hate to remember how cold I was to you then." She shook her head, cuddling closer to him. "And yet all that time ago, when we hardly knew each other, our minds achieved Union."

"I realized later it was a sign of our Grace bond. I just had no idea we could both experience it like this when one of us is still mortal."

"Maybe your mind magery makes it possible for us. Or maybe my mystery affinity does it. Do you think it will happen more often, now that we'll be together all the time?"

He caressed her face, pushing her tousled hair back. "I hope so."

He reached for her thoughts again. He sought the paths that had led him so near her and turned mere impressions into words, made her inner voice into magic. Her eyes glazed, and she rested her forehead on his. Her thoughts wrapped around him as always. But he fumbled for the connection he had just felt while they had made love. It did not come to him. He did not hear her voice in his mind.

"I'm not sure I know how to open our Union on purpose." He tried not to feel disappointed. It was already extraordinary that they had enjoyed even a touch of what was to come. But now that the connection escaped him, a powerful sense of longing knocked the wind out of his sails.

She stroked his chest. "You aren't used to that. It must be difficult for you."

"I admit, I have seldom encountered the limits of my power. What good is it to be one of the three most powerful Hesperine thelemancers in history if I can't…mind-feast…with my Grace as much as I please?"

"Mind-feasting," she said with relish. "Don't worry, my love. We don't have long to wait. Soon, I will be a Hesperine, and we will have everything our hearts desire. Forever."

Lio and Cassia's story continues in
Blood Grace Book 5, *Blood Union Part One.*
Learn more at
vroth.co/union1

GLOSSARY

Abroad: Hesperine term for lands outside of Orthros where Hesperines errant roam, meaning Tenebra and Cordium. See **Orthros Abroad**

Adelphos: false name assumed by Chrysanthos to hide his identity as a war mage from the Hesperines.

Adrogan: ambitious Tenebran lord, a younger son who travels to Orthros to make his fortune. Once one of Cassia's unwanted suitors, now betrothed to Biata.

Adwene: Konstantina's Grace, a formidable Imperial scholar in his mortal life and now a thirteen-hundred-year-old intellectual of Orthros.

Aetos: winged messenger of the gods in the Tenebran and Cordian pantheon. First scion and eldest son of Kyria and Anthros, the most powerful among the lesser deities known as the Fourteen Scions.

affinity: the type of magic for which a person has an aptitude, such as light magic, warding, or healing.

Aithourian Circle: the war mages of the Order of Anthros, sworn enemies of the Hesperines, who have specialized spells for finding and destroying Hespera worshipers. Founded by Aithouros in ancient times, this circle was responsible for most of the destruction of Hespera's temples during the Last War. Oversees the training of all war mages from Tenebra and Cordium to ensure their lifelong loyalty to the Order.

Aithouros: fire mage of the Order of Anthros who personally led the persecution of Hespera worshipers during the Last War. Founder and namesake of the Aithourian Circle, who continue his teachings. Killed by Hippolyta.

Akanthia: the world comprising Tenebra, Cordium, Orthros, and the Empire.

Akesios: god of healing in the Tenebran and Cordian pantheon. The third scion, or third son, of Kyria and Anthros. A lesser deity alongside his brothers and sisters, the Fourteen Scions. Men with the affinity for healing magic become mages of Akesios.

Akron: highest-ranking mage in the Order of Anthros, who holds the ultimate authority in the Order that dominates all other mages.

Akron's Altar: the altar in Corona upon which the Order of Anthros executes heretics by immolation, where many Hesperines have met their deaths.

Akron's Torch: an artifact of the Order of Anthros, which holds great magical power and symbolizes their authority. Prometheus stole it from the Hagion of Anthros, enraging the Aithourian Circle. Its whereabouts have been unknown since his capture.

Alea: one of the two Queens of Orthros, who has ruled the Hesperines for nearly sixteen hundred years with her Grace, Queen Soteira. A mage of Hespera in her mortal life, she is the only Prisma of a temple of Hespera who survived the Ordering.

Alexandra: royal firstblood and Eighth Princess of Orthros, the youngest of the Queens' family. Solaced from Tenebra as a child. She raises silkworms for her craft. Lio's childhood sweetheart.

Alkaios: one of the three Hesperines errant who saved Cassia as a child. He retrieved the ivy pendant from Solia's body for her. A light mage known to travel with his Grace, Nephalea, and their comrade, Iskhyra.

Amachos: false name assumed by Dalos while he was in disguise as the royal mage of Tenebra.

Anastasios: Ritual rirstblood who Gifted Apollon, founder of Lio's bloodline. He was a powerful healer and Prismos of Hagia Boreia, who sacrificed his life to help Alea protect their Great Temple from the Order of Anthros's onslaught.

Andragathos: god of male virtue and righteous warfare in the Tenebran and Cordian pantheon. The seventh scion and youngest son of Kyria and Anthros. A lesser deity alongside his brothers and sisters, the Fourteen Scions. See **Knightly Order of Andragathos**

Angara: goddess in the Tenebran and Cordian pantheon who blesses warriors with morale in battle. Often portrayed wearing golden armor and bearing a sword. The second scion and eldest daughter of Kyria and Anthros, a lesser deity alongside her brothers and sisters, the Fourteen Scions.

Annassa: honorific for the Queens of Orthros.

Anthros: god of war, order, and fire. Supreme deity of the Tenebran and Cordian pantheon and ruler of summer. The sun is said to be Anthros riding his chariot across the sky. According to myth, he is the husband of Kyria and brother of Hypnos and Hespera.

Anthros's fire: a flower commonly grown in Tenebra, used by humans in combination with the herb sunsword to ward off Hesperines.

Anthros's Hall: the god Anthros's great hall beyond the mortal world. Tenebrans and Cordians believe that those who please Anthros in life are rewarded with an afterlife in his Hall with his company of eternal warriors.

Anthros's pyre: Anthros's eternal, holy flames, where he punishes those who displease him.

Apollon: Lio's father, an elder firstblood and founder of Orthros. In his mortal life before the Ordering, he was a mage of Demergos. Transformed by Anastasios, he was the first Hesperine ever to receive the Gift from one of the Ritual firstbloods. Renowned for his powerful stone magic and prowess in battle, he once roamed Abroad as one of the Blood Errant. Known as the Lion of Orthros. Now retired to live peacefully in Orthros with his Grace, Komnena.

apostate: rogue mage who illegally practices magic outside of the Orders.

Apprentice's Toddy: an alchemical infusion for Hesperine sucklings or young mages whose magic has begun to manifest. Remedies the discomfort and anxiety that accompany blooms of power.

Archipelagos: land to the west of the Empire comprising a series of islands, which maintains strict isolation from the rest of the world. See **Nodora** and **Matsu**

Argyros: Lio's uncle and mentor in diplomacy and mind magic. Elder firstblood and founder of Orthros from Hagia Anatela, Gifted by Eidon. Graced to Lyta, father of Nike, Kadi, and Mak. An elder firstblood and founder of Orthros like Apollon, his brother by mortal birth. Attended the first Equinox Summit and every one since as the Queens' Master Ambassador. One of the most powerful thelemancers in history, known as Silvertongue for his legendary abilities as a negotiator.

Ariadne: an apprentice mage of Kyria who accompanies the Semna and Pakhne to Orthros. One of the mages who helped the Hesperine embassy take Zoe and the other Eriphite children to safety.

Arkadia: Lio's cousin, daughter of Argyros and Lyta. Solaced from Tenebra as a child. With her mother's affinity for warding and aptitude for the battle arts, she serves as a Master Steward in Hippolyta's Stand.

Astrapas: Timarete's Grace, Lyros's father.

Atalanta: bloodborn Master Steward of the Stand who used her running skills to rescue humans from heart hunter territory. Martyred when their liege-hounds hunted her down.

Athena: two-year-old Eriphite child Solaced by Javed and Kadi. Younger sister of Boskos by birth and blood. The severe case of frost fever she suffered as a mortal damaged her brain. While the Gift has healed her, she is still recovering lost development.

Aurelio: most famous minstrel in Tenebra and Cordium, whose songs are universally beloved.

Autumn Greeting: ancient courtship festival of Tenebra. When a woman shares this dance with a man, it is considered a promise of betrothal, after which their fathers will arrange their marriage.

Avior: woodland god in the Tenebran and Cordian pantheon.

avowal: Hesperine ceremony in which Graces profess their bond before their people; legally binding and an occasion of great celebration.

Baltasar: Hypatia's firstgift, birth son of her Grace, who joined her bloodline. From the Empire like his father, Khaldaios. A scholar and member of Konstantina's Trial circle.

Bamaayo: word for "mother" in Queen Soteira's first language.

Baruti or **Baru:** Hesperine scholar and Fortress Master in the Prince's Charge; a theramancer and the librarian of Castra Justa, responsible for dangerous magical tomes and artifacts Chargers discover in the field. Began his mortal life in the Empire and chose to become a Hesperine at the First Prince's invitation; alumnus of Capital University.

Basilis: title of a non-royal female relative of the king, outside of the line of succession.

Basir: Hesperine thelemancer and one of the two spymasters of Orthros, alongside his Grace, Kumeta. From the Empire in his mortal life. His official title is "Queens' Master Envoy" to conceal the nature of their work.

Bellator: Tenebran free lord who kidnapped Solia and held her for ransom inside Castra Roborra before murdering her. Led the short-lived rebellion that ended there with the Siege of Sovereigns.

Benedict: First Knight of Segetia, Flavian's best friend, who harbors unrequited love for Genie. Cassia trusts him and considers him a friend, despite his hostility toward Hesperines as a devotee of Andragathos. Travels to Orthros as Lord Titus's representative during the Solstice Summit.

Biata: young Tenebran lady who is one of Lady Hadrian's followers and frequents her weaving room. Prone to gossiping. Betrothed to Lord Tyran.

Blood Errant: group of four ancient and powerful Hesperine warriors who went errant together for eight centuries: Apollon, Nike, Rudhira, and Methu. The only Hesperines errant who have ever carried weapons, they performed legendary but controversial deeds in Hespera's name.

blood magic: type of magic practiced by worshipers of Hespera, from which the power of the Gift stems. All Hesperines possess innate blood magic.

Blood Moon: Hesperine name for one of the two moons, which appears red with a liquid texture to the naked eye. Believed to be an eye of the Goddess Hespera, potent with her blood magic.

Blood Union: magical empathic connection that allows Hesperines to sense the emotions of any living thing that has blood.

bloodborn: Hesperine born with the Gift because their mother was transformed during pregnancy.

bloodless: undead; a corpse reanimated by a necromancer, so called because blood no longer flows through its veins, although it has a semblance of life. Often used as an insult by Hesperines.

Bosko *or* **Boskos:** ten-year-old Eriphite child Solaced by Javed and Kadi. Elder brother of Athena by birth and blood. Harbors anger over what the children suffered and is struggling to adjust to life in Orthros.

Caelum: Solia and Cassia's thirteen-year-old half-brother, only son of King Lucis, crown prince of Tenebra.

Callen: Perita's loving husband. Once a guard in Lord Hadrian's service, he lost a promising military career due to a leg injury he suffered during his unjust imprisonment. Now serves the royal household of Tenebra as Cassia's trusted bodyguard.

Cassia: Tenebran lady, illegitimate daughter of King Lucis and his concubine, Thalia. Secretly a traitor working with the Hesperines from within the Tenebran embassy. Deeply in love with Lio, she hopes to secure peace so she can stay with him in Orthros forever.

Castra Justa: the stronghold of the First Prince and base of operations for the Prince's Charge.

Castra Roborra: fortress in Tenebra belonging to Lord Bellator, where he held Solia captive and ultimately murdered her. Site of the Siege of Sovereigns.

Chalice of Stars: Nike's legendary round shield, which she uses along with the Stand's hand-to-hand combat techniques.

Changing Queen: Queen Hedera of Tenebra, the Mage King's wife and co-ruler during the Last War. As a Silvicultrix, she was a powerful mage in her own right. Her own people knew her as Ebah. Also known as the Hawk of the Lustra and associated with her plant symbol, ivy.

the Charge: see **Prince's Charge**

charm: physical object imbued with a mage's spell, usually crafted of botanicals or other materials with their own magical properties. Offers a mild beneficial effect to an area or the holder of the charm, even if that person is not a mage.

Chera: goddess of rain and spinning in the Tenebran and Cordian pantheon, known as the Mourning Goddess and the Widow. According to myth, she was the Bride of Spring before Anthros destroyed her god-husband, Demergos, for disobedience.

Chrysanthos: war mage from Cordium with an affinity for fire, rival of the late Dalos. As the Dexion of the Aithourian Circle, he is one of the highest-ranking elites in the Order of Anthros. An adroit politician born to an aristocratic family in Corona.

Cordium: land to the south of Tenebra where the Mage Orders hold sway. Its once-mighty principalities and city-states have now lost power to the magical and religious authorities. Wealthy and cultured, but prone to deadly politics. Also known as the Magelands.

Corona: capital city of Cordium and holy seat of the Mage Orders, where the main temples of each god are located, including the Hagion of Anthros.

the Craving: a Hesperine's addiction to their Grace's blood. When deprived of each other, Graces suffer agonizing withdrawal symptoms and fatal illness.

Daedala: Prisma of Hagia Zephyra. Ritual firstblood and Gifter of Timarete.

Dakarai: Grace of Kitharos, one of Nodora's fathers. A dancer and drummer from the high veld of the Empire.

Dalos: Aithourian war mage who disguised himself as a Tenebran and conspired with King Lucis to assassinate the attendees of the Equinox Summit. When the Hesperines' ward stopped him, his spell rebounded, killing him with his own magic.

Dawn Slumber: deep sleep Hesperines fall into when the sun rises. Although the sunlight causes them no harm, they're unable to awaken until nightfall, leaving them vulnerable during daylight hours.

Demergos: formerly the god of agriculture, now stricken from the Tenebran and Cordian pantheon. His worshipers were disbanded in ancient times when the mages of Anthros seized power. According to myth, he was the husband of Chera, but disobeyed Anthros and brought on his own death and her grief.

Demetrios: royal firstblood and Third Prince of Orthros, the Queens' second-eldest son.

Departure: contingency plan that dates from the founding of Orthros, when Hesperines feared the Last War might break out again at any time. If the Queens invoked the Departure, all Hesperines errant would return home, and the border between Orthros and Tenebra would be closed forever.

Deukalion: bloodborn firstgift of Apollon and Komnena, Ambassador in Orthros's diplomatic service who has devoted his career to improving relations between Orthros and Tenebra. While in Tenebra for the Equinox Summit, had a secret affair with Cassia and helped her stop Dalos's assassination attempt. Upon his return to Orthros, he discovered she is his Grace. He is determined to free her from her duties to Tenebra and persuade her to stay with him for all time.

Deutera: respected mage at the Temple of Kyria at Solorum, the Prisma's right hand and trusted confidant.

Dexion: second highest ranking mage in the Aithourian Circle, second in command to the Synthikos and destined to succeed him.

Discourses on Love: Orthros's canon of erotic texts.

Divine Tongue: language spoken by Hesperines and mages, used for spells, rituals, and magical texts. The common tongue of Orthros, spoken freely by all Hesperines. In Tenebra and Cordium, the mages keep it a secret and disallow non-mages from learning it.

dream ward: specialized spell used by Gift Collectors to shield their minds from Hesperine thelemancers.

the Drink: when a Hesperine drinks blood from a human or animal; a non-sexual act, considered sacred, which should be carried out with respect for the donor. It's forbidden to take the Drink from an unwilling person. *Or* Hesperine sacred tenet, the commitment to thriving without the death of other living things.

Ebah: see **Changing Queen**

Eidon: Prismos of Hagia Anatela. Ritual firstblood and Gifter of Argyros.

elder firstbloods: the ancient Hesperine founders of Orthros. Gifted by the Ritual firstbloods. See **Apollon, Argyros, Hypatia, Kassandra, Kitharos, Timarete**

elder Grace: the Grace of an elder firstblood.

the Empire: vast and prosperous human lands located far to the west, across an ocean from Tenebra. Comprises many different languages and cultures united under the Empress. Allied with Orthros and welcoming to Hesperines, many of whom began their mortal lives as Imperial citizens. Maintains a strict policy of isolation toward Tenebra an Cordium to guard against the Mage Orders.

the Empress: the ruler of the Empire, admired by her citizens. The Imperial throne has passed down through the female line for many generations.

envoy: according to common knowledge, a messenger attached to the Hesperine diplomatic service. In fact, envoys are the Queens' spies who gather information from the mortal world to protect Orthros and Hesperines errant. See **Basir, Kumeta**

Epodos: Kitharos and Dakarai's firstgift, Nodora's eldest brother. Solaced from Tenebra as a child, he is Orthros's leading bard and a member of Konstantina's Trial circle.

Equinox Oath: ancient treaty between Orthros and Tenebra, which prescribes the conduct of Hesperines errant and grants them protection from humans.

Equinox Summit: peace talks in which the Hesperines send ambassadors from Orthros to meet with the King of Tenebra and renew the Equinox Oath. Each mortal king is expected to convene it once upon his accession to the throne.

Ereba: elder firstblood from Hagia Notia, Gifted by Eukairia. Martyred during the destruction of the temple, she did not survive to become a founder of Orthros.

Eriphites: worshipers of the pastoral god Eriphon, branded heretics by the Order of Anthros. The last surviving members of their cult are twenty-four orphaned children recently brought to safety in Orthros thanks to Cassia and Lio. See **Zosime, Boskos, Athena**

Eriphon: lesser deity, pastoral god known as the Herder of Demergos, whose worship was also banned during the Ordering.

errant: a Hesperine who has left Orthros to travel through Tenebra doing good deeds for mortals.

essential displacement: process by which necromancers can transfer the magic of one person, the source, into another person, the vessel, through a third person called the channel. The vessel must die for the source to reclaim their power.

Eudias: young war mage from Cordium with an affinity for weather, including lightning. Compelled to join the Aithourian circle due to his magic, he does not relish their murderous plots. Apprenticed to Dalos, he reluctantly assisted his late master in Tenebra and now answers to Chrysanthos.

Eudokia: Hesperine youngblood, one of Lio's Trial sisters in Orthros. Solaced from Tenebra as a child. An initiate mathematician, calligrapher, and accomplished scholar. Daughter of Hypatia.

Eugenia: young Tenebran lady, believed to be Flavian's cousin and daughter of his late uncle, Lord Eugenius. In fact she is his sister, the daughter of Titus and his concubine Risara.

Eukairia: Prisma of Hagia Notia. Ritual firstblood and Gifter of Ereba.

Evander: see **Evandrus the Younger**

Evandrus the Elder: Tenebran free lord who assisted Lord Bellator in Solia's kidnapping and joined forces with him inside Castra Roborra during their rebellion.

Evandrus the Younger: son and heir of Evandrus the Elder, who died with him at Castra Roborra during the Siege of Sovereigns.

familiar: the animal companion of a Hesperine, bound to them by blood.

the Fangs: Prometheus's famous twin swords.

the Feast: Hesperine term for drinking blood while making love.

Ferus: a Tenebran free lord, the most threatening of Cassia's unwanted suitors, until she exposed him as a traitor. Now in exile in the eastern Tenebrae.

Festival of the Rose: five nights of celebration during the Hesperine Winter Solstice observances. Each festival is dedicated to a petal of Hespera's Rose, representing the Goddess's blessings. See **Ritual, Gift, Drink, Sanctuary, Grace**

fire charm: a charm created by a fire mage that those without the affinity for fire can use to light a flame. In Tenebra, they are rare and valuable because only a war mage of the Aithourian circle can make one.

First Prince: see **Rudhira**

firstblood: the first Hesperine in a bloodline, who founds the family and passes the Gift to their children.

Firstblood Circle: the governing body of Orthros. Every firstblood has a vote on behalf of their bloodline, while non-voting Hesperines can attempt to influence policy by displays of partisanship. The Queens retain veto power, but use it sparingly.

firstgift: the eldest child of a Hesperine bloodline, first to receive the gift from their parents.

flametongue: rare herb whose oil can be used to fireproof armor or clothing against mundane flame. Offers no protection against magefire, but still prized by the few royals and nobles who can afford it. The Order of Anthros forbids anyone but their mages to grow and prepare it.

Flavian: young Tenebran lord, son of Free Lord Titus and heir to Segetia's seat on the Council. Despite his family's feud with Hadria, he is admired by women on both sides of the conflict as a paragon of manhood.

fleeter: a person from the Archipelagos. See **Honorable Families**

Font of the Changing Queen: stone fountain on the grounds of Solorum Palace that dates from the time of the Changing Queen. This historical monument is a subject of legends, which say it ran with blood the day the Mage King died.

foregiver: a Hesperine's ancestor who gave the Gift to their bloodline in the past.

the Fourteen Scions: see **Scions**

free lord: highest noble rank in Tenebra. Has a seat on the Council of Free Lords and heredity authority to vote on whether a king should receive the nobility's mandate.

Gaius: aging Tenebran lord loyal to Free Lord Hadrian who travels to Orthros to represent him during the Solstice Summit.

Galanthian: Tenebran free lord with lands in the cold northern region of the kingdom. Father of Nivalis.

gargoyle: mythological creatures with fangs, horns, and wings, which are said to be Hespera's familiars, created from her blood. Hesperines believe they guard the gates of her divine Sanctuary to protect it from Anthros and the other gods.

Genie: see **Eugenia**

geomagus: mage with an affinity for geological forces, who can use their magic to conjure heat from the ground or create artifacts like warming plates for heating food and drink.

the Gift: Hesperines' immortality and magical abilities, which they regard as a blessing from the goddess Hespera. The practice of offering the Gift to all is a Hesperine sacred tenet.

Gift Collector: mage-assassin and bounty hunter who hunts down Hesperines for the Order of Hypnos using necromancy, alchemy, and fighting tactics.

Known for adapting common items into weapons to skirt the Orders' religious laws against mages arming themselves.

Gift Night: the night of a person's transformation into a Hesperine, usually marked by great celebration.

Gifting: the transformation from human into Hesperine.

Glasstongue: see **Lio**

glyph: sacred symbol of a deity. Each god or goddess in the pantheon has a unique glyph. Often used as a pattern in spell casting or carved on shrines and temples.

glyph shard: a fragment of the glyph stone from the Shrine of Hespera where Lio and Cassia fell in love. Although Chrysanthos destroyed the sacred site, its Sanctuary ward lives on in the stone Cassia took from it.

glyph stone: the capstone of the doorway of a shrine, inscribed with the glyph of the deity worshiped there, where any spells over the structure are usually seated.

the Goddess's Eyes: the two moons, the red Blood Moon and the white Light Moon; associated with Hespera and regarded as her gaze by Hesperines.

Gorgos: master mage from the Sun Temple of Anthros at Solorum who aspires to become royal mage.

Grace: Hesperine sacred tenet, a magical bond between two Hesperine lovers. Frees them from the need for human blood and enables them to sustain each other, but comes at the cost of the Craving. A fated bond that happens when their love is true. It is believed every Hesperine has a Grace just waiting to be found. See **Craving**

Grace braids: thin braids of one another's hair that Graces exchange. They may wear them privately after professing their bond to one another, then exchange them publicly at their avowal and thereafter wear them for all to see to signify their commitment.

Grace-family (Grace-son, Grace-father, Grace-sister, etc.): the family members of a Hesperine's Grace; compare with human in-laws.

Grace Union: the particularly powerful and intimate Blood Union between two Hesperines who are Graced; enables them to communicate telepathically and empathically.

Great Temple Epoch: the historical period when the Great Temples of every cult flourished across Tenebra and Cordium, and all mages cooperated. Came to a cataclysmic end due to the Ordering and the Last War.

Great Temples of Hespera: powerful, thriving temples where mages of Hespera worshiped and worked their magic in peace, before they were branded heretics. Razed during the Last War.

Gregoria: royal firstblood and Fourth Princess of Orthros, the fourth child and second-eldest daughter of the Queens.

Guardian of Orthros: see **Hippolyta**

Hadria: domain of Free Lord Hadrian, located on Tenebra's rocky western coast, where the seas are treacherous.

Lady Hadrian: Lord Hadrian's wife, a mature lady above reproach in the court of Tenebra, admired for her graces and respected for her political acumen.

Lord Hadrian: one of the two most powerful free lords in Tenebra, who commands the fealty of many other free lords and lesser nobles. His family has been feuding with Segetia for generations. Known for his loyalty to the throne, but also for honor superior to the king's.

Hagia Anatela: one of the four Great Temples of Hespera that flourished during the Great Temple Epoch, located in the eastern part of the continent. See **Eidon, Ourania**

Hagia Boreia: one of the four Great Temples of Hespera that flourished during the Great Temple Epoch, located in the northern part of the continent. See **Alea, Anastatios**

Hagia Notia: the southernmost of the four Great Temples of Hespera that flourished during the Great Temple Epoch, located in Corona, where the mages of Hespera co-existed with the mages of other gods. The first temple to be razed during the Last War in an unprovoked, surprise attack by the Order of Anthros. See **Khariton, Eukairia**

Hagia Zephyra: one of the four Great Temples of Hespera that flourished during the Great Temple Epoch, located in the western part of the continent. See **Daedala, Thelxinos**

Hagion of Anthros: the most powerful and sacred temple of Anthros in Corona, where the Akron presides over the Order of Anthros.

Hammer of the Sun: Apollon's famous battle hammer, which he wielded while Abroad with the Blood Errant. He left it in Tenebra when he brought Komnena to Orthros.

Harbor: bay in Orthros around which Selas was built. The founders landed here when they first escaped Tenebra and found refuge in the unsettled north.

Harkhuf Addaya Khemkare: Imperial human guest visiting Orthros to study theramancy, a cousin of the Empress. Xandra's share.

harlot's kiss: Tenebran and Cordian name for roses which, as Hespera's sacred flower, are forbidden to be grown there.

Healing Sanctuary: infirmary in Orthros founded and run by Queen Soteira, where humans are given care and Hesperines are trained in the healing arts.

heart bow: traditional gesture of devotion to the Queens of Orthros, a deep bow with one hand over the heart.

heart hunters: warbands of Tenebrans who hunt down Hesperines, regarded by their countrymen as protectors of humanity. They patrol the northern borders of Tenebra with packs of liegehounds, waiting to attack Hesperines who leave Orthros.

Hedon: god of pleasure and chance in the Tenebran and Cordian pantheon, patron of sexual acts and gambling. Styled as the god of fertility and prosperity by the Order of Anthros in their attempts to promote morality.

Helene: royal firstblood and Sixth Princess of Orthros, the Queens' sixth child and second-youngest daughter.

Hephaestion: a mage of the Aithourian Circle during the Last War, the war mages' most brilliant military strategist and inventor of magical siege engines.

Because of his sexual relationship with another man, his fellow war mage Gladius, Aithouros expelled him from the Order, punished him for apostasy, and took credit for his ideas.

Hespera: goddess of night cast from the Tenebran and Cordian pantheon. The Mage Orders have declared her worship heresy punishable by death. Hesperines keep her cult alive and continue to revere her as the goddess of the moons, Sanctuary, and Mercy. Associated with roses, thorns, and fanged creatures. According to myth, she is the sister of Anthros and Hypnos.

Hespera's Rose: the most sacred symbol of the Hesperines, a rose with five petals and five thorns representing Hespera's sacred tenets. Frequently embroidered on clothing or represented on stained glass windows. Based on real roses, which are the Goddess's sacred flower and beloved by Hesperines. The mages uproot them wherever they're found in Tenebra or Cordium and punish those who grow them for heresy.

Hesperine: nocturnal immortal being with fangs who gains nourishment from drinking blood. Tenebrans and Cordians believe them to be monsters bent on humanity's destruction. In truth, they follow a strict moral code in the name of their goddess, Hespera, and wish only to ease humankind's suffering.

Hesperite: human worshiper of Hespera, persecuted as a heretic by the Orders.

Hippolyta: Lio's aunt, Graced to Argyros, mother of Nike, Kadi, and Mak. Greatest and most ancient Hesperine warrior, a founder of Orthros. Known as the Guardian of Orthros for her deeds in Tenebra during the Last War and for establishing the Stand.

Hippolyta's Gymnasium: gymnasium in Orthros founded by Hippolyta, where she trains the Stand and Orthros's athletes compete.

Hippolyta's Stand: Orthros's standing army, founded by Hippolyta. Under her leadership, they patrol the border with Tenebra as Stewards of the Queens' ward. So few of the peaceful Hesperines take up the battle arts that Nike, Kadi, Mak, and Lyros are the only Stewards.

hold lord: Tenebran lord who holds a homestead in the eastern Tenebrae.

Honorable Families: noble bloodlines that rule the Archipelagos from aboard their fleets of dynastic ships.

House Annassa: the residence of the Queens of Orthros, the Hesperine counterpart to a royal palace.

House Komnena: Lio's family home in Orthros, seat of his bloodline, named for his mother.

Hulaic Epochs: eras of pre-history before the Great Temple Epoch, known only through oral traditions.

the Hunger: a combination of sexual desire and the need for blood, which Hesperines experience with their lovers.

Hylonome: bloodborn from Orthros's history who starved herself to death on the top of Hypatia's Observatory after the death of her Grace.

Hypatia: elder firstblood and founder of Orthros from Hagia Anatela, Gifted by Ourania. Grace of Khaldaios and mother of Kia. Orthros's greatest astronomer, who invented the Hesperine calendar.

Hypatia's Observatory: tower in Orthros established by Hypatia, where Hesperine astronomers study the heavens and teach their students. Every Autumn Equinox, Orthros's diplomats watch for the Summit Beacon from here.

Hypnos: god of death and dreams in the Tenebran and Cordian pantheon. Winter is considered his season. Humans unworthy of going to Anthros's Hall are believed to spend the afterlife in Hypnos's realm of the dead. According to myth, he is the brother of Anthros and Hespera.

In Sanctuary: Hesperine term for the current historical era, marked from the date of Orthros's founding.

initiate: Hesperine who has achieved initiate rank in their craft or service, more advanced than a student but not yet of full rank. Attained after the young Hesperine completes a significant crafting project or research treatise that meets with their mentor's approval.

Initiation: see **Trial**

Ioustin *or* **Ioustinianos:** First Prince of the Hesperines, eldest child of the Queens of Orthros. Lio's Ritual father. Solaced from Tenebra as a child. Once a warrior in the Blood Errant known as the Blood-Red Prince, he now leads a force of Hesperines errant known as the Charge. Young Hesperines call him Rudhira, an affectionate name given to him by Methu.

Iskhyra: one of the three Hesperines errant who saved Cassia as a child. She gave the Mercy to Solia. A warder known to travel with Alkaios and Nephalea.

Iulios: royal firstblood and seventh prince of Orthros, the seventh child and youngest son of the Queens.

ivy pendant: wooden pendant carved with a triquetra of ivy. Secretly passed down from one Tenebran queen to another and finally, from Solia to Cassia. Imbued with Lustra magic and connected to the Changing Queen in some way, it allowed Cassia to access secret passages inside Solorum Palace.

Javed: Lio's Grace-cousin, avowed to Kadi, father of Bosko and Thenie. From the Empire in his mortal life. Has an affinity for healing and now serves in Orthros's Healing Sanctuary.

Kadi: see **Arkadia**

kaetlii: word in the tongue used by Tenebrans to train liegehounds, meaning the person the dog is bonded to and will protect until death.

Kalos: the Charge's best scout, who uses his tracking skills to find Hesperines errant who are missing in action.

kalux: Hesperine word in the Divine Tongue for clitoris.

Kassandra: Lio's Ritual mother, an elder firstblood and founder of Orthros. Ritual sister to the Queens, who Gifted her, and mother of Prometheus. An Imperial princess in her mortal life, she became the first Hesperine from the Empire and secured Orthros's alliance with their Imperial allies. Now the Queens' Master Economist who oversees Orthros's trade. Has the gift of foresight and as Orthros's oracle, guides the Hesperines with her prophecies.

Khaldaios: elder Grace, avowed to Hypatia, father of Kia. From the Empire in his mortal life.

Khariton: Prismos of Hagia Notia. Ritual firstblood and Gifter of Phaedros.

Kia: see **Eudokia**

King of Tenebra: see **Lucis**

Kings and Mages: Tenebran and Cordian name for the game Hesperines call Prince and Diplomat.

Kitharos: elder firstblood and founder of Orthros from Hagia Zephyra, father to Nodora. One of the Hesperines' greatest musicians.

Kleos: royal firstblood and Fourth Prince of Orthros, fourth child and second-youngest son of the Queens.

Knight: Cassia's beloved liegehound. Solia gave him to Cassia as a puppy so Cassia would have protection and companionship.

Knightly Order of Andragathos: holy warriors who adhere to a strict moral code and persecute Hesperines in the name of their patron god. See **Andragathos**

Komnena: Lio's mother, still rather young by Hesperine standards. Fled a life of squalor as a Tenebran farmwife and ran away to Orthros with Apollon, who Gifted her while she was pregnant and raised her son as his own. Now a respected mind healer. As the Queens' Chamberlain, she is responsible for helping newcomers to Orthros settle and adjust.

Konstantina *or* **Kona:** royal firstblood, Second Princess of Orthros, the second child and eldest daughter of the Queens. From the Empire in her mortal life. As the Royal Master Magistrate, she is the author of Orthros's legal code and an influential politician who oversees the proceedings of the Firstblood Circle.

krana: Hesperine term in the Divine Tongue for vagina.

Kumeta: Hesperine light mage and one of the two spymasters of Orthros, alongside her Grace, Basir. From the Empire in her mortal life. Her official title is "Queens' Master Envoy" to conceal the nature of their work.

Kyria: goddess of weaving and the harvest in the Tenebran and Cordian pantheon, known as the Mother Goddess or the Wife. Her season is autumn. According to myth, she is married to Anthros.

Laskara: Timarete's firstgift, Lyros's elder sister. One of Orthros's most renowned sculptors, know for her contributions to art and mathematics.

the Last War: the cataclysmic violence sparked by the Ordering sixteen hundred years ago. When the Order of Anthros sought to suppress all resistance to their authority, magical and armed conflict ravaged Tenebra and Cordium, destroying the civilization of the Great Temple Epoch. Peace came at the cost of the Hesperines' exile and the Order of Anthros's victory, while the Mage King secured his rule in Tenebra.

Laurentius: favored warrior of the Mage King. Worshiped Anthros, but loved Hesperite mage Makaria. After the Orders martyred her, he sacrificed himself in battle. Went to his funeral pyre with his amulet of Anthros and her votive statue of Hespera.

liegehound: war dogs bred and trained by Tenebrans to track, hunt, and slay Hesperines. Veil spells do not throw them off the scent, and they can leap high enough to pull a levitating Hesperine from the air. The only animals that do not trust Hesperines. They live longer than other canines and can withstand poison and disease.

Lio: see **Deukalion Komnenos**

Lion of Orthros: see **Apollon**

Lucis: current King of Tenebra, who reigns with ruthlessness and brutality. Born a lord, he secured the crown by might and political schemes, and he upholds his authority by any means necessary. Cassia has never forgiven him for Solia's death.

Lysandros *or* **Lyros:** Lio's Trial brother and Grace-cousin, avowed to Mak, Solaced as a child from Tenebra. Also a warder and warrior serving in the Stand.

Lyta: see **Hippolyta**

Mage King: King Lucian of Tenebra, who reigned sixteen hundred years ago, widely considered by Hesperines and mortals alike to have been a great monarch. He and his wife, the Changing Queen, made the original Equinox Oath with the Queens of Orthros. A fire mage and warrior, he ruled before the Mage Orders mandated that men must choose between wielding spells or weapons.

mage of dreams: mage of Hypnos with an affinity for thelemancy.

Mage Orders: the magical and religious authorities in Cordium, which also dictate sacred law to Tenebran temples. Responsible for training and governing mages and punishing heretics.

Mak: see **Telemakhos**

Makaria: Hesperite Sanctuary mage martyred in the Ordering. Lover of Laurentius. Centuries later, Lio and Cassia fell in love at the shrine of Hespera she once tended near Solorum.

manteia: paradigm of magic that includes praeternatural affinities such as mind magic, foresight, and necromancy.

Martyrs' Pass: the only known passage to Orthros through the Umbral Mountains. Site of Aithouros's last stand against the Hesperines when he and his war mages tried to pursue them into Orthros.

Matsu: Nodora's Ritual mother and the only other Hesperine from the Archipelagos. A beloved thespian and fashion leader in Orthros.

Menodora: Hesperine youngblood, one of Lio's Trial sisters. Daughter of Kitharos and Dakarai. An initiate musician, admired vocalist, and crafter of musical instruments. She is one of only two Hesperines from the Archipelagos and the immortal expert on the music of her mortal homeland.

Mercy: Hesperine sacred tenet, the practice of caring for dead or dying humans.

methodological deconstruction: an application of magic by which a scholar can use observation and deduction to reverse charms and spells by mages of other affinities.

Methu: see **Prometheus**

Midnight Moonbeam: black-and-white dwarf goat kid, one of Zoe's two familiars.

mind healer: see **theramancer**

mind mage: see **thelemancer**

moon hours: by the Hesperine clock, the hours corresponding to night, when Hesperines pursue public activities.

moskos: Hesperine term in the Divine Tongue meaning testicles.

Muse of Orthros: Hesperine whose service is music, dancing, or poetry.

Namenti: Tenebran coastal city on the southern border, near Cordium.

Nephalea: one of the three Hesperines errant who saved Cassia as a child. A warder known to travel with her Grace, Alkaios, and their comrade, Iskhyra.

New Guest House: guest house for visiting mortals on the docks of Selas, built four hundred years ago.

newblood: Hesperine youth, no longer a suckling child but not yet an initiated youngblood.

Nike: see **Pherenike**

Nivalis: young Tenebran lady, one of Lady Hadrian's followers who frequents her weaving room. Daughter of Lord and Lady Galanthian. Her three younger siblings died in a past epidemic of frost fever. Betrothed to Deverran.

Nodora: see **Menodora**

the Oath: see **Equinox Oath**

Oracle of Chera: mage with the gift of foresight, appointed by the Orders to serve in Corona. The affinity is so rare that usually only one woman is born with it in each generation.

Order of Anthros: Mage Order dedicated to the god Anthros, which holds the ultimate religious and magical authority over all other Orders and temples. Bent on destroying Hesperines. War mages, light mages, and warders serve in this Order, as do agricultural and stone mages.

Order of Hypnos: Mage Order devoted to Hypnos, which holds authority over necromancers, mind mages, and illusionists. Oversees rites for the dead, purportedly to prevent Hesperine grave robbing, but in practice to stop rogue necromancers from raising the dead. The Order of Anthros's closest ally in their effort to destroy Hesperines.

Ordered Time: Tenbran and Cordian term for the current historical era, which they mark from the Ordering.

the Orders: see **Mage Orders**

Orthros: homeland of the Hesperines, ruled by the Queens. The Mage Orders describe it as a horrific place where no human can survive, but in reality, it is a land of peace, prosperity, and culture. Located north of Tenebra.

Orthros Abroad: the population of Hesperines who are errant in Tenebra at any given time. Under the jurisdiction of the First Prince, who is the Queens' regent outside their ward.

Orthros Boreou: Hesperine homeland in the northern hemisphere, located north of and sharing a border with Tenebra.

Orthros Notou: Hesperine homeland in the southern hemisphere, near the Empire.

Orthros Warmbloods: unique breed of horses originated by Hippolyta. Hesperine blood magic gives them intelligence, strength, and longevity superior to mundane horses.

Ourania: Prisma of Hagia Anatela. Ritual firstblood and Gifter of Hypatia.

Pakhne: eldest daughter of Free Lord Galanthian, sister to Nivalis. Happily left her life as a lady to become a mage of Kyria. Travels to Orthros as one of the Semna's attendants during the Solstice Summit.

Perita: Cassia's handmaiden and dearest friend. Wife of Callen. Has assisted Cassia in her schemes ever since Cassia helped her save Callen from prison, and she delivered crucial information that enabled Cassia to save the Hesperine embassy from Dalos's assassination attempt.

Phaedric Terror: historical event during the Last War, when Phaedros sought to cure the world's ills by turning all humans into Hesperines. His campaign of forced Giftings resulted in many deaths and inflamed the conflict between Hesperines and the Mage Orders.

Phaedros: mage of Hespera and brilliant scholar from Hagia Notia, Gifted by Khariton. The only survivor of the temple's destruction by the Aithourian Circle. After he perpetrated the Phaedric Terror, he lost his status as an elder firstblood. Now lives in eternal exile under the midnight sun.

Pherenike: Lio's cousin, a warder and warrior second only to her mother Lyta in strength, a thelemancer second only to her father Argyros in power. Solaced from Tenebra as a child. Known as the Victory Star, one of the Blood Errant alongside her uncle, Apollon, and her Trial brothers Rudhira and Methu. After the surviving Blood Errant's campaign to avenge Methu, she remained Abroad alone and has now been missing in action for over ninety years.

Philo: see **Theophilos**

Prince and Diplomat: board game and beloved Hesperine pastime; requires strategy and practice to master. See **Kings and Mages**

Prince's Charge: the force of Hesperines errant that serve under the First Prince.

Prisma: highest ranking female mage in a temple.

the Prisma of the Temple of Kyria at Solorum: powerful mage who leads the women of her temple with pragmatism and kindness.

Prismos: highest ranking male mage in a temple.

Prometheus: legendary Hesperine warrior and martyr. Bloodborn to Kassandra and descendant of Imperial royalty. Known as the Midnight Champion, he was a member of the Blood Errant with his comrades Nike, Rudhira, and Apollon. Captured by the Aithourian Circle before Lio's birth. Orthros still mourns his death.

pyromagus: mage with an affinity for fire.

the Queens: the Hesperine monarchs of Orthros. See **Alea**, **Soteira**

the Queens' Couriers: young Hesperines who serve Orthros as messengers, delivering correspondence and packages throughout Selas.

the Queens' Terrace: a terrace at House Annassa that fulfills the function of a throne room, although the Queens sit together on a modest bench, and their terrace is open to all.

the Queens' ward: the powerful Sanctuary ward cast by the Queens, which spans the borders of Orthros, protecting Hesperines from human threats.

Rainbow Aurora: brown-and-white dwarf goat kid, one of Zoe's two familiars.

rhabdos: Hesperine term in the Divine Tongue meaning penis.

Ritual: Hesperine sacred tenet. A ceremony in which Hesperines share blood, but in a broader sense, the whole of their religious beliefs.

Ritual circle: area where Hesperines gather to perform Ritual, usually marked with sacred symbols on the floor.

Ritual firstbloods: the eight blood mages who performed the Ritual that created Hesperines. As the leaders of the Great Temples of Hespera, all except Alea were martyred during the Ordering. See **Alea, Anastasios, Daedala, Eidon, Eukairia, Khariton, Ourania, Thelxinos**

Ritual hall: central chamber in Hesperine homes where the bloodline's Ritual circle is located.

Ritual parents: Hesperines who attend a new suckling's first Ritual or who give the Gift to a mortal who becomes a Hesperine as an adult. They remain mentors and trusted guides for eternity. Comparable to Tenebran temple parents.

Ritual tributary: Hesperine who establishes their own bloodline rather than joining their Gifter's family.

Rose House: the newest guest house on the docks of Selas, built in recent years by Apollon and Lio for Komnena's use.

royal firstbloods: the Queens' children, who are to establish their own bloodlines in order to share the Annassa's power with their people.

Rudhira: see **Ioustinianos**

Sanctuary: Hesperine sacred tenet, the practice of offering refuge to anyone in need. *Or* Hesperine refuge in hostile territory, concealed and protected from humans by Sanctuary magic.

Sanctuary mage: a mage with a rare dual affinity for warding and light magic, who can create powerful protections that also conceal. Queen Alea of Orthros is the only mage with this affinity who survived the Orders' persecution of Hespera worshipers.

Sanctuary Rose: a variety of white rose that originated in the Great Temples of Hespera. The only vine that survived the Last War now grows in Princess Konstantina's greenhouse, and she has propagated it throughout Orthros. Traditionally, each person who requests Sanctuary is given one of these blooms in welcome.

Sanctuary ward: ward created by a Sanctuary mage, which can both protect and hide those within it. Strong Sanctuary wards require the caster to remain inside the boundaries of the spell. Should the mage die there, their sacrifice will increase the ward's power and sustain it indefinitely.

Scions: lesser deities in the Tenebran and Cordian pantheon, the fourteen children of Anthros and Kyria, comprising seven sons and seven daughters. Each has their own cult and mages.

Sea of Komne: the sea that separates mainland Orthros from the landmass where Tenebra and Cordium are located.

Segetia: domain of Free Lord Titus, landlocked and known for its gentle hills.

Selas: capital city of Orthros Boreou.

Semna: elderly former Prisma of the Temple of Kyria at Solorum, who travels to Orthros for the Equinox Summit to spread her goddess's teachings to the Hesperines.

Severinus *or* **Severin:** son and heir of Severinus the Elder, who tries to mitigate his father's abuses against their people.

shamisen: long-necked, three-stringed musical instrument from the Archipelagos favored by Nodora.

share: human or immortal with whom a Hesperine is romantically involved, sharing blood and intimacy.

Siege of Sovereigns: King Lucis's assault on Castra Roborra after the murder of Solia. Ended the rebellion of the nobles who styled themselves the sovereign free lords and resulted in the death of every living thing in the fortress.

Skleros: master necromancer and Gift Collector who holds the Order of Hypnos's record for completing the most bounties on Hesperines. Expert in essential displacement.

Slumber: see **Dawn Slumber**

Solace: Hesperine sacred tenet, the practice of rescuing and Gifting abandoned children.

Solia: late Princess of Tenebra, King Lucis's legitimate daughter and heir before the birth of his son. When she was seventeen, rebel lords kidnapped her. Lucis refused to ransom her or collect her remains and ensured all witnesses perished in the ensuing Siege of Sovereigns. Nobles and commoners alike still mourn her.

Solorum: ancestral capital of Tenebra, royal seat of the king.

Solorum Fortress: castle built for the defense of the capital by seven successive kings over the course of two hundred years. The Hesperine embassy lodged here during the Equinox Summit due to the humans' fears.

Solstice Summit: diplomatic negotiations between Tenebra and Orthros marking the first time a mortal embassy from Tenebra has ever entered Hesperine lands. An unprecedented event proposed by Lio in an effort to build on the tradition of the Equinox and rescue relations between Tenebra and Orthros.

sophia: title of a Hesperine whose service is teaching and scholarship.

Soteira: one of the two Queens of Orthros, who has ruled the Hesperines for nearly sixteen hundred years with her Grace, Alea. Originally from the Empire, she was a powerful mortal mage with an affinity for healing before leaving to found Orthros alongside Alea.

speires: symbolic hair ties Lyta gives to trainees when they begin learning the battle arts. Stewards wear them as part of their Stand regalia.

the Stand: see **Hippolyta's Stand**

starflake: evergreen tree that thrives in Orthros's climate. Its fruit, which it bears in winter, is sweet with a tart aftertaste, a beloved Hesperine delicacy.

stepping: innate Hesperine ability to teleport instantly from one place to another with little magical effort.

Steward: see **Hippolyta's Stand**

Summit Beacon: bonfire on the border between Tenebra and Orthros, which the King of Tenebra lights to announce to the Hesperines he wishes to convene the Equinox Summit.

Sun Temple: see **Temple of Anthros at Solorum**

sunbound: mild Hesperine curse word.

Sunfire Poison: alchemical poison concocted from sunsword and Anthros's fire. Lethal to Hesperines at the right dose, in smaller amounts it can reduce them to mortal strength and ability.

sunsword: herb commonly grown in Tenebra, used by humans in combination with the flower Anthros's fire to ward off Hesperines.

Synthikos: highest ranking mage in the Aithourian Circle, who commands the war mages and has powerful influence over the Order of Anthros as a whole.

Telemakhos: Lio's cousin and best friend. Exposed as a child in Tenebra due to his club foot, Solaced by Argyros and Lyta. A warrior by profession and warder by affinity, he serves in the Stand. He and his Grace, Lyros, are newly avowed.

Temple of Anthros at Solorum: temple in Tenebra's capital, once an ancient site of outdoor Anthros worship that was later walled and roofed by kings. The temple of the royal mage, where the king and his court attend rites.

Temple of Hedon: any temple dedicated to the god Hedon, where the Orders allow prostitution and gambling in order to control and profit from such activities.

Temple of Kyria at Solorum: most influential and respected temple of Kyria in Tenebra, located near the royal palace. Houses orphans and provides healing services to the surrounding area. Due to their reputation and magical power, the women here enjoy a great degree of autonomy.

Tenebra: human kingdom south of Orthros and north of Cordium. Agrarian, feudal society ruled by a king, prone to instability due to rivalries between lords. Land of the Hesperines' origin, where they are now persecuted.

the Tenebrae: former name of Tenebra, a plural indicating the free lords' independent domains under the nominal rule of a king affirmed by the Council. King Lucis has since changed the name to Tenebra, singular, to symbolize how he has united the kingdom under his absolute power.

thelemancer: a mage with an affinity for thelemancy, or mind magic, which gives them the power to manipulate others' thoughts and control their Wills.

Thelxinos: Prismos of Hagia Zephyra. Ritual firstblood and Gifter of Kitharos.

Thenie: see **Athena**

Theophilos: ancient Hesperine, Orthros's greatest master crafter of stained glass, who mentored Lio in his craft.

theramancer: a person with an affinity for theramancy, or mind healing, who can use magic to treat mental illness.

Thorn: Rudhira's two-handed sword, which he carried as one of the Blood Errant and now wields as he leads the Charge.

Timarete: elder firstblood and founder of Orthros from Hagia Zephyra, Gifted by Daedala. Mother of Laskara and Lyros. One of the Hesperines' greatest painters.

Titus: free lord of Segetia, one of the most powerful men in Tenebra, who commands the fealty of many other free lords and lesser nobles. Segetia has been feuding with Hadria for generations.

Trial circle: age set of Hesperines who go through the Trial of Initiation together. They consider each other Trial sisters and brothers for the rest of their immortal lives. Although not related by birth or blood, they maintain strong bonds of loyalty and friendship for eternity.

Trial of Initiation *or* **Trial:** Hesperine rite of passage marking an immortal's transition into adulthood.

Tychon: young war mage with an affinity for fire, Chrysanthos's apprentice. Zealous in his devotion to his master and the Aithourian Circle's cause.

Union: Hesperine sacred tenet, the principle of living with empathy and compassion for all. See **Blood Union**

veil hours: by the Hesperine clock, the hours corresponding to day, when Hesperines Slumber or devote their private time to friends, family, and lovers.

veil spell: innate Hesperine ability to cast magical concealments that hide their presence and activities from humans or fellow immortals.

veiled blood seal: Hesperine spell for securing confidential correspondence.

Vigil of Thorns: five nights of meditation during the Hesperine Winter Solstice observances. Each vigil is dedicated to a thorn of Hespera's Rose, representing the Hesperines' sacred duties. See **Mercy**, **Solace**, **Will**, **Union**, **Gift**

Vulgus *or* **the vulgar tongue**: common language of all non-mages in Tenebra and Cordium.

war mage: mage with an affinity for fire, lightning, or other type of magic that can be weaponized. The Order of Anthros compels them to dedicate their lives to the Aithourian Circle.

warder: mage with an affinity for warding, the power to create magical protections that block spells or physical attacks.

Waystar: Hesperine fortress, Orthros's first refuge for those crossing the border from Tenebra. Hesperines errant who use weapons must leave their armaments here before crossing the Sea of Komne to Selas.

Will: free will, willpower. *Or* Hesperine sacred tenet, the principle of guarding the sanctity of each person's freedom of choice.

Winter Solstice: the most sacred time of the Hesperine year, when they celebrate Hespera with the sacred Festival of the Rose and Vigil of Thorns.

Xandra: see **Alexandra**

youngblood: young adult Hesperine who has recently reached their majority by passing the Trial of Initiation.

Zoe *or* **Zosime:** Lio's little sister, a seven-year-old Eriphite child Solaced by Apollon and Komnena. Loves her new family and idolizes her brother for his role in saving her from Tenebra. Has yet to heal from the emotional wounds she suffered as a mortal.

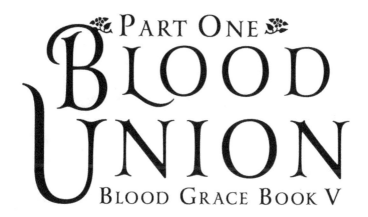

PART ONE
BLOOD UNION
BLOOD GRACE BOOK V

She's ready for her eternal future with him.
But the past won't let them go...

The night Cassia has fought for is here. At last, she'll drink Lio's blood and join him as an immortal Hesperine, fulfilling their Grace bond. But then an unexpected guest returns to Orthros with a revelation about the past she never imagined. Secrets lay hidden in the illustrious Empire, where she must travel with Lio to uncover the truth.

Lio has risked everything for his Grace before, and he'll do it again. He'll stand between Cassia and the politics pulling her back toward the human world. He'll push his magic to new limits to keep her safe. Even if it destroys his life's work as a diplomat - or Cassia's trust in him.

Steamy romance meets classic fantasy worldbuilding in Blood Grace. Follow fated mates Lio and Cassia through their epic love story for a guaranteed series HEA.

Learn more:
vroth.co/union1

Blood Dream

A Blood Grace Story

The nightmare is over, but can they live their dream come true?

Cassia is finally free to stay with Lio. Safe in Orthros and done with human politics, she's ready to celebrate with him and her immortal family. And yet she feels uneasy in her new home.

Lio wants the start of their life together to be everything Cassia dreamed. But he can tell something is wrong, and she's trying to hide it. Now there's nothing to keep them apart. So why is she pulling away?

They've defeated necromancers, war mages, and the tyrant king so they can be together. Can they win against the personal specters that threaten their happily ever after?

This touching and steamy Blood Grace bonus novelette is set after the events of Blood Sanctuary Part Two.

Get Blood Grace 4.5 for free
when you sign up for my newsletter!
vroth.co/dream

ACKNOWLEDGEMENTS

HERE WE are at Blood Grace Book 4. Rapid releasing (or even re-releasing) four books in four months is a wild adventure. I quite literally couldn't have managed this without the amazing network of supportive family, author friends, readers, bloggers, and indie publishing professionals.

It's amazing to realize that hundreds of people have been part of this process at some point, in all kinds of ways big and small. There are certainly too many of you to name. But if you're reading this, and you touched this project at all, know that I'm thinking of you by name and appreciating the time you took to help me realize my goals as a creative.

First and foremost, my gratitude to readers. You're the reason we're all here. Thank you for keeping books thriving in the digital age and making it possible to be an author.

To my wonderful coven on the FaRo Authors Discord, hugs and watermelons. May charrot bless your creative endeavors. Thank you to my unreasonably sexy ladies, tea time companions, cover testing buddies, and stabby enemies-to-lovers friends. I love you all so much. I'm grateful to our established authors who mentor us with wisdom gained from experience and to our new authors who bring such energy and talent to the group. I so appreciate everyone who has come to my release parties, offered feedback on a million details from blurbs to bedposts, beta read, reviewed, reshared, or held my hand late into the night picking out music for reels. Know that I'm here for you anytime you need a second opinion, a shoulder to cry on...or carebear lasers.

To Patricia, thank you for one of the loveliest working relationships in my author career. It's a privilege to have your beautiful work gracing my books. You are absolutely amazing, and I look forward to many future collaborations!

Gratitude to my Ko-Fi donors for contributing to my artwork-funding goal in Argyros's favorite currency, cups of coffee! I'm well-caffeinated and touched by your generosity.

Ko-Fi Donors
Anastasia R.
Brittany C.
Brittany H.
Kaija W.
April O.
Bridie N.
Lisette M.
Trish H.
Julia G.
Sthepanie C.
Leigh H.

As ever, I'm deeply grateful to my incredible Ambassadors for Orthros. In honor of everything you do out of pure love for books (and because we've added new friends to this list!) I want to recognize each of you by name again.

Author-Ambassadors
Steph @slpraterwrites
Dani @authordanimorrison

Editor & Research Ambassador
Brittany @brittany.wilson1764

PA & Ambassadors Coordinator
Kaija @strictlybookish_kai

Ambassadors

Abi @words_and_dreams
Abigail @a_reads_alot
Ahana @tohearts_content
Alex
Alisha
Angela
Anshul @stories.buddy
Ashleigh
Aurora @AuroraLydia
Barbara
Brandy @better_0ff_read
Bridie
Brittany @bookwyvernlovestea
Carole
Cheyenne
Christine @
anxioustattooedandbookish
Deborah
Emily @thehamsterreads
Erika @theenchantedshelf
Haley @thecaffeinated.reader
Heather @_the_forgotten_books
Jessica @reddoorromance
Jessica @readbelievelove
Jordie @bookish.and.blonde
Julie @1bookmore
Kadie
Keshia @808bookdr
Kris @a_bookish_dream
Kristen
Kristin @madhattersfolly_reads

Leah @leahlovestoread
Madhu @mabookyard
Megan @bookish_megeen
Melissa
Nadine
Nancy
Nat
Nicki @starseternal182
Nicole @starsbooksandtea
Nina
Patricia @myromancehasnolimits
Raley
Riley @paperroselibrary
Rishma @bookaddict__ril
Sahana @books_and_draws_
eclectic
Samantha @
bookobsessedandblonde
Sarah @books.and.tea.princess
Sarah @theheavycrownreads
Sharon
Sherri
Shreya @my_fair_fiction
Sonya
Stephanie
Tammy
Tara
Taylor @tmo_reads
Tia @tiaisreading
Whitney

ABOUT THE AUTHOR

VELA ROTH grew up with female-driven fantasy books and classic epics, then grew into romance novels. She set out to write stories that blend the rich worlds of fantasy with the passion of romance.

She has pursued a career in academia, worked as a web designer and book formatter, and stayed home as a full-time caregiver for her loved ones with severe illnesses. Writing through her own grief and trauma, she created the Blood Grace series, which now offers comfort to readers around the world.

She lives in a solar-powered writer's garret in the Southwestern United States, finding inspiration in the mountains and growing roses in the desert. Her feline familiar is a rescue cat named Milly with a missing fang and a big heart.

Vela loves hearing from readers and hopes you'll visit her at velaroth.com.

CPSIA information can be obtained
at www.ICGtesting.com
Printed in the USA
LVHW042343211222
735706LV00001B/38